ALSO BY JACLYN DOLAMORE

Dark Metropolis

GLITTERING SHADOWS

JACLYN DOLAMORE

HYPERION

LOS ANGELES   NEW YORK

First Edition, June 2015
10 9 8 7 6 5 4 3 2 1
G475-5664-5-15091
Printed in the United States of America

Library of Congress Cataloging-in-Publication for Hardcover
Dolamore, Jaclyn.
Glittering shadows / Jaclyn Dolamore.—First edition.
pages cm
Sequel to: Dark metropolis.
Summary: Rebels grow anxious behind closed doors while Thea, Freddy,
Nan, and Sigi are caught in the crossfire of the revolution which has left bodies
lining the streets of Urobrun, but as the battle lines are drawn, the greater
threat of losing magic forever casts a dark shadow over the land.
ISBN 978-1-4231-6331-2 (hardback)
[1. Fantasy. 2. Magic—Fiction. 3. Revolutionaries—Fiction.] I. Title.
PZ7.D6975Gl 2015
[Fic]—dc23   2014041986

Visit www.hyperionteens.com

To Kathy Dolamore Gould, all-around fun and supportive aunt who listened to me ramble on about my stories when I was just a wee thing

GLITTERING SHADOWS

ONE

Marlis Horn came from a long line of unpleasant women. They were known for being too smart for their own good and for lacking feminine delicacy and sentimentality. Marlis was quite proud of this heritage.

But the opera was what always undid her. She didn't care for the raucous jazz other girls enjoyed, but the acoustics in the Theatre Urobrun were so magnificent. Music seemed to come from every corner and fill her soul with stories of love and bravery, death and revenge.

She clutched her opera gloves together as the hero, Siegfried, perished, stabbed from behind. The heroine, Kriemhild, curled over Siegfried's body, singing of her despair in a powerful soprano, her hair tumbling across the front of her dress in long, fair braids. The stage lights were upon her so that she seemed to glow in her white dress, but her eyes were dark. So dark, so angry—so powerful. She would avenge his death.

If something terrible ever happened, I would be like Kriemhild, Marlis thought. *I would take action.*

She had seen this opera three times before, but it had never seemed as real as it did tonight. She couldn't shake the feeling something was about to happen. All her life, Marlis had sometimes heard odd, ominous music at night, but today it had happened even in the middle of breakfast. She always felt it meant something, but she had long since stopped telling Papa when she heard it; he dismissed it as the result of an overactive imagination, and gave her that awful medicine that made her feel stupid.

Marlis wasn't a child anymore. She would not risk anyone knowing that her mind veered into strange places. The world was already too quick to dismiss an ambitious girl as crazy.

"Look, Paul's across the way." Ida brought Marlis back to the real world, and for once Marlis was almost glad for it. Usually she just put up with her. Being the daughter of the Chancellor unfortunately meant spending a lot of time paired with the daughter of Vice Chancellor Walther. Ida enjoyed the opera merely as a social event, and all night she'd been peering at other audience members through her opera glasses, sometimes waving or stepping out to talk to someone.

"Yes, I see him," Marlis said.

"He's cute, isn't he?" Ida replied, the glasses still held to her nose. "I hear he's getting really good at tennis. Have you ever played with him?"

"I haven't," Marlis whispered. "But maybe you should pay attention. It's almost over."

"Thank goodness." Ida settled back into her chair. "What's going on again?"

"Shh." Marlis started to lift one finger to shush Ida, but she saw Papa's attention slide her way. Papa had suggested lately that she ought to be friendlier with other girls. Boys, too, for that matter. He admired her focus, but said anyone who aspired to politics ought to be good at making friends.

Marlis expected no one told Kriemhild to make friends. *Not even God can hide you from my vengeance,* she sang, and in the next cycle of the opera, to be performed later in the season, she would stop at nothing—setting fire to the palace and striking down the man who murdered Siegfried with Siegfried's own sword.

If only I lived in the days of warrior queens and Papa was the king instead of the Chancellor. I'd learn to fight, and everyone would love me for fending off barbarians.

As the curtain closed on Siegfried's funeral pyre, Ida stretched. "I'm going to find Paul and say hi. Do you want to come with me?"

"I'm not interested in Paul."

"I never said you had to be interested! Maybe we could just play doubles with him and Heini sometime."

Papa gave her a pointed look.

"I guess," Marlis relented.

The house lights had come on, so the opera house had lost a little of its gilded mystery. The curtain was down, the room filled with the din of cheerful upper-class voices. Marlis threw her white fur wrap around her shoulders.

Papa's senior adviser, Volland, shoved aside the curtain to their box. His lean face was white, his necktie not quite straight.

"What are you doing here, Volland?" Papa frowned. "I thought you were going to get some sleep tonight."

"Mr. Chancellor, sir, something's happened. You need to leave at once."

Marlis felt as if she'd swallowed stones. The unsettling feeling inside her all day suddenly found its direction. She didn't know yet what had happened—but she already understood it was bad.

"Is everything all right?" Mrs. Walther clutched at her jewels.

"I'm sure it's nothing," Vice Chancellor Walther said, putting an arm around her.

Down in the gallery, a man underdressed for the theater was running up the main aisle shouting something. The crowds that had been clearing out leisurely suddenly began to rush. Volland waved his hands at the Walthers, getting them moving. Additional guards were waiting to usher their party out.

"It's the Valkenraths, sir," Volland said, as they hurried down the back stairs. "The rebels have been gathering around Roderick Valkenrath's house, and . . . the workers are escaping."

"*What?*" Papa thundered. "How could this be? Where are the Valkenraths, then?"

"No one's seen them. But we've only just gotten word of this."

"I can't imagine they'd betray us," said Vice Chancellor Walther, who was a friend of Gerik Valkenrath. Mrs. Walther whimpered softly—she was certainly full of feminine delicacy and sentimentality, her diamond earrings sparkling through her soft blond waves. Ida shot Marlis a panicked expression.

"Put the army on full alert," Papa said. "We need to get this under control at once."

TWO

arlis couldn't remember when she'd last seen so many guards, especially with all branches of government stretched so thin. The Walthers climbed into one car in the motorcade, while she and Papa climbed in the second with Volland. Marlis managed not to show any panic outwardly. She wasn't sure she even felt panic yet.

Since she was a child, the city had been using magic to bring back the dead to work in secret underground. The government had kept them concealed for eight years now. Who was to blame for this breach, Marlis wondered.

Freddy was the key to all of this, the only one with the power to bring the dead back to life. But he was only seventeen. If he had revealed the secret—well, the Valkenraths were his guardians, and she wondered if they hadn't driven him into it.

She didn't like either one of them. When she was a girl, Gerik used to pull a quarter out of her ear and tell her to smile more. As for Roderick, she could appreciate his cool demeanor, but she didn't trust it one bit. But Papa did. He'd known them both since they were in school together.

"How . . . did you find out about this?" Papa asked Volland, putting an arm around Marlis. He was a little breathless from rushing down the stairs.

"The police received several calls about a commotion in the neighborhood. The neighbors thought maybe the rebels were staging a protest at Roderick's house, but when the officers responded, they discovered people in work suits, looking confused. At this point, they contacted the guard."

The city police didn't know about the underground workers. Only her father's private guard was aware of them.

"Has anyone accounted for Freddy?" Papa asked.

"He's missing, too."

"I worry he might have something to do with this. He's of the age when boys do foolish things." He looked at Marlis. "You just saw Freddy at the Stanglers' tea. Did he seem any different than usual?"

"He *has* seemed different lately." Marlis kept looking out the car window. It didn't seem possible that at this very moment, the revived dead were sharing the same fresh night air as they were. Here along the Wahlenstrasse, the streetlamps cast their glow on broad empty sidewalks. "But that's no surprise—you let him go out at night with a girl. I imagine it was quite a shock to his system."

"That was very controlled," Papa said. "Gerik was with them at all times."

The only girls Freddy was normally permitted to see were

Marlis and Ida and the other daughters of top officials. But magic ran in family lines. Eventually they would need someone else who could revive the dead, so Freddy must have children, and it certainly wouldn't be with the daughters of top officials.

"But the girl is a peasant from Irminau," Marlis said. "Maybe she's with the rebellion."

"She's a rustic?" Papa snapped. "Gerik should have told me."

"Papa, you know how Gerik is with women. Can't you just imagine him winking at Freddy and saying, 'Go on, I won't tell'?" She shot a look to Volland. He agreed with her about Gerik.

"I'm afraid I can imagine it." Volland grimaced.

"Gerik wouldn't endanger the entire city!" Papa said.

A handful of people ran down the sidewalk, dressed in black. Everyone in the car glanced at them. Rebels, Marlis thought. Not the workers, who would be in uniforms. She didn't see weapons in their hands, and the guards outnumbered them for now. But her eyes tracked them until they were out of sight.

"Gerik might very well have been with them. But even with a chaperone, some women have a way of getting a point across," Volland said.

"It wouldn't be hard to convince Freddy that we're his enemies," Marlis said. "You've kept him like a prisoner."

Papa's eyes were fixed on the lights of the guard car in front of them. "Well, we will get this situation in hand."

The guard car hit the brakes, and now their car stopped too, pitching all their heads forward. "What now?" Volland said.

There was shouting ahead. A flashlight beam swept by, but

Marlis couldn't see much. She had to fight an urge to open the car door and run into the street—she hated being trapped like this, even behind bulletproof glass.

A reddish glow rose in the distance, as if something had been set on fire. The car had stopped next to one of the city's parks. Expensive apartments with small balconies overlooked the rose-bushes. Even at night, such a place looked welcoming—but she saw more rough-looking people running past the car.

And then—the world shattered.

A light as bright as the sun blinded her. A wave of force rumbled the ground. Papa's arms clutched her tight. A tower of fire and smoke shot toward the sky ahead, burning hot, dying back quickly. Her mind scrambled to make sense of this—was it a bomb? The word "bomb" sounded odd in her mind, like she scarcely remembered what it meant.

She could hardly breathe, Papa was holding her so tightly. Or was it just that she had forgotten how to breathe? She pressed her face to his jacket, shutting her eyes. His body was warm and solid, the only thing that felt safe.

Marlis felt every nerve in her body, every finger and toe. Her thoughts didn't venture into fears or hopes. She could only think of facts, as if she were studying sentence structure or photosynthesis. *I might die now.* That was just a fact.

I can't be afraid to die. Mama has already done it. She tried to think of it like jumping across a chasm, with her mother holding out her hands on the other side to catch her.

"It went off up there—" Volland had unbuckled his seat belt. "I can't see—"

Marlis loosened her grip on Papa. Another fire burned now, closer ahead.

Someone struck the back window of the car with a rock. The glass held.

"Reinforcements," Papa said, seeing uniformed men run by with rifles at the ready. "They'll see us home. We'll be all right."

Marlis watched as a guard shot a man in the street. She couldn't yet absorb that she was in the middle of gunfire and angry shouting voices, just a few blocks from home. The motorcade was trying to turn around. Their driver reversed a little, then cut the wheel far left, going slowly to avoid the pack of guards, but one of the guards motioned for the car to keep moving forward instead.

A head slumped sideways onto the window. Volland jumped. The face slid away, unconscious. The man could have been a younger version of Volland himself—thin, scholarly looking, light-brown hair.

In another moment, the car was moving forward again, bringing into view the crumpled, burning chassis of an identical vehicle. "That's the Walthers' car," Papa said, jerking forward in his seat to see better. "The bomb . . ."

Their driver jerked the wheel to avoid a piece of the bumper. Marlis couldn't see bodies through the flames. But they had to be there. They hadn't lived. No one would have lived through that explosion. Ida might have burned to death, or maybe the bomb tore her up first.

Marlis twisted the ribbons fastening her wrap around her shoulders. She looked the other way. The bodies of rebels

littered the sidewalk like fallen toys. Guards on the street sig-
naled all clear and waved them through.

"The rebels—" Papa was trembling. He punched the seat
ahead of him, his face flushed, his eyes bulging with rage.

"Papa, please. Your heart."

"Damn my heart," he retorted. "Damn me for letting this
happen."

⊙–⊙–⊙–⊙

They did not go home that night. The Chancellery had the
thickest walls in the city, with bunkers a few stories below the
ground floor. Papa and his ministers could meet there, keeping
the wives and children safe beneath their feet. Papa saw her
safely down the stairs to windowless bedrooms dressed with
old imperial furnishings, fringed floor rugs, and paintings of
tall ships. The Chancellery itself had been renovated on the
surface, but the building was over two hundred years old, and
the decor down here must be at least seventy.

"You're safe now," Papa said. "Try to get some sleep."

She scoffed. "Sleep? I want to know what's going on."

"You'll hear as soon as we get a clear picture. Stay with Mrs.
Wachter."

A few of the women were in the gloomy sitting room.
Wilhelmina Wachter, wife of General Wachter; Ada Rasp, wife
of the domestic affairs minister, who was playing jarring idle
notes on the piano in the corner; Mauritza Baum, wife of the
head of the Chancellor's guard, and her little boy, who was
sleeping on her lap. Marlis saw them, but she also saw the empty

space that would have belonged to Ida and Mrs. Walther. Ida's face, melted beyond recognition. Ida's lace and blue silk gown, charred to nothing.

Marlis kept thinking of the bomb, the guards, the fallen bodies of the rebels, but it seemed as abstract as Mrs. Rasp's tuneless fiddling on the piano. Part of her felt that Ida was still in the opera box, waving at Paul.

Wilhelmina rose, her dress rustling. She hadn't been at the opera, but she looked like she'd come from a dinner party, in dark green silk. "Are you all right, Marlis?" Wilhelmina, while too distant to be considered a surrogate mother, was still the closest thing Marlis had since her own mother's death. She admired Wilhelmina, and Wilhelmina was both kind and candid with her.

"What will happen now?" Marlis asked, and then bit her lip. That voice was too scared to belong to her. "I mean, we know so little. I hate not knowing. Is it all over, if the workers have gotten out?"

"*Something* is certainly over," Wilhelmina said. "And I can tell you the workers *are* out. I saw them on the streets around Roderick Valkenrath's house, and the rebels are popping up everywhere."

Mrs. Rasp let out a shuddering cry. "My god, how long before they overpower us even here? If they think we used magic to force people into slavery, it'll be like the Revolution all over again. They'll be hanging us in the square."

"But *didn't* we use magic to force people into slavery?" Wilhelmina asked. Although she had a forceful presence, she looked pallid, or maybe it was just the lighting in the basement.

"I suppose you think we deserve to be hanged?" Mrs. Rasp asked.

"Shh," Mrs. Baum said, stroking her boy's hair when he stirred a little.

"Of course not," Wilhelmina said. "I know why we did what we did. But—" She shook her head and glanced at Marlis again. "You might as well have a seat. I know you won't sleep. For now, we can only wait."

Marlis pulled out from under her dress the necklace her mother had given her as a child—gold in the shape of a real human heart. Mother had loved science; Marlis thought of her every time she rubbed the familiar shape between her fingers.

The women sat, talking sometimes, falling into heavy silence other times. At some point in the night, the power flickered. Wilhelmina had candles at the ready. The workers underground had managed some of the electric plants. But the power remained on—for now.

Marlis finally fell into fitful sleep in her chair. A child's wailing woke her again. More women had joined them. Now Mrs. Alberti sat at the piano. The ornate cuckoo clock on the wall said it was six in the morning. Some of the wives had gathered at the table around a pot of coffee, speaking in hushed tones.

Marlis rose, shaking off her bleariness. "Has there been any news?"

"Not much," Wilhelmina said. "It sounds like we might be down here longer than we thought, though. We haven't seen your father, but I spoke to my husband. The military have their hands full, so they want us to stay under guard."

"Did he say what's happening out there? Have they found the Valkenraths? Freddy?"

"Roderick is dead," Wilhelmina said. "They found his body underground. That's all we know of him. Apparently the streets are madness—fires and riots. People beat a police officer to death in Langstrasse. They're trying to get it under control." She spoke calmly but looked pinched. Beside her, Mrs. Baum dropped her face into her hands.

Marlis went into the hall and paced. Down here, she heard nothing, felt nothing. What did the world look like outside these walls? When she stepped into the light of morning, would it be transformed? She wanted to be at her father's side, hearing every detail. Here they were, all the ladies crowded in a concrete hole, like inanimate valuables tucked into the cellar for safekeeping.

I can't bear this blindness.

Marlis tried to go up the stairs. A guard stopped her at the top. "Sorry, Princess. Your father said not to let you up."

"I won't bother him. I won't say a word. I'll stay outside the meeting chamber. It can't be any more dangerous up there."

"I wouldn't be so sure," the guard said. "The crazies might just find a way to storm the Chancellery. I heard they have more magic than anyone expected."

Her heart beat faster.

"But don't worry." He spread a hand hastily. "The military's out in force."

The door above the guard opened. Volland! He would always spare her a moment. "What's going on?"

"It's bad, dear," he said gently, walking past the guard. "All of the workers are dead. It happened a few moments ago, at sunrise. Freddy must have ended his magic."

"He *chose* to kill all those people?" She adjusted her vision of the world outside—now seeing the streets littered with bodies.

"It's possible he may have been killed himself. Although we had protection spells on him, spells can be broken. If he dies, his magic dies with him. But for it to happen right as the sun rises does suggest a deliberate action to me—that he, or his captors, chose to end the workers' lives at dawn. We can only speculate for now."

Marlis clenched her fist, smothering just how disturbed she was at the idea of losing not just Ida but also Freddy. She'd grown up with both of them. "Freddy never got to . . . I mean, he was so young."

"He may have betrayed us," Volland said, but he sounded sympathetic.

"Even if he betrayed us . . . it's our fault, really. We never really—I don't know. We didn't give him much respect."

"You might be right. But it's too late now." Volland patted her shoulder. "Can you tell the others? I just wanted to share the latest news."

"Of course."

She watched Volland's scarecrow-lean body dash back up the stairs. The door shut her out once again.

THREE

Thea tried to lose herself in the smell of coffee, the familiarity of her own kitchen, of filling cups and stirring in sugar and milk.

Trying not to think of those last moments with Father. Watching his spirit slip away. Holding his hand as it went still and lifeless. She had to leave his body on the street, covered by her coat, and walk home with Mother.

Stop.

She handed one cup to Freddy, who stood close to Thea in the kitchen, crowded between the cabinet and chipped enamel sink. The rest she distributed around the small table adjacent to the kitchen, where Nan, Sigi, and her mother occupied all three of the chairs. Coffee would do little to battle the exhaustion in their eyes, but it was nice to do some small thing for the people she loved.

"We need to make a plan," Nan said. "Freddy isn't safe here. Everyone will be looking for him." Her voice was a little sharper than Thea remembered. Nan was always tough, but never so serious. Now she seemed all edges and angles, and her face matched—it was thinner, her cheekbones standing out, her blond cropped hair ruffled and unwashed.

"Maybe you should introduce me to your friends, Thea," her mother said. "I know I haven't been myself, but I do remember you mentioning Nan before. Didn't you two work together?"

"Yes," Thea said, "at the club." She looked at Nan uncertainly. *What are you, anyway?*

Nan hadn't explained much to Thea, either. There hadn't been time.

Nan looked at the table. "So much has changed since we worked at the club. I didn't know how to explain. I still don't. Sigi's mother, Arabella von Kaspar, told me I was a Norn. I'd never heard of it, and she had to dig up these dusty books to try and convince me. All I knew was, I'd always felt different, and the description matched—that Norns can't see colors, for instance."

"I *have* heard of Norns," Thea's mother said.

"You have?" Thea asked.

"Yes. In the north, there is a festival dedicated to them. They're believed to be the guardians of magic and the sacred forest. But I don't know much more than that. I lived in southern Irminau."

"And you didn't die, Nan," Thea said. "Do you have some kind of magic?"

"I think so, but I don't know how to use it. I don't really know much of anything." Nan shrugged like she was trying not to show how much this distressed her.

Thea's mother turned to Freddy. "Now, you—I see, with

your silver hair, that you're a sorcerer. A powerful one. You had something to do with what happened. . . ."

He glanced down. "I had everything to do with what happened."

"That's not quite true," Thea said. "They made him do it. The government took him from his family when he was a child because he could raise the dead. That's why he has to hide now, so they don't try it again."

Thea's mind flashed back to the kiss they had shared out in the hall, just minutes ago. *My first kiss, shared with a boy whom everyone will be hunting for.* She'd imagined her first kiss would be a joyous thing, but the memory lingered bittersweet on her lips. Nothing about Freddy felt safe.

"Are you the one who brought back my husband?"

"I brought back all of them." Freddy's eyes were still pointed at the floor.

"This is the sort of thing we left Irminau to avoid." Mother put a hand on Freddy's shoulder. "Don't apologize, Freddy. If they forced you into it, then . . ."

Mother had plenty of stories about life in the village where she had grown up, but she didn't talk much about why she and Father left their home in the neighboring country of Irminau. Now she said, "When we came to Urobrun, we were promised a land without magic."

"But," Sigi said, "is that really better? I used to walk the streets taking photographs of people. I remember—" She tapped her left temple impatiently. "My memories are still coming back. It's almost there. I think I'd hurt myself. Twisted my ankle, maybe. This old man was on the street and he healed me, but he looked panicked the whole time, and as soon he was done, he ran away. As if I was going to go tell the police or something."

"It would be painful, I'd think, to be able to heal people but feel like you were forbidden to do it," Thea said.

Sigi nodded. Thea didn't really know Sigi—she had come out of the underground with Nan—but Thea felt an affinity with her. Sigi was just another ordinary girl, albeit a wealthy one. She was short and plump and likable-looking, with a head of wild brown curls and a few faint freckles. "My mother was Arabella von Kaspar, the leader of one of the revolutionary groups. She talked about it all the time, how magic should be free."

Mother twisted her loose hair into a coil. She still wore it unfashionably long. "Magic should be a gift. But shortly after I got married, King Otto called for all the magic users in the country to register at the palace, and they didn't leave. I couldn't have children in a place like that. Magic didn't run in our families, but sometimes it appears out of nowhere." She opened a drawer, scrounged a couple of pins, and put her hair up.

It's been so long since I've seen Mother fix her own hair. With the bound-sickness that tied her by magic to Thea's missing father, she forgot the simplest things. Thea had to remind her to put on stockings before leaving for church, or how to make eggs.

"I shudder to think of Irminau's response to this," Mother continued, her hand now moving to the photograph of Father in his army uniform. "When they hear how much trouble this country is in, King Otto will surely take advantage."

"What can you tell us about King Otto?" Nan asked. "How much of a threat do you think he poses?" Her fingers twitched like she wanted to take notes.

"The papers make him out to be rather foolish," Thea said. "They say he just builds models of his castle and has portraits painted of himself in costumes."

"Well, *papers*," Sigi said. "They'll say anything that sounds entertaining."

"King Otto was no fool when I lived in Irminau," Mother said. "Conniving and eccentric, yes. But a lot of people in Irminau love him. He can seem like a father figure, and has built a strong national pride. But then he began taking steps to round up the magic users, and all of us with our eyes open left if we could."

"How many kinds of magic users are there?" Nan asked.

"Healers and garden witches," Mother said. "Nearly every village had those. Then there are elemental powers, also fairly common, and witches that handle basic connective spells like binding magic. But I have no idea how many types of rare magic, like reviving, might exist."

"Why didn't the magic users rebel," Freddy asked, "if that's where Otto's power comes from?"

"Some of them have favored positions at his court," Mother said. "And magic users are such a small section of the population. They are appreciated, but also feared. Many people back home saw King Otto's tough laws simply as keeping magic under control.

"But to answer your original question," Mother continued, "Urobrun once belonged to Otto's kingdom, and all the wars this nation has fought since trace back to the original battle for independence."

"If Otto decided to march his army in here, would Urobrun be able to fight back?" Nan asked.

"The military is already stretched thin," Freddy said. "And who knows what will happen here after today."

Nan's eyes darted quickly across each of them. "That's why we need to try and find a safe place to hide," she said. "To protect ourselves—especially Freddy—from the Chancellor's forces and Irminau's, and even the revolutionaries."

"Maybe with my father?" Sigi ventured. "He wasn't involved with the revolutionaries. He hasn't lived with my mother for years. And his apartment's swank—it's over on Parc. We'd have to sleep on the floor, but at least there's a good pantry to raid."

"I'm worried someone might find us there," Nan said.

"I bet he could find us a place with some friends," Sigi said. "He and I do get along better than Mother and I did. He's a bit of a lout, but I think he can keep a secret."

"It's better than staying here. We need to get on the move immediately."

Mother's hands were clenched around her mug of coffee, but she hadn't taken a single sip. "You should do what you need to do," she said softly, touching the back of the chair like it was an anchor. "I know you'll return safely."

"You don't know," Thea said, hesitant. She wanted to go with her friends, but she wanted just as much to stay with Mother, who had been sick for so long. Now she was sharp and well, bringing a sense of comfort Thea hadn't felt in years.

"You'd go crazy with worry if you stayed here," Mother said.

Thea squeezed her hand. Mother was her old self, except that the old Mother wouldn't have let Thea leave. Mother had just lost the man she loved, the man she had been bound to by magic. Thea met her eyes with the fears she wouldn't voice. "Just swear to me you'll be here safe and sound when I get back, too."

"I promise," Mother said. "I might get a few more supplies." Outside the window, people were hauling bags of food. "The smart ones are getting provisions now, before they're gone."

"Maybe you should pack some clothes," Nan told Thea, "quickly."

Thea didn't have that many clothes to begin with, so it wasn't hard to sweep the contents of her wardrobe and vanity into a bag. Winter was coming, and she had abandoned her coat as a shroud for Father's body. At the time, it had not seemed important. Coats could be replaced. Now she wondered if that would be true. Having packed the clothes, Thea threw in her book of old fairy tales from Father Gruneman, then snapped her bag shut.

Her mother hugged her so tight that Thea let out a tiny croak of pain.

"Be safe," Mother said, her voice breaking.

"If worse comes to worse, I still have Father Gruneman's gun." Thea picked up her purse, feeling the weight.

"That poor man," Mother said. "Though I'm not surprised he was in deep." On top of everything else, last night Thea had to break the news to Mother that their beloved priest had been killed for his involvement with the revolution.

Then the four of them ran out into the street, leaving Thea's mother behind.

"Let's take the back way down Arch Street," Thea said.

In front of Thea's apartment, it might have been any other day. The sidewalks were flush with the pure, golden light of morning. It seemed wrong to have such a beautiful, cloudless sky when the city was full of the bodies of lost loved ones.

Several long paces behind them, a man was hunched into a gray coat, the brim of his cap pulled down over his face. Nan looked back at him suspiciously.

"Thea, maybe I should carry the gun," Nan said in a low voice.

Thea wouldn't argue with that idea. She didn't like having responsibility for the weapon; even in self-defense, she wasn't sure she had the guts to shoot someone. As she handed over the purse, the man walking behind them glanced up.

FOUR

Last night Freddy had escaped his prison. No guards had followed him underground. For the first time in his life, every turn of the path, every decision was his own.

He didn't want to let that freedom go. He had to fight an urge to clutch Thea's hand tighter and run, as if he could outrun his fate.

"The candy store is closed," Thea commented. "Maybe all the shops are. It already feels like the war all over again."

Freddy followed her gaze to a tiny shop tucked ahead in the narrow street. Tiered towers of flower- and fruit-shaped marzipan in the windows, colored pink and green and orange, caught the eye even from a distance.

He veered closer to the window, to peer in for just a moment. Thea followed easily, their shared touch adding a new element to conversation.

"Come on!" Nan said. "What are you two doing? We don't have time!"

Where one man had been behind them, now there were two. They were picking up their pace—and looking at Freddy.

He instinctively clutched his hat, although his silver hair was hidden.

"You three, *run*," Nan said, her voice tense. "I'll distract them."

The men each took out a gun.

Freddy cursed and put a protective arm around Thea. They wouldn't hurt him when they needed his magic, but they could hurt anyone around him.

"Stop!" one of the men shouted. "We don't want to harm you." He was the shorter of the two, their appearance otherwise concealed under coats, hats, and scarves.

"Wait—I know you," said the taller one, whose dark brows were furrowed in concentration under the brim of his hat. He was looking at Sigi. "You're one of the workers! Why aren't you dead?"

Sigi stiffened. "I certainly was not!" Her upper-class accent grew more pronounced.

He looked at her feet. "How about those worker-issue boots, then?"

"Who are you?" Sigi demanded.

"I was one of the guards underground."

"You work for the Chancellor?" Nan asked, stepping forward, putting Sigi behind her.

"No, I was spying for the revolution. We are with the Hands of the White Tree." He motioned to his companion. "I'm Max and this is Will. We have a safe place here in the city where you can hide."

"If you're here to help us, why were you shadowing us down the alley?" Freddy asked.

"We wanted to make sure it was you," Will said. "And—we weren't sure if you'd trust us."

"Good call there. I don't trust you," Freddy said. "I already told one of your men I want to be left alone."

"That wasn't one of *our* men," Will said. "Probably someone from one of the other revolutionary factions. Sebastian doesn't want you to work for him. He just wants to make sure you're safe."

"Who is Sebastian?" Freddy asked. "And why should I trust him?"

"Sebastian," Nan repeated. "I've seen some of his tracts."

"The name sounds familiar." Sigi's nose scrunched thoughtfully. "He's young, isn't he? I think my mother mentioned him."

"He's our leader, and he's an Irminauer. So are we." Will looked at Freddy and held a hand out slightly, as if offering the kinship of shared rustic heritage.

But plenty of Freddy's enemies were Irminauer.

"He's young but he knows what he's doing," Max said. "You must realize your magic is too important for you to be wandering around. Come with us, for your own good."

"For my own good," Freddy scoffed. "That's what they all say." But it was dangerous for him to be out. It would take just one wrong person glimpsing his silver hair. Should he trust them? Could he?

The men glanced at each other briefly.

Then Max shot Freddy.

FIVE

After fumbling with the clasp of Thea's purse, Nan had the gun in her hands.

"Stop right there," she warned, "or I'll shoot back."

Freddy staggered behind Nan.

"Are you all right?" Thea asked Freddy.

"It hit me." He sounded bewildered, and now Nan glanced back to see him pulling up the leg of his pants. A bruise was already darkening, but a gunshot should leave more than a bruise.

"It *did* hit me," he insisted.

Sigi picked up something small off the ground. "Here's the bullet."

"There must be—some kind of protection on me," Freddy said. "I never knew."

Nan's focus whipped back to the revolutionaries.

"Are you Nan?" asked Will. The eyes peering out under his cap looked deceptively friendly.

Nan kept her hands steady around the weapon. She had never held a gun before, but this feeling was familiar. Like she had held weapons in other lives, held a man's fate in her hands many times before.

"Sebastian would like to see you, too. He knows what you are. He wants to help you find the answers."

As Nan feared, Arabella must have told others about her. But Arabella got her information from other revolutionaries. What if Sebastian *did* know something? She still needed more answers than she'd been given. She only knew bits and pieces—the strange song in her head, her defiance of death, her inability to see colors. She couldn't stop thinking of the flash of color she had seen from Sigi's kiss.

Green. She had known its name, her gray world peeled back to allow a glimpse of beauty.

"Don't trust them." Freddy stood up again. "They just shot me in the leg."

The men exchanged a more serious glance. Their eyes said *Whatever it takes.* Nan recognized that look. She probably had it, too. So it would be a test of who really meant it. She met Thea's eyes and looked up ahead at a break between buildings, a narrow lane leading back to the busier street. Thea nodded almost imperceptibly, acknowledging the escape plan. They had to communicate with a look all the time when they worked together at the Telephone Club. Hopefully Sigi and Freddy would know to follow.

Thea grabbed Freddy's hand and started to run.

Max fired again.

A pained scream cut through Nan's ears.

Thea let go of Freddy's hand. Her left hand was covered in blood. The bullet had cut through Thea's hand and stopped when it reached Freddy's protected skin. Nan registered all of this in a split second, and then she fired back at Max's knee.

Anger pulsed through her hands. With a little less self-control, she might have shot to kill. But she'd be no better than Arabella, who killed Rory Valkenrath without giving him a chance for redemption.

The bullet struck. She heard the crack of impact, like it hit a wall. But Max didn't bleed.

So, he was protected like Freddy. *I should know how to get out of this,* Nan thought. Unknown magic thrummed inside her; she had started to use it with Rory, and she felt it now, but she didn't understand her power, didn't know what would happen if she let it out.

"Why did you hurt *her*?" Freddy lunged toward Max and grabbed his arm, shoving his hand toward the ground, trying to wrest away the gun. Will had his gun out too, but he had taken a step back.

When he saw Nan's gun train on him, he held up his hands. "We didn't want to hurt anyone. I swear."

"That's hard to believe," Nan said.

Max dodged Freddy's fists. He moved with the experience of training, his evasion as graceful as the way he used Freddy's miss to knock him off balance and punch him back. Freddy staggered, and Max kicked him to the ground.

"Max!" Will looked as horrified as Thea, who was rushing toward Freddy's fallen form, a stain of blood spreading on her sweater where her hand was tucked under the wool.

"Please!" she shouted, her voice wild with pain. "Please, stop!" She put her good hand to his bruising jaw.

"Max, all these gunshots! What are you thinking? The police are going to come!" Will said. "We have to get them out of here." His eyes implored Nan and Thea. "Your hand will be all right, miss. We have a healer. You won't want to go to the hospital. They're already dangerously crowded with people wounded in the uprising."

Nan lowered her gun, and Max lowered his, too. There was still a gleam in his eye she didn't trust. But Thea was badly hurt. And Will was right. If their fight alerted the police, that would be worse.

Freddy seemed to be thinking the same thing. He lifted his hands in a gesture of surrender, but his eyes were dark.

"I'll come with you," he said, "but your healer had better be good."

SIX

"Let's get a bandage on that to stop the bleeding." Will glanced at Thea, all business now. He unbuttoned his coat to access a small bag slung across his chest and took out a roll of bandages.

She stepped back into Freddy's arms when Will tried to get close. "Don't touch me." Tears of pain blurred her eyes. Max had fired at them like he shot people every day.

"I shouldn't have done that," Max said abruptly, as if he read her mind. "I don't know what got into me. I won't hurt you anymore." He held up his hands.

Thea let Will wrap her mangled hand. The pain had stolen her speech. She wanted to cry but she wouldn't give them the satisfaction. The world was a blur; she was aware of climbing into the spacious backseat of a clunky black car, and Freddy putting his arm close around her, but she must have passed out after that, because the next thing she knew, she was in a stranger's arms as he carried her into a sunlit room and placed her in bed.

"Don't worry," he said. "Ingrid's going to take care of you."

"Where did my friends go?" she asked, panic rising.

"I'm going to meet with them now."

"Are you Sebastian?" She thrashed her head back and forth, writhing as if she could escape the searing in her hand, only vaguely aware of Sebastian himself. He was young, as Sigi had said.

He gave her a cup of medicinal-smelling liquid. "Drink that for the pain. It'll be over soon."

She took the liquid, and sleepy warmth immediately rushed over her.

A little later, she opened her eyes when she heard something rustle. A girl was at her bedside. This must be Ingrid, slight and small-featured, with fair hair spilling over her shoulders. She looked young, but Thea had the sense that she was older than she appeared—something about the shadows under her gray eyes, and the way she sat so still. When she saw Thea was awake, she tilted her head like a bird. "Are you feeling any better?" Her accent was rustic and thick.

"A little." She felt drowsy and stupid. It would be so easy to succumb to the cheerful numbness of drugs. *Stay alert.*

"Where am I?" she asked.

"We have houses to stay in, throughout the city, that belong to our friends. This house belongs to Mr. Schiff, the zeppelin builder. Isn't he kind? I think this room must have been his daughter's." On the nightstand was a porcelain doll in a dusty pinafore, a stuffed bear, and a glass of water. The wallpaper was striped yellow and cream with chains of small roses, while the white bedspread was embellished with frills.

"You're a healer?"

"Yes. I'm a Norn—like your friend." The harsh sounds of her accent contrasted with a certain dreaminess of tone.

"Norn," Thea repeated, trying to fix the idea in her fuzzy mind. She still didn't really understand what Nan was. "My friends—they're with Sebastian?"

"Yes. I expect they'll have plenty to say. Sebastian always does." Ingrid was gazing at the sunlight beaming through the window as she spoke. She suddenly put a small, cool hand on Thea's arm, trying to pull it away from her chest. "I need to look at it."

Thea winced and drew back. "It's—it's all right," she said, although it wasn't. "Can you just find Nan for me?"

"First I need to see your wound." Ingrid took a firm hold of Thea this time. She pulled the bandage away from her skin—slowly, with careful little fingers. Ingrid's hands could've belonged to a child.

Fibers clung to dried blood, and Thea sucked air through her teeth.

"It hurts," Ingrid said gently.

"Of course it does." Thea's voice shook, especially when she saw the wound laid bare again. If it were anyone else's hand, she might have looked away from the torn red flesh.

"I'll soothe the pain," Ingrid said, but Thea already felt the pain melting away, even though her hand looked awful. "How's that?"

"A lot better."

Ingrid bent over and rummaged around on the floor. When she came back up, she had Thea's book of fairy tales. "I saw this poking out of your bag. Running away with clothes and lipstick and a book of Irminauer tales?" She smiled a little. Her teeth were neat and straight.

"Father Gruneman gave it to me when I was little," Thea said. "At my father's memorial." She thought Ingrid might know Father Gruneman, since he'd been a revolutionary leader.

"Father Gruneman must have understood that the forest always calls us home, even here in the city," Ingrid said, putting the book in front of Thea and opening it to an image of a girl in beautiful stylized robes plucking a mushroom from the forest floor. "The pictures are lovely."

Thea glanced at her uncertainly. She was still holding Thea's wounded hand, her touch featherlight but never breaking contact. "Are you going to heal my hand?"

"Yes, of course I am. But it might hurt a lot, just for a moment. Have some more medicine"—Ingrid poured from a bottle on the nightstand—"and look at your beautiful book."

Thea took the medicine. "It'll be all right, though?" she asked. The medicine had deadened some of her fear, but in the back of her mind she thought that if she lost the use of some of her fingers, she wouldn't be able to work many places anymore.

"It will be fine very soon." Her voice was even, soothing. Thea heard the actual words less and the rhythm more. The words were like water running over rocks, constant and sweet, and she closed her eyes.

"Your voice is like a song," Thea said. "My mother used to sing to me when I was sick." Mother sang all the time, before her sickness. Sometimes it was annoying, Mother throwing open the curtains and waking her up for school singing. But other times it was nice. She wished Mother were here now.

"I could give you a song," Ingrid asked. "It will help."

"Okay."

Ingrid began to chant—it was more like a chant than a song—long, beautiful tones. The music seemed to spin its way into the picture of the girl in the forest, so the colors grew brighter and Thea could almost smell moss and earth. Ingrid's hand upon her arm was like a thread to another world, not unlike that fairy-tale forest that was a little bit frightening but also full of wonder. Anything could happen. The chant filled her with a sense of Ingrid's power.

Thea felt something bite her wrist, heard a grinding, and her eyes snapped away from the book.

Ingrid held a bone saw in one hand, driving the blade just above Thea's wrist with long, slow strokes. The saw was bright with Thea's blood, but Ingrid had put cloths down so none would drip onto the bedspread or the carpet. Thea saw this through a haze of soothing tones and visions. She tried to say something, but her body was too dulled to speak or move. Ingrid's eyes were half-closed, almost dreamy, as her lips moved with her strange song, but when she saw Thea looking, her note trailed off.

"I'm sorry if it still hurts a little." Ingrid's words retained their rhythm. "I didn't think I'd be giving this gift to you. But one must trust in fate."

SEVEN

"Wait here. I'll get Sebastian." Will had shown Nan, Freddy, and Sigi into the cellar of a labyrinthine home, one of the grand old mansions overlooking Mecklinger Park.

As soon as he climbed the stairs, Sigi squinted after him. "Sebastian wants Freddy, and he knows something about you," she told Nan. "But I'm not very interesting. I'll scope out the place while you talk to them."

"Just don't get shot," Nan said.

"They are trigger-happy, aren't they? Well, hopefully they've gotten it out of their system. I can be quite charming if I feel like it." Sigi fluttered her lashes, her tone light, but Sigi always joked when she was tense. Her mother had traded her life for Sigi's last night; Nan couldn't imagine what she must be thinking now.

Nan handed Sigi the purse with the gun. No one had confiscated it; hopefully that showed some measure of mutual trust, but she'd feel better if Sigi had a weapon. "Don't get lost, either. This place is as big as a hotel."

"That I can't promise." Sigi moved to the stairs.

Freddy was peering over the long table; at least twenty chairs fit down its length, and maps of the city and the nations of Irminau and Urobrun were spread out, with a few points marked. Shelves stocked with tins of food lined the walls. Barrels and sacks of grain, beans, and wine occupied much of the empty floor space. If they stayed, Nan imagined she'd be eating better than she had in a long time.

Thea was unconscious when they arrived and had been whisked away to the healer over their protests.

It didn't matter anyway, Nan thought. Clearly, they were not in control here. Guards had watched them pass through the outside entrance, their purpose clear despite the fact that they wore plain clothes and not uniforms.

Nan thought Sigi might run into guards and be ushered back down to the cellar, but moments passed and Sigi didn't reappear. Boots thumped down the stairs, followed by a disheveled dark suit and a scruffy face. The young man was already holding out his hand before he reached the bottom. "Sorry about all of the trouble. Sebastian Hirsch." He gripped Freddy's hand. "I'm so embarrassed by the whole incident."

Nan was too surprised to return the handshake with her usual grip when he moved on to her. She had expected Sebastian to be a younger version of Rory or Arabella—arrogant, authoritative, wealthy enough to own this house. Instead, she got what looked like an unshaven college student. At a second glance, though, he did have the appropriate revolutionary look: half-laborer, half-intellectual; dark-haired with eyeglasses, strong hands, penetrating eyes, and military posture.

"I can't believe you would send your men out with orders to shoot," Freddy said. "Thea is innocent in all of this. Her father just died this morning. And now she's had to take a *bullet* for me."

Sebastian gripped his hands together. "Well, I think we've had a gross misunderstanding." His voice was aristocratic, but not the way Sigi's voice was. His was the rougher tone of a wealthy Irminauer. Even their nobility sounded like they came from the deep, dark wood. "What I *told* them was to bring you and Nan to safety. Obviously I didn't want anyone to be hurt. That would belie the whole mission. I did say that you might not trust us, and as a *last resort*, they could use force if necessary. Max is one of my best men. He's got a bit of a mouth on him sometimes, but violence isn't like him."

Sebastian paused, studying Freddy. "I know you're reluctant to trust me after this, but my concern is that you're safe. I'm not sure how many people Arabella told about you, or how many government officials know you exist." His attention shifted from Freddy to Nan. "You're Nan, aren't you?"

She bristled. "How much did Arabella tell you about me?"

"Arabella didn't *want* to tell me anything," he said. "She didn't like me. But in this case, she needed information. She approached me asking about Norns. It took a while to tease out the fact that she'd found one."

"So you were the one who gave her the book I found at her house?"

"Probably. I heard you went to one of her parties, but of course she left me off the invitation list. What an audacious woman." He pulled out a chair. "Have a seat, if you like. We have a lot to talk about. Do you mind being called Nan? Arabella wouldn't tell me your last name."

"It's Nan Davies. But Nan is fine. I never knew my parents anyway." Nan sat on the edge of the chair, her guard still up.

"Well, I'm glad to have found you looking none the worse for wear this morning. Not everyone was so lucky."

She glanced down. It was still hard to believe that every other person she'd met underground was dead now.

He leaned back in his chair and crossed his legs on the table, like he was settling in for a story. "One of your sisters is here."

"You mean—another Norn?" She sat up straighter, more hopeful that he really might have answers for her.

"There are three of you in Irminau, and Ingrid—"

"We aren't in Irminau," Nan said. "I wasn't even born there."

"Details, details. The river unites Irminau and Urobrun in spirit if not in borders." He took his feet off the table and spread his hands across the map depicting the two countries. "And you must know that we were one country, two hundred years ago." He pointed at the northern region of Irminau. "The river Urobrun originates from the mountains here and flows through the great forest of Irminau." He traced the line of the river through Irminau, the larger of the two countries. Urobrun was like a small triangle snipped off the tip of Irminau, but it had much of the fertile land and access to the sea. "Magic flows from the forest to the river, spreading to the people who live near it, losing potency as it goes until finally it reaches the sea."

"I've seen stories about magic coming from the forest, but does it really?" Freddy asked.

"The stories are true." Sebastian pointed at Freddy with a pencil. "Magic comes from the great tree called Yggdrasil." He flourished the pencil along with the name. "Every year the Norns would bring water from the river Urobrun to water the roots of Yggdrasil, and in return, magic would flow out of the tree and to the people."

Yggdrasil. That name stirred the ghost of a memory within her.

Home, whispered a voice inside her. Nan remembered the wind whispering through the dense green leaves, felt the rough texture of the bark beneath her fingers. Then she shook her head, trying to dispel the thought. She was a city girl who had never even seen a forest. A tree? Her home definitely wasn't a tree.

"Do you remember it at all?" Sebastian asked.

"No," she lied.

"That may be because of the tragedy. Someone killed you and your other sister, in your previous lives."

Every word he spoke stirred fresh images. Two women: one dark-haired and serious, the other just a young girl. *My sisters.* It didn't seem possible that she could have family, stretching across more than one life, when she had grown up feeling so alone.

"Ingrid was the only Norn left to protect Yggdrasil," Sebastian continued. "One night the tree was felled by men from Urobrun. They even dug up the roots. This pivotal moment helped lead to the war. Ingrid worried the destruction of the tree would disrupt your memories."

"So the Urobrunians destroyed the tree . . . in order to destroy magic?" Nan asked.

"Exactly."

"But it obviously didn't work," Freddy said. "Magic isn't gone."

"Ingrid planted a new tree from seeds she had saved. But it hasn't been the same since. Children are rarely born with magic now." He looked at Nan again. "The main revolutionary force in the city wanted to free the workers and overthrow the Chancellor in favor of a fair and open government. But we—the Hands of the White Tree—look past that. The people of Urobrun can say they don't need magic and call the people of Irminau backward rustics—but this country will always be a part of Irminau, with Yggdrasil at its heart."

"You want unification?" Freddy asked.

"It only makes sense. Each country has different resources. And each is messed up in a different way."

"So what about the Norns?" Nan asked. "How do we fit in?"

"You should all hear the music of fate—the wyrdsong."

"The sounds I hear at night," Nan said softly, amazed at just how much he knew, that he could put a name to the song in her dreams.

"So you do still retain that connection," he said. "Ingrid will be glad to hear it. The wyrdsong guides you. It'll help you know how fate is meant to go."

"I sensed that," Nan said. "I tried to use it on Rory Valkenrath, when I was trying to convince him that he needed to release the dead. I thought somehow that if he heard it, he would understand. And I think it was working, until Arabella shot him."

How strange it was to hear she had such responsibility, and Sebastian was so much more forthcoming than Arabella.

"So . . . you're the leader of all this?" Freddy asked. "You still haven't explained how that happened."

"My father oversaw a small duchy in Irminau," said Sebastian with a shrug. "So I'm fairly well-versed in everything from military operations to taxes."

"How many men do you have?" Nan asked. "What's the plan?"

"About five hundred, all told," Sebastian said. "This is the central base. We occupy two other buildings as well—Bauer Hall and Reuenthal House."

"It'll take more than five hundred men to unify Urobrun and Irminau," Freddy said.

Sebastian looked unfazed, leaning back in his chair. "Yes, the UWP is much larger than us, for now."

"The UWP?" Freddy asked.

"The United Workers Party," Nan said. "The Valkenraths didn't let you read the paper, then?"

"Afraid not." Freddy crossed his arms.

"The UWP are the dominant revolutionary group in the city," Sebastian said. "We'll support them to keep the city from falling to Irminau." He pushed back his sleeve to check a wristwatch. "I'd rather not allow King Otto and his magic users to gain a foothold here."

A young man walked halfway down the stairs and peered in. "Sir, Karetzky is here with a report."

"Ah, a messenger." Sebastian lifted a hand. "I'll be there

soon. Tell him to wait in my office." He turned back to Nan. "Make yourselves at home. There's a spread of food upstairs, if you're hungry."

She could barely recall the last time she'd eaten. Food seemed an alien concept.

"What about Thea?" Freddy asked. "How long does healing take?"

"You'll be the first to know when Ingrid is done," Sebastian said. "But don't worry. She's a miracle worker with wounds."

EIGHT

Thea tried to scream. Her brain and voice fought to connect, and a hoarse sound tore from her throat. Ingrid's eyes met hers.

Her eyes were a clear gray that bored into Thea's soul. *Trust.* She kept singing, her voice more beautiful than any song of earth. The sound seemed to match Thea's thoughts—shape her thoughts, even. Pain fell away.

She had seen her father die with the sunrise. She had held his hand and watched him go. She had seen a man rotting in the depths of the underground, workers shot on the street, her mother left alone with sorrow written on her face. So many terrible things she wanted to wipe from her mind, so many burdens she wondered how she could bear. Ingrid's song, Ingrid's eyes . . . they offered release.

Forget these pains. Don't think. Let the world's song beat with your own heart, and nothing you have seen on earth will matter.

All the dark memories that pulsed in Thea's heart grew buoyant. If she just opened her hand, they would fly free, and she would be free of them.

Father—Mother—

Her jaw trembled with uncertainty. The motion of the saw reverberated up her arm as her bone split clean in two. The split was like the calm after the storm—the grinding gone silent, her arm set free of ugly memories. Ingrid's hand gripped her arm just above her wrist, and Thea felt her blood held back by Ingrid's will. Then the wound began to seal, skin climbing over blood and bone. Everything she saw and felt seemed far away, like reading a horror novel on a sunny day. It wasn't real.

Her injured hand had dropped onto the cloths. It was just a dead thing now, like her father's body with his soul gone out of it.

Scream. Scream! Please, scream! Stop her!

Ingrid seemed to notice her distress, and smiled at Thea, the sun streaming through the windows catching her fair hair so she looked radiant as a painted angel. And then she held up a new hand, a splendid wooden hand with neatly articulated little fingers. Designs were burned into the wood, curls and patterns, the kind of dreamy images that might float in one's head just before falling asleep at night. Ingrid was like a *nightmare*—

A *dream* come to life, Thea thought, with her strange melody and her wise eyes.

Ingrid held the wooden hand to the stump where her old hand had been, and Thea could feel that this was not just any wood. It was alive. As soon as it touched her, it began to put out roots that crawled through her skin, tickling beneath, wending their way inside of her. Filling her with everything she had lost.

All the pain was gone now.

Ingrid let the last note die softly. Then she cocked her head again. "Does your hand feel better?"

"Yes." Another answer teased at her mind. But why? Of course she felt better.

Now when she looked at her left hand, she didn't see the wood, but the perfect match to her right. The pale hue of her palms, the thin lines webbing across, the pinker shade of her fingertips, the veins running beneath—it was all there. And the wooden hand moved exactly as she wished it to, even though it only had the ghost of sensation. No one would know it was wood, except Thea.

"Even you will forget," Ingrid said, seeming to read her mind.

Yes, I will forget, she thought. *It's better than new.*

"This wood is from my tree," Ingrid said.

"Your tree?"

"My Yggdrasil." Ingrid looked slowly at the ceiling, like she was following the line of branches above her head instead of a hairline crack in the plaster. "The sacred tree of Irminau. It's the most beautiful place, Thea. I wish we could go there now, so you could feel its magic running all through you. You would feel such serenity. But now you have a little piece of it. Do you feel it?"

A vision flashed over Thea's head: the bright spring green of a tree's branches filling the room, blocking the ceiling from view entirely. It brought her back to childhood, to summers in the forests outside the city visiting Uncle Peter or her mother's dear friend Antje. But this was the tree of all trees. A tree so strong and magnificent that she almost thought she heard the rustle of its leaves across the miles. "I do."

Ingrid's eyes dropped back down to meet Thea's, and the vision broke. "But you mustn't tell anyone. There isn't enough magic to go around."

"Like Freddy's magic." Thea understood. "We can't tell anyone, because he can't bring back every person that dies. And you can't give everyone a piece of Yggdrasil."

"Yes. You understand." Ingrid wiped away the blood smeared on Thea's arm. "I'm glad you came. There are never many girls around here, and I've missed my sisters. I hope you'll help me protect my tree."

"Of course I will," Thea said, eager to have purpose. She was no longer just a sixteen-year-old girl who had left school and become a waitress, a girl who had fallen in with Freddy by accident and could not match his power.

Ingrid had trusted her with something great.

NINE

Sebastian showed Freddy and Nan to a dining room. Sigi was already there, eating a sandwich piled high. The remnants of lunch were spread across one end of the grand table: breads, cold cuts and boiled sausages, cheeses, sliced potatoes, pickles, butter, horseradish, and mustard. Only a lifetime of manners kept Freddy from grabbing food by the fistful. Thanks to his constant use of magic, he was always hungry, and last night he had worked some of the strongest magic of his life on an empty stomach.

"I hope the conversation went well," Sigi said.

"It was . . . interesting," Nan said, making a slight face.

Freddy quickly assembled a sandwich and folded it into a napkin. "I'm going to find Thea. I can't imagine healing takes longer than this."

"Good idea," Nan said.

Freddy nosed around downstairs as much as he could without seeming overly suspicious, but only found common rooms—dining room, music room, a ballroom that was quite creepy in its empty expanse, a front parlor and a back parlor, and a few miscellaneous rooms of chairs and paintings. The house overlooked a vegetable garden out back, and even now in November, a gardener was out picking lettuce. *Magic,* Freddy thought, wondering how many other sorcerers worked for Sebastian.

He headed for the stairs and almost collided with Will on the second-floor landing.

"Oh—hey," Will said. "I was just going to ask you—we have a few nice empty bedrooms. Want to come see which you'd like?"

Freddy frowned. Had Will been ordered to keep him from the third floor? The question was casual enough, but it seemed like Will had just been standing there—and choosing a bedroom sounded uncomfortably permanent. "I want to check on Thea first. It's been a while."

"Ingrid will let you know as soon as she's ready, I'm sure. I don't want to disturb her. But Thea is in the best of hands, I can tell you that. Ingrid's so gentle."

Soft footsteps were padding down the stairs. "How sweet to say. All in a day's work." A slight blond girl appeared in view. Her eyes fixed on Freddy. She reached out to touch his silver hair before she was all the way downstairs. When he flinched back, she laughed gently. "No need to be shy. I've just never seen the like on someone so young!"

"Are you Ingrid? I need to see Thea." He knew he sounded rudely blunt, but he didn't care.

"And she would like to see you," Ingrid said.

"How is she?"

"Wonderful." She waved for Freddy to follow her up.

Thea was in bed sitting back on a pile of fluffy pillows, but her eyes lit when she saw Freddy. Her left hand looked good as new. "How are you feeling?" he asked.

"A little drugged, but . . . good." She smiled up at him. "Don't worry. You look so concerned. Sit down."

Freddy pulled over the wooden chair, picking up a bottle of medicine on the nightstand. It looked similar to the stuff the maid gave him when he had a headache, but he had never seen Thea look dreamy. The room smelled very clean. "What happened?" he asked. "What did she do?"

She waved her fingers. "She fixed it, obviously. What about you, did you learn anything? Did you meet Sebastian?"

"Yes. He had a lot to say about Nan and the Norns. Ingrid is one, too."

"She told me about the tree."

"Yggdrasil?"

"I could almost see it, the way she spoke. To think we never even knew it existed! It must be the most beautiful place."

"Thea, can you tell me more about the healing? Did she give you anything else to take besides this medicine?"

"Her magic takes the pain away. It made me dream." Her expression shifted to something haunted, and then she reached for his hand. "I need a dream. It was nice to forget everything for a minute."

"I know." He gripped her hand back. Her fingers felt solid and warm. "I'm glad you're all right."

"Freddy . . ."

"Yes?"

She shook her head. "Nothing. I felt like there was some-thing I needed to tell you, but I can't even think of it."

"Are you sure?"

"Must've been a dream I had after I passed out."

This feeling of wrongness had been creeping into Freddy's mind from the moment Max shot Thea. Could he have done it deliberately to provide a reason for Ingrid to be alone with Thea? If they knew so much about Freddy already, they might also suspect he had feelings for her. That he trusted her. That he'd lost everything from his own bedroom to his cat to all the people he'd known, and she was his only anchor.

And also, his weakness.

TEN

Who was Nan Davies?

According to Sebastian's story, nobody. Her name and face were just a mask to put on for this life. She was supposed to help the Hands of the White Tree protect Yggdrasil. She must never again dream of owning her own shop or go out at night to the Telephone Club to work with Thea and joke with customers.

She would never again be an ordinary girl.

"So what did Sebastian say?" Sigi asked. "Does it match what my mother told you?"

"He knows a lot more than Arabella did. There are three Norns, and one of them is here. He said I'm supposed to . . ." She hesitated.

"What?"

"It sounds stupid when I say it aloud. Actually, it sounds stupid even if I *don't* say it aloud."

"I'm sure it's not stupid," Sigi said, leaning on the table.

"I'm supposed to bring water to a sacred tree in the north called Yggdrasil."

"That's all? But why?"

"So the water can carry magic throughout the land to the people. It preserves balance. I told you it sounded stupid."

"It sounds *mystical*. Where is this tree?"

"In Irminau. But—the tree was actually destroyed right before I was born."

"So then there's nothing to do?" Sigi poured a cup of tea from the pot on the table, although it had obviously gone cold.

"I don't know. He says Ingrid planted a new tree. She's another of the Norns. He called her 'my sister.' I suppose I should talk with her."

"Nan." Sigi tilted her head to one side. "Whenever you talk about this stuff, you know, you seem different . . . unhappy. Like you're being shipped off to boarding school."

"Maybe I just need to understand it better." She chewed her thumbnail a moment, remembering how her boss used to harass her about that habit. "I've always sensed I was different from other people. If it's my fate, how can I fight that?"

Sigi was quiet. She sipped her tea and made a face.

"You don't believe in fate, do you?" Nan asked.

Sigi shrugged. "I don't know. It just doesn't seem right that you have no choice about your own life. I mean, how do we know Sebastian and Ingrid are right?"

"I've tried to have a normal life," Nan said. "I had a normal job, and I planned to be a dressmaker. I would still love to have that life, but it never works. I can't shake that feeling, telling me I have some larger purpose to fulfill."

"But it seems like that feeling goes against your own heart. How could it be right?" Sigi stared into the teacup, now half-empty. "I guess it's easy for me to say."

"No—you're right," Nan said. "That's my problem. Everything Sebastian told me feels right and wrong at once. I have to find out more, even if it means . . . losing a part of myself. The Nan part."

She hoped Sigi understood that she would have given anything to have a normal life, to see colors and go to dances and yearn to be touched and kissed.

"You'll always be Nan," Sigi said. "Nan is already kind of strange, after all." She shot her a quick, shy smile and started making herself a second sandwich. "If you don't want to lose these aspects of yourself, then I think you should fight for them, no matter what these people say. I mean, they aren't gods, right?"

"Not exactly, but—there is a weight to all this I can't explain. Yggdrasil feels important. And I have these memories of it. . . ."

"New memories?"

"I guess they're actually old memories, but new to me, yes. I remember the way the tree felt. It was so beautiful. I felt so safe there." She shook her head. "I'm also afraid to remember more. I'm afraid something I've gained here will be lost."

"Like seeing colors?"

Nan nodded. "I'd like to understand art better. Hear music the way it should be. Your pictures . . . I understood them."

"They're black and white," Sigi said. "I guess that's why."

"It's more than that. They captured humanity in a way I understood. They were lovely."

Sigi looked away, embarrassed by praise. "You should eat something, by the way."

"I'm not hungry."

Sigi took a piece of bread and slapped a thick layer of butter on it. "This is an art you can try to appreciate: the art of bread-making."

Nan realized she was hungry after all once she took a bite. Sigi was right: Eating was a pleasure of the real world, too, and she felt more like herself tasting the fresh bread and golden, salty butter. She hadn't eaten this well in weeks.

"I'd like to have my camera," Sigi said. "My mother might have kept it, but if you think her house isn't safe, I could pay my father a visit. Probably should, even if we aren't staying there. He'd give me some money."

"I'd like to see how the city looks, anyway," Nan said. "And if he lives on Parc, that isn't far."

"Oh no!" A not-quite-unfamiliar voice cut into their conversation.

Nan whirled behind her.

"Don't tell me you're thinking of leaving." The much-mentioned Ingrid walked in, with a mysterious smile on her lips. Nan didn't need an introduction to recognize Ingrid. She *knew* this girl. While she couldn't place the details yet, everything about her was deeply familiar—her rustic accent, her soft steps, her ageless eyes.

But there was also something . . . different. Wrong. Like walking into her own bedroom and feeling someone had entered and moved things around.

Ingrid held a hand out to Nan. "Verthandi!"

Verthandi.

Nan shivered at the name, a buried part of her mind stirring from amnesia.

"Ingrid," Nan said, feeling another name tugging at her. "Skuld?"

Ingrid caught her breath, and tears sprung to her eyes. "You *do* remember."

Nan held up her free hand—Ingrid was clutching the other. "I don't remember much."

"You remember our names, though. It's a start. I'm so glad it's *you*."

The word "sister" crossed Nan's mind, but she was wary of voicing it. She had always been alone, abandoned by her parents, taken in by a guardian who was distant if kind. To have a sister—to have family—she hardly knew what to make of that. She would have wanted it more if it didn't mean turning her back on everything else she'd known.

Ingrid finally let go of her hand and touched Nan's cheek instead. "You look so very tired."

Nan shied back from the touch. "Well, I was shot yesterday by Roderick Valkenrath, when he was trying to test my mortality. Freddy brought me back to life."

"I see, I see."

Sigi looked thoughtful. "Freddy brought Nan fully back from the dead," she said. "So, if Nan died—in her life before— couldn't you have had a reviver bring her back then?"

"Revivers are rare." Ingrid sounded weary. "But—it doesn't matter. When they killed her the last time, they didn't leave anything to chance. Just rest for now. The sooner you remember, the sooner you'll be using your powers to fight with us. You'll remember me and the past we've shared."

"Will I?" Nan glanced at Sigi, who was watching this quietly.

"Yggdrasil's death has weakened us. It gave your human life more of a hold on you. I started to know what I was from the time I was eight or nine years old, but of course, the tree had not been destroyed at that time. I worried you might never remember. Now that we're together, I'll help you and you will understand everything, in time."

"Is it true we've lived many lives?" Nan asked. "Do you remember all of them?"

"I remember what I need to remember. Urd is the Norn of the past. She's the one who writes things down."

"The Norn of the past?"

Ingrid nodded. "We each have a different role when it comes to the fates. I sense the future, you sense the present, and Urd is always looking back."

"Is Urd here too?"

"She is still lost."

"How old *are* you?" Sigi asked. "How old was the tree?"

"I've long since lost count," Ingrid said, waving a hand. "The number doesn't matter. What does matter is that we understand our purpose."

"So," Nan said warily, "is there something I should do?"

"I have brought water to the tree, and I have men protecting it. That's the least of our worries. The most difficult task we've had through the years is keeping the tree safe from kings and rulers that want to exploit its powers. You have already acted according to your deepest instincts in saving the reviver and bringing him to me, so his powers can once again be used for good."

"Well, I didn't exactly *bring* him to you," Nan said.

Ingrid's eyes turned briefly hard. "Verthandi, you must remember where your power comes from and what it's meant for. Don't let *anything* distract you, or it would be the end of everything. Yggdrasil would die, all the magic in the land would die, and we would be mortal."

Mortal. She made it sound like such a dirty word.

ELEVEN

It was two o' clock in the afternoon now, at least fifteen hours since their escape from the opera house, when Marlis's father finally found her scribbling diary entries on scrap paper in an empty bedroom.

"Come rain or shine, you won't neglect the diary. I'm glad you're eating," he said, noticing an empty bowl on the nightstand.

"Have you eaten, Papa?"

"I'm not hungry."

"What would Mother say?" Marlis chided.

"Something about vitamins." He smiled slightly, but it faded quickly. His face looked lined and old in the low basement light, as if he'd aged years since she'd last seen him. "The people are demanding I speak."

The sound of the crowd had been building, the dull roar audible even in this underground sanctum. There must be thousands of them, for their voices to reach here. "You won't, will you? Surely it isn't safe."

"Wachter urged me not to, but I'm going to address the

people through the radio. I spoke to Minister Unger, and we agree that it might be comforting for you to say a few words after I do."

"Me?" This was truly an honor, to be permitted to address the people for the first time during such a crisis. "What should I say?"

"Unger has a short speech written for you. The people may not trust me, or any of the cabinet, at this moment, but to hear the voice of a young girl—and I thought it would please you." He smiled and handed her a paper.

She glanced over the words, a little disappointed to see simplistic pleas for peace and unity.

"I wrote the last few lines," Papa said. "About supporting our military. I know that's important to you, so I'm sure you can deliver them with true passion."

Marlis was known for her volunteer work at the military hospital. The newspaper often depicted her in that guise—the angelic nurse who sat by a wounded man's bedside. It was half-accurate. She cared about the soldiers, but they gave her plenty in return: thrilling stories of battle and war. This speech was the voice of that fictional girl from the newspapers. She didn't like that girl very much. "I could say more than this," she said, "something with substance."

Papa put a hand on her shoulder. "The people need comfort from you. You're the one who will tell them everything's going to be all right after I tell them what's happened. They want to believe every word of this speech, so you must speak with conviction."

She understood, now: This was another version of his "Politics is a game" speech. "Are you really going to tell them what happened?"

"We've decided to divert the people's attention to Irminau."

Marlis understood—the original justification for bringing back the dead was the losses in the war with Irminau. And since that war, King Otto had remained an unpopular figure, with the papers deriding his lavish lifestyle in his extravagant palace, Neue Adlerwald.

"Won't blaming Irminau for something we did be an invitation for another war?" she asked.

"Probably, but I'd rather go down as a unified nation fighting Irminau than have a civil war on my hands."

"I just wonder . . ." She tapped her fingers on the table. "This seems like it could be an opportunity for us. In Irminau, magic users are subjected to the demands of the king, and here, magic is outlawed. Yet people now know that you still used magic when given the chance. That makes us look hypocritical. This is our chance to relax our policy and make magic users *want* to support our side."

His posture turned rigid. "Princess . . . we can't let magic users run free. How many people here have magic? One out of a thousand, perhaps? Think how much power that tiny minority could hold over everyone else, the resentment it would brew if they could do whatever they pleased."

"There would still be laws, of course."

"History has shown that when sorcerers flaunt their power, unrest is sure to follow."

"History has not shown that. Look at the reign of King Maximillian. He employed magic users to police one another, but he also encouraged them to use their skills."

"That was over two hundred years ago. I'd say he was lucky." He put a hand on her shoulder. "A few sorcerers won't change things, and they'd be more trouble than they're worth. We need to move toward a modern world, not return to the past."

"A few sorcerers could tip the balance." But Marlis knew she had already lost him. She couldn't find a way to make Papa see that this was right. He would do what he felt was right. Why couldn't he see?

"Can you take a moment to rehearse the speech and then come to the broadcasting chamber?"

"Of course," she said, shoving back another wave of disappointment at the thought of the speech. She needed to embrace the words, even if they weren't her own.

Politics is a game.

TWELVE

Thea was changing into a fresh dress from her bag when she heard a man yell from downstairs: "The Chancellor's speaking!" Her hand still felt numb doing the buttons, but she managed. Freddy was waiting for her in the hall. Downstairs, a few men were gathered around a radio in the front parlor.

The Chancellor spoke with gravity. "A great tragedy, one I am sorry ever had to be made known . . . This dark magic, I'm afraid, began during the war. It is the result of a secret spell that Irminau used upon our brave men."

"That *Irminau* used?" Freddy whispered indignantly.

"We are not a magical nation, as Irminau is"—the Chancellor's tone was faintly condescending—"and so we still do not fully understand the workings of this magic, and certainly we did not know any antidote when it first entered the country. I know some of you, last night, saw loved ones you had thought dead. I am sorry to tell you that they *were* dead when you saw them, in the fullest sense of the word. The magic from Irminau reanimates the dead—but they are not the loved ones you knew. They return with extremely violent tendencies and few memories of their old life. We managed to keep them contained while we looked for a cure—until last night. Words cannot express my sympathies for what occurred last night."

For a moment, the radio speakers brought nothing but silence.

"He's blaming it on Irminau?" asked one of the men gathered close to the radio.

"Good old Nikki, can't fault him for consistency," said a man with bushy eyebrows. "A liar to the end."

The Chancellor went on, "With the assistance of our scientists, we were able to develop an antidote to the violence and madness that these unfortunate citizens had succumbed to. However, a dose of this serum lasted for mere hours. We could not let them go free. We were hoping to develop a cure, but when last night's outbreak occurred, for public safety, we were forced to use any means necessary to stop them—"

Behind Thea, Nan and Sigi entered the room. "Feeling better?" Nan whispered.

Thea lifted her hands. "Good as new."

"Better be," Nan said. "They shot you, and I still don't understand why."

Beside Thea, Freddy murmured, "He's dragging Marlis into this?"

The Chancellor had just introduced his daughter.

"Do you know her?" Thea knew the Chancellor's daughter from reading the society pages, although they had a dutiful and almost disappointed tone when they reported on Marlis. She never hosted costume parties or balls, and she was never spotted out at nightclubs. She was mostly seen at political events, and they tried to describe her dresses in glowing terms, but there seemed to be only so many ways they could call something "delightfully simple" or "basic, but elegant."

"She was about the only kid I was allowed to play with growing up," Freddy said.

"Really? You played with Marlis Horn? She seems very serious. What did you play?"

He rubbed his chin. "Battle, usually. I was the only one who'd play that stuff with a girl. I don't think it was ever just a game to her, though. She wants to go into politics like her father, and I bet she'd aspire to the military if she was a boy."

"I never knew. The paper just says she doesn't dance and loves to knit. The reporters don't seem to like her."

"Knit?" Freddy laughed, and then paused. "Wait. She does knit socks and scarves for soldiers in the hospital. She'll clean wounds and talk to dying people and everything. I can't think of any other politician's daughters who would do that."

"Should I be jealous?" Thea smiled.

"If I ever give you reason to think I have feelings for Marlis, you'd better suspect something's wrong with my head. She was always too patriotic for me, but I do wonder what will happen to her, if the Chancellor is removed from power."

On the radio, Marlis was speaking in a measured tone that contrasted with the youthfulness of her voice. "Last night, when I realized what was happening, I was scared. What will happen to my country? What will happen to me? But fear is not our way. We are a brave nation, a nation that rises to a challenge. We have fought for our land and for our voices to be heard. It's in these dark hours that we are tested. I know we will not fail, not even in this moment when the odds against us seem greatest. . . ."

"It seems so strange," Freddy said, "to think I was around these people just yesterday. I feel a million miles away now."

"Good thing," Thea said. She felt a little giddy, just feeling *safe*. Maybe it was an illusion, but the walls of this building seemed so secure. She was surrounded by men who were mostly her father's age, with her father's accent, and sometimes even a suggestion of her father's features. They had plenty of food and all her friends were here. Except Mother.

Mother—

She kept feeling like there was something she needed to tell Freddy. To remember.

Father—

No. *Why are you thinking of Father?* She twisted her hands, replacing the grief with the soothing image of Yggdrasil's branches above her head. *Don't think of Father. Don't think.*

THIRTEEN

"I just came from Republic Square." A man with white-blond hair staggered into the front parlor where Freddy was still hanging around the radio long after the Chancellor's speech. The man's clothes reeked of the acrid smoke that had been faint on the air. "They've been bringing the dead to the square and burning the bodies. Hundreds of them." He gripped the arm of the fellow who was trying to help him out of his coat. "It's horrible."

"Burning them?" Freddy asked, the faces of all those men and women he had revived flashing through his mind.

The man didn't even seem to hear him. "The bodies were everywhere. The smell was everywhere. I'll never forget it. It was worse than anything I ever saw in the war."

"Come on, Ulrich," one man said gently. "Let's get your coat off, get you a drink."

Sebastian came in with a few papers in his hand and leaned in the doorway. "Listen," he said, "I've gotten an update from the UWP. They built the funeral pyres for the workers. This morning the military was piling the workers in trucks, carting them off to a mass grave." He pulled off his brimmed gray cap and crumpled it in his hand. "People started bringing the bodies to Republic Square as a spontaneous protest."

"So the Chancellor could choke on the smoke of what he's done," an angry-looking man with thick round glasses retorted. "That's fitting." Some of the other men hung their heads. Freddy edged to the door. No one was looking at him, or speaking of his involvement, though it wouldn't be much of a leap.

"Even though this isn't an ideal burial," Sebastian said, "it is progress. The people aren't just accepting the Chancellor's lies. They're pushing back. I hope you will all try to pull yourselves away from the radio and eat a good dinner while we still have fresh food, because the next few days will be busy."

"Dinner!" Thea grabbed Freddy's hand. "Let's go. I barely got any lunch. And you're always hungry, aren't you?"

He let her tug him along, but she was definitely too eager. The news of the burning pyres—that might include her father's body—hadn't registered.

The house had lost electricity. A few lamps lit the dining room table, which was spread with a buffet, as even this large table wouldn't fit half the occupants of the house. They got in line and grabbed plates, then found a quiet spot to sit in a dim room near an old piano. They didn't talk much as they ate. Freddy knew something was wrong, but he didn't relish forcing Thea to remember her father's death.

As he scraped the last pieces of fried potato off his plate, the piano lid was lifted, and men started bringing in lamps to brighten the room.

"Oh, is there going to be music?" Thea asked.

"Every night," said the pianist. "Keeps our spirits up, so why stop now?"

"I never suggested you should stop," Thea said, now flashing a smile at Freddy.

Thea had a flirtatious smile; he wanted to just give in to whatever that smile wanted, but he knew this wasn't her. Normally, she would look worried. She would talk about her friends, about the revolution, about her mother.

Somber conversation filled the room as instruments were tuned, and then the musicians began to play a sentimental air. Freddy didn't know any of the popular music, since Gerik had never allowed him a radio. Thea was swaying in her seat and mouthing a few words. She leaned closer to him. "Do you want to dance?"

"I don't know how."

"What better time to learn?"

"I'm pretty sure a better time will come along than today."

She leaned her head on his shoulder. "Oh Freddy, this is the first time you've ever been free! Come on!" She grabbed his hand. "Let me teach you to dance." Her eyes were soft and merry in the low light. He could still remember the taste of her kisses.

One dance couldn't hurt. "Just one."

They stood up and stepped close. She positioned his arms and glanced down at his feet. "Let's try this—step—step—left, left . . ."

Freddy kept glancing up to survey the room. Men stood around talking, some tapping a foot to the music while others danced a little. A few were just watching Thea and Freddy, which made him nervous. Maybe they were just happy to see a girl around. Or maybe they were wondering about the powers that his hair made so obvious.

Ingrid was nowhere to be seen. In the corner, Sebastian did a little ragtime shuffle, twirled one of his men around in jest, and accepted a glass of whiskey. Something about him gave Freddy a twinge of recognition.

"He's kind of an odd character, isn't he?" Freddy said.

"Yes, but I think I like him. Maybe it's the Irminauer accent." She looked briefly sad—briefly *herself*. Her left hand twitched in his grasp.

"Does it hurt?" he asked.

"No! It doesn't hurt at all!" she said, too vehemently.

"Let me see." He pulled her hand close to his face, like he meant to kiss it—he wanted to look natural.

"It really doesn't hurt," she said. "Really, it's fine." She was breathing rather quickly. Her face now reminded him of the night when he told her what he really was, that he'd brought her father back from the dead.

"That's it," he said, stepping out of the dance position.

"What? Freddy, what?"

"You're not yourself. We need to—" He broke off, noticing Ingrid entering the room. She looked at him and smiled a little. It wasn't a friendly smile.

Can she read Thea's mind? Does she know I'm suspicious? He'd found that if he concentrated on a person he'd brought back to life, he could feel their emotions. Maybe Ingrid could, too. Maybe she could go even farther.

He didn't want to be in the same room with her.

71

"I'm just talking nonsense, aren't I? I'm sorry. I want to dance; I'm just too tired," he told Thea. "Let me show you to your room. I can't leave you alone down here with all these men."

" 'These men.' Don't be silly. I worked at a club, remember? This is about the most honorable lot I've ever been around. You go on, get some sleep, I'll be fine." She was already stepping back, catching Sebastian's eye.

Sebastian. He damn sure didn't want her dancing with the leader of this whole operation, but he didn't know what to do about it without making a scene.

Best just to find Nan. Thea couldn't get in too much trouble in an hour or two. Hopefully.

Where *was* Nan? He hadn't seen her in a while. He'd brought her and Sigi back to life, though, and still felt the ghost of a connection to them. Following the thread of magic, he found their bedroom, where Sigi appeared to be asleep while Nan read by candlelight.

"Freddy," Nan said, putting the book aside. "Where's Thea?"

"Probably dancing with Sebastian."

"With Sebastian?"

Freddy walked in, close enough to whisper, "Thea barely seems to remember anything that happened yesterday."

Nan didn't look surprised. "I thought she seemed strange, too. I feel like there's a spell at work."

"I'm worried everyone might be under that spell. And I suspect Ingrid can hear anything we say to the people she's enchanted. I have a connection to the people I work magic on, and I'd guess she's more powerful than I am."

"When I met Ingrid, I had an immediate sense that something was off." She tipped some of the wax out of the candle as it sputtered. "But the spell can't be that easy to cast, or we'd all be under it. She had to get Thea alone for a while."

"Still. What do we do, if it's true?" Freddy asked.

"I don't know yet." Nan rubbed her forehead, looking weary, her face gaunt in the candlelight. "But I will. Just stay alert."

FOURTEEN

"In need of a dance partner?" Sebastian approached Thea, while watching Freddy's retreat. "Where's he running off to?"

"He's tired."

"And you're not? How is the hand feeling?" He took her hand in his. His fingers were covered in ink stains and he had a fading summer tan—he didn't spend all his time behind a desk.

"Almost back to normal. It's numb, but it moves."

"Good to hear." He shifted his grip. Thea put her hand on his shoulder. When he put his other hand on her back, she couldn't help being aware that he was—not taller than Freddy, but certainly stronger. It wasn't Freddy's fault that his magic had weakened him . . . but it was more than that. Sebastian had a strong presence. One could just *tell* he was the leader— even among men who were older.

And even in just a few steps she could tell he really knew how to dance, as if he'd had proper lessons. The band was mostly playing music from her parents' generation, old ragtimes.

While she barely knew what to do with them, she could follow his lead.

"I had a chance to meet your friends properly," he said. "The reviver, the Norn, and Arabella von Kaspar's daughter. I can see how those three might have come together, but you're still a bit of a mystery." He looked like he expected something intriguing.

"It's disappointing, I'm afraid," she said. "My parents were rustics in a bound marriage, so when my father was brought back from the dead, it made my mother sick. I worked at the Telephone Club, in Lampenlight—"

"I know of it," he said.

"Freddy came in one night, and when I touched him, I saw a vision of the moment he brought my father back from the dead."

Sebastian nodded. "You have a connection to your parents' connection. And Freddy had a connection, too. Magic is like that. Why was Freddy in the club to begin with? I'm surprised they let him out."

"I think his guardian felt bad that Freddy was so restricted." Thea's cheeks warmed, recalling her shame when she discovered that Freddy was supposed to find a girl to bear his children and pass on his magic. She wouldn't tell Sebastian that. "He wanted him to have a little fun. That's where I came in. I wanted to know what was going on so I could save my parents. We went underground and . . ." Her mind resisted going back there. *Don't think. You're safe now.*

"You don't have any magic, correct?" Sebastian asked.

"No, just an ordinary girl."

"I'm *not sure that's true.*"

"I don't know much about you, either. Where are you from? I can't place your accent."

"My father is a baron in Irminau."

"Royalty? Oh dear. Should I have curtsied?"

He laughed. "Please don't. I'm hardly royalty. It's a tiny, tiny remote scrap of land, and my older brothers are free to squabble over it."

"Older brothers? I really would've thought you were the oldest."

"Do I seem bossy?" His dark eyes danced. The room seemed too warm, and her stomach twisted. She kept trying to think of Freddy, and a terrible part of her wanted to forget him, forget the kiss, forget everything.

"Potentially. You must've gotten yourself into this position somehow."

"Much of it is thanks to Ingrid, really. She has the power, but no interest in being a leader. She says it is her job to steer us, not to rule."

"So Ingrid appointed you the leader?"

"Well—boy, you ask a lot of questions, don't you? With such a penetrating expression, too. Have you thought of becoming a reporter?"

"No." She smiled—no one had ever really told her she should *become* anything.

"Or a spy. I might have use for a spy-reporter. I hope you'll be sticking around."

"I'm sure I will. I like it here." The bouncing ditty the musicians had been playing ended, and they started up a more romantic tune: "I'm Thinking of Her."

I'm thinking of her . . . while I'm dancing with you . . . I'm sorry my kisses are not ringing true . . .

Maybe it wasn't that romantic after all. Thea and Sebastian both stepped back from each other at once.

"I should find my friends," she said, patting her hair even though everything seemed in place. She felt disheveled.

"Of course," he said. "Get a good night's rest. I'm sure tomorrow will be another big day. I'd better turn in myself." He lifted a hand as final acknowledgment and then started talking to one of the other men as if nothing had happened.

Nothing *had* happened. She was just having a fickle moment. Sebastian was very attractive—so what? Freddy was her silvery sorcerer boy, though he hadn't been much fun today. He seemed worried about something. Why worry, when they were finally safe? She couldn't seem to worry right now if she tried.

And it wasn't like I told Freddy I'd marry him. She had kissed him, however. Or did he kiss her? She was having trouble remembering what had even occurred.

It wouldn't seem so confusing in the morning. Shadows and rhythms just had a way of turning things upside down.

FIFTEEN

Thea woke up abruptly, disoriented. She rubbed her hands together—the left one still didn't feel normal. Ingrid could probably fix it, but she had an inexplicable resistance to approaching Ingrid.

She slid her palms together for a few moments, then her mind wandered back to dancing with Sebastian and her hands no longer seemed important. He seemed even more intriguing after a night's sleep.

She dressed and fixed her hair as best she could. Her curls were starting to fall out, and her winter dresses seemed so drab.

Freddy knocked on the door, and she slapped on a smile. "I'm sorry," she said, "I know I slept for ages."

"You needed it, I'm sure." He frowned. "I just wanted to check on you."

"That's sweet. I'm fine, thanks."

He lingered silently in the doorway, watching her button her shoes, and her hands felt clumsy under his gaze. "I'm fine," she repeated.

"Do you want to go check on your mother this afternoon? Maybe we could bring her some food."

"You can't go anywhere. It's dangerous."

"I'll leave if I have reason to leave," he said. "We should at least send word."

Pain twinged down her wrist. She couldn't think of Mother—it hurt to try. All those awful things were in the past, and she had to focus on the future. She could tell Freddy was already worked up about it, and she didn't need him worrying over her. "You're right. I'll talk to Sebastian."

"Did you end up talking to him last night?" Freddy asked, walking beside her down the hall.

"A little."

"I'd like to know more about him, such as why men twice his age follow his orders. Is he really who he says he is?" Freddy rubbed his chin. "I sure wish I had access to a good library. I'd love to see if there is a Sebastian Hirsch in the records."

She stopped at the top of the stairs. "You don't need to be so suspicious. He said last night it's because Ingrid appointed him the leader. And she's a Norn, so she would know who ought to run things, wouldn't she?"

When she stopped, Freddy stopped too, leaving a distance between them. "I hope so," he said.

Thea remembered the moment she had stood in the tunnels underground with her arms around him. He seemed suddenly like another person, and she wasn't sure how it had even happened. Or was *she* the different person? She had, once again, the feeling that there was something she wanted to tell Freddy, but she couldn't grasp it.

Is this how Mother felt when the bound-sickness began?

She forced a small smile before hurrying off, looking for Sebastian. One of the men from the dance last night—Marco, with the thin mustache—directed her back upstairs to Sebastian's office.

"Good morning," Sebastian said, and then looked at the clock on the desk. "No, never mind. Good afternoon. Can I help you with something?" He was holding papers in one hand and frowning at a typewriter, then after another second, he looked up.

"Maybe. I . . ." She couldn't remember why she'd come here. "I don't know what to do with myself, honestly. I'd like to help the cause. I was thinking of what you said last night, about needing a reporter-spy."

"Yes." He lifted a finger. "Unfortunately, I don't need you yet. It's very chaotic out there. Still, sit down a minute, if you like." He motioned to a heavy leather chair. Besides his modern clock with a sleek black plastic case and the paper-strewn desk, the room was obviously still the domain of its former owner Mr. Schiff, with stately-old-gentleman trappings: dark wood wainscoting, hunting motifs carved into the mantle around the fireplace, paintings of ships at sea, and models of the Schiff zeppelins poised around the room.

When she sat down, Sebastian got up and paced around to the front of the desk, as if only one person was allowed to sit at once. "I know it's less glamorous, but how are you with nursing? I don't mean anything gruesome, of course—that's Ingrid's domain. Just bringing around blankets and food, maybe talking to people a little, making them comfortable."

"That sounds a lot like waitressing. . . ."

"You don't sound excited."

"I'll do what needs to be done. I just liked the idea of being something more than a caretaker. It wasn't what I dreamed of when I was a little girl. I had to leave school when my mother was sick, and options for women are few enough as it is—and without an education . . ."

"Well, I don't care if or where you went to school, I promise you that," said Sebastian. "I'm hoping we'll have some of the Irminauer refugees soon, and when we do, it would be useful to have someone attending to them with open ears and a dash of charm so they'll feel comfortable and willing to lend us their abilities. In the meantime, you could check on the men who were injured over the past couple of days."

"I could do that."

"Ingrid can direct you. She's probably downstairs."

"Ingrid?" Thea stood up as something in her froze.

"What's wrong with Ingrid?" He sounded like he really wanted to know.

She couldn't speak. *Yggdrasil . . . washes the pain away. . . .*

He took a step closer to her and reached for her left hand. Thea had wanted him to touch her, but now suddenly she was afraid. She pulled her hand back and covered it against her chest, recalling the pain, gritting her teeth against the memory.

"Thea," he said.

Do you know what happened? What is this terrible feeling? Why can't I speak? She wasn't breathing as she stood expectantly, feeling his eyes might hold the answers.

"Ingrid," he said, "knows what needs to be done. You should talk to her."

She let out her breath. "Yes."

"She might seem a little strange, but her magic is a gift."

She let her hands drop to her sides, allowed relief to seep in. "Yes."

He lowered his gaze and everything was normal again. "If you can just help her out for now, I'll find you more exciting things to do later. You'll feel sorry for all those poor schoolkids stuck behind a desk." He glanced at his typewriter. "Speaking of . . . I'd better get back to my half-finished antigovernment screed."

"Are you the one who writes all those papers I see around town, with the capital letters? 'DOWN WITH THE ELITE! LONG LIVE THE BROTHERHOOD OF THE WORK-ING MAN!'" She shook her fist.

"I try to be a little more subtle than that, though subtlety does *not* work as well as you might hope. You write two thousand words of a well-reasoned argument, and all anyone cares about is the comic on page three of the Chancellor getting kicked in the tender bits by a worker."

"So you should've been a cartoonist."

"Evidently." He smiled and went back to the typewriter while she left to find Ingrid.

SIXTEEN

Although the attic was cold, Marlis had spent the morning there, her frigid fingers scribbling down what had happened to record in her diary later. Out the wavy old glass of the attic windows, Marlis could see a sliver of Republic Square past the Chancellery roof, the ground completely covered by a sea of people who hated her father.

Wilhelmina found her sitting against a trunk with her knees pulled up. "Marlis?"

Marlis dropped her legs and brushed her skirt down, suddenly feeling that her posture wasn't very dignified.

"Do you want luncheon? It's getting dark up here."

"Yes, thanks. I just needed quiet."

After two nights cooped up, Wilhelmina was able to arrange for the women and children to move to the Wachters' house. It was close to the Chancellery and accessible via old tunnels. A stone wall surrounded it, providing a natural defense where a guard unit could camp, and the bedrooms were far more numerous and hospitable than the Chancellery's bunkers. Marlis wasn't used to sharing space with so many other people.

"Tired children are too much," Wilhelmina said, understanding. "I only had one; I don't know how anyone can handle six or seven. They'll quiet down and eat with the nannies. Then again, we've got Mrs. Rasp and her opinions at our table. I might prefer to eat with the children."

The lunch spread was thin for the city's most prominent wives; mostly things that would spoil if they weren't used. Marlis guessed Wilhelmina had given the kitchen detailed instructions on rationing the food in case this dragged on. At least they still had electricity, they still had maids. The danger didn't feel real, with everyone sitting around all day, talking and drinking tea and coffee from dainty cups.

Mrs. Rasp was indeed the first to make a barb about the meal, once the pleasantries were out of the way. "Very practical of you to offer such simple fare, Wilhelmina. I know I certainly don't have an appetite after that *smell*."

"Horrid." Mrs. Stangler shuddered.

"I still don't see how those people can burn their own loved ones," Mrs. Rasp continued. "It's barbaric. No rites, no attempt at a proper burial at all?"

Wilhelmina was uncharacteristically quiet.

"*This* just doesn't seem like anything good people would do," Mrs. Rasp continued. "This seems like heathenism to me."

"I think we should be responsible for proper burial," Wilhelmina said, poking at her salad. "We promised free cremation for the poor, and we dragged them from their peaceful death instead. It's the least we could do, not to let these poor souls decompose in the gutter or toss them in a mass grave."

"Oh, I suppose now you'll act like you had no part in this,"

Mrs. Rasp said. "Wasn't your husband the one who destroyed the tree?"

The tree.

Marlis had never heard anything about a tree, and yet she sensed it was important. But if it was significant, wouldn't Papa have told her? Didn't he tell her everything important?

She was beginning to wonder.

Wilhelmina shot Mrs. Rasp a stern look. "You know you shouldn't be talking about this."

"It's all going to come out," Mrs. Rasp said, tugging on her earrings fretfully. "It's all going to come out, and they're going to twist everything we did. We'll be lucky to have our heads a few weeks from now."

"The rebels are not going to behead anyone," Wilhelmina said firmly.

Marlis kept thinking of the speech she'd given. She'd said those words on the radio, and everyone heard them. The more she considered it, the more they jumbled inside her. They didn't feel true. And what Papa said to the people was a lie. Coming after him, she might as well have given his speech, too.

You know it's just politics. She tried to swallow that thought along with her cold cuts.

What will become of me if I stand on the wrong side? Everyone will know I lied. But what could she do if Papa wouldn't listen to her ideas? She wouldn't turn against her own father. Better a liar than a traitor . . . right?

"And now I hear the worst kind of rustics are pouring across our borders and no one is there to regulate them. They're going to join up with the revolution. God save us from whatever dark magic these forest folk have dreamed up," Mrs. Rasp said.

"My cousin said when she was in Irminau as a young woman, she met a girl who was possessed by demons—cursed for sleeping with a married man," Mrs. Stangler said. She always liked a bit of gossip when her children were out of the way. "Her family turned her out, so she lived on the streets. If she touched you, you'd get warts, they said."

"Yes, demons, mind control, curses." Mrs. Rasp shook her fork. "I would rather be hanged than have anything to do with demons."

"Oh my," Mrs. Rosen said, sounding almost amused.

"People *are* born with magic here, too, you know," Wilhelmina said. "So if it's true, we might as well be suspicious of our own citizens. I'd rather they come here than join King Otto's army."

"Or, they could be Otto's spies," Mrs. Stangler said, undeterred.

They knew nothing, really. They all had the same vague reports and occasional news from their husbands. The border breach seemed far away compared to the pictures of the revolutionaries and the pyre of the dead on the front page of the newspaper. Freddy's lifework, all of the city's hidden power, reduced to a pile of dirty dangling limbs and grainy black-and-white faces.

Marlis approached Wilhelmina after the meal. "Thank you for lunch," she said. "I appreciate you hosting all of us."

"Of course." Wilhelmina smiled gently. She was not that gentle of a person, and her smile was disconcerting. "I'm sorry about the conversation. They're just scared."

Marlis wouldn't admit she was scared. She liked to think she wasn't. An uncertain, unpleasant feeling kept turning around inside her. She thought of the speech one minute and Freddy the next, then the protestors and the car blowing up with Ida inside it. Ida's light, flirtatious manner had often annoyed Marlis, but now she wished for her company, to keep her mind off things. Ida would have laughed at Mrs. Rasp's nonsense. "What do you think will happen, really?" she asked, in a voice barely above a whisper.

Wilhelmina paused. Marlis, unfortunately, knew that pause. Her mother had paused that way when Marlis asked her if she was going to die. "I think your father and my husband and all the men taking care of this country are trying their best to keep things together in a difficult situation. But some of the decisions that were made . . ." She looked at Marlis for an uncomfortably long moment. "We took it too far."

"What was Mrs. Rasp speaking of? The tree?"

Wilhelmina squeezed her hand. "Dear, at this point, the less you know, the better."

"Father always tells me things," Marlis said. It sounded petulant. She was going crazy with being pent up.

"We could be brought to trial. It's better if you can't answer questions." She drew away from Marlis, returning to the other women across the room, who were conversing in voices that occasionally grew heated.

Marlis lingered alone in the empty half of the room, catching sight of herself in a decorative mirror. Although she was not especially pretty—she'd once heard her great-aunt describe her as "all bones and nose"—she had always liked her appearance.

She thought she looked intellectual and older than her years, with her dark bob and straight bangs framing serious brown eyes behind round glasses.

Right now she saw only vulnerability—slender shoulders and full lips slightly parted in worry. She pressed them together, staring at her reflection.

But behind her own eyes, she thought she saw a flash of someone else.

Urd.

She covered her ears reflexively, then lowered her hands quickly. She felt silly. No one had spoken. It was just nonsense in her mind, the fancies she usually smothered surfacing in these traumatizing days.

SEVENTEEN

When Nan woke that morning, Thea was still sleeping. Nan stared at her peaceful face for a long moment. If Ingrid had enchanted Thea, she owed it to her friend to dig deep until she found out what was wrong.

First, she needed some fresh air. The thought of spending time close to Ingrid was repellent. Deep down she knew something was very wrong: Ingrid was not the Skuld she had known. But if Nan reached for answers, she might become Verthandi. Maybe she wouldn't even care about her friendship with Thea anymore. It seemed logical to assume that Yggdrasil's destruction had given her a closer connection to other people, even if it was hanging by a thread.

She hurried from the room, heart pounding with guilt, and found Sigi downstairs eating breakfast.

"Do you still want to go to your father's place and find a camera?" Nan asked.

"Oh yes."

She thought the guards might try to stop them leaving, but they just told them to be careful. The only sound on the street was the rustling of dry leaves in the wind. The smell of smoke still lingered in the air, and Nan tried not to think where it had come from.

Sigi had her hands thrust deep into the pockets of her black wool coat. She was short, and these were men's coats they had swiped from a dusty closet, so the hem grazed the tops of her boots, and the broad shoulders swallowed her. While it might have looked comical, nothing about Sigi was comical just now. She looked pensive, the wind tossing a wild dark lock across her brow.

"You know when someone dies," she said softly, "and the world keeps turning even though it feels like it should stop, because you're so sad? The way the city looks today is how I thought it should look when someone dies. Everything's stopped."

Nan nodded.

"I don't like it much after all," Sigi said.

They had walked to the end of the street now, passing the boarded-up subway station. The air was sharp, the sky overcast. It seemed too early for snow, but Nan wouldn't be surprised to see a few flakes. A policeman on the corner regarded them as they passed.

The next corner marked the boundary between the residential district and a row of shops with apartments above. Here, a lamppost was plastered with papers describing missing people. Although the disappearances had been going on for a long time, Nan had never seen so many notices about them. They were all written on crisp new paper, probably posted since the night the workers escaped.

"So many missing." Sigi grabbed one of the papers, with a girl's graduation picture taped to it. "I remember her underground, I think. A tall girl who never talked. She lived in the bunks below ours." She squinted up and down the street. "Do you think they've cleared all the bodies out of the square?"

"You don't want to go there, do you?"

"Not really. No. It would be awful. But I have this feeling like I need to do *something*, and I'm helpless."

"I think they probably have cleaned things up by now," Nan said. "They'll want to hide as much of this as possible." She understood the desire, realizing she had been unconsciously scanning the landscape for bodies left behind, as if she simply needed confirmation that the events of last night were real.

Sigi walked in a silence Nan didn't disturb for a block and a half. Sigi kept looking all around, even up at the top stories of the buildings, as if she was searching for some sign.

"Do you want to walk by the square anyway?" Nan finally asked. "Maybe it would provide some closure. We could pay our respects, or something."

Sigi shook her head. "No, but—maybe we could get a drink. Toast to them. I feel that being sad doesn't do anyone any good. Even though I am sad, I want to pretend I'm not."

"Sure."

Usually Parc was one of the brightest of streets, where wealthy people drove their automobiles up and down the boulevard and parked to shop for clothes and jewels and trinkets only they could hope to afford. On this quiet afternoon, mannequins in the latest fur-trimmed coats and winter gowns posed in dim windows next to shuttered doors.

"I hope he's home," Sigi said, looking ahead to a modern apartment building. The front of the building was a clean white edifice rising above the overhang of the lobby, with curved white balconies bending behind like an abstract paper sculpture. "It's nice to see something familiar."

The lobby was a large spare room with big windows, everything made of angles. The doorman acknowledged Sigi with a nod of recognition. She laughed quietly. "My father must not have even told the doorman I died."

They rode the elevator to the fourth and highest floor. The doors swung open onto a white hallway with electric lights in diamond-shaped fixtures edged in black. There were only two apartments on this entire floor, with the hall leading to the exit stairway. Sigi knocked. Her brow was sweating.

The door swung open. "Sig? By god, 'zat you?" The man standing in the doorframe shared Sigi's stocky build and dark curly hair. He was swarthier, with a suggestion of beard and mustache, and wearing an untucked cotton shirt and matching trousers. They looked like clothes rich people brought back from cruises to warmer climes, and they had fresh paint stains as well as older, faded ones. Nan wondered how colorful he was to other people's eyes.

"Yeah, it's me."

"Your mother kept saying you were still alive." He hugged her in a very ordinary familiar way. "Come in. Who's your friend?"

"This is Nan. She's . . ." Sigi trailed off, apparently deciding not to explain at all. His eyes looked Nan up and down with approval.

"You girls want something to drink?" He was in the kitchen now—the apartment was very open, the spaces partitioned by half-walls in a way that seemed fashionable, though Nan was not too familiar with fashionable apartments.

"No. Well, I don't know. Wine, maybe. Just a glass," Sigi said, shedding her coat onto the back of a chair.

"So were you never really dead?" He took out glasses.

"I *was* dead."

"You didn't really kill yourself, did you, Sig?" His voice was almost a whisper now.

Sigi twisted away from him and Nan both. "I'm sorry. . . ."

He took off his glasses and wiped them off, like he was avoiding eye contact. "Your mother's in so deep, I wondered if maybe someone killed you to get to her, and she was trying to cover it up. But however it happened, how did you come back?"

"That's the thing—" She locked eyes with him as he handed her the wineglass. Her bottom lip quivered slightly.

He put a hand on her shoulder. "It's okay."

"No, it's not. Mother's dead. She gave her own life for me."

He looked taken aback for a moment, as if he didn't know how to process this and maybe didn't even believe it. "She was probably knee-deep in trouble," he said, trying to reason through it. "All that revolutionary business. Would've gotten herself shot if she hadn't— Not really surprising—"

"It just feels like—" Sigi broke off, as if deciding he wouldn't understand.

He hugged her again, his eyes wide. "Sweetheart, your mother was crazy. Don't feel bad about this. Don't feel bad."

"Aren't you even going to mourn her at all?"

"We had quite a history," he said heavily.

She just cried against his chest briefly, and he stroked her hair. He handed Nan her wineglass over Sigi's shoulder, but he looked uncomfortable, as though he wasn't used to sharing emotions with his daughter.

Nan shifted her feet, trying to seem invisible during this private moment. The apartment was disheveled, with shoes sitting in the middle of the floor and the remains of what looked like a small dinner party at the table and around the kitchen. Each wall was dominated by a large painting—an abstract, a portrait of him, a modernist café scene.

"Sig, do you need a place to stay?" he asked, his voice rough but gentle.

"No, I could use a little money, though. I don't have anything. My camera, my clothes . . ."

"Money, camera, clothes. All you ever needed, right? You can take my camera or anything else. Look in the closet, see if any of Gretchen's clothes fit you."

Sigi wrinkled her nose. Whoever Gretchen was, she didn't seem pleased at the idea of taking her clothes.

"Are you sure you don't want to stay?" he continued. "For dinner, anyway. I'd like to know you're safe. It's crazy out there. I was just heading out the door to check on a friend. Can you hang around for a bit? Sit back, finish up the wine, eat anything you want. I'll be back in no time."

He opened a drawer and tossed her a pair of keys, which she didn't catch and had to pick up off the floor. He grabbed his coat and paused before leaving. "I love you, kid."

"I love you, too," Sigi said. She looked pained as he closed the door, and took a deep, shuddering breath. "I knew he wouldn't want to hear it," she said. "He can't deal with the bad stuff. He never wants to talk. I bet he doesn't even have a friend to meet. He doesn't want me to see him cry. He'll go have a drink and talk to a bartender about it instead."

"I understand," Nan said. "I knew some of those men at the club. They'd come talk to me, and sometimes they'd comment that they could talk to me but not their own kids. I don't know why that is."

"Well"—Sigi wiped a few tears away—"should I look at *Gretchen's* clothes?"

"Does he have a lot of mistresses?"

"A revolving door." She took a long drink of wine. "In some ways, though, I'm comforted that he's acting exactly the same as he always does, even as the world crumbles around him. Can you believe my mother married him?"

"I've seen stranger matches."

"Oh, you would have stories about that, too."

"So many. Thea tells them better, though."

"I guess I've seen it all, taking my photographs, but I don't take many of couples," Sigi said. "Maybe I should. I like the old people sometimes. When they're holding wrinkled hands together. It's sweet. My parents would never last that long with anyone. Should I top off your glass?"

"I'm good."

As Sigi started to walk toward the bedroom, she paused in the living room. The sofa faced the balcony. The entire wall was glass, filling the room with sunlight. All the furniture was angular and new. Sigi's mother's house had been full of older well-crafted wooden chairs and tables; this stuff was not so much crafted as designed, each lamp and table like pieces of a puzzle that you'd imagine might somehow fit together into a giant cube. Sigi paused and tapped her fingers to her lips.

"I could photograph you *here*," she said. "If you still want me to photograph you."

"I do," Nan said. "I definitely do. But why here?"

"You fit into this room perfectly. Cool and modern."

"Ironic," Nan said, "considering I am apparently ancient."

"This room captures what you want to be, doesn't it?" She held up her hand, twitched with sudden purpose, and rushed into the bedroom.

Nan was about to follow when she caught a glimpse of her reflection. She had almost forgotten she was wearing this shapeless dress.

I certainly don't want to be immortalized in this ugly thing. She glanced at the hall where Sigi had disappeared, hearing rummaging. Nan wasn't self-conscious, but Sigi might be alarmed to walk back in and find Nan standing in her underwear.

The idea of making Sigi blush was tantalizing. Was it attraction to Sigi herself, or was it attraction to the idea of attraction?

She imagined Sigi's kiss and the world flooding with color. *That's all I want.*

Her skin was warmer now. She ran a hand along her neck, looking back at her reflection. She was more accustomed to her face with makeup on, but Sigi had never known her that way. Her bare face was more androgynous. It was still hard to believe that one guard underground had taken her for a boy.

Nan Davies, she thought. *That's who you are.*

She reached for the hem of her dress, crossing her arms to sweep it over her head. Loose as it was, she didn't have to struggle to get it over her shoulders. It was crumpled on the floor in a moment, baring her thin shoulders to the mirror. She was still wearing underwear from her imprisonment, a plain cotton chemise and drawers, and stockings Thea had loaned her that morning.

"Okay . . ." Sigi's voice moved into the hall. "He got a new camera, so—" She broke off when she reached the doorway. "Um—"

"I'm not wearing that ugly old thing for the picture," Nan said.

"What if my father comes back?"

"It doesn't *show* anything."

"It sure implies a lot." Sigi was flushed, but she couldn't stop staring. "You really want me to photograph you in your underwear?"

"Why not?"

Sigi's eyes clicked over into a mode Nan recognized, from surprise to thinking about the shot. "Sit down on the couch," she said. She moved to the window, fussing with the curtains. Nan sprawled across the cushions. Even though she had not been nervous about changing for gym in school or wearing a short skirt at work, this moment felt different.

Sigi messed with the camera for a little while, her lips pressed together thoughtfully. She looked up and caught Nan's eyes.

"Stay like that," she said softly. "Just like that." She took one picture, told Nan to look toward the dining table for a profile shot, and took another. "Maybe put an arm up over your head. Lean back?"

After a few more shots, Sigi stopped and regarded Nan for a moment. "I don't usually take photographs like this. I'm a street photographer. I like to look for the beauty in ugly things, but you're just . . . beautiful. I don't know if I can do you justice."

"You can certainly flatter."

"I mean it," Sigi said. "You don't seem real. A photograph might ruin you, might turn you into an ordinary girl." Then she suddenly looked pained. "I'm sorry. That's actually what you wanted, isn't it?"

"If you see that in me . . . I don't mind. I don't see it. I see that I'm different, but not the beauty."

Nan didn't know how to describe the way Sigi looked at her. The word "hungry" sounded too crude. Closer to awe, but also more than that. She felt as though in giving Sigi permission to look at her so closely and capture her on film, she had offered Sigi some of her power.

"You know," Sigi said, "the thing about art is that it's like a quest that never ends. You always have something in your head that is so beautiful, and you never manage to create it. Sometimes you come close. And that moment . . . is madness. It's so fleeting. If you've tasted it once, you have to keep searching. You look like that moment."

"Like madness?"

Sigi just looked at her.

Nan stood up from the couch and kissed her hard. She kept her eyes open. Colors flashed in her vision—gold and brown furniture and the blue sky out the window. Her heart hammered. *Just let me hold on to this . . . let me feel.*

Sigi's mouth was yielding and tasted like tears. Her eyes were closed and Nan heard a little catch in her throat. She touched Nan's back, lightly, like she didn't want to trap her. Nan ran her fingers through Sigi's wild hair.

Nan was afraid to stop because she didn't want to lose the colors. Or this feeling.

Sigi was the one who pulled away. "Nan . . ." She looked like she knew it was about more than her.

"I don't ever want to go back," Nan whispered. The colors in the room had muted, but they weren't gone, and Nan couldn't stop staring. The room was so different now. There was the gold upholstery and a blue vase and a green houseplant. Everything was brighter. "I don't want to see Ingrid again."

"I understand," Sigi said. She didn't need to say *but.* It was already in the room with them.

Nan walked over to the crumpled dress, picked it up, and slipped it back on. When she poked her head through the collar, the room was gray again.

EIGHTEEN

"This was one of my old haunts," Sigi said, pointing at what appeared to be an old carriage house converted into a restaurant, wedged between crumbling mansions that had been converted into apartments. The sign said THE BIRD'S NEST. It was open and appeared crowded and dim inside.

"I didn't know you lived in the Pinsel-Allée district. This isn't far from where I grew up. I was just over on the bad side of the university."

"It's bad here, too, sometimes. Artists like to fight more than you'd think." Sigi grinned, shoving the door open so a wash of noise and cigarette smoke came over them. Hardly anyone was sitting at the tables; students and bohemian types were standing around talking about the protests and the workers and criticizing the Chancellor. Some looked roughed-up or even had blood on their clothes.

Sigi waved Nan to the bar. They perched on stools. "Two glasses of wine," Sigi said. "A decent red. We're honoring the dead." She smiled briefly at Nan. "That rhymed. Unintentional.

It's the poetry in the air. I hope you like wine—I think we need something classy for our toast."

"I agree." Nan put an elbow on the bar counter, enjoying the atmosphere. The thick air reminded her of the Telephone Club. "They must not have power here either," Nan commented, noticing candles flickering on the bar. As they had shared an awkward meal with Sigi's father where he mostly talked about his own life, the sun had climbed down the sky.

"Here you are, ladies." The bartender put down their glasses.

Nan had no more taste for wine than she had for food these days, but she lifted the glass. Sigi met Nan's eyes. She swallowed. Nan could see she was just trying not to cry.

"To life," Nan said softly.

"To sunrise," Sigi replied, even softer. She took a drink. "You know, we could still stay with my father, if you don't want to go back to Ingrid. As you can see, he and my mother both like to talk about themselves—he's harmless."

"I have to go back. I don't think they'll let Freddy leave, and Freddy and I both suspect Ingrid put Thea under some kind of enchantment." Nan kept her voice low. She didn't trust anyone, even in the anonymity of a noisy restaurant.

"You didn't tell me about that!"

"I was going to—I just wanted to think about other things. We don't know much more than that, anyway. Thea just isn't acting like herself."

"Do you think Ingrid has some power to make people forget, the way we did underground?" Sigi asked, swigging more wine.

"I don't know what Ingrid can do," Nan said. "That's the problem with magic. You never know what it can do. Maybe that's why I seem to have trouble using mine. I don't like the idea of it much."

"If we got Thea out of there, do you think the spell would fade?"

"But what if it didn't?"

The door of the Bird's Nest was constantly opening and closing, with some people popping in just to skim the room looking for friends, while others joined the conversation. One young man who had just walked in suddenly approached them and looked at Sigi.

Then he stepped back as if he'd seen a ghost, his pale face dumbstruck. "Sigi," he said.

"Helmut? What's going on?" Another fellow approached the first. Everyone seemed edgy, ready to react at the slightest sign of distress.

"Hel," Sigi said, quickly putting down her drink and lifting her hands. "It's all right."

"You were dead!" Hel pointed at her. "Were—were you underground?"

"*No.*" Sigi's eyes darted around the room as strangers turned to look at her. "Hey, why don't we step outside and talk?"

"You can talk in here," a girl said. "Is it true what he's saying? Did you find a way to come back from the dead? They're lying to us, aren't they? The Chancellor? About the spell?"

This barrage of questions seemed to paralyze Sigi. Nan stood up. "Everyone, please, calm down. It's a simple mistake. She's fine. I'm not sure who you are"—she looked at Hel—"but she isn't, nor has she ever, been dead. I've been with her. Who is this, Sigi?" She shot Sigi a dramatic, accusatory glance, hoping everyone would see this as a case of misunderstanding, that Sigi had lied to an old lover or something.

"She was dead," Hel said. "I saw her body. Margie—her roommate—rang me up when she found Sigi dead in her apartment."

Sigi seemed to snap into awareness, snatching up her camera bag, grabbing Nan's arm, and rushing for the door.

"Hey, wait!" Hel cried. He grabbed Nan's arm, trying to stop them both.

Nan shoved him back, knocking him into the people behind him, then she kept running with Sigi. They darted down the closest alley before the bar crowd could rouse themselves to follow, and then turned again from there.

"Taxi," Sigi said, spotting a cab. "Taxi!" She flung out her arm, running into the street to stop the driver. They rushed into the backseat and told the driver to return to Sebastian's headquarters.

"We should have thought of that," Nan said. "Old acquaintances."

"I *did* think of it," Sigi said. "I wanted to see old friends and explain. I didn't think they'd be afraid of me—at least, not once I told them."

"Well, we don't know how the situation in the city must look from the outside, with the workers appearing last night and the Chancellor's story. People must be terrified. I'm sure once things calm down, you can explain."

"That makes sense. But seeing Hel look at me like that . . ."

Sigi brought the camera bag into her lap and put her arms around it.

"Was he a good friend?"

"I had a lot of good friends. Hel and I have known each other since we were kids; he was practically my brother. Margie was a good friend, too. Hilarious, and she'd take good care of you. And Hilda, and Helena . . ."

"You have a lot of friends," Nan said, feeling suddenly aware of her own isolated life.

"I did. They'd love you, too."

"I don't know." Nan tried to keep the conversation moving, unsure if any group of people would truly "love" her. "Maybe you could write them letters explaining—it might be less shocking for them that way."

"You're right. It was careless of me to hope I'd run into them and think they wouldn't question what happened. I just yearn for normalcy."

"You and me both."

NINETEEN

On his fourth morning at the Hands of the White Tree headquarters, Freddy woke to gunshots.

When he came downstairs, a small crowd had gathered, watching as Will and a wiry man named Johan dragged a limp body into the house.

"Anton and Roger were on guard duty," Will said. "Roger's nowhere to be found, and Anton's dead."

"Roger *shot* Anton?" Sebastian hurried into the center of the commotion, wearing clothes he looked like he'd slept in. "Did anyone see him?"

"Max, Werner, and Keller went out to find him."

"Bring Anton to my office." Sebastian ruffled his hair and then looked at Freddy. "Can I talk to you?"

I knew this was only a matter of time. "You can talk to me," Freddy said. "From there, we'll see."

"I don't force people to use magic," Sebastian said, walking with him down the hall to the stairs. "Let me make that quite clear."

"I assume this is the introduction to some heavy persuasion, then?"

Sebastian threw up a hand. "I do want to know why one of my men would shoot another." He stopped at the door of his office, nodding at Will and Johan. Ingrid had come up behind them, and Sebastian shut the door once she'd stepped in, leaving the men outside.

"This *is* what your magic was meant to do, Freddy," Sebastian said, "allowing this man to have his final say."

Freddy half-listened, feeling his power pulse in the presence of the dead man. He had never noticed the change that came over him when his magic had an opportunity. He had never gone without it.

Ingrid cocked her head at him. Her eyes were dark in her pale face. Yet, she didn't seem sad. Freddy wasn't sure what she was thinking.

His fingers itched.

"Arabella said I had to stop working my magic, that it was making me sick."

"That is true, to a point," Ingrid said. "But this will be a mere fraction of the effort the Valkenraths put you through, and there are herbs that help offset the ill effects."

He wanted to believe her, wanted to give in. She would say anything to get him to work for them.

"It isn't any healthier to suppress your magic than it is to use it too much." She came closer, looking up at him—she was quite small, barely reaching his shoulder. Her face was plain, and her dress was simple and longer in the hem than was fashionable. She had to be twice his age. Yet the word that into his mind when she looked at him was "seductive." If he listened to her speak for too long, he might do anything she asked.

He thought of Thea. He had seen little of her the past few days. She helped Ingrid tend to the injured, and she seemed more interested in chatting with Sebastian and his men than seeing him. She danced to the evening music and didn't pester him to join her. She still hadn't checked on her mother.

I can't let her get to me.

He turned on his heel. "If I revive one person, it will lead to more and more. And soon you'll have someone you don't want to let go."

"Freddy, one thing I swore I'd never do," Sebastian said, "is force a magic user to work. But don't you want to know, too? What if Roger brings word of you back to whoever he works for?"

"We could all be in danger," Ingrid said, "including your girl."

Sebastian's expression was brooding as he gently checked Anton's pockets. Freddy thought he must be casting for a way to convince him. *I'd do the same thing, if it were someone who died working for me.*

"I'll do it," Freddy said. "On one condition." His whole body was growing warm with power, though he knew this was an illusion; he was a slave to his magic more than it gave him power.

"Yes?" Sebastian said.

"I believe Ingrid put a spell on Thea, a spell that was meant for me. If you're really working for a righteous cause, you don't have to enchant us to have our help."

Ingrid regarded him with such a dark look that he felt a chill of fear. Her look went far beyond her fragile appearance. Those eyes belonged to something ancient.

"All I did," Ingrid said, "was show her Yggdrasil. When Thea saw Yggdrasil, she forgot her human suffering. It may seem like she has become a little heartless, but she has simply connected with the greater love of the entire universe. She'll grow stronger and stronger because of it."

Sebastian stood like a statue as she spoke, until the last moment, when a small frown tugged at his mouth.

"Do you have anything to say, Sebastian?" Freddy asked.

Sebastian looked at Ingrid, briefly. Then he said, "No."

"No?" Freddy threw up a hand. He realized he should probably be more delicate for the sake of his friends, if not self-preservation, though he was too frustrated for delicacy. "I don't know what madness you have *him* under," he said, pointing at Sebastian, "but I have gone through too much to see Thea forget all about her mother."

"I'm not under any madness," Sebastian replied, but the response was oddly delayed. "What are you accusing Ingrid of?"

Ingrid came closer again. She touched Freddy's hand in a familiar way. "So suspicious, Freddy . . ." Why didn't he stop her? "I understand, seeing you spent all those years with the Valkenraths. You don't trust other people. Give Thea time: She will remember her mother as soon as she's ready."

"And when will that be?"

"It's her decision. I haven't put anything in her mind that wasn't already there." Ingrid turned Freddy's hand over, like she was reading his palm. "Such power in these hands. You've never known what it is to do *good*. Wouldn't you like to find out? I can feel the magic burning inside you. You don't have to hold back."

Freddy felt short of breath. Trying to resist Ingrid and his magic at once . . . it was too much.

"I just want to prove that I *can* hold back," he said.

"You can't," she said. "Can you?" She nudged his shoulder, pointing him toward Anton. His skin itched, his hands burned, and he knew he couldn't walk out of this room and leave the dead man behind.

He placed his hands on Anton and kept them there until the man's eyes opened, the magic coming in a tingling rush of relief. Anton looked at the three faces hovering over him. "*Roger,*" Anton said.

"Yes? What happened?" Sebastian put a hand on his arm.

Anton stared glassily back at him for a moment and then said, "God, I thought maybe it was a dream."

"Not a dream," Sebastian said. "He shot you."

Anton took a few tense breaths and then said, "This morning I rummaged in Roger's coat pockets. I wanted to bum a smoke. I found a letter."

"From whom?"

Ingrid held up one hand and took Anton's hand in the other. She glanced quickly at Freddy. "Anton may want to talk to you in private, Sebastian."

Freddy crossed his arms. Maybe she could make him use magic, but she couldn't make him leave Anton's sight.

"Whatever Anton has to say, I trust Freddy with it," Sebastian said. "He's worth the risk."

"I'm telling you," Ingrid said. "Freddy has no loyalty to Yggdrasil. Until he swears his allegiance, it's just too dangerous."

"I will answer for any negative consequences," Sebastian said. "Anton, please, go on. Tell me about the letter."

Ingrid paced to the side of the room, trailing her fingers along the wall.

"It was from the king," Anton said, looking unsure about Freddy himself. "Asking for information about you."

"You mean Roger is working for Otto?"

"Yes. I asked Roger about it when we started our shift, and he wouldn't answer. It was obvious he was a spy for Otto, and we got in a quick scuffle. I was trying to get his weapon from him, and he shot me. Did he get away?"

"Seems he did," Sebastian muttered.

It had been years since Freddy had seen a photograph of Crown Prince Rupert of Irminau, but as Sebastian spoke to Anton, the pieces fell together with such satisfaction that he smiled.

"Ah," Freddy said. "*Now* I know why you seemed familiar."

TWENTY

Freddy couldn't have a conversation with Sebastian until Anton had said his final words and asked Sebastian to bless him for the afterlife.

"I'm not a priest," Sebastian said.

"You're my sovereign. It's good enough."

Sebastian glanced uncomfortably at Freddy, and then took Anton's hand and said a prayer for him. Then Freddy let Anton go. It was getting easier to break the magic, though he doubted it would ever be truly easy.

"Ingrid, let me talk to Freddy alone," Sebastian said, as Will and Johan carried Anton's body away.

Her eyes flashed at him, but she said nothing. She walked out stiffly, her face pinched with hurt. Freddy almost felt as if Sebastian had been looking for an excuse to tell him the truth.

"Prince Rupert," Freddy said. "The last time I saw you in the newspaper, you lost a leg skiing and then drowned while swimming in the river. Was any of that true?"

"Ingrid was able to heal my leg, and the drowning story is what the servants told my father."

"How did Ingrid heal a missing leg?"

"I'm not quite sure. She had me in a healing trance. She's quite powerful."

Freddy was beginning to recognize the distant stare through half-closed eyes that showed Sebastian had lost himself to Ingrid's enchantment. "So you think Otto knows your identity? Does he believe you really drowned?"

"It isn't unreasonable to suppose I did drown," Sebastian said. "I lost my leg the winter I was sixteen, and all that spring and into the summer I was recuperating and extremely depressed. He sent me to his summer retreat with my most dearly loved servants in the hopes I would cheer up. As far as he knew, I wanted to die, but he does have spies peppered throughout the revolution. It's impossible to say if Roger suspected my identity or not."

"So you ran away from home deliberately when Ingrid healed your leg. Why leave that position of power?"

"I have no power as long as my father is alive. He abuses people, and he's killed people I loved—magic users, drained dry until they're dead. I want to help them, but obviously I can't simply kill my father: I have to build an army worthy of challenging him."

"Why did you come here?" Freddy asked. "Why not incite rebellion in Irminau first?"

"It was easier not to be discovered here," Sebastian said. "Working in Irminau? That's the kind of thing he would see coming. Besides that, I love Urobrun, even with all its flaws. This is how I imagine the future. Or at least, it's a start. And Ingrid agrees with me."

"Ingrid," Freddy said. "She certainly doesn't seem happy with me."

"She is cautious around people who haven't sworn an oath to Yggdrasil. She knows I'd do anything to protect the tree—she doesn't know that about you. She'll warm to you, I'm sure."

If Ingrid had every person in the house bewitched, then even if he and Nan found proof of her wrongdoing, they wouldn't be believed. Sebastian sounded perfectly sensible—until it came to Ingrid. He would have to tell Nan about this right away, but how could they fight an enemy that lurked inside the mind?

TWENTY-ONE

That afternoon, Sebastian's men returned with thirty or so weary, grateful refugees from Irminau. They were hungry and exhausted, and some were sniffling and coughing with winter colds. Thea saw echoes of her parents in their kind, weather-beaten faces and humble trunks of clothes and valuables.

Their unofficial leader was an older woman with long gray hair, wearing bits of silver finery along with her shabby clothes. When Thea brought her soup and a blanket, the woman glanced over her bobbed hair, geometric knit sweater, and pleated skirt as if she was an alien species. She reminded Thea of her grandmother. Thea had only met her once, before the war, when trips across the border were easier. In her fuzzy memory, Grandmother had worn the same kind of silver rings on her fingers. "Those are lovely," she said, motioning to the woman's hand. "Are they very old?"

"Yes, very old. They came down to me from my great-great-grandmother."

"I wish my family kept things like that," Thea said. "My

parents left Irminau when they were young. They had nothing."

The woman cracked a small smile. "An Irminauer girl? Really? You look like a movie star."

Thea laughed. "You haven't seen a real movie star yet."

It was strange to think of movie stars still existing in this new, torn-up world. She felt as if all the glamorous clientele of the Telephone Club must surely have vanished the moment the workers saw the light of day.

After she tended to the Irminauer family, Ingrid told her to dip a cloth in a cup of herbal tea for Max, who had gone out drinking and come home with two black eyes. When he saw her come into the room to tend to him, he turned away.

"You shouldn't be helping me," he said. "Not after what I did to you."

"Don't worry, I'm fine. Close your eyes." The tea smelled unpleasant, and reminded her of something her mother would've made for her when she was sick. *Mother . . .*

"I didn't mean to do it." He grabbed her arm, the warm cloth falling off his face, his breathing growing rapid. "I didn't want to shoot you. Or anyone. Something came over me—"

Thea laughed uncomfortably. "Really, you sound possessed! I told you, I'm fine. You're just shaken. Get some rest."

"No one deserves to be hurt like that. No one deserves any of this! I don't want it, but—it was done. She said it was for the best."

Thea gently yet firmly removed her arm from his clutches and stood up out of reach. "What do you mean?" she asked. "What was for the best?"

"M-my hands . . ." He put a hand over the compress and started to cry.

"What about them?"

"She—had a saw—"

Thea broke into a cold sweat. She hurried from the room, leaning against the wall outside Max's door. *What's happening to me?* She couldn't seem to catch her own thoughts. She was already forgetting what Max had said, but a sick feeling lingered, a snatching at something she wasn't sure was there.

Yggdrasil—

Yggdrasil is always there.

⊙–⊙–⊙–⊙

That evening, when the musicians began to play, Nan crossed the room and held out her hand.

Thea laughed. "You can't dance!"

"Maybe I could learn, if I keep trying."

"You think?" Thea took Nan's hands. Sometimes, when it had been slow at work, the Telephone Club girls would dance a few lively steps together, encouraging the crowd to get going. Nan never participated, because she was so terrible. Thea tried to lead her now, and it was still hopeless, her steps always out of time. When Nan stepped on Thea's foot, her ears flushed and she glanced at Sigi, who had just walked into the room with some papers in hand. She waved at them.

Sebastian walked in and started chatting with Max, along the periphery, and now Thea was blushing, too.

Nan glanced over her shoulder and saw the focus of her attention, even though Thea had tried to mask it by looking away. She raised her eyebrows at Thea. "He isn't the reason you've been acting so weird, is he?"

"I don't know what you mean. I haven't been acting weird."

Nan nodded, seeming distracted. "So do you like him?"

"I don't know him."

"You know what I mean! Do you *want* to know him?"

"Maybe. I don't know what's come over me! I never used to fall for anyone and . . . now I'm confused. I kissed Freddy, but Sebastian is so handsome."

"Handsome men are nothing new," Nan said. "It must be more than that."

"I feel as if we share something," Thea said, unsure how to explain.

Nan stopped her poor attempt at dancing and clutched Thea's hand. "Thea, I just want to talk to you." Her husky whisper was barely audible over the instruments. "Whatever Ingrid did to you, please shake it off."

"All Ingrid did was to show me a purpose," Thea said, though she felt, once again, the sense of other thoughts and feelings, smothered behind a veil. "I don't know why you and Freddy seem so . . ." *Afraid of her. Afraid of her. Nightmare. Ingrid. Blood.*

Thea tightened her own grip of Nan, riding a sick wave of panic she couldn't voice. "She did . . ." *Speak.* "She did something."

"What did she do?" Nan demanded.

Thea shook her head, her mind a blur of pain and terror. Whatever had happened was too terrible to tell Nan. If she told Nan, she would have to face that awful thing.

"Damn it," Nan said, as the door swung open and Ingrid entered. She was looking right at them. Thea pulled away from Nan, feeling as if she had betrayed Ingrid.

Sebastian noticed all of this from the side of the room. He walked over to Ingrid. "Something wrong?"

"No," Ingrid said, her forehead wrinkled with tension so she almost looked her age for once.

"The way you charged in here . . ."

"I just wanted to see how things were going, to make sure everyone's comfortable. I feel as if the mood has been a bit unhinged."

Sebastian took a sip of the drink in his hand and glanced around. "If this is your idea of unhinged, you might want to take a step back, because I was thinking of removing my jacket."

"You should be working, Sebastian," Ingrid said, and then she smiled her neat little smile. She could've been a movie star herself, Thea thought, the type who could play a little girl for decades.

As she departed, Sebastian did toss his jacket aside, and he gave Thea and Nan a crooked grin. "I don't know what's gotten into her lately."

"I'd sure love to know myself," Nan said, her tone sharp. She squeezed Thea's hand, and left them.

"Do you ever get the feeling—" Sebastian began. Then frowned.

"That something is wrong?" Thea asked softly. Even though

Ingrid was gone, she kept seeing that terrible look she'd had in her eyes when she pushed the door open.

"Maybe," Sebastian said. "It reminds me, sometimes, of my childhood bedroom. I swore it was haunted, but I never saw the ghost. I just felt that someone was there, watching me. Or that someone was speaking in the next room, yet when I opened the door, the room was empty." He laughed sharply. "That makes me sound like I'm losing my mind, and I don't have time for that."

"I feel the same way." Thea took a step closer so she could whisper. "Like someone's watching us."

He looked at her, and she saw an echo of her own thoughts in the way his expression suddenly set as sure as an egg poured into a hot pan. *Don't speak of it anymore.*

He reached for her shoulder, almost fumbling, and drew her close, while he still held his drink in one hand. "We should just dance," he said, shutting his eyes. "Live in this moment. This is the first chance I've had to relax in days."

She took the drink from his hand, drank the last sip, and put it aside. Whatever it was, that odd touch of madness that sometimes crept into her mind, it was shared. It bonded them in some unseen way that only their eyes seemed to understand. She would never have put her head on any other man's shoulder, but she found herself now doing just that, spreading her hand across his back to feel the way his muscles shifted as he danced, the warm soft-and-hard of his skin beneath the thin cotton of his shirt. She shut her eyes.

When she opened them, Freddy was standing in the doorway. As soon as she noticed him, he left, his expression unchanged.

TWENTY-TWO

"Hel wrote back," Sigi said, flashing the letter at Nan as she walked away from Thea.

Nan was still lost in her worries over Thea; she had to run Sigi's words back over in her mind. "You didn't even tell me you sent a letter."

Sigi pushed the doors open, heading back into the hall. The sound of the music grew muffled as the heavy doors shut behind them again. "I've been so nervous about what he'd say, I didn't want to talk about it. He understands now, though."

"Did you tell him the truth?"

"Not exactly. I didn't give him many details about what it was like underground. And I didn't tell him about Freddy. I just said my mother gave up her life for mine, and it was a rare spell that I didn't know existed. After that, I tried to sound like my old self, to ease his mind. I asked him a lot of questions about how things are going for him. He likes attention."

"I see he wrote a lot in response." The letter looked to be at least five pages, covered front and back in small handwriting.

"Brevity isn't his strong suit. He spent three pages just giving me a detailed account of what happened to him the night the workers got out. 'At approximately two forty-five p.m., I was wakened by shouting outside the window, so I reached for my robe and hurried downstairs to see what was the matter, finding three young men who looked dirty and distressed. They started to explain the horrifying circumstances, and I tried to invite them up for cheese toast, but they insisted on—' Well, anyway. You can tell he's a dear, can't you?"

"Sure," Nan said, although she was not usually quick to call anyone a "dear," and certainly not on such scant evidence. She could tell Sigi was eager to share her friends; despite apprehensions, Nan tried to play along.

"He invited us to a gathering tomorrow morning. University classes have been canceled all week, so no one has much to do, and the curfew has ruined evening parties."

"Oh—you told him about me?"

"Of course I told him something."

Nan glanced at the doors again, wishing even more that Thea was her old self. She needed someone to talk to about this. Should she even try to pursue normal friendships now? What would she say at a gathering? At least Sebastian had sent for some other clothes for her and Sigi, and they weren't bad.

The door creaked open. Ingrid slipped out. "What are you two doing?" she asked suspiciously, as if they would discuss huge secrets right in the hallway.

"Nothing much," Nan said.

"Oh?" Ingrid shot Sigi a look as if she wanted her to go

away, but Sigi stayed put. "I have seen so little of you, sister. I hope you're concentrating on regaining your memories and your powers."

At night, the memories crept in. Ingrid in her youth, a slip of a girl in a dark green dress and apron, her long blond hair braided and coiled around her head, with a few wisps floating out to soften her face. Her bare, dirty feet curled beneath her as she peeled apples. She never liked to stay inside. Their small cottage was built under Yggdrasil's branches, with just enough room for their three beds and three chairs and a hearth for cooking, where Urd liked to read by the fire.

Nan swallowed. Even the beautiful memories frightened her beyond words. They belonged to a stranger.

"You have been remembering," Ingrid said. "I see it in your eyes. Why do you fight it? Why don't you want your old life back?" When Nan didn't answer, she glanced at Sigi again. "Do you want to lose everything?"

Nan narrowed her eyes. "No, I certainly don't," she said. "You were different, in my memories."

"We were so happy together before Yggdrasil's destruction. Such a thing had never happened, in all our years. Of course, it *will* grow again. And when it does, we can be happy as we were." Ingrid smoothed her hand down the front of her dress, fretfully, like she was looking for comfort. "Good night, Nan."

Nan's stomach flipped as she watched Ingrid leave the room. She didn't want to sleep, fearing she might recall more of her sister in young and merry days. *I must have loved her once, more than I love Thea, or anyone in this life. The old me probably would have protected her above all.*

Something dark has a hold on her, too.

"Nan?" Sigi asked. "You look so troubled."

"She's right. I do have memories of her. And all I know is that something's wrong." Nan pressed her fingers to her temples. "I'd like to meet your friends. I need to think about something else."

⊙–⊙–⊙–⊙

The guards didn't want them to leave the next morning. "Sebastian's tightening security after what happened to Roger," they told them.

"I can assure you I'm not reporting to any enemies," Nan said. "Sebastian wouldn't force me to stay, I'm sure." She was certain of this now; Freddy had told her and Sigi Sebastian's true identity yesterday. Sebastian must know that she knew, and since he clearly wanted this kept secret, she was sure he wouldn't challenge her.

"No, but—"

"We won't be gone long."

The streets had more people on them now, the mood changing from withdrawn fear to a desperate energy. They had to stop for a pack of factory workers marching by, waving United Workers Party flags, the group including some wives and older children. At the university, students milled around the wrought-iron fences surrounding the dorms. Someone had climbed the university clock tower to hang up a sign that said BETTER TO DIE ABOVE THAN SLAVE BELOW, so anyone checking the time would see it.

Sigi said Hel was studying architecture at the university and lived on the third floor of one of the grand old apartments with a mansard roof and elegant balconies. The hallway smelled of baked goods. When Sigi knocked, a girl opened the door and immediately threw her arms around Sigi.

"I thought Hel was playing a trick on me!" she cried. Then she slapped Sigi, although not hard. "Why did you die in our apartment?"

Sigi looked pained. "Is there any good answer to that question?"

"No. Of course not. But—never again. God bless your poor mother. Did she really trade her life for yours?"

Hel swept over and kissed Sigi's cheek. "I told you not to talk about it."

"Easy for you to say. You always liked magic more than I do," said the girl Nan assumed was Margie. More faces had crowded around. One girl grabbed Sigi's hand while another shoved Hel out of the way to hug her. Nan already felt overwhelmed.

"This is Nan," Sigi said, pulling her into the fray. "We met underground. Nan, this is Hel, Margie, Hilda, Lena, Doris, and *there's* Martin, I wondered if you were here."

"Hello," Nan said, quietly counting the people in her head. Seven people, including Sigi. That wasn't a lot, so why did it seem like so many, when they were all looking at her?

Luckily they didn't ask anything of her. "Can you tell us what's happening?" Lena asked Sigi, as they all sat down on the tidy white sofa and gathered chairs. She was a tall girl with sallow skin, full red lips, and a small chin. "All we have are rumors and lies."

"What happened underground?" Margie asked. Her eyebrows seemed almost perpetually raised, making her blue eyes even wider. "Or is too painful to speak of?"

"We didn't have it as bad as some," Sigi said, launching into an explanation of the serum that tore their memories away, the drab meals, the rote tasks. Nan noticed she left out the more uncomfortable parts, such as the way Rory Valkenrath would prowl around the cafeteria. Sigi had been terrified of him. And she didn't speak of what happened to the revived workers without the serum—that it had also kept them from decaying and hungering for blood.

Nan hadn't thought of all this much since arriving at Sebastian's. Thinking of Rory reminded her of that taste of her own power. She had tried to use the wyrdsong on him. *I was so close to showing him his own wrongdoing.* Although she hadn't quite understood her power, it felt so right.

Hel was moving back and forth through the arched passage between the kitchen and living space, setting out bread and jam, cheese, and sliced apples. Nan hadn't gotten a very good look at him in the dim bar the other night. Now he seemed rather harmless—quite tall and big-boned yet gentle, clearly a pampered rich boy in an argyle sweater and neatly pressed slacks, his hair parted to the side and curled over one eye. She caught him looking at her here and there.

Nan stayed mostly quiet throughout Sigi's story, from the underground to the escape, to Sebastian's revolutionary group. Her friends were gripped.

"Should we join up?" Lena asked. "We could help the revolution."

"Sebastian sounds handsome," Doris said, although Sigi hadn't said one word about him being handsome.

"No," Sigi said. "I don't want any of you to get hurt."

"So it's all right if you keep getting hurt?" Margie said.

"Well—we're still not even sure we can trust Sebastian," Sigi said.

"Why?" Doris asked.

Sigi looked at Nan with a crumpled brow. She hadn't mentioned Nan's involvement, and was clearly struggling with how to explain.

Nan thought of the party at Arabella von Kaspar's house. She had felt just as uncomfortable there, among people with some inkling of what she was. The first time she had met Sigi, she'd gone upstairs to escape the crowd. *I can never fit in, because I can never explain. It ruins everything when I do.*

"I think it's best we don't talk about it yet," Nan said. "We don't want to spread rumors ourselves. If Sebastian is trustworthy, I wouldn't want to ruin his reputation."

"Oh dear. So mysterious." Doris sighed.

The crowd began to break up now into two smaller groups. "I still have a lot of your things at our place," Margie was telling Sigi, "if you want to get them."

"Sure, we could come by." Sigi kept trying to work Nan into the conversation, but Nan remained an awkward presence, always standing around listening to everyone else talk.

"Nan?" Hel approached her while Sigi was talking to Margie. "Would you like a drink?"

"Just me?" Nan asked, since he hadn't offered anyone else a drink.

"You look like you could use one."

"I actually don't care all that much for drinks." Then she felt bad for rejecting his hospitality. "If you have tea . . ."

"I do. I have a few varieties, if you want to see which you'd prefer."

She sensed that he wanted to get her alone, although she didn't know why. This put her on edge even more, but she still followed.

"You don't like meeting lots of new people much, do you?" he asked, as they stepped into the kitchen. "I feel exactly the same way."

"Oh—" *Is that all?* Nan was relieved. By now, she almost expected strangers to drop heavy information into her lap. "I guess I'm sort of a loner."

He nodded. "It took Sigi ages to get me out of my shell. Even now, I prefer to play waiter instead of leading the conversation. You might have noticed. I'm sorry we're all so loud."

"You're fine." Nan smiled a little. "I'm glad to see Sigi enjoying herself. She told me she's known you a long time."

"Truth be told, I'm still unsettled, seeing her alive again." He filled the kettle and put three different tins of tea on the counter. "But I'm glad. We grew up playing together. Our mothers are good friends, and we didn't really get along with our mothers, either of us, though we got along with each other. She got me through some hard times in boarding school, writing me supportive letters."

"That's nice." Nan chose one of the teas, without really caring.

"She means the world to me." He hesitated. "I'd let her stay with me in a heartbeat, if she needed it, but she seems to want to stick with you."

Nan felt pierced with guilt, as if Hel sensed her own confused feelings. "I definitely want her to enjoy a long, happy life, since she's gotten this second chance," she said.

"I hope she does. I didn't realize how fragile she was, until the—the suicide."

"We're all fragile in certain ways, I suppose," Nan said, looking through the passageway to the living room, seeing Sigi laugh heartily over something Margie had said.

In the living room, Lena turned to the phonograph and put on a record. A song began to play, a jerking, screeching sound that Nan recognized as jazz. Sigi looked at Nan and then turned sharply. "Oh—I'm sorry, Lena, maybe not yet. We—uh—had some bad memories of music underground. They played it sometimes to . . ."

"It's all right," Nan said. Sigi was never a good liar, anyway, and Nan was used to hearing music all the time, unpleasant as it was to her ears. "Really," she said, when Lena looked unsure. "Sigi loves music. I'm the one who has bad memories, but I really don't mind at all."

She had never been around a phonograph, though. She certainly hadn't had one at home, and a live band played at the club. Something about the bell shape of the horn unnerved her.

Why?

An answering memory flashed into her mind.

A cold white room with only a cot and a table. Her hands and feet, shackled so she couldn't move quickly. And when she did move, she stumbled. Her mind was hazy.

She remembered a man sitting beside her. And a phonograph. "I hear you don't like music," he said. "That it disturbs your powers."

He was speaking gently. She wouldn't look at him. Her skin was hot with hatred.

"I don't want to do this to you, god knows," he said, "but you have to stop fighting. I'll protect you and your sisters and Yggdrasil—I *need* my magic users, though, Verthandi. Is it so unreasonable to ask that they serve their king? Is it?"

Nan shuddered violently, remembering days upon days—or was it weeks?—of tinny music and shackled hands.

"Your tea is ready," Hel said.

"Thank you." Nan gripped the cup, even though it almost burned her fingers. She didn't want to embarrass herself around all Sigi's friends by revealing her shock, but now that she remembered King Otto's face, it was all she could think about.

TWENTY-THREE

"Marlis? Your father would like to see you. He's sending a car."

"It's safe?" Marlis looked at Wilhelmina hopefully. She was tired beyond words of being cooped up with the other women and children, and the weather had turned too cold to hide in the attic.

Wilhelmina smiled humorlessly. "Safe enough, I suppose. They've cleared the rebels out of Republic Square."

Marlis wasn't used to Papa keeping her at arm's length like this. He usually liked her to be involved, but he would also want her to be safe. *He wants me for something else. Another speech, perhaps.*

She had always dreamed of giving speeches to the people. The words she had already said still haunted her, however. They weren't her own.

You know that's how it works.

She wished she knew how to talk to Wilhelmina, to share her hesitations with someone else, but since her own mother died, she had kept her deepest thoughts inside her head. Sharing them felt too uncomfortable, as if no one would understand. She could have attended a thousand balls, worn the finest couture gowns, made endless small talk—all the things Papa urged so she would fit in—but people would always sense the farce. She didn't want to play the woman's role on the political stage.

But Papa was trying his best to give her what she'd always wanted.

She couldn't climb into a car without thinking of Ida's death, and she shoved that back, trying to remember the powerful deaths that had happened in the opera, not the real ones. *Kriemhild wouldn't brood, she would do something.*

The drive to the Chancellery only took a few minutes, and Papa awaited her inside, pulling her into an embrace. "Have you been all right at the Wachters'?"

"Fine."

He took her arm and started walking, leaning close. "It hasn't been made public yet—we caught Gerik Valkenrath this morning."

"He's still alive?"

"Oh yes. He was trying to escape by boat. He swears he has no idea where Freddy is." Papa's grip on her briefly tightened. "You were right, I think—this all happened because Gerik was reckless. He won't own up to it—says he always had the situation under control—but his story has more holes than a wheel of cheese. He let Freddy talk to rustic girls without supervision. I'll bet the boy's running around with the rebels as we speak."

The hall of the Chancellery was so vast and hard and cold. The marble floors had a grayish sheen that matched the light struggling through clouds outside. The chill wrapped around her down to the bone. "Freddy was getting too old for the way he was kept," Marlis said.

Papa gave her a hard look. "Marlis—Freddy wasn't going to grow up. You know that. That's why he needed an heir."

Marlis drew her arm away from his touch.

"I'm not telling you anything new," Papa said.

She remembered one of her birthdays, asking Papa if Freddy could come to the party. No, Papa said. Freddy couldn't go anywhere, he was sick. She wasn't told the secret then, though as she got older, she found out in bits and pieces: *Freddy isn't really sick, he has powerful magic. That's why he's so tired sometimes. That's why his hair is silver. Freddy's magic does so much for this city; he's terribly important. Indispensable. You're old enough to know the truth now. You can keep a secret.*

No one ever said outright that Freddy's magic would kill him, but it was alluded to in so many little concerned comments. Of course it wasn't new. Of course she'd known.

"Don't look like that, Princess," Papa's voice cajoled gently. "Look how many young rustics just threw their lives away this week. Freddy would have died having made a difference."

She bit back the sick feeling inside her. She knew Papa didn't *like* the idea of draining Freddy's life away. Freddy wasn't really different from the young men who were drafted in the war. It only disturbed her because she was one of the few people with the privilege of watching him grow up under the weight of his magic.

Papa exchanged a muted greeting with a few other ministers they passed in the hall. "We need to find him," he continued, turning the corner. "We can't let power like his fall into enemy hands. I wondered if we might lure him out."

Volland walked out of one of the meeting rooms and lifted a hand in greeting. "I've just sent on the documents," he said. "And you'll meet with Taussen tomorrow."

"Yes, yes, I'll look it over. I'm talking to Marlis about Freddy."

"Ah." Volland's expression was neutral. *Being neutral is my job,* he told her when she teased him once about being expressionless. "Is she amenable?"

"He hasn't told me the plan yet," Marlis said.

"Beating around the bush, are we, sir?" Volland teased. "Your father and I were disagreeing this morning about how to approach the situation, Marlis. I think we're on the same page now. We feel you might have the best chance of saying something on the radio that would compel Freddy to return home, if he is at all able to do so."

He paused as Lieutenant Acherbaum rounded the corner, walking purposefully like he was trying to catch up with them, even though they weren't moving. Acherbaum stopped in front of Papa and saluted, hand slashing the air.

"Acherbaum!" Papa said. "Let me extend my sincere apologies: I heard your unit sustained heavy losses against the revolutionaries."

"Thank you, sir." There was a curious insistence to Acherbaum's tone that made Marlis nervous. He should have little reason to approach Papa like this when Papa was so busy; he was a second-tier officer. "I suppose a few lives are a small price to pay for this country. Especially when you can bring them back again."

"You misunderstand," Papa said, as Volland placed a protective hand on his shoulder. "We never had that capability. Dark magic brought them back, we could only attempt to control it."

"Liar!" Acherbaum shouted. "You're a liar! You could have used that magic to bring back *good* men."

"This is not the time and place for this discussion," Papa said, even as one of the guards moved toward Acherbaum.

"You betrayed us!" Acherbaum pulled out a gun. Three shots happened almost at once—Acherbaum firing once, twice, and then the guard. Papa fell back, caught by Volland, clutching his stomach.

"You—" Acherbaum gurgled, and then he turned his gun on his own head.

Acherbaum's blood splattered onto Marlis. She ripped off her coat and flung it to the floor.

"Papa! Papa!" She knelt beside him, trying to pull open his coat. Beneath the black wool, bright-red blood stained his shirt. Marlis had never seen a color as vibrant as the blood all over Papa, all over the floor, all over her hands. "Hang on!"

"Marlis." He grabbed her arm. "I'm so sorry. I love you. I love you so much."

"Don't—" He never told her that. She knew, and that unspoken knowing was all she needed. "I love you too," she whispered, realizing this could be her only chance.

"But—I need to tell you—You should know—you are— more than my daughter. There's a letter hidden in my desk—at home—my office there—left drawer." He seemed to shiver, his eyes bulging slightly and unfocused, as if struggling with the Grim Reaper. "Your mother loved you, too. You *were* our daughter. Please . . ."

He spasmed, and that was the last of him. More guards had gathered around, trying to keep panicked officials at bay. In those few moments where it was only Marlis and the dying light in Papa's eyes, the empty hall had filled up with gibbering voices and rushing footsteps. Someone shouted for the doctor, while someone else cried out, "He's gone!"

Volland looked at her. He had heard every last word Papa said. She could hardly see him through the tears in her eyes. She couldn't speak. She held on to Papa's arm, blocking out all the commotion around her, seeing only his face. The only person who loved her. The only person she loved. A doctor rushed in, but she knew it didn't matter. Only one person could have any hope of mattering, one little fox who had eluded the chase of the hounds.

She clutched Papa's hand tight as they loaded him onto a stretcher.

"He's alive, barely," Volland announced. "Everyone get back, let them get through." He took Marlis's arm and pulled her off Papa. She was stunned into silence. *He most certainly isn't alive.*

Everyone else was moving around her, guards following the stretcher, ministers running to and fro, Acherbaum's body pulled up, leaving a slick pool of blood on the floor. Despite all this movement, Marlis felt as if time had stopped.

Volland stepped in front of her, placing a hand on her shoulder. "Come with me a moment. Please."

She jerked back. "I don't want to be touched. I don't want to go anywhere."

"Come on," he said, even more gently. "We need to talk. To find Freddy."

She forced herself out of the haze of pain. "I'll follow you," she said quietly.

He didn't lead her far, ducking into an unoccupied meeting room. "We can't lose your father now when everything is already so unstable."

"Is that why you said Papa was alive?"

"Of course. We have an understanding among the higher staff that we would use Freddy in any case like this. We would have brought back Vice Chancellor Walther, if he hadn't died in an explosion. But—of course, to do this, we must find Freddy."

"We will *get* Freddy," she said. "I'll do whatever I must do. First I have to get home." She knew Volland had heard every word of Papa's strange mutterings.

Volland didn't ask questions. That was how he was; he knew she would tell him more the moment she felt like it, and he could be patient until then. "Of course," Volland said. "Go home and then tell me what you need. We'll figure out a plan."

"I'll hurry," she said.

The ride home seemed both ponderous and miserable. She had never wanted so much to sob, but the tears stayed locked in her throat. As the guards ushered her into the house, she overheard the chauffeur comment, "Nothing warms that girl up," as if she were heartless just because she wouldn't show him her grief.

All the household staff and aides had heard that her father was in the hospital fighting for his life, and they wanted to fuss over her. She told them to go away, knowing how cold she must look to them, with her face severe and her eyes dry.

She locked the door to Papa's office and yanked drawers from the desk until she found a letter in a hidden compartment.

If you are reading this, something must have happened to me. I can't imagine it will ever come to that, but I must plan for every contingency, and I love you. I want you to be safe. I know you will doubt my love after you read this letter, but I hope you will be able to come back to it later, for confirmation of what you know to be true in your heart.

The heart in question was already sinking into her stomach. She read quickly—the letter was quite long, as Papa was always verbose once he got going.

We've always said you look like your mother. And it's true. I think sometimes she loved you more fiercely than her own blood because of it. Your mother would never admit she believed in coincidences, much less miracles, but I know that was what you meant to her. To both of us.

You were adopted, Marlis. Your mother was unable to conceive. And we had reason to keep you close and safe.

In the forests of Irminau, there is a monastery dedicated to seeking out the children they call "the Nornir." The monks and many rustics believe there are three women reborn over and over, who protect the magic that comes from a sacred tree deep in the forest, and that this magic is a tool God uses to influence human fate. If a Norn is born into a family that can't properly care for her, the monks will offer the child a home.

Let me be blunt—I never believed in that nonsense. Magic is simply a force—a weapon, more often than not. But I can't deny that magic seems to crop up more often in the north, closer to the tree. My job is to protect my country. To destroy that weapon. So we destroyed the tree. Either we would destroy magic entirely, or we would destroy a powerful symbol of Irminauer belief. And then we tried to capture the Norns. You were the only one we could find, a babe in the care of monks who swore you were sacred.

If the legends were true, magic would have died with the tree, but magic still plagues us.

If the Nornir still live and you are what the monks believed, you would have grown into my enemy and manifested magical abilities, but you, my dear Marlis, seemed to follow in our footsteps. You share my political ambitions and your mother's scientific curiosity and her way of looking at every angle before forming a conclusion. A guardian of fate? A tool of gods? I scoff at the idea. You have grown into a modern young woman—without magic.

Could the lore of the Norns have been wrong all along? Perhaps so. You seem to believe in this world we have built. I hope you will keep fighting for it and not against it. I hope you will forgive me for my dishonesty and understand the measures I took to find out the truth, and then to protect you from it, because my love for you is one thing that has always been true.

The letter was dated several months before. She wondered if his words were still true. She had tried to persuade him to accept "barbaric" magic.

She paced the room fervently, crumpling the letter in one hand and twisting her mother's necklace in the other.

"You left me . . . to find this after you were dead?" she whispered aloud. The whisper only made the house seem emptier. The guards and servants outside the room made no noise. Papa's office was cavernous, the light on his desk failing to chase away the shadows in the corners. "Did you ever mean to tell me?"

She was not his child. She had never spent nine months tucked inside her mother to emerge into their arms. She had been born far away to complete strangers. And she was—

What was this? A Norn? What did that mean? She didn't even know who she could talk to about this. What to do, what to *think*?

She finally stopped pacing at the window. The sky was so heavy and gray that she wouldn't be surprised to see the year's first snow. She was so alone, always. If Papa were truly to die, every day might look as heavy and gray as this, even if the sun was shining.

But he lied to you anyway. Just like he lied to Freddy. He didn't trust you to handle the truth. What other reason for hiding it away in this—cowardly—letter!

She threw the letter at the wall. Her shoulders shook.

You can't tell me this after you've escaped into death. You're going to look me in the eye and tell me why I should still fight for you.

TWENTY-FOUR

"We have word that the Chancellor may have been killed," Sebastian said, making a general announcement to the gathered men.

Over the past few days, Freddy's mind had turned away from the world he had left, but Sebastian's announcement brought his past back into sharp focus.

The Valkenraths, the Chancellor . . . the glittering, controlled world of the government elite had felt so immutable when he was captured in the heart of it. It was hard to imagine it could be so changed.

"Though we only have hearsay to go on now," Sebastian continued. Standing next to him in front of the tall drawing room windows was Yann, from the same revolutionary group as Arabella. Freddy had punched Yann the night the workers escaped, so he would recognize him anywhere. Yann noticed him, too, though he didn't look surprised. He must have known the reviver was with Sebastian.

"We don't know who shot the Chancellor," Yann said. "Whoever executed this plot, they weren't from the UWP circles. Of course, the radio says he was merely injured. One of our spies in the capital swears this is just a story, and he's always been reliable."

No doubt if the Chancellor was dead, they must be scouring the city for Freddy more fiercely than ever.

"Everyone in the Chancellor's circle has surely been holding their breath these past few days, waiting to see if Irminau will capitalize on Urobrun's vulnerability and initiate war," Sebastian said. "The government won't want to make this public knowledge yet, to buy some time."

"What if King Otto marches right in?" Will asked. "Can we stop him? Can anyone?"

"The UWP has a plan," Yann said. "We want to establish a citizen army as quickly as possible. That's why I'm here, to see if you'll help us."

"Of course we will," Sebastian said. "The sooner we can secure the city for the revolution and get the Chancellor's camp out of the picture, the better chance we'll have of fending off King Otto when he makes his inevitable move."

"Things are obviously advancing very quickly," Yann said, motioning to Sebastian's hand, which clutched a stack of papers. "I wondered if you'd be able to attend a strategy meeting tomorrow morning as soon as the curfew lifts?"

"I'll be there."

Yann nodded and left.

"I'll be damned if Yann claims the country," a burly dark-haired man said, once Yann was gone. He looked like he'd enjoy snapping Yann in half.

"I don't think Yann will personally 'claim' the country,"

Sebastian said. "Anyway, Yann's just the messenger. Brunner is now the head of the radical UWP, and I rather like him."

"But you're our leader, Sebastian," Aleksy said.

"Well," Sebastian said, "Brunner has greater numbers and is quite competent as a military leader. At this time, he will serve better. Even if we don't agree with the UWP entirely, King Otto has a lot of magic on his side, and we have to be able to present a unified front against him."

"I agree with Sebastian," said Heffler, a thickset man with serious eyes who seemed well-respected. "We don't have the numbers to operate on our own. All the rebel groups in the city are falling in with the UWP right now if they know what's good for them."

Sebastian took a few strolling steps along the vast floor rug, which had grown rather dirty with all the coming and going. "I doubt the UWP will ultimately gain control of the country," he said. "At least, not these current leaders. They're stepping into a huge mess. Things *will* go wrong, and someone will be blamed. If the Chancellor is already out of the way, the next group to step in will likely also suffer. Even I'm not entirely sure what direction to go in yet. Let the UWP make the mistakes first: While we'll support them in their efforts, we will distinguish ourselves enough to step out of their ashes."

"What if they are successful?" another man asked. Freddy didn't know his name, but he had a lion's head of hair.

Sebastian shrugged. "Let's worry about that when it happens."

A man ducked his head in, to share what he'd just heard on

the radio: "Now they're reporting that they've caught Gerik Valkenrath."

Thea had come in through the side door during Sebastian's speech, wearing an apron from her nursing duties. At this news, she looked at Freddy with concern and started moving through the crowd to reach him. Despite last night, he wanted to soften when he saw she still cared. *It's not her fault if she's enchanted,* he tried to remind himself as he rushed toward the radio. Freddy had expected to hear one of the officials delivering the grave news; he didn't expect to hear Marlis.

"We are still looking for Gerik's ward, Frederick. I would like to assure him that he will not be blamed for Mr. Valkenrath's actions, and I will personally see to his safety and comfort if anyone has any news of his whereabouts." She spoke clearly and pointedly, and he could almost see her eyes flashing with frustration.

"We are also seeking two accomplices of Gerik's, Karl and Marianne Lang. They are considered to be very dangerous, and if anyone has any further information about them, I beg you to come to the Chancellery."

Freddy sucked in a breath. Damn Marlis.

"Are you all right?" Thea whispered.

He nodded, not wanting to confide anything in her when he couldn't trust her.

Now Gerik himself was permitted to speak. Freddy's old guardian sounded like a stranger, his easy, arrogant manner replaced by a voice that was low and subdued.

"I want to apologize to all of you for the events of the other night and all the years that preceded it. I was in charge of the effort to cure this disease, and I take responsibility for this breach of security. In my shock and, admittedly, my cowardice, I did not come forward when I should have, but I am as appalled as anyone that Irminau would do this to our people. We must not allow them to win. I hope justice will be served."

Freddy approached Sebastian as the crowd broke up. "Can we talk?"

Sebastian nodded. "In my office."

Ingrid followed. Freddy shot her a glare. "Just you and me, Sebastian."

After shutting the door, Sebastian sat down, found a cold half-empty cup of coffee, and took a swig.

"That broadcast was a thinly coded message to me," Freddy said. "Karl and Marianne *Linden* are my parents. She can't state outwardly that she's looking for me because I'm the reviver, but she can toss out a threat. She'll punish my parents if she can't have me."

"So you want to go back to the Chancellery?"

"I have to go."

"And suppose they decide they'd like to torture you and find out where you've been? And you lead them right back to me?"

"They don't want to torture me," Freddy said. "I can do a lot for them. They want my power."

"Maybe that's true, but . . ."

Freddy kept thinking of Thea in Sebastian's arms. He didn't want to bring that up now—he didn't like showing that kind of weakness, and it seemed so petty. As for Thea or Sebastian, he didn't know what was going on in their heads. Sebastian probably didn't know Thea had kissed Freddy, and Thea might not even remember. *Don't take it out on him.*

"I think I can help you," Freddy said. "I came from that world, and they need me. I know Marlis, and her love for her father could be a weakness—I'm the only person who can keep him alive. I can get some good information for you, and they won't kill me. What other person can you send into the enemy den knowing they won't kill him?"

"Bah," Sebastian said, sounding defeated. "I can think of a hundred bad things that could come of this."

"I can think of bad things no matter what path I take," Freddy replied. He wondered if maybe a part of him wanted to go to Marlis because at least he knew what she was about. He didn't have to constantly guess if he was around enemies or friends, like he did here.

"Are you going to bring the Chancellor back?"

"I might. And he'll know every breath he takes is thanks to me."

Sebastian dropped a few stray pencils into his empty coffee cup as if they were thoughts he was sorting out, and then glanced up. "Ingrid said you can't control your magic. I do know you can end someone's life, of course—we've seen that. But do you think you'll be able to keep a handle on the situation under pressure?"

That was Freddy's weakness. He loved using his magic, and he still hated releasing people into death. When he let all of the workers go, many of them had been injured by the Urobrun Army. He had seen and even felt their pain. That made it easier. But to kill the Chancellor would be a challenge.

No, not to kill him. He's already dead. I can't forget that. "I will admit that controlling my magic has been difficult in the past, but I've learned a lot since then."

Sebastian looked torn. "I have to think of my men, to keep them safe."

"I'm leaving Thea here. If I thought I was putting her in danger, I wouldn't go." He couldn't help a possessive note entering his voice. Part of him wanted a challenge from Sebastian so they could get it all on the table, but that wouldn't do any good if they were enchanted. *I just have to focus on helping her.* "I can manage this. You asked me to trust you, and I have to ask you the same."

Sebastian tapped his fingertips together, thinking it through, then said, "All right. I don't like it, but I'll trust you."

TWENTY-FIVE

Thea couldn't believe what she was hearing. "Freddy, stop and think about this for a moment! They offered no proof that they have your parents."

"I realize that." He seemed distant. "But I think there is something I can do there, as opposed to here, where I can only sit around and wait."

"We're all waiting right now. All I've done is bring trays of food and fluff pillows! Our time will come."

His brows twitched, betraying his worry, but he still sounded firm. "I hope so. For now, you're safe here. And I'll be back."

"You can't promise that," Thea said.

He took her hand and held it. His silence explained it all. He didn't want to go, but he would.

Down the hall, Ingrid had been talking to Sebastian in a low tone just outside his office; now she looked at Freddy. "You can't possibly be leaving us just when we need you most," she said.

"I'm afraid I am."

"Sebastian—you're letting him go?"

Sebastian scratched his head. "Well . . ."

"You can't possibly."

"I can't tell my men I believe in freedom and then force Freddy to stay. And Freddy has a point—in many ways, he has the upper hand."

Ingrid's expression was fierce, and Thea felt uneasy. Freddy ought to trust Ingrid. He was thinking of his parents, who might not even be in danger, when Yggdrasil *was* in danger. "Freddy, if the Norns don't think you should go, then you shouldn't go," Thea said.

"I'm going. I'm sorry." He looked past her to Sebastian.

"I'll get someone to escort you," Sebastian said.

He said softly to Thea, "I hope I can explain later."

When he let go of her hand, she felt a strange sensation— the quick twinge of pain that sometimes appeared down her forearm, and then nothing at all. She touched her palm where Freddy's hand had just been.

"Feeling all right?" Ingrid approached Thea once Sebastian and Freddy had left.

"Yes, of course." Thea shook her head.

"I'm sure that announcement took you aback, just as it did me." Ingrid straightened her angular shoulders and walked over to Thea. "Sebastian should not let Freddy go. I'm not sure what impulse guides him sometimes."

"I know Freddy's hated being cooped up here, and we all feel helpless. I know someone must do these smaller tasks, but—" She sighed.

"If you wanted to do something more important—"

"I do."

"If you were willing to fully embrace the protection of Yggdrasil, you could tap into its power, too."

"How?"

"Come with me. I'll show you."

Ingrid led Thea into her bedroom, and they settled on her quilt. The room had one small window, and the curtains were drawn, the sunlight creeping in only around the edges. Their knees were close as Ingrid took her hands. A brief twinge of discomfort rang through her—she was not usually so intimate with people. She wanted to snatch her hands back. Ingrid smiled a little. Her eyes were round and blue, her lashes fair. "You already have some of Yggdrasil inside you, from when I healed you. But right now—" She paused, as if she heard something in the silence. "You must not be afraid if it leads you to dark places. I don't know if you're ready to accept that. Magic is always a marriage of darkness and light."

"What does that mean?"

"Where does the strength for my magic come from? I can't give and give, I must also take." Ingrid drew back, like she was suddenly uncomfortable with how much she had said, but she still held Thea's hand. "Thea, do you know what I did to you?"

Thea flexed the fingers of her left hand. The movement was perfect. "You healed my hand."

"More than that."

"You . . ." The memory was like sliding her hand into ice. "You cut off my hand."

"Good," Ingrid said. "You have to be able to accept, first, the difficult choices I made for Yggdrasil. If you had not given

149

a piece of yourself to Yggdrasil, you would not be able to have its power. Give and take, you see."

Shouldn't a sacrifice like this be chosen, not forced?

Thea kept her thoughts quiet. She didn't want Ingrid to withdraw her gifts. And maybe in the haze of her pain, she had chosen this. "I understand."

"I will teach you the first spell. It will help keep you safe if anything happens. Close your eyes and imagine Yggdrasil."

Thea summoned to mind an image of Yggdrasil's thick trunk, the branches that spread toward the golden light of the sun. She felt its warmth as clearly as if she stood beneath it, on a perfect June day, with the air lazy and fragrant.

"Think of the piece of Yggdrasil that is a part of you, and imagine it spreading through you until you become joined with the tree itself. You are no longer soft flesh and bright blood that can easily spill: You are as strong as the trunk of a tree that has stood for longer than any human memory."

Thea remembered now when Ingrid had given her the wooden hand, how she had felt as if tiny roots were threading up her arm. She twitched, briefly alarmed by the memory, and opened her eyes. The sight of Ingrid calmed her again. Ingrid's eyes were closed, her chest slowly rising and falling with deep breaths.

Thea surrendered to the feeling of something greater than her urge to protect her own body. "I feel it," she whispered.

"The more you give yourself to Yggdrasil, the stronger you will become."

"I want to be strong." Thea's heart was beating faster. If she could get closer to Yggdrasil, feel its magic, then she wouldn't need anyone.

"I don't get to teach magic to other girls," Ingrid said. "It reminds me of when I was with Verthandi and Urd."

"Your sisters?"

"Yes. Nan is Verthandi."

"It fits, somehow," Thea said. "Does she always look like Nan?"

"Her appearance changes, as mine does. And yet I think she always does look like Nan. Strong." Ingrid smiled. "That was good, for your first attempt. You should try to connect with Yggdrasil every day, and if anything bad happens, tap into that connection. The strength of the tree will be inside you, and if you've succeeded, bullets will glance off you and blows will lose their power."

"I'll be protected from pain," Thea said softly, seeing the leaves of Yggdrasil grow even brighter in her mind.

"Remember to keep it a secret. I wish I could give it to everyone, but I can't."

"Of course," Thea said. "I would never tell a soul."

TWENTY-SIX

Two guards trailed Freddy, staying back just enough that he couldn't forget their presence. Not many people were out to begin with. Behind the gates of fancy homes in the neighborhood, children cried and dogs barked. The park was abandoned.

On Kesslerstrasse, the shops were open again. The butcher had empty windows and a line out his door. Women exited, clutching small paper-wrapped parcels as if they were gold. Stores selling everything from shoes to musical instruments had their window displays stocked. The clothing store had an elaborate display of painted mannequins wearing ladies' fall day dresses in dark red and green with pleated knee-length skirts. However, no one opened the doors, no one lingered at the windows. The most popular spot in the row seemed to be the barber, where a crowd of men spilled into the street, talking, gesturing, smoking. "What a bunch of lies!" one man kept shouting.

The clock shop was where Freddy was most tempted to linger. He couldn't remember his early years spent at home, but the sound of multiple ticking clocks must have been constant background noise. It could have been the sound of all his life. He had tried to cling to his past. With books instead of his father's guidance, he taught himself to repair broken clocks. Gerik brought them to him, indulging the hobby.

Now these clocks, ticking out of reach behind a shop window's glass, felt symbolic of the future. He wouldn't be fixing clocks anymore. When he was the Chancellor's prisoner, he needed to dream of that other life. Now, he had to think of making his own decisions about his power.

It was a short walk to Republic Square, and he couldn't avoid it forever, though he couldn't separate it from the image of a burning pyre of workers' bodies.

Of course, all that was over. The square, which was ordinarily a popular place for picnics, was blocked off to pedestrians, with a few armored military vehicles parked around. The protestors had been cleared out, although their detritus remained: Bits of trash, handkerchiefs, papers, and photos littered the park. A flock of geese drifted around the fountain.

But in front of the statue The Maiden of the People, a tall stone figure bearing a sword and the flag of the Republic of Urobrun, was a circle of burned grass as wide as a small house. The Maiden's expression looked more aggrieved than noble. And just across the street, the Chancellery loomed.

Doubt crept up on Freddy. The Chancellery was familiar, yes, and he missed familiarity. He had forgotten how formidable the building was: The government might be modern, but no one had felt the need to replace the Imperial architecture of one hundred years ago, white columns soaring toward statues of soldiers on horseback and angels blowing trumpets. Only the bright flags of the Republic, hung in pairs on the front of every government building, stated that the Empire was dead.

He walked up the wide, empty stairs, approaching the guards. They stared at him from afar, their weapons in easy reach. His existence was known to so few, he didn't expect to be recognized.

He held up his hands. "I'm Frederick Linden," he said. "You've been looking for me."

The moment he said his name, they started moving toward him. One of them grabbed his arms, yanking them behind his back.

"Hey!" Freddy said. "Ease off. I came of my own will."

More guards had already crawled out of nowhere. They jostled him inside without saying a word to him, and he wondered if maybe he was wrong—maybe they meant to hurt him after all. Perhaps they considered his crime to be so grave that they would execute him.

They dragged him into a small room, locking him inside. The only comfort was that the room was nicely furnished with the red upholstered chairs ubiquitous in government buildings. If they meant to kill him, surely he would be thrown straight into a dank cell? Or was this wishful thinking? Suddenly he found the hundred bad things Sebastian had mentioned were all in his mind at once.

The door opened, and Marlis entered with the Chancellor's adviser, Diedrich Volland, and two guards. Freddy recognized these particular guards—they had been among the ones to stand outside the door when he revived people.

He felt limp with relief, even though it wasn't warranted.

"It *is* you," Marlis said. She seemed so much her normal self that it made her radio broadcast seem like a bad dream. "Where have you been, Freddy?"

"Laying low. I didn't know who might be looking for me. I'm glad to have made it here safely." He wanted her to feel they were on the same side, at least for now.

"I'm glad to see you as well. I'm sorry for locking you up in here. We're trying to minimize the number of people who know your role, so the guards were told you were a suspected rebel leader and not to ask you any questions until we arrived. We are in dire need of your services."

"In what way?"

"Come with me."

The inside of the Chancellery was as quiet as the outside. The place felt like a giant funeral parlor, with the few men they passed wearing black and speaking only in soft voices.

"We have a lead on your parents, Freddy," Marlis said, as they walked into the courtyard to meet their car. "I hope you can help me, and I will be happy to help you in return."

"What do you want from me?"

"My father," she said, her tone growing heavier. The driver opened the door for them, and Marlis climbed in first. Volland was last, keeping Freddy between them.

"I want to see my parents delivered to safety first," Freddy said.

"I'm not asking you to bring back thousands of people. Just one." She sat stiffly. She didn't wear her grief—that wasn't her way. He knew how much her father had meant to her.

155

"It's wrong," he said. "When I was kidnapped by Arabella von Kaspar, I—"

She interrupted him. "As if she was trustworthy! Of course she would say it was wrong!"

"Listen to me!" he said. "I found out that magic has a balance, and if it's disrupted, there are consequences, and there are even guardians—" He stopped. He knew she wouldn't believe him about the Norns. She had always seemed to lack any imagination, and even he had found the story hard to swallow at first, so she would surely scoff.

"Guardians?" she pressed. "You don't mean Norns?" She said "Norns" like the word was a snake she held by the tail.

"You know about it?" Freddy asked.

"A little. What do you know?"

Freddy was careful with the truth, trying not to implicate the people he'd left behind. "The morning before the dead escaped the underground, the Valkenraths asked me to revive a girl I had already revived before. She had been shot and died a second time. Normally, this wouldn't be possible because the revived can't die from a mere gunshot wound. The girl told me she was a Norn."

"What is it that the Norns supposedly do?" Volland asked.

"They have powers that allow them to intervene when humans abuse magic," Freddy said.

"What kind of powers?" Marlis asked.

"I don't know," Freddy said.

"Do we have anyone we can spare to check the archives for more information?" Marlis asked Volland.

"I can manage without Brewer," Volland said.

"Then get him right on it."

It only took a few minutes to reach the Chancellor's home, where Marlis promptly got out and crossed her arms impatiently. She had always acted as if she expected to rule in her father's stead, and now it seemed like she thought the day had already come. Volland even seemed to be taking orders from her.

Marlis led the way. She was wearing a plain gray silk dress he had seen her wear many times before. Two guards brought up the rear, with Freddy in the middle. Volland had parted from them along the way, probably to give the order to Brewer, who Freddy thought might be Volland's secretary.

The Chancellor was lying in state on his bed. Freddy had never seen the Chancellor's private chambers. He felt like an intruder, seeing a painting of his late wife gazing upon him from the wall, a pile of newspapers on the nightstand, the slippers on the ornate rug. In Freddy's mind, the Chancellor was always standing, speaking forcefully, with every situation under control. Now he looked pale and small beneath the heavy canopy, eyes closed, hands folded.

"How are you keeping him preserved?"

"Bathed in serum. It has a few uses, rather like baking soda." Freddy could see the silent temper in Marlis's face now. Even as a child, she had grown cold and fierce rather than crying when she was upset. She bit her thin lips, and gently smoothed her father's brow, creased so he looked harried even in death.

"Revive him now, and I will assure your parents' safety," she said.

"I want to see them first."

"I'm afraid it can't work that way," she said.

"You need my magic."

"I do, but do I need your cooperation? You take pleasure in using your magic, I know."

This was the test. He knew her weaknesses, but she knew his, too. She was poised yet tense, an animal waiting to strike.

"Marlis, we shouldn't act as enemies," he said. "Don't you realize how precarious all of this is?" He spread his hands to indicate the wider world.

"Of *course*. I'm sure I know much more than you do." He saw the beginnings of tears in her eyes. "Please, just bring him back and do *not* let him go until I say so." She turned to the wall abruptly, smoothing her hands over her face and hair, and then adjusting her glasses.

He stepped closer to the Chancellor's body, feeling the familiar itch of magic in his fingers. He knew now that he couldn't allow people to live, and when he let her father go, she could harm his parents anyway. His only chance to gain the upper hand was to show Marlis he meant business.

"I can't agree to the terms," he said. "I can't let him live."

She looked at the guards. "Tie him."

Freddy had seen the guards quickly subdue the people he revived when they were occasionally panicked and violent. Now he received the same rough treatment as one guard grabbed him and the other pulled up a heavy wooden chair. They didn't care if they bruised his arms or scraped his skin as they held him down with iron arms and bound his legs to the chair.

"Marlis!" He twisted his head to look back at her. The chair faced the Chancellor. "Is this really how you want it to go?"

She wasn't watching the guards, and stood by the window, clutching the curtain in one hand. Sunlight turned loose strands of her dark hair to red-gold.

The guards yanked his hands forward and reached for the Chancellor's hands. The dead man's cold hands were pressed into Freddy's and tied there, forcing his magic to flow. It had always flowed with a touch, and now he had to choke it back with everything in his power.

That meant touching death, touching the clammy, soft hands of the man who, along with Gerik and Uncle, had forced him into a childhood of imprisonment. His throat was tight and painful. Holding back magic felt oddly like choking back tears. Now the guards were roping his chest to the back of the chair, and then his elbows to the arms. He couldn't even speak. It took everything in him not to revive the Chancellor.

"Leave him," Marlis said, and he heard her walk from the room quickly. She *was* ashamed she'd done this to him. He heard it in her voice and her step.

He was faced with the ghastly sight of the Chancellor, now with his arms extended toward the chair like Freddy was a macabre puppeteer. Every instinct inside of Freddy screamed to bring life back to these cold hands and that slack face.

He tilted his neck back to look at the ceiling. The urge was dampened, ever so slightly, if he didn't look at the man. He was breathing fast, wiggling his feet against his bonds, restless to work, and he still felt the Chancellor's slack skin forced against his fingers.

I will bring you back, he thought. *I'll let you say good-bye to your daughter. But not yet. Just—not—yet.*

His hands were growing warmer, and his face, too, as if he were running for his life. The magic seemed like it would boil inside him if it wasn't used. He had never resisted like this before. The Valkenraths brought him the dead and praised him when his work was done. Arabella said he had become addicted to the feeling, that he wouldn't feel this way if the Valkenraths hadn't pushed him into it.

He shut his eyes, battling silently. A wave of cold nausea passed over him, even as his hands and face were sweating. The tingling feeling that always came with magic danced up his arms and down his spine and then behind his eyes.

His eyes opened again. The ceiling was plain white plaster but he saw stars and flashes. He kept staring until they faded and his heart slowed its beat to an everyday rhythm.

It was a silent fight, leaving him spent and relieved. The magic seemed subdued. He could still feel it at the ready, though he had control.

No clock was in view, and time seemed to crawl. He sat exhausted, trying not to think about the unpleasant position he was in. He heard footsteps creaking outside the door occasionally, but no one entered. How long could Marlis stand to wait?

TWENTY-SEVEN

Marlis couldn't stop pacing Papa's office, couldn't stop the tears from running down her face, couldn't stop the sick feeling twisting inside her. A part of her wanted to confide in Freddy, but she didn't know where he'd been or what he'd heard. Papa first. Freddy later.

She was only vaguely aware of Volland in the background, speaking to someone at the door, then doing something at her father's desk.

"Marlis," he said.

"Yes?" She stopped pacing.

"It's going to be all right."

Gentle words made it worse. "It's not," she snapped. "I don't need to be patted on the head."

Even though her ire didn't rattle him, something had, she realized. She could see it in his eyes. "Brewer found a report on . . . Well, a little before you were born, our intelligence in Irminau captured and killed a young woman with persuasive powers who spoke of 'rustic myths like the Norns and the sacred tree.'"

"They killed her?"

"According to the report, she was too dangerous to keep alive because of her ability to enchant."

Volland still hadn't said anything direct about Papa's dying words. She drew a quick breath. "Did you know I was adopted, Volland? Did you know any of it?"

"No. I've only worked for your father for eight years. No one spoke of it. I'd imagine very few people know; he wouldn't want that known."

Wilhelmina knew, Marlis thought, remembering the talk of the tree at lunch, and the odd way Wilhelmina had looked at her when she asked about it.

He added, "I really don't have any idea what it all means, but we'll find out. Plenty more archives to search."

We'll find out. This comforted her much more than "it'll be all right." Little else about this did. She didn't dare think too deeply about that report.

Footsteps suddenly hurried toward them down the hall, and a hand pounded on the door. Marlis opened it to see a trusted courier from the Chancellery. "Mr. Volland, an urgent message for you, sir, from General Wachter."

Volland took the proffered note, unfolded it, read it. Then he shook it a little and looked at it again, as if he was hoping the words might rearrange themselves. He looked at her. "We have a response from Irminau. They are demanding that the Chancellor retract his statements and confess the truth to the people by tomorrow night. They'll declare war otherwise." He folded the paper. "It's no less than we expected."

"We should show this to Freddy," Marlis said. "Perhaps it

will motivate him." He was being so stubborn. Of course, she would probably act the same way, in his position, but Freddy used to be agreeable. Or maybe "resigned" was the better word. She used to think him a bit weak-willed; now she wondered what it felt like to grow up knowing you were different. *Knowing you were stolen away.*

The guards outside Papa's bedroom would have notified her at once if they heard any word from him, but a new rush of tears threatened when she saw Freddy sitting there, still and controlled with Papa's lifeless hands beneath his.

"We've heard from Irminau." She held the letter in front of him.

He read it quickly and looked at her. His eyes held a hardness she'd never seen before. "Would your father take that course?" Freddy asked. "Would he confess?"

"I don't know," Marlis said. "I *do* know that if Irminau invades, they'll crush us as long as we're in this state, and you'd be quite a war prize."

He took his time answering, as if he wasn't worried at all. But he had to be.

"I will revive your father, Marlis," he said. "However, his presence won't save us from war. You will have to let him go, and soon."

She tried not to show her relief. She'd begun to worry he really would be that stubborn. "Fine."

His magic began to work immediately. Color returned to her father's face. His hands twitched. She could see how much effort Freddy had put into resisting as relief flooded his face.

"Untie him quickly," she told the guards, as her father's eyes

163

blinked open. "And then leave us, please. Get Freddy out of here."

"Where am I?" her father asked. "What happened?"

The guards had freed her father's hands first, so she could bring one of them to her heart, to feel his warmth again. "You were shot," she said.

His eyes searched the ceiling, his expression confused. "Acherbaum!" He sat up with the sudden memory. "And I told you—didn't I tell you—the truth?"

She shook her head, not wanting Freddy to know anything, then shot a significant look to the guards. Freddy already looked suspicious. The guards had just cut Freddy's feet from his bonds. She waited for them to usher him out before she said another word, but instead she found herself sniffing back more tears.

"Did you find the letter?" Papa asked, once they were left alone.

"Yes."

"I'm dead?" he whispered.

She nodded.

He pulled her to his chest. His tight embrace felt like an apology. "We have serum, don't we?" he said. "Was the assassination covered up?"

"It was," she said. "The people think you're recovering. But—Freddy says he can't let you live, that it goes against the order of things."

"I won't have terms dictated to me by a mere peasant boy, Marlis, you know me better than that. It won't be hard to get him to cooperate."

She grew rigid and drew back. "Papa, when Acherbaum shot you, do you remember what he said? He was angry that you used Freddy's magic on peasants while his men died fighting the rebels. Now that your men know you can bring back the dead . . ."

"They shouldn't know," Papa said. "That isn't what we told them. I understand the rebels have circulated that story."

"But it *is* the truth. Their story is the *truth*."

"It certainly isn't the whole truth. Truth is quite a malleable concept to begin with."

She clutched her hands together tightly. His words chafed. What she used to see as clever maneuvering, she now saw only as lies. Lies that no one was spared from, not even her.

He was also so close to being lost to her forever.

"Irminau is demanding you confess that this was your doing and not theirs," she said, "or they'll declare war."

"And yet, if I confess, people will lose their trust in us entirely. The inexperienced rebels will have their victory over us, and Irminau will march in anyway." He frowned. "I know we're in a corner, but I'd rather go down fighting. There is always a chance of victory. With surrender, there is nothing, especially to a man like King Otto."

She nodded slightly. She agreed that Irminau would go to war with them one way or another. This was the first time she had heard Papa admit that they had no option, they would lose no matter what they did.

Did she believe that? No. If he accepted magic users . . .

They'd already been down that road, and he had refused her flatly.

"Papa," she said, "I want you explain something to me."

"Of course, Princess." He tried to reach for her hand, but she pulled back.

"Did your men kill a Norn? Before I was born?"

"I was Vice Chancellor, then," he said. "I didn't give the orders." He frowned.

"And then you kidnapped me when I was a baby. Did you ever think I might have been the same Norn your men had just killed, newly reborn?"

"I hardly believed in all that stuff," he said, drawing his hands back.

"You believed it enough to kidnap a child! I read the letter, but I don't understand. Why did you take me in if you thought I had dangerous magic? Or . . ." A new thought occurred to her. "Did you oppress my powers somehow?"

"No, Princess. I did not. I don't even have that ability." He sighed. "We weren't sure what we were getting into. We knew that the Norns' tree they call Yggdrasil was a powerful symbol for the people of Irminau, and they claimed that it was the source of magic. Our army destroyed the tree before you were born, and some of our men brought back samples of the wood. We found they had astonishing power. Later, we used them to make the serum."

"The—serum—?" She struggled for words, because although this was the first she had heard of it, an instinctive revulsion rose within her, as if she had heard the serum was made from chopped-up pieces of human flesh.

"We knew then that at least some of the story was true.

The tree had potent magic. However, magic was not destroyed along with the tree, as we'd hoped. Your mother thought we should try to learn more about the forces at play. She thought we should try to bring a Norn here and see if they really have the powers legends ascribe to them. So we found you."

"You stole me away"—she twisted her heart necklace—"to be one of Mother's science experiments." She'd always been proud of her mother's fierce intelligence and curiosity; now she saw it in a whole new light.

"Marlis, your mother loved you like her own. We both did. Besides that, you had already been separated from your family. I don't know what course of events brought you to that monastery, but you had no mother there."

"You went to Irminau?"

"I have detailed reports. Marlis, you know how it works. Let's not fight at such a time. It all turned out, didn't it? You've never had any magic. Those monks would have been disappointed, but your mother and I certainly weren't."

"But the music I hear. You told me it was nonsense. Sometimes I think I have a different name. Maybe I do have magic. Maybe it never felt safe to . . ." She bit her lip. "I mean, I saw what you were doing to Freddy."

"Well, if I suppressed your magic somehow, I have done you a favor. What good has magic done? Very little that I see! Even here—it's gotten me into this mess. If Irminau didn't have magic, I wouldn't have to resort to it either. I wouldn't have been tempted into evil as I was! And now that boy has *my* life on a string! What good is that?"

"At least I get to speak to you now!"

"Acherbaum killed me because of Freddy!"

She rose, feeling very cold. *Acherbaum killed you because of your choices. Papa, you're wrong.* The words seared through her mind like a comet—she let them pass and did not speak them. He was going to die. Serum couldn't—shouldn't—save him. She didn't even want to see it pass his lips, knowing now where it had come from. If death hadn't shown him that he was wrong, nothing would.

Soon she would be alone.

TWENTY-EIGHT

The Chancellor exited his bedroom and returned to the Chancellery without thanking Freddy. Marlis emerged alone, glancing at the guards who had been keeping watch so he couldn't listen in. "As long as you keep Papa alive, you and your parents will be safe." Marlis wouldn't meet his eyes.

"The Chancellor won't even talk to me?"

"He has too much work to do."

"What's wrong?" Freddy smothered his anger at being brushed off, even though it reminded him of the way Gerik treated him. He didn't want to let her go without getting anything out of her. "You seem upset."

"Of course I'm upset," she said, her tone formal. It had never been easy, finding cracks in the Marlis facade.

He took a step closer to her. "You know I hold your father's life in my hands, whereas you haven't even found my parents yet. If there's something going on, you might want to tell me. Why are you looking for information about the Norns?"

"I—" She shook her head and glanced at Volland. "If there

is some girl with powerful magic running around, I need to know more."

"You'd already known of the Norns when I mentioned them. What have you heard?" Freddy asked, searching her face for a spark of emotion.

Her face was so still she might have been a porcelain doll as she walked away wordlessly. Keeping everything under the surface was telling in its own way, Freddy thought. *If she weren't affected, she would have snapped back at me.*

As Marlis left, Volland returned to Freddy with an expression of polite apology. "I'll show you to a room where you can rest and have something to eat," Volland said.

After that, servants began a parade of Freddy's favorite foods. The struggle against his magic had left him even hungrier than his regular magic did, and he didn't know when he would ever see the like of such food again. Maybe no one would. Fine sliced meats and veal in gravy with wild mushrooms and mashed potatoes. The frothy clouds of whipped cream, the apple strudel, chocolate tortes. He thought of old stories where witches fattened people up to eat—they wouldn't have much luck fattening up Freddy. No matter what he ate, his face always looked a little too thin.

Just when he was tiring of this feast, Marlis opened the door. "Freddy, I would like to talk to you alone for a minute, please."

She dismissed the guards and the maids, and perched rather rigidly on a chair.

"I hope you have enjoyed the meal," she said. "I thought you must be hungry, hiding out as you were."

"I'm not sure 'enjoyed' is the right word, when I know

people are out there battling over what's left, worrying about the winter."

"How worldly you've become in a week," she said, but the barb lacked teeth. Her eyes were shadowed. "I have no one else except him, you know."

"I know." He was softer now.

"He's in a meeting discussing how to proceed, but it isn't the same as before. I see it that way, although I'm not sure if he does. I do realize that now—you hold his power. And that is no way to live." Her lips formed a tight frown. "He can't last for long."

"No."

She drew out a handkerchief that had been balled inside her hand and twisted it. "Please tell me everything you know about the Norn you met."

"I don't know much more. Why don't we see what your records say?"

"You needn't look so smug, Freddy, you don't hold the power here. You hold my father's life, nothing more, and you know if you let him go, there would be nothing stopping us from bringing you harm."

He hadn't been aware he looked smug, but now he raised his eyebrows. "Really? You don't think my powers will be useful in the future?"

"I know we've already run your powers dry." She wasn't meeting his eyes again. "I know if you keep using magic, your body will start to break down."

If she wanted to rattle him, those were the words to do it. He ran a hand through his hair, remembering Arabella's talk of abused witches—first every strand of their hair turned silver, and then it fell out. "I imagine I must still have some years of magic left in me before I'm dead. And if you don't care about my welfare at all, you'll be willing to take those years from me. Your father would."

The conflict within her was visible in her silence, in the handkerchief twined around her fingers. Her admission that her father couldn't last for long wasn't just about the precarious nature of Freddy's magic. She no longer agreed with her father. Something had opened her eyes.

"Marlis," he said softly. "Did something happen . . . besides your father's death?" He had almost said, *Did something happen to upset you?*, catching himself just in time. Marlis would surely get defensive if he accused her of being upset.

"Why would you think that?"

"You don't seem like yourself."

"Well, neither do you. You're keeping secrets."

"You're the one who seems to be unraveling, though. Tying me to a chair? Why not just talk to me? Your father told you something that has shaken you so badly that I don't think you know where to turn."

Her brown eyes lifted to his, flashing anger. She shot out of the chair and walked slowly to the window. Her fingers spread along the sill. She lowered her head. "I don't," she whispered.

He slowly got to his feet, to approach her, but she waved her hand at him not to come. "I can't talk to you either. I can't trust you. I can't trust anyone." She turned to the door, and now he did hurry to her side to stop her.

Although he couldn't quite call her a friend, she was from

the same world, and even more so if she'd also been told lies. "You could trust me, but it has to be mutual."

She shut her eyes and spoke quickly in a rough voice, as if the words burned her throat. "He told me I'm a . . . Norn."

The third Norn? Right under my nose?

The confession seemed oddly fitting. She had always seemed serious for her years, holding herself solitary, observing more than she spoke. It was more than her behavior, though: It felt like the hand of fate, that his path would have traveled alongside a Norn almost from the beginning.

"Is he your real father?" he asked.

"It doesn't matter."

"Doesn't it?"

She looked unsure. "Well—it matters that he didn't trust me with the truth. I know you weren't told much about what you were really doing and why. I don't think that was right."

"Did *you* know what I was really doing? That I brought back soldiers who had done nothing wrong, and they never saw their families again?"

"I didn't," she said in a low voice.

"Where are your real parents?"

"I never had them. He said I was stolen from a monastery." She shook her head as if she thought this was nonsense.

"In Irminau?"

She was silent. She'd looked down on Irminauers. It was tempting to be truly smug at this point, but he wanted to earn her trust more than ever. She *must* come with him. "I've met the other Norns," he said. "There are three of you, and the two others are in this city. They're looking for the third."

"They're looking for me," she repeated, like she was finding the whole thing hard to accept. "What do they want with me?"

"They want your help."

"Doing what?"

"Well . . . that's where it gets complicated. The other two Norns aren't quite in agreement. That's why I think they need you—to balance things out."

"Where have you been, Freddy? Who are you with? How do you know so much all of a sudden?"

To tell her about Sebastian would be dangerous. Sebastian had feared Freddy might talk under duress. "The others are with a man who escaped from Irminau. I think he sees the potential in the good things about this country."

She sniffed. "And you've met him?"

"Yes."

"What does he want with Urobrun?"

"He wants to defend Urobrun from King Otto's army and also to see new leaders in Urobrun—a regime where children aren't kidnapped and lied to, and magic users aren't banned in public and exploited in private." He tried to sum it up in a way she might appreciate. If he mentioned that Sebastian wanted to unify Urobrun and Irminau, it would scare her off.

"Lofty goals. But I won't see this country overrun by radicals."

"Look, I know you don't see me quite as an equal—"

"I never said that."

He scoffed. "You didn't have to say it. I don't want to see this place turn into a mess either. I have my own hesitations about the revolutionary movement, but who will replace your father among the current leadership? And do you trust them? Would they listen to you at all?"

A sour expression came over her. "I'm sure they would not."

"You should come with me," he said. "Your father will have to pass on—the future is still ahead for you."

"You're asking me to leave behind everything I know because of some story."

"Is it a story?" he asked. "Or are you Urd?"

She looked thoughtful, her eyes far away, and somehow older. "I know that name," she whispered.

TWENTY-NINE

"Last night," Sigi whispered to Nan at breakfast, "when you went to bed, I got talking to Andre about how he met Ingrid."

"Who is Andre?" Nan asked.

"He's the one with all the sisters," Sigi said, as if Nan would know who that was.

"So what did he say?" Nan asked.

"He was at a protest. It turned violent, and he was hurt. He said Ingrid appeared like an angel and healed his wounds. I asked what the wounds were and how she healed them, and he said he didn't remember."

"I can't help wondering if she's spreading her magic too thin. She's always looking around like she's paranoid about something."

"So the whole thing might topple with one nudge." Sigi flicked her finger at the air.

"Mm." Nan had been haunted for the past couple of days by the memory of King Otto holding her captive. He knew exactly how to harm a Norn—the pain of music, how the wyrdsong worked, how they would be reborn after death. She had gone to him for help, to save Yggdrasil. He had held her there for weeks and finally—did he kill her, or did she manage to kill herself? Why didn't he help her, if the tree was what provided him with magic users? What had happened after that?

Whatever had happened, Ingrid could no longer be trusted for answers.

"I'm losing you again," Sigi said. "Are you having another memory?"

"Just thinking." Walking home from the gathering at Hel's two days ago, she had told Sigi about the memory of King Otto, though she didn't relate details. She felt so vulnerable speaking to anyone about the memories that seemed to assault her at unexpected times. Even the pleasant ones—Skuld's hutch of rabbits, or Urd's potato stew.

Thea peered in the room, plate of bread and cheese in hand, her hair freshly curled. "Why are you two hiding out in here?"

"It's quiet," Nan said. They had purposefully sought out this room in the far corner of the house.

"Well, Sebastian is back from the UWP meeting. He's making an announcement in a few minutes, and I thought you'd want to listen."

The men were gathered around the drawing room. The pocket doors had been opened to accommodate everyone. Nan, Sigi, and Thea pressed in at the back.

"Well," Sebastian said, taking a drink of coffee, "I'd say it was a success. The UWP is making a valiant effort to stop fighting with one another and mobilize. A few key figures have been killed over the past week, and that's shaken everyone into action. They held an election, and Brunner is now officially the UWP president."

"They are planning a coup d'état," Heffler said, "and we will support them. The first stage begins tonight."

"I'll be acting as field leader for this mission," Sebastian said. "Heffler will be my second in command. I'll need one hundred and forty men, so we'll be recruiting from our secondary bases as well. Once they arrive, I'll hold a planning meeting. Will, you'll be serving as third in command under Heffler. Most of you will be going with Heffler, while I need about twenty men to follow me for the first phase."

Sebastian called for volunteers to fill a few more positions. When he mentioned a medical unit, Thea lifted a hand. "I could go as a nurse."

Nan looked at her with alarm. "What are you doing?"

Thea moved closer to the front of the room—it had cleared out a little, as some of the men had left after receiving their orders. Sebastian scratched his cheek. "Nursing on the battlefield is going to be a lot uglier than here. That's no place for you, and you don't really have any training."

"No place for me? Why shouldn't it be?"

"It's dangerous. Everyone else who's going has combat experience."

"I think she could be very good at it," said Ingrid as she wrapped her hand around Sebastian's, pulling it down from his thoughtful pose. "She could assist Dr. Keller. A woman's touch is always appreciated, and Thea has the touch."

Sebastian looked blank. He nodded at Thea. "Tell Dr. Keller

you'll be going with him, and he'll tell you what you need to know."

Nan grabbed Ingrid's arm before she could go. "Thea can't go into *battle*."

"She won't be in battle," Ingrid said, "she'll be support. She can handle it. Trust me."

"Nan, I've got to do something," Thea said. "I want to do something that matters."

"And you will," Ingrid said. She motioned to the door, keeping Thea close.

"Should we go with her?" Sigi asked.

Nan hesitated. *I've been running away from my fate. What if Thea is killed because I couldn't figure out a way to end this enchantment?*

Ingrid must have a purpose for Thea, she thought, to have bothered with her in the first place.

"No," she said at last. "If the men are leaving, and I can search the house without Ingrid's people breathing down my neck, maybe I can find answers."

THIRTY

Once the rest of Sebastian's unit arrived, he called everyone back into the drawing room, where a hand-drawn map had been tacked to the walls. It was standing room only, and so warm with body heat that Thea would never have guessed cold autumn winds blew outside. She was sweating and shivering at once, adrenaline already beginning to rush through her.

"Tonight we are launching a series of simultaneous attacks to destroy what remains of the Chancellor's government. Our task is perhaps the most difficult," Sebastian explained. "We're going to capture the Urobrun Production Arsenal, take what weapons are in the warehouses, and destroy their operations."

The room erupted with raised voices. One of the men managed to make himself heard over the rest: "Destroy them? What about Irminau? How will anyone fend them off without the arsenal?"

"With the weapons we have, with magic, and by recruiting from the king's army," Sebastian explained. "Yes, destroying the country's primary munitions supplier may have some unfortunate consequences, but we have to force the government's hand. They can't grow their army without weapons to give them."

The voices settled to a murmur yet didn't stop.

"Winter will come early this year"—Ingrid lifted a hand for their attention—"and it will bring much snow. I sense it."

"The king's army can't move through the winter," Sebastian said, "but the news can. We'll have months to send whispers over the border of a new leadership here in Urobrun, one that is friendly to magic. And when the spring thaw comes, the king will find that all his sorcerers have a renewed hope of freedom here."

This suggestion finally settled the room.

"Now, as for this operation—we're departing at nightfall," Sebastian continued. "We'll split into three groups and take separate routes. Any guards you run into must be dealt with quickly before they can alert the Chancellor's forces."

Sebastian grabbed a cane propped against the wall and pointed at the map. "This is a map of the supply base, drawn from an inside man at the UWP. He said the place usually has about fifty guards; I'd expect that will be at least doubled right now."

Even based on the drawing, the arsenal looked formidable. It was depicted as a large square of wall with a guard tower at each corner, surrounded by a fence with guard stations at the gate. Within these two layers of defense were the buildings themselves—one for production, one for offices, and three for storage.

Sebastian tapped the spot on the map depicting the guard stations at the fence. "Most of you will go with Heffler and Will to attack from the front. First, cut the phone lines. Next take out the guards at the gate, and then the patrol inside and the towers." Now the tip of the cane was moving all over the place. "You're going to set explosives to breach the wall. Meanwhile, I will be coming in through the sewers in back with about twenty of you. We'll take out the guards in the office and turn off the power. From there, we just have to clean up the rest, get the weapons onto their delivery vehicles, and destroy the factory.

"Even though it's after hours, some workers will probably still be in the factory," Sebastian added. "Try not to harm them. They may sympathize with us, but if they don't cooperate, capture them."

Preparations consumed the rest of the daylight hours. The men seemed ready; many of them had fought in the previous war, and although in recent years their missions might have consisted more often of distributing banned literature, that held plenty of risk, too.

"Finally, a good, straightforward fight," she heard Will say.

When night fell, they gathered in the main hall. Thea stood at the back with Dr. Keller, a leather satchel with bandages and salves hung at her hip.

Sebastian gave the order for them to proceed quietly. Outside, the air was bitter cold, more like January than November. High winter clouds blocked what little moon there was, and the streets were so dark that occasionally she heard someone stumble.

Thanks to the curfew, the streets were empty and the late-night streetcars Thea once rode home from work no longer ran along the rails. The automobiles of late-night revelers sat safely in their garages. It was as though the apocalypse had come and gone, sucking all the life from the city. Thea was glad they didn't have to pass through the Lampenlight District; she couldn't bear to see it dark and empty.

As they reached more public areas of the city, their march halted. Thea stood on her tiptoes and craned her neck both ways, trying to see why. "Probably guards up ahead," Dr. Keller whispered.

Someone shouted, the sound quickly cut off by scuffling. A gun fired, then a return shot. Thea drew closer to the wall of the building they were passing, pierced by a sudden memory of other gunshots. She clutched her hand, then she remembered the magic Ingrid had taught her. There was nothing to fear.

"Get him!" a man yelled ahead, and suddenly a guard was running toward Thea. He shoved her out of his way. Dr. Keller sidestepped her and tried to grab the man's coat, but he was running too quickly.

"Back up, girl!" someone shouted. Dr. Keller jumped out of the way just before a round of bullets punched holes in the guard's back. He was running and falling at once, leaving his legs sprawled at an odd angle before he went still.

Fresh blood leaked over the sidewalk. Thea watched it slowly spread across the concrete and seep into the cracks.

Dr. Keller grabbed Thea's arm. "Keep up. We need to move."

"He's dead!" Thea gasped.

"Remember, you have the strength of Yggdrasil," Dr. Keller said.

Thea cast her mind back to that vision of strength. Ingrid had chosen her, thought her worthy of this, and there was no time to question. It was easy enough to detach from the situation—it had happened so quickly in the darkness. The man probably only had seconds to register he'd been shot before he was dead on the ground.

Quietly but quickly they were moving again, the cold air sharp in Thea's lungs, rushing down streets that all seemed the same in the shadows, until they reached the arsenal.

It was just outside the factory district, on the eastern edge of the city. The fence had three layers topped with barbed wire, and beyond that was a stone gate, with the guard towers rising up behind it. It was big. Really big, it seemed to Thea, to be conquered by their group, which suddenly seemed so small.

They were still some distance away when Sebastian halted and motioned for his smaller group to split. Silently, he and Heffler exchanged a salute, and they started moving around the back. A few other men moved toward the telephone poles. Thea's breath came in frosty clouds as she waited for the order to move again.

The men shimmied up the telephone poles. Wearing black, they could hardly be seen. The men on the ground advanced closer to the guard posts at the fence. Spotlights whipped around from the towers, though there was no sign of alarm.

Out of the right corner of her eye, motion. Split telephone wires fell toward the ground. One of the men raised an arm to signal.

Heffler lifted a hand. "Advance!" he shouted. His voice boomed through the darkness over the rattle and click of guns being aimed and readied. The men opened fire.

The arsenal sprung to life, returning fire. The voices of the guards crying alarm sounded indignant at first. The lights from the guard towers turned toward them. Sirens rang.

At the first exchange of fire, Thea went rigid. A memory shoved its way into her mind, past all her defenses: the night her father died. They had been running down the street trying to reach her mother when a military vehicle had driven by and fired on them. Her father knocked her to the ground and protected her, so she didn't see it, only heard it. He was badly hurt, and she had to leave him in the alley.

She'd forgotten until she heard the sound.

I shouldn't be here.

But she wanted to be strong. Though her father surely didn't want to go to war, he had. She was working to save Yggdrasil, and Yggdrasil would keep her safe in return, keep her strong.

After the men broke through the gate and ran toward the arsenal, a few fallen forms were left behind. Two of them were already lost, she could see at a glance. Two more were bent over, clutching wounds. Dr. Keller checked on all of them.

"Swab some alcohol on that and bandage him up," Dr. Keller ordered, pointing Thea to one of the injured men, who clutched his arm, while he tended the other, who was worse off, having been shot in the side.

Thea opened her bag and worked quickly. She felt very calm as long as she didn't think.

There were still tears in her eyes. Why? Why couldn't she

get these pained memories of Father out of her mind, when she needed to be brave? He would have been brave.

As she patched up the injured man, gunfire and shouting and cries of pain battered her ears, and she kept seeing the bodies of the fallen out of the corner of her eyes. Father had always been such a peaceful man: He was gentler than her mother, in many ways. Was "brave" the right word for how he might have felt in a place like this?

A pang shot through her heart. It didn't seem quite right. He had been fighting against his own homeland: He must have been sad more than anything.

The spotlights sweeping across the broad lawn of dead winter grass between the fence and the arsenal walls abruptly shut off. A few whoops of triumph went up from their men. Sebastian's group had been successful, then. Dr. Keller had a flashlight, and he found her and took her hand.

"Over here," he said, and when she didn't respond right away, "Are you all right?"

She heard a falling scream, like a man had been shot off a wall. Such an awful sound.

"Keller!" A man called out. "We need a medic!"

Dr. Keller turned the flashlight that way. Ulrich was dragging a younger man forward, blood soaking his shirt around the stomach.

"Lay him down gently," Dr. Keller said. He tore open his shirt.

This man was one of the younger ones, his face pale and frightened. "I want my mother."

Mother. Everything kept reminding Thea of the moments

she couldn't let her mind return to: her mother's sickness, her father's death. She turned away in desperation, her left hand itching, her mind crowded with memories.

A voice shouted warning. The grounds suddenly lit with brightness. She dropped in blind panic as an explosion rocked her.

Then she remembered that blowing the gates open was part of the plan. Her thighs and arms shook as she pushed them up again. Her hands were wet with frigid dew. She watched as the men rushed the gate to meet the guards inside. Although their pounding footsteps shook the ground beneath her, it felt like a dream. The perimeter was almost empty of people now . . . except the dead.

"Thea! Come help over here!" Dr. Keller called her name from the deep shadows around the arsenal walls.

Thea's arms were shaking violently, and she had only taken two steps toward Dr. Keller when she halted at the sight of a man lying dead in the grass. His eyes were open, sightless and staring. A bullet had torn through his stomach, and his shirt was stained dark with blood. She didn't know this man's name, but he was from the house—she'd seen him just yesterday, bringing pine boughs from outside to fill the vase on the dinner table.

I don't want to be here. I never wanted to be here. I don't want to fight. I want to see Mother.

She ran away from Dr. Keller without knowing where to go. She couldn't roam the streets alone. She veered to one of the guard stations. Maybe she could just wait out the battle.

Past the door, Thea could just make out the silhouettes of

two men. Of course. The guards would be dead, too. Today they were the enemy, though they worked for her own government, and they might very well be as ignorant of what was going on as she had been just weeks ago. No, the word "enemy" didn't feel right. She stepped closer, clutching her bag. "Hello? Is anyone alive?"

The silence pierced her. The little room was quiet with death. The body closest to her feet was slumped on the ground, only the rounded shape of his back visible. The other body had been shot in the head, his eyes untouched and glassy, but his blood fanned violently across the table behind his skull. And they were so young. They couldn't know anything. She didn't know anything.

She crouched and opened her bag, staring at the bandages and medicine like she should be able to use them, to fix something. There was nothing she could give them except a prayer. She searched for words Father Gruneman might have said, tears streaking her cheeks, but couldn't remember them.

Yggdrasil whispered in her ear, with the voice of Ingrid. *Don't think. Listen to me, and nothing you see on earth will matter.*

"No . . . !" Thea struggled to get the word out. She needed to think, needed to feel. She needed to remember what she had lost and who she still had. Father and Mother were not worth giving up, not even for the protection of Yggdrasil, not even if the memories came with such pain.

Ingrid cut off my HAND—

Her eyes opened wide as she wrapped her thoughts around the truth, all those moments where she had struggled to scream, to tell Freddy or Nan something. She still heard Ingrid's whispers, her song, in her mind. She had to stop it before it got a hold of her again.

She grabbed her left hand and wrenched it.

Something inside her arm tore, and she gasped with pain. It was stuck to her on the inside. *This* is *your hand, Thea. What are you trying to do?*

"No, no, no . . ." She took the scissors from her bag for cutting bandages, shut her eyes. *Would this hurt? No—it doesn't matter—do it!* She stabbed the back of her hand and hit hard wood. Her eyes opened. She felt nothing. There was a brief flash where she saw the true hand beneath the illusion, and then the magic took over again.

It wasn't going to let her go.

She was sweating, her mouth dry, trapped and desperate. The fog was closing in on her mind, and it was only the stark horror of these dead men that kept it from claiming her. If she walked away, she would never remember this.

She pulled the cold fingers of one man's arm away from the gun he'd been holding when he died. Her teeth chattered. Her hand shook. She held her hands as far away from her as she could, and put the barrel against her left. She turned her head away and pulled the trigger.

Wood splinters shot across the guard station. The illusion shattered, the strange symbols of magic burned into the wood torn apart. It was still attached into her skin; before she had time to balk, she pulled on the hand again. Wood broke free from flesh. Little roots had sprouted from the base, bright with

Thea's blood. Ingrid's magic must have healed her arm when it was severed, but those little spots where the roots had worked into her bled and stung.

She stared at her pale, slender arm, now ending with just a stump. Everything she had ever accomplished with that lost hand flashed through her mind.

The shock made her oddly focused. She took off her coat and pulled the bandage from her bag. She started wrapping it around the stump, wrapping and wrapping, like she could smother the whole thing away forever. Then she buttoned her coat over her left arm. She didn't want anyone to see this, didn't want to talk to anyone about it. She didn't want to touch the wooden hand again, but after a moment of hesitation, she quickly dropped it in her bag.

She stood in the door of the guard station, facing out. Shots echoed inside the arsenal walls. Her heart was in her throat. She couldn't help Dr. Keller anymore; she could only watch and wait. The calm she had enjoyed over the past week was gone, and memories pushed their way in—all the death and pain, and all the stupid things she'd said to Freddy and Nan when she didn't care.

It hadn't even hit her until now that Freddy could be dead, for all she knew. She'd had no fear under Yggdrasil.

In a few more minutes, the shots died down. She heard Sebastian shout, "Get the—" Only the first two words rang clear over the din.

When truck engines rumbled to life, she finally moved forward, clutching her arm beneath her coat.

Within the arsenal walls, dozens of men ran back and forth,

loading trucks with crates of weapons, herding along a few captured workers. The lights were out, so beyond the immediate activity within the gate she only saw the shadows of large buildings against the sky and flashlights bobbing along. A few men hurried out of the largest building. Explosions shattered the window glass. She ducked behind a truck, clutching her heart. That was the factory, she remembered, visualizing Sebastian's map. No one was paying attention to her at first, and she didn't see Dr. Keller.

Walter, who played the piano in the evenings, spotted her and ran over. It was odd to see a pianist now running around with a gun. "Are you hurt, Miss Thea?"

"Just—my arm. I'm fine. I tripped and bruised it."

"Here, why don't you sit in the truck?" He urged her along toward one of the idling vehicles and opened the passenger door with a gentlemanly air. "Such a young girl shouldn't be in a place like this anyway! What was Sebastian thinking?"

"It was my fault. I insisted."

He shook his head. "We'll be moving once we get it all loaded up." He shut the door.

Thea could hardly bear the wait to get back to a safe, warm bed, but at the same time, she knew there was no escape from this. Unless Ingrid could fix it.

Ingrid had better be able to fix it.

THIRTY-ONE

A few men had been left on guard; other than that, the house held only the injured, the refugees from Irminau, and Sigi and Nan.

And Ingrid, of course. She had gone to her room as soon as the men left. Nan wondered if she slept, free of worries because she had no friends, no loved ones. She had hoped to search Ingrid's room—that wouldn't be possible now. Sebastian's office? She found it unguarded, but also locked.

His bedroom, on the other hand, was open. He had a modest room, much like the one Freddy occupied. The bed was unmade, with a map open on the covers and his pajamas tossed across a bedpost. There wasn't much in it, except for a travel-worn black trunk she found under the bed. She tried to lift it. It held something of decent weight, and was locked, too. She quietly pried open drawers until she found a key.

She cracked the trunk open to reveal a prosthetic limb made for someone who had lost their leg just below the knee.

This is nothing new, she thought. When Freddy related that Sebastian was Prince Rupert, he also said that Prince Rupert had lost a leg, and supposedly Ingrid had restored it in a "healing trance." Seeing the truth of it before her was a harsh reminder that magic was not this powerful: It took a great sacrifice to bring Sigi back to life; it would take a great sacrifice to bring back a lost limb.

She shut the trunk and marched downstairs to Ingrid's room before she lost her nerve.

Ingrid's face was expressionless when she answered Nan's knock. "Yes?" Her fingers toyed lightly with the plain collar of her dress.

"What did you sacrifice to restore Sebastian's leg?"

The fingers dropped. "Nothing. The sacrifice was made when Yggdrasil was destroyed."

"And what happened to *Thea* when you were supposed to heal her hand?"

"I'm not willing to explain my plans to you as long as your sense is compromised."

"How is my sense compromised? All I'm trying to do is figure out what the hell kind of game you're playing!"

"You are lured by the human world. You've lost the person you used to be." Ingrid's severe expression lightened, a brief flash of hope crossing her eyes. "We used to be one another's family. Yggdrasil was our home. I know you remember."

"Sometimes . . ."

"You remember me. You told me I used to be different." Ingrid spread her fingers and rubbed them against her palms. "I remember me, too. I don't want to be this way. If you would help me, we can all be happy again." She looked up.

Nan gently pushed the door open and entered Ingrid's small

cave of a bedroom. "Ingrid, what are you doing? You've made Thea forget her mother, the one person she's worked so hard to protect. How could that be the right thing to do?"

"Thea was in pain. She's happier without those memories. She'll remember her mother again after she has fully realized Yggdrasil's power. Nan, you must realize, even as you are looking for humanity in yourself, humans are looking for something that transcends those feelings inside of themselves. That's why they go to church. But I can show it to them, so they see beyond their everyday lives and work for a greater purpose."

"You mean, for you. They do what you want them to do."

"For Yggdrasil!"

"Yes, Yggdrasil," Nan said. "Your story goes that Urd and I were killed by the Urobrun Army and the tree was destroyed. You planted a new tree, thus saving magic, but it's been weakened ever since. And you have now found a way to enchant people into loyalty by healing lost limbs or wounds. Am I on the right track?"

"Somewhat."

"Somewhat? I'll say, somewhat. Because I have a memory of being held captive and tortured by King Otto, and I sense he was the one who killed me. Why didn't you tell me that?"

"I don't wish to dwell on the events of that year. It's unimportant."

"Unimportant? The king is still alive. You're working for his *son*. No—his son is working for you. I don't see why you need to use magic if Sebastian is really on your side. Did you do this to get revenge? Is Sebastian really his father's enemy?"

Ingrid's laugh was brief and sharp. "Sebastian hates his father as much as I do. I swear to that."

"Then what is the lie?" Nan leaned close enough to Ingrid that her breath fell upon her sister's cheek.

Ingrid turned away, giving no answer. "I'll call the guards if you threaten me."

"I'm not threatening you, though I might if you don't drop the enchantment on Thea. If you want to lie about King Otto, fine—I'll find another way to get answers. Leave my friends out of it."

"She'd been shot badly," Ingrid said.

"Not that badly."

"If I drop the enchantment—"

"What?"

"I swapped her hand for one I had made from Yggdrasil."

"Swapped?" The red squares on Ingrid's quilt suddenly flashed into Nan's vision. She saw the color of blood.

"Verthandi, I didn't hurt her! I took her pain away."

"Thea has faced so much, and what you've done to her now—"

"I *have* saved most of these men," Ingrid said. "They lost arms, legs, fighting in these ridiculous wars. Once the war is over, if they're left broken, no one cares. They're lucky if they don't have to beg. You've seen them now, fighting for me, for Yggdrasil, with purpose and pride. They need me—and I need them."

"But Thea didn't need you."

"She did, in her heart. I could feel her desire to be free from her grief. Still, I didn't want *her*. I meant for it to be Freddy."

"How can you possibly think you're in the right?" Nan shook her head. "And you said 'most' of these men. Did you cut off anyone else's limbs unnecessarily?"

Ingrid's stony silence was an admission of guilt.

"So every man in this house has a limb made from Yggdrasil?"

"Not *all*. Sebastian's closest circle."

"Can you give them back what they lost?"

Ingrid laughed sharply. "I already did! I gave them a piece of Yggdrasil. There is nothing better than that."

⊙–⊙–⊙–⊙

Tears pricked at Nan's eyes and clogged her throat. When Sigi walked into their bedroom, she couldn't speak until she had swallowed them down.

"I spoke to Ingrid," she said.

"What happened?"

Nan's voice was surprisingly calm as she explained what she knew, even as her heart rode on the waves of a stormy sea. "If I fix the enchantment, it means Thea's life will never be the same, and there's nothing I can do. Even if the revolution is a success, I can't give her back her hand."

"That means all the men, too, and Sebastian? They're all crippled?"

"She said it was only Sebastian's inner circle, but how could she have done this to even one person?"

"Nan, can you get control of the magic somehow?" Sigi asked. "Instead of her?"

"I don't think so. It's like Yggdrasil's magic is hers now." Nan spread her palms on the wool blanket spread across her bed. The itchy fabric helped ground her. "I don't understand what Ingrid is doing, and maybe I need to stop trying. When Sebastian comes back, I'm going to try to break the spell on him."

THIRTY-TWO

Thea swallowed back a lump in her throat as she rushed up the stairs looking for Nan, still keeping her injured arm concealed. Downstairs, the men were dragging in cold air along with crate after crate of firearms stolen from the arsenal. The upper floors were almost abandoned—except for Sigi and Nan's voices, coming softly from their bedroom.

They went silent when they saw her. "Thea," Nan said, with such gravity that Thea wondered if she somehow already knew.

Thea's voice left her. She couldn't describe that moment in the guard station. Instead, she opened her bag and dropped the wooden hand onto her bed. The thin roots had turned reddish-brown with drying blood. Sigi jumped at the sight of it, but Nan only echoed the grief in Thea's own eyes.

"You figured it out," Nan said. "I know what Ingrid did to you. When you left, I confronted her."

Thea shut her eyes and hugged her concealed arm. "Can she fix it?"

She already knew what the answer would be, and Nan's heavy pause confirmed it. "No . . . and there are others."

Thea wanted to scream. Throw things. Find Ingrid and choke the life out of her—but even the thought of two hands wrapped around Ingrid's neck reminded her of her loss. "What can we do?"

"We should start by approaching Sebastian," Nan said. "He's the leader."

"Sebastian . . ." Thea remembered dancing in his arms, like it had been a dream. A dream where they both struggled to speak and could not. And yet, she still remembered how safe she felt in Sebastian's arms. Was he really missing a hand? A foot? What if it was worse? She couldn't imagine him ever being as vulnerable as she felt right now.

"Her influence isn't easy to break," Thea said, gesturing to the wooden hand on the bed. "I had to shoot the hand to break the spell."

"Is Sebastian downstairs?" Nan asked.

"Yes. They're bringing in the supplies now, and last I saw he was directing."

"Maybe if we show him this—" Nan grabbed the hand. "Seeing it might snap him out of it. We need to hurry. Ingrid can sense things through the enchantment."

"I could keep an eye on Ingrid for you," Sigi offered. "Try and distract her if she starts to follow you."

"Perfect," Nan said. "Thea, are you able to do this? Or do you want me to try to explain on my own?"

Although Thea still didn't want to speak of her hand, she

did want Ingrid's power to be known. She didn't want to spend even one moment alone, waiting, wondering. "I can do it."

On the ground floor, Sebastian was supervising the movement of crates into the basement and holding his ubiquitous cup of coffee. Thea found herself noticing his hands in a new way, wondering if they were real, wondering if they would pull his hand free and find ink stains on wooden fingers.

Nan approached him boldly while Thea watched, thankful she had Nan on her side. She couldn't imagine handling this on her own. "I need to talk to you," Nan said. "Urgently. Can someone else take over for you?"

"I think it's under control, really. I'm just being bossy." He raised his eyebrows. "Did something happen?"

"Yes. There is another traitor in your ranks."

The word "traitor" snatched his attention. He motioned them to his office, and didn't ask questions until they were behind closed doors. "What happened?"

Nan jumped right in. "When Thea's hand was shot, Ingrid amputated her hand and replaced it with one formed from the wood of Yggdrasil."

He looked at Thea. His expression was the same as it had been when they danced—like words were trapped behind his eyes. She didn't want him to see her this way—a girl with a missing piece, with shattered confidence. She forced herself to speak. "I couldn't seem to think of my parents. I practically abandoned my mother. Deep down, I knew she had—*crippled* me—but I could only think of Yggdrasil."

"The injury must have been more serious than you realized," Sebastian said, speaking calmly, as if he didn't quite comprehend what she was saying. She could imagine that his mind must be working much as hers had, whispering in his ear to ignore the truth. "Ingrid would never harm someone unnecessarily."

"I've had trouble remembering, too," Thea said. "Some moments I knew the truth, then I couldn't seem to speak. Sebastian, I know you have those moments, too, when you remember your own mind."

Sebastian's face was turning ashen. "She's a Norn," he said. "She knows how things should be. She told me—" He smacked his hand against the edge of the desk. "What are you trying to do to us?" He leaned forward, muscles tense, looking like he was battling a physical pain. "She made choices out of a dire need. She had no allies, no one she could trust, and the only way to build the force she needed was to make this pact. She heals an injured man, and they swear their loyalty."

"You're repeating her words," Nan said. "A part of you belongs to her."

He looked like he was struggling to speak. Thea glanced at Nan quickly. She didn't want Nan to do anything yet. "You have to fight her off," Thea said. "She's told you things you wanted to hear. She's helped you forget terrible memories, told you about the power you could have . . ."

"Ingrid isn't evil," he said. "She has to make hard choices. Leaders always do."

Thea opened her bag and took out the wooden hand. She didn't say anything, just thrust it at him; the hand itself, with the hole shot through it, and the dangling bloodstained roots, told the story.

"I—" His voice dropped to a whisper. "I'm sure she's done this for a reason."

"She's not the Ingrid I knew," Nan said. "And the reason is misguided. You can't have her guiding the thoughts of your people. Did you make a pact with her? Freddy said she healed your leg after you lost it. I've never heard of a healer who can regenerate legs."

He looked furious. "What you're asking is something I cannot ask of these men. You don't know what you're talking about. Why should I listen to you? You weren't there when Yggdrasil was destroyed."

"Sebastian, please," Thea said. "The magic is making you say these things. You have to fight her off."

Her pleas only seemed to send him into a panic. He made a move to the door, and Nan grabbed his jacket. Thea scrambled to help her, hooking her arm around his. He shoved her back easily.

"We can't fight him, either. He's protected by Yggdrasil," Thea said.

Nan grabbed the hand he was holding the coffee cup with and splashed the liquid in his face.

"Guh!" He wiped his eyes, and she tackled him, knocking him onto the floor. He kicked her back.

Thea looked around wildly. She spotted the walking stick he'd been using to point at maps earlier. It was an antique with a finely worked silver ram's head handle. Sebastian lunged to grab it when he saw it swing toward him. "Not that!"

Thea whipped the stick out of his grasp and then swept it sideways, full force, toward his head. Maybe he was protected, but he obviously didn't want her breaking his possessions against his own head.

He ducked. Nan jumped on top of him and pushed his face into the floor. "Thea, hold him!"

Thea sat awkwardly on his legs. "Nan I don't know how to get his leg off." Her left arm, still buttoned under her coat, itched to be free and useful, but without a hand, an arm wasn't good for much.

Meanwhile, Sebastian was rocking beneath them, trying to throw off their weight. "Ingrid!" he shouted.

Nan slapped her hand over his mouth. She grabbed a fistful of his hair and pulled his head up. "I don't want to be violent with you. Please. Fight her off."

"*Mmf!*"

"Look, I—ow!" Nan withdrew her hand, bitten. Sebastian reached back and shoved her sideways, and with another heave managed to get out from under them, even as Nan tried to drag him back down again.

"I don't want to hurt you," he said, holding up his hands. "You need to back off."

"Thea, give me that cane." Nan whacked his right shin with the cane and it cracked in two. The only pain in Sebastian's face seemed to come from what she'd done to a well-crafted object.

"Right one, then?" Nan said.

"I will not allow you to have it," Sebastian said. He glanced at the door, obviously wondering if Ingrid or anyone was ever going to hear all this scuffling and intervene.

With a trembling hand, Thea worked open the buttons

of her coat. She flinched, not from pain but from a mix of shame and horror, as she pulled the bandage away. Maybe she shouldn't be vain at such a time, but at this moment what hurt the most was the loss of the sheer beauty of her hand.

She lifted her left arm toward him. "Look at me. Max shot my hand under Ingrid's orders. That's why he was so upset when you questioned him. The other day, when he came back from chasing Roger, he started to cry. He tried to tell me that Ingrid took his hands. He's your man. You need to take responsibility for him and for me. For all of your men. If I can fight this, you can, too."

Sebastian had gone very pale. She saw the weight settle into his eyes, understood all too well the pain of accepting the truth. A part of her wanted to stop him. She didn't want to see him without a leg any more than she wanted to see herself without a hand. His mouth set, as he seemed to muster his resolve. "Help me . . . do it."

"We will," Thea said. "Sit down."

"Hurry," Nan said. "I can't believe Ingrid hasn't come. She *must* know."

Sebastian sat in his desk chair and rolled up the right leg of his pants. Nan quickly grabbed his leg with both arms and pulled. The illusion briefly broke, revealing the wood, but it didn't give. Sebastian winced. Thea grabbed his hand, worried they might lose him again.

"Let me . . ." Nan put her hands on his leg more gently, and she began to chant. Thea remembered the wyrdsong from Ingrid. It sounded softer from Nan, which was strange when she had never thought of Nan as soft. The illusion vanished again and the leg broke free just below Sebastian's knee, leaving a clean stump with spots of blood where the leg had rooted, just like the end of her arm.

Nan stopped chanting and dropped it like a hot stone. The little roots that had sunk their way into his mind and soul were longer and deeper than on Thea's hand, although some of them seemed withered and stunted, as if they represented the part of Sebastian's mind that had fought against Ingrid.

Thea shuddered.

Sebastian gripped the desk, his eyes squinting shut with the stinging pain of the torn roots. The pain of Thea's own wounds sharpened with sympathy. "Oh *no*," he said. "Now I do remember everything."

"What do you remember?" Thea asked, trying to sound gentle, although her stomach was tied in a knot. She felt like she'd broken him.

"Something inside me knew the truth all along—that every time we approached a wounded man and offered him help, he was giving up his freedom to choose his own fate. I've known that *I* was trapped, that my choices weren't always my own either, but I couldn't seem to fight it off. And look, I can live without a leg. Some of those men will have a harder time."

"They should be able to choose, at least," Thea said. "I watched my mother lose her mind from bound-sickness over the course of years. I'd rather give up my hand than my thoughts."

"If they want to stick with her by choice, maybe there's nothing we can do," Nan said. "But then you shouldn't be able to trust them either."

"What do I have to fight with now?"

"Ingrid said your inner circle was affected," Nan said. "How many?"

"Perhaps fifty men," Sebastian said.

"You still have plenty of healthy men without their numbers. And the ones who are injured can surely still do something," Thea said, although maybe this was her own wishful thinking.

"You were raised a prince," Nan said. "You learned a few things about running a country that Ingrid could never have taught you. The military strategy: She didn't have anything to do with that."

"No, she didn't," he agreed. "All of my education was founded around learning how to rule."

"Wait—a prince?" Thea glanced at Nan.

"Sebastian is the prince of Irminau."

Suddenly everything about Sebastian was cast in a new light. She'd been dancing with a prince. She'd just helped break the enchantment on a prince. And not just any prince—the son of the king her mother had fled. King Otto was just a name in the newspaper to her; to Sebastian, he was a *father*.

"How stupid I am," he said. "I met Ingrid in the forest when I was recovering. She seemed so kind; she must have been plotting all the while. She gathered these men under the banner of my family name."

"But not all of them know you're the prince," Thea said, "right?"

"No. Just the ones who have been with me the longest, the ones sworn to Yggdrasil." He sighed. "Considering how difficult it is to break free of the magic, I'm not sure how to address my men. Maybe I should talk to them one by one?"

"What we really need is to force Ingrid's hand," Nan said. "We have to get her to lift the spell, or it will be very difficult to make the men understand."

"Then we'll speak to her first. Bring her here."

Thea picked up her coat from where it had dropped on the floor and started to button it over her arm again.

Sebastian watched her, guilt in his eyes.

"We're in the same position, so you don't need to pity me," she said. Her tone was harsh. She couldn't help it. She pitied herself. Her beauty had given her a job that paid better than any other opportunity for a girl of her station. She was so aware of the loss, and so aware of how hollow the loss sounded in the face of larger disasters.

"I hope being sorry isn't the same as pity," he said. "I don't pity you—I know how odious it is to be pitied. I just want you to know that at least you won't want for livelihood, as long as I'm in a position to give anyone a job."

"I want more than a livelihood," she snapped, then looked away. *It's not his fault. It's not his obligation to give me a purpose.* He had suggested she might be a reporter or a spy, but that was before, when they were both under the enchantment. Now the idea sounded ludicrous. A spy needed anonymity, which a one-handed girl would lack. A reporter needed poise, and hers was shattered.

"Sebastian!" Aleksy was suddenly pounding on the door, sounding frantic.

"What is it?" Sebastian called.

"Why did you send Ingrid over to Bauer Hall?"

Sebastian hid the wooden leg behind the desk and put his

elbows on the desktop like everything was normal. "Come in, come in."

Aleksy ran inside, glancing at Nan and Thea with very brief confusion. "I'm sorry if I interrupted anything."

Sebastian waved his hand impatiently. "What do you mean, Bauer Hall? She has no reason to spend time at the secondary bases."

"Ingrid just left with a bunch of men. She said you wanted them to change posts; I don't understand why you wanted Will and Heffler and everyone to go."

"Damn it," Sebastian said. "I don't think that's where they're going."

THIRTY-THREE

The dream tore Marlis from sleep. For a moment, she didn't recognize the spartan walls of her own bedroom, couldn't recall her own name. Then it all rushed back like the first breath after a dive.

The books.

She had dreamed of the books.

Diaries and journals she had kept throughout time, recording everything she had done, everything her sisters had done, every enemy they faced, every twist and turn of their own powers. So that they might remember. So that they might not repeat their mistakes.

It was a cold night, yet sweat soaked her nightgown. The books were her only clear memory. The rest came in snatches—faces and moments, none of them clear, just teasing dreams that made her feel unsure of who she was or who she had ever been.

She glanced around the shadows, wishing she were not alone. She took deep breaths, taking in the sight of familiar furniture, a heavy walnut bedroom set that had belonged to her late grandmother.

She really was my grandmother. I am *Marlis Horn,* she thought fiercely, and she had to wipe tears from her eyes. That memory of the books was too concrete, and too tempting, to ignore.

The books were buried beneath one of Yggdrasil's roots in a box, an enchanted box that only she could open.

Could Papa's men have captured the box?

She didn't sleep the rest of the night. It was hard just to keep her feet under the covers. Sometimes she had to pace, to release all the energy pent up inside her; other times she drifted to the window and stared at the moon.

In the morning, she was already dressed when the maid, Elsie, brought breakfast. "No, thank you," she told the young woman. "I'll eat later. I need to see Papa."

"He's already left," Elsie said. "Something terrible happened last night, I think. I don't know what it was, but he rushed out before the sun had risen."

"I never heard anything!"

"They were whispering. They didn't want to wake you and Mr. Linden."

"Right, 'Mr.' Linden." Marlis huffed. Papa clearly wanted to keep Freddy out of his business as much as possible. The less Freddy knew, the less likely he would try to influence policy by dangling her father's life in front of him—that was the reasoning, she was sure, though Freddy wasn't likely to stand for it long.

"Papa can be so stupid," she muttered, going back to the breakfast, pouring herself tea with loads of milk and sugar.

Elsie bobbed her head and departed, clearly not wanting to be implicated in any word against Papa.

Marlis had no desire to talk to a maid anyway. She wouldn't be any help with these problems. Quite likely no one would, except perhaps her fellow Norns. That meant leaving with Freddy. What of Papa then?

If only Mama were here. She might understand.

Might. Even then, Marlis wasn't sure. Marlis wondered what Mama had thought of her, in truth. Marlis had a feeling Mama didn't believe in Norns. She probably felt she had rescued a poor ordinary girl from being brought up by monks. But then, it was such an odd thing to do, for her parents to agree to raise a baby from Irminau.

Marlis stirred her tea like it was the pool of an oracle and an answer might bubble to the surface. She wondered if Mama would like the idea of her husband living thanks to a thread of magic and a serum made from a tree. Marlis doubted it. "It's time," she would have said, the way she said when she was dying, dragging the words through her congested lungs. "Everything lives and everything dies, and when we die we become part of the soil that helps trees and flowers grow," she told Marlis, adding with a smile, "Unless you're a cow or a pig, and then you get eaten. So be sure to plant flowers on my grave, and when they grow, that will be me saying hello."

Papa must die.

Marlis wiped her nose. No, she liked Mama's words better. *It's time.*

She had to think of the future now, and the future would not have her parents in it. The future was leading her to her own past, one they didn't share. She scribbled a note with one hand while she ate her breakfast with the other. *I might have new information. Very important. I don't know who I can trust besides you. Please see me as soon as possible, alone.* She called Elsie back again.

"Will you have this sent out to Volland immediately?"

"Of course, right away."

⊙–⊙–⊙–⊙

Volland appeared several hours later, without her father. "What is it?"

"I remembered something last night. I've always kept a diary, you know."

He nodded. Volland could appreciate these things; at thirty-five, he was the youngest man on her father's staff, a precocious scholar in his earlier days. Marlis could still see the gawky student in him despite the polish he must have acquired over the years.

"There was a box underneath Yggdrasil with all of the diaries I kept . . . before. In other lives. Is there any chance they may have been recovered by the army when the tree was destroyed?"

"I'm sure I would have heard of something like that. Seems more likely they're still right where you left them." More heavily, he said, "In Irminau."

"Or else the other Norns have it. And *they* are here in the city."

"How do you know that?"

"Freddy's seen them."

212

His brow furrowed. "Well, we ought to bring them here, in that case."

"I don't think they'd come willingly. I must go to them."

"Would you be safe?"

"Am I safe now?" she asked.

His posture shifted to concession. "Not at all, really. There was a multipronged attack last night. The production arsenal was destroyed, the east end armory was raided, and so our weapons supply lines have been disrupted. The revolutionaries are committed to taking over the government, clearly. I hope they're prepared to fend off Irminau."

"Without the arsenal, even?" She put a hand over her heart. "Were there many casualties?"

"We lost about a hundred men, and a hundred more were captured. This wasn't a military engagement, though—it was an attack on a strategic point. We weren't guarded as heavily as we should have been."

"A hundred men is a lot, in context. Well, here is what I think. Papa's death is quite clearly inevitable, and so is our downfall. The Republic, I mean. Papa as good as said so."

"Yes, he has," Volland agreed. "At this point he wants to go down in a blaze of glory."

"And what do you think of that?"

"It isn't what I would choose." For the first time, his expression showed a hint of fear.

"I know you've often been the voice of reason to my father," Marlis said, "but I think he's beyond that now." She glanced down. "I wondered if you might go with me to find the others." She couldn't quite admit that she didn't want to be alone, and

Freddy wasn't enough. She wanted someone older and, in many ways, wiser.

Volland tapped his hands together, smiling in an anguished way. "A week ago I would never have considered a suggestion like this—now everything's gone crazy, hasn't it? I want to believe in miracles. I want to believe that all of this means something. I've always thought you were unlike other children."

"And I'm not such a child anymore," she added.

"If I leave, I'll be considered a traitor," Volland said. "I couldn't return."

"Not necessarily," Marlis said, not wanting to frighten Volland off. "Once we find the books, we can always come back. If the information in them has any value to the government for the impending war against Irminau, no one will care that you left, only that you came back with them."

"Do you plan to bring the books back here, then?" She could hear his uncertainty, as if he also realized she didn't quite belong here anymore.

"We'll see what I learn from them." She tried to smile, as if she knew what she was doing, though it didn't feel genuine. "This place is slipping through my fingers, Volland, whether I try to hold on to it or not. I'd rather . . . let it go. By my own choice. I've already said good-bye to Papa." Marlis wanted to cry again. This was real. This was a farewell to everything she had ever known, not just people but also places and things. Every little thing. The three-hundred-year-old painting in the western wing of the house of a woman making stew while her children played on the floor, their emotions palpable across the ages. The way the light fell on her favorite chair on an autumn afternoon, the best place to read in the whole house. How the horses in the stable perked up eagerly and came forward for apples when she visited them.

She had been a child here, and when she left, that would be gone. When she saw those books, she would have to face that her life went far beyond this place, whether she liked it or not. That her name had been Urd before it was Marlis.

But.

It is time.

THIRTY-FOUR

"Let them go, Aleksy," Sebastian said. "Those men, the ones who left, are bewitched." He frowned and tapped his fingers on the desk. "Please . . . tell the others something. I have to think about this for a moment."

"Bewitched?" Aleksy asked.

"I'll explain it to everyone soon. I just need to compose myself for a minute. Please."

"Yes, sir."

Sebastian dropped his head onto his crossed arms on the desk. He stayed like that for a long moment. He had been so calm throughout this crisis in the city; now Thea wondered how much of that Sebastian was real.

Nan looked at Thea. Her expression was grim. "Sebastian, where do you think Ingrid is going? Is there someone she would turn to?"

He lifted his head and pulled at his hair. "There is one man who wants Yggdrasil's power to continue more than anything, because he relies on it."

"King Otto?" Nan said.

"Yes."

"Do you know something about this?" Nan demanded. "Does she have some kind of history with Otto?"

"I know nothing," he said. "The day I met her, she got me under her spell."

"I'm going after her," Nan said, snatching up Thea's wooden hand. "I have to find out what this is all about. I'm taking this, so I have evidence."

"You're leaving?" Thea asked, not wanting her to go, though she realized the scope of Nan's life went beyond this place.

Nan gave Thea a quick embrace. She didn't smell like Telephone Club smoke as she once did—now she seemed clean as snow. "I hate to abandon you now. I could still use a good chat with you, and I bet you could, too."

"Yes. But . . . we can have it when you get back."

Nan's eyes held a hundred apologies and explanations. "I need to hurry so I can catch up with her. I feel like I'm the only person who can stop this."

"Listen, when you get there—" Sebastian lifted a hand before she could run out. "Look for a woman named Jenny. She's kept in the place they call the Mausoleum. Tell her I'm well, and ask her if she knows anything that might help. You can trust her."

"Thank you, I will." She was out the door in a flash of green skirt and heels.

Sebastian looked at the desk. "Maybe I ought to start smoking a pipe. I've heard it's relaxing, and it's an excellent prop, besides. It might make me seem more authoritative."

Thea sat down on the edge of the desk near him. She could

see he had no idea what to do. She didn't feel like making light of the situation.

When she didn't respond, Sebastian lifted his eyes to hers. Even now, he had a strong presence. His eyelashes were short and dark, so his eyes seemed sharply defined. She could tell he was thinking about a lot of things at once. His eyes didn't stay put—they kept glancing toward different objects in the room, putting together pieces. She had a fleeting thought of touching his unshaven cheeks.

The thing about Sebastian was that he had seemed safe. Now she knew he actually wasn't.

"Do you still have bandages in that bag of yours?" he asked.

She had forgotten she carried it. "Yes."

"My leg is bleeding from the—thing." He held out a hand, and she gave him the satchel. He pulled up the leg of his pants, and she wasn't sure if she should avert her eyes, if he was self-conscious as she was, but he started talking matter-of-factly as he unrolled the bandage. "I am quite sure we can't blame Ingrid for my accident, unless she can grant wishes."

"You wished to have an accident?" Thea asked, confused.

"No, not *really*. Only in the way you wish for things when you're angry. My father, you see, is deathly afraid of injury. He never goes anywhere without a healer or two at his side, and that extended to me. Whenever I hurt myself as a kid, I was immediately healed. No cuts, scrapes, bruises, skinned knees for me. And it might *sound* nice—" He rolled the bandage around the stump of his leg, just below the knee, and secured it.

"It sounds intrusive," Thea said.

"Exactly."

"But just being royalty sounds like that. In books, anyway. Like you have no privacy."

"It's true. I just think he's a bit more unhinged than some kings."

"Too inbred?"

His brow wrinkled. "I don't know if I like the implications of that statement."

She almost smiled. "So a part of you wanted to have an accident just to mess up your father's careful safekeeping?"

"You're jumping to conclusions." He half-smiled back. "But sort of. I was an athletic kid, and all those healers of my youth had made me feel invincible. I always wanted to ride the wildest horse in the stable."

"And ski the most dangerous slope, I suppose?"

"Yes, although I was on a moderate slope when it happened. One I thought I knew well. There's a life lesson for me, I guess. Can't get too comfortable."

"How did the accident happen?"

"I don't remember it. I lost control, and it's a blur from there. When I woke up, they said I tumbled down the mountain and twisted my leg. The healers couldn't save it. It *was* terrible. But—the look of horror on my father's face was almost . . . Well, I can't say it made it all worth it; let's say it put the fire into me to find something else to do with myself." He reached for her hand, and his grip tightened around her fingers. "You will find new opportunities, too."

"All I had to go on was my looks." Her voice was a little hoarse with the admission. Back then, she hardly dared admit that she hated leaving school. It just hurt too much. She *had* to leave school, so all she could do was tell herself that working at the Telephone Club was the best thing she'd ever done.

"Well, I know a little something about that, too. The prince with the prosthetic leg is a lot less romantic than the prince who is known for his athletic prowess. Your talents go beyond your looks. The thing about sports, or maybe anything, is that the people who win the races and the tournaments are the people who can put aside their fear and do what needs to be done. And you're obviously one of those people, or you wouldn't be here." He gave her fingers a final squeeze before letting them go. He looked sad now. Despite his encouraging words, he was surely thinking of his own loss.

"What are you going to do?" she asked. "You need to tell the men something before that dark-magic rumor grows a life of its own."

He sighed. "Maybe a part of me knew something was wrong, because I brought my prosthetic leg with me to Urobrun. It's under my bed in a trunk. The key is in my nightstand. Maybe . . ."

"I can get it," she said.

Thea walked into his bedroom uninterrupted. She could hear a noisy, continuous murmuring downstairs.

He wasn't using the Schiffs' master bedroom—he'd chosen a small guest room much like Freddy's. She couldn't resist a glance around. The only photograph beside his bed was of a dog. No girls. The dog photograph wasn't just a snapshot, it was a studio portrait on sturdy cardstock in a velvet frame.

It gave her a fuzzy feeling. It was a little much to get a formal portrait of a dog, but it was also sweet.

Thea didn't want to have these feelings about Sebastian. It didn't feel right to toss Freddy over like that. Her mother married the first boy she ever loved. Her father married the first girl he ever loved. It felt, in some way, like the way love ought to be. Like in fairy tales.

But no one loved the sorcerer, in the fairy tales. They loved the prince.

She shoved these thoughts aside and knelt to peer under the bed. She had to use her left arm to support herself while she pulled out the wooden box. The pose didn't feel right without her hand, and the wounds from pulling out the wooden hand were a little tender.

She opened the box and looked at the prosthetic leg. It was made of a lightweight metal, connected with straps to a leather thigh harness with laces to secure it. It didn't look very comfortable. Of course, she had seen war veterans with various prosthetics. Crude ones for the beggars and the poor, sometimes no more than a peg. This one was obviously well made, but seeing the leg was like ice down her spine, a reminder that no prosthetic could come close to the real thing.

The ice turned to fire as she recalled dim memories of Ingrid cutting off her hand, that smile on her face as she said, *One must trust in fate.* "Bitch," Thea whispered. It felt good to speak her hatred aloud.

She hurried back to Sebastian. After securing the straps and laces, Sebastian winced when he stood, and his attempt to walk looked painful and off-balance. The leg didn't quite fit. "I guess I've grown a little since Ingrid found me," he said. He cursed and pounded the desk, and his accumulation of empty coffee mugs with spoons in them all jumped and clinked. "If word gets out that I've lost a leg, people might start to think about the one-legged prince whose death was a little bit suspicious."

"What are you going to tell them, then, if not the truth? How are you going to explain this?"

"I need more time to think."

"Well," she said, "I don't think you have that."

He took a deep breath.

THIRTY-FIVE

Nan found Sigi downstairs talking to Adrian, a tall young man who worked in the kitchen.

"What's going on?" Sigi asked. "Ingrid just left with a group. Adrian said they grabbed some food on their way out."

"I need to go after her."

"You'd better not go without me," Sigi said. "Let me get my camera. Adrian, could you pack us some food?"

Nan suppressed a smile. Sigi might have tried to escape the socialite life she'd been born into, but she still possessed the ability to give breezy orders.

"They won't be very fast," Sigi said, as they shoved their clothes into a bag. "They carried out two trunks that looked heavy. Say, isn't that Thea's valise?"

"Yeah, she'll understand, though. Come on." Nan shouldered the bag, and they rushed down the stairs. Adrian had a parcel of food and a flashlight ready for them.

"You're the best," Sigi said. "I hardly know you, but you're the best."

They stepped out into the night. *This cold air blows down*

from Irminau, Nan thought. The neighborhood felt forbiddingly large when they were planning on leaving it behind.

"Do you know where she went?" Sigi's whisper produced a cloud of frigid breath.

"No, though I think I know where she's headed." Nan's skin tingled, intuition pricking at her temples. She proceeded cautiously, staying close to the wall around Mr. Schiff's house. Usually guards were posted at the corner, near the old subway station, but she didn't see them. She crept forward, Sigi just behind her.

Sigi stopped. "Is that a body, there? By the subway station?"

Nan had been looking for people standing, not collapsed, but Sigi was right: There was a human-size lump of darkness at the entrance to the subway station. She approached a little faster now, and the lump didn't move.

It was one of the Chancellor's guards, and he'd been shot. The subway entrance was open, and she saw another man slumped halfway down the stairs.

"Ingrid's work?" Sigi asked.

"I think so."

Nan started down the stairs, trading the brisk breeze of a winter night for air that was damp and still.

"Some of them are probably still down here." Sigi's eyes turned haunted. "The dead."

They were several miles from the spot where the workers had escaped—but some of them could have come this way. She held out her hand.

"Where *is* she headed?" Sigi asked, as they descended the

concrete steps. The station was now inhabited mostly by spiders—or at least, the ghosts of them. Nan switched on her flashlight, and wherever she pointed it, ragged gray webs floated from ceilings and between turnstiles. The musty smell roused memories, but there was no sign of death.

"To King Otto."

"Really? Isn't he abusive to magic users? I thought her whole philosophy was about respecting magic users."

"I expect she plans to control him the way she did Thea and the men here."

"What are you going to say when you find her?"

"I don't know. I thought maybe I could show them all Thea's wooden hand and use the wyrdsong." Nan didn't know if the wyrdsong would work on her own sister and all the men she had already used the wyrdsong on, or if she could use it effectively on such a large group.

"Maybe we should just play along. Pretend you had a change of heart. Go to Irminau with her."

"But . . . King Otto? I don't want to go there."

"I've never known you to be scared," Sigi said. "I know Otto locked you up and killed you, but so did Valkenrath, and you weren't afraid of him."

"Things have changed. I've seen colors. I've heard music. . . . I feel that I'm changing, that maybe I don't have to be stuck in this same pattern anymore. But if I go to Irminau . . ."

"Irminau is where it all began," Sigi said, "and where it all ended. Maybe you need to go there, to finish whatever is going on."

In the distance, voices echoed faintly along the tunnels like ghosts. "That must be them," Nan said.

Sigi's eyes went briefly wide at the sound. "All right. We're doing this."

Nan squared her shoulders and moved ahead.

The voices grew louder and closer. They turned a bend in the track and saw flashlights faintly illuminating the silhouettes of a large group of people.

"*Ingrid!*" Nan shouted.

Sigi jumped. "Try not to give me a heart attack."

Nan heard a few guns being readied, but she couldn't see much besides the flashlights now pointing in her face. Sigi held up her hands, and Nan did the same.

"Ingrid, I'm sorry," Nan said.

"Sorry?" Ingrid sounded tense.

"I broke Sebastian's tie to Yggdrasil. I know that's why you left. I thought it was the right thing to do, but . . . it wasn't. I understand that now. I don't want you to go. We're—we're family." She still hoped maybe she could convince them to turn around.

"I was the one who made a mistake. I thought when I found you, things could be as they were, that you would understand what I did," Ingrid answered. "I realize now that I am alone. Cut your ties to Yggdrasil and . . . and find what happiness you can." As she spoke, the men watched with blank faces.

"I—I want to go with you," Nan said. "I want to see Irminau and Yggdrasil. I've grown up here in the city. Maybe if I could *see* . . . I would understand."

Ingrid clasped her fingers together like she was considering this idea. "Is that really what you think? I thought you didn't believe in our cause anymore."

"I was caught in the shock of the moment," Nan said. "But when you left, I thought of all the years we've shared. I want you to be as you were, with your long hair and bare feet and your pet rabbits."

"I don't want to let you go either," Ingrid said softly. "I want to fight at your side, I just don't trust you."

"You outnumber us," Nan said. "Do you have to trust me? I wouldn't have come if something didn't draw me to you." She held out her hand. She wanted to believe the Skuld she had known still existed.

Ingrid's hand reached out, but she didn't step forward. A gap stood between them—of space and trust. Ingrid looked so small, the only girl in the crowd, standing in her pale-colored dress. Nan wished she could grab her and shake the pain out of her. *Let them go, Ingrid! Let them all go. Forget whatever terrible things you saw, and be the girl you used to be.*

She grabbed Ingrid's hand instead. They were going home.

THIRTY-SIX

Marlis couldn't tell Papa she was leaving. And she couldn't be there when Freddy let him go, because today could not be that day. She wanted Papa and all the other ministers to be busy with their meetings, late into the night, while she slipped away.

She had already said good-bye.

Now, how to get out of the Chancellery with Freddy and Volland? Pairs of guards stood at every door, along with a few posted across the street. They were supposed to protect her, and she couldn't imagine how she'd get past them.

She gathered Freddy into the fold to plot. "Uncle—Valkenrath's house connected to tunnels that led to the workers," he said. "He talked about their history, how they were part of an older system that once connected to the palace. Does this house connect, too?"

"Papa never mentioned that our house did, but—"

"It must," Volland said. "This house predates the Republic. It was first built for the Duke of Schwarzwasser. The old nobility must have had ways to sneak out and find one another."

"Well, then, we'd better look for the door," Freddy said.

"I never go in the cellar," Marlis said. "It's very gloomy. Seems like a good place to catch one's death."

"I doubt anyone has ever died from going into the cellar," Freddy said.

Marlis gathered candles and matches into her coat pockets, then walked ahead of them to the door. She waited a moment, making sure no guards or servants were watching, then opened the door slowly, so the noisy creak would alert Freddy and Volland.

The cellar felt older than the rest of the house, like a dungeon, with claustrophobic ceilings and ancient brick walls. Two small doors formed of old planks led in two different directions; she chose the one farthest from the kitchen, because the space under the kitchen was used for storing food and wine. This room was a catchall of junk better suited to the trash: dusty jugs with broken spouts, pine boughs that had shed their needles with old garlands wrapped around them, rusty tools of unknown usage.

She was beginning to wonder if this quest was futile when her candlelight danced across an old loose door propped against the wall. She clambered over the barrels and boxes to peer behind it, where the edge of a hidden door came into view. "Could this be it?"

Volland and Freddy pulled the heavy old door away and lowered it gently to the ground. The second door was locked into a frame with a plank across it to hold it shut; they removed that, too, and used a rusty crowbar to pry it open. The door hadn't been opened in ages and had settled against the frame.

Behind it was a narrow tunnel that sloped downward and traveled as far as the candle could see.

"We've found the beginning," Volland said. "Now the only problem is, where do you suppose we can get out without drawing attention?"

"Valkenrath's house linked to the entire underground," Freddy said. "The subway system. Old catacombs. Everything."

Two steps in, Marlis could already see the path ahead was going to split. The tunnel smelled like trapped time. It was difficult to imagine it would ever connect to something as modern as subways.

⊙–⊙–⊙–⊙

Just when she feared they might be lost in a labyrinth, the tunnels intersected with the subway system. Not only were Marlis and Freddy too young to remember the subways, they were never in the position to have used them. But Volland did.

"This brings back memories," he said, as they walked by a car abandoned on the track. "I used to ride these cars every day. Freddy, what part of the city are the revolutionaries in?"

"Mecklinger Park."

"Are they really?" Volland sounded understandably shocked. Few neighborhoods had a better reputation than Mecklinger Park. Papa always spoke as if the rebels met in smoky dives and abandoned warehouses. "Well, that isn't far at all. We just need to follow the signs. Watch your step, Princess."

Volland led the way to the station. It was very close indeed— they had only walked for ten minutes, if that. Even though she didn't have memories of the subway, she hated to see a part of her city forgotten like this, smothered in dust and sadness. "Wait," Freddy said, lifting his head as if he heard something. He shoved past the broken turnstiles. She could see morning light hitting the tops of the stairs.

A corpse was slumped a few steps from the exit, in the uniform of her father's guard.

"He's only been dead for an hour or so," Freddy said. "Should we find out who killed him?"

"Don't touch him," Marlis said. She had never been squeamish, but suddenly she felt she'd had enough of seeing the doors open and close on death. "Is this the right station?"

"Headquarters is a few houses down," Freddy said.

"Then let's just hurry on ahead."

Freddy looked at her strangely. She imagined that he expected her to want to know how one of her father's men died. But he didn't question her order as he led the way toward the house. Even for this street, it was grand, set back behind a stone wall like the Wachters', rising up three stories plus attic. The rebel guards recognized Freddy, and they bristled at the sight of Volland and her.

"It's all right," Freddy told them. "They're with me. They're joining our cause. I want to see Sebastian right away."

The men were edgy, hands on weapons. They were strapping, rustic men with hair flopping in their eyes and sturdy, plain wool clothes—such a far cry from the sharp uniforms and regulation haircuts of her father's guards and soldiers. They made her nervous, too, like they might not follow rules of good conduct.

The guards showed them into a massive entrance hall. All the empty space was above their heads—the floor was packed with curious, uneasy men. The room was loud with conversation, her name rippling back through the room as she was recognized. It seemed they had already been gathered before she arrived. *Celebrating the arsenal raid, no doubt.*

The men cleared out a path for someone. This must be the revolutionary leader. The revolutionary leader? No, surely it couldn't be. He was just a scruffy young man, leaning on a cane and limping badly.

"Freddy," he said. "Safe and sound. Thank goodness for that." He shook Freddy's hand. "But—"

"This is Marlis," Freddy said. "I know a lot of you already think you know who she is, but there's more to it than that. She wanted to come."

He hadn't spoken the word "Norn." He hadn't called her Urd. She was relieved he had left that off for now. "Yes," Marlis said, "as events have unfolded rapidly in the capital, I have realized how much of the truth I didn't know. And my father's top adviser, Diedrich Volland, agreed to come with me."

Volland bowed, hesitated a little, and then offered his hand. Marlis wondered what he must be thinking, having left the hallowed halls of the Chancellery with all the distinguished men in well-pressed suits for this disheveled lot.

"I'm Sebastian Hirsch," the leader said. "Nice to meet you, Mr. Volland. And Miss Marlis."

She hadn't expected his voice to sound so distinguished. His accent was Irminauer, though well-bred; it relaxed her a bit. "I certainly hope to be here as a friend, if we can find common ground in our goals."

"Let's talk in the parlor. And I'll thank the rest of you not to eavesdrop." He waved the three of them on, while he walked slowly. He sat down with obvious relief in the room's most comfortable chair, while Marlis just barely sat at all, on the very edge of the couch, with Volland next to her. Freddy stayed on his feet, lingering by the mantle.

"Were you injured in the raids last night?" she asked. "On the arsenal and supply bases? I presume you participated?"

Sebastian nodded a little, like that was a given. "I lost a leg," he said, "to make a long story short."

"A leg? Not tonight—you would be in no condition to walk," Marlis said. Of course, he might have a healer at hand, but he looked far too in control to have suffered a grave injury. He sat in his chair like it was a throne, while she felt so out of her element. "You were foolish to destroy the arsenal: We'll need those weapons when King Otto inevitably tries to wage war."

"What have you told her, Freddy?" Sebastian asked.

"I told her about the Norns," Freddy said, picking up a decorative paperweight that had been sitting on the mantle and tossing it from hand to hand. She suspected he was relishing her discomfort here, after what she'd done to him.

"Well, it's no secret now," Sebastian said. "I'll tell you the same thing I just told my men. Ingrid, who has been by my side for the past three years, had my loyal men and me under an enchantment. She is *not* a military or political strategist, however."

"Who figured it out?" Freddy asked.

"Thea and Nan," Sebastian said in a lower voice. "And Nan's gone. She went after Ingrid."

"They're gone?" Freddy furrowed his brows.

"The other Norns?" Marlis asked, clutching her hands around her knees.

Sebastian nodded.

Volland tilted his head at Marlis slightly. She understood that look; she took it as, *Don't lose your composure, Princess. Ask him a question.* "What is your plan, Mr. Hirsch? From what I understand, the rebels are hoping to overthrow the government and establish their own."

Freddy looked impatient. "For goodness sake, Marlis. Just tell him why you're here."

"The UWP is trying to work that out," Sebastian said, acknowledging Freddy's comment only with a sideways flick of his eyes. "I agree with them that—"

"The UWP," Marlis interrupted, unable to contain herself. The rebels had killed Ida and danced around the Chancellery with their crude homemade signs. "What are they good for except destruction? Do they really have any plan for what to do once they've ousted—if not assassinated—the current leadership?"

Sebastian held up a hand. "Marlis, I don't work for the UWP. I work with them right now, because they have the people's ear. I agree with you: I don't think they know how to govern. And my dream goes farther than theirs. I want to bring Irminau and Urobrun together as one democracy."

"And govern yourself?" Marlis sniffed. "You look very young."

"Twenty. Yes, it's unfortunately young."

"I imagine you'd have to establish a monarchy to rule at such a young age," Volland said. He sounded both concerned and defeated—he'd left her father for an inexperienced youth. "The people won't accept that."

"Enough." Freddy put down the paperweight and walked almost between them. "Sebastian, I know Marlis. By the time she sleeps on it, she'll put two and two together. This is Prince Rupert of Irminau. You might remember he had a skiing accident and supposedly drowned shortly thereafter."

"Prince Rupert?" She took in the sight of him all over again, trying not to recoil. His shoulders had tensed as Freddy spoke, his head leaning slightly sideways as if Freddy's words were blows. "You're *his* son?"

He straightened up again. "I know my father is a terrible king. That's why I left. I have no wish to use my royal blood to any advantage."

"Does your father know you're alive?"

"Not that I'm aware."

"Freddy, you told me he was the king's enemy—you could have mentioned he was also his *son*."

"I thought it might make you feel better," Freddy said. "I thought you'd appreciate his credentials. The lost prince. It's like something out of one of your operas, isn't it?"

"My operas," Marlis repeated, still stunned. "It is, but . . . if life were an opera, half of us would be dead at the end."

"I am King Otto's enemy," Sebastian said, his hand in a fist on his knee. "Make no mistake about that. The only advantage I got from growing up in Neue Adlerwald is that I learned how government works."

She glanced quickly at Freddy. It was not lost on her that he had spilled Sebastian's secret and not hers. But he was waiting.

Sebastian pushed his glasses up his nose and leaned a little closer in to her. "What about you? You mentioned mutual goals. What are you thinking?"

"I have always been faithful to my father and the Republic. However, I recently learned I wasn't told the whole truth. I didn't realize the depth of what my father asked of Freddy, and he also lied to me. When he thought he was dying, he told me I'm . . ." She stopped, shook her head. "I *am* a Norn. Urd. I knew that name before I knew what it meant."

"When she told me, I knew I had to bring her here," Freddy said.

"Urd," Sebastian repeated. "It's true?"

Freddy nodded.

Sebastian spread his hands, like he wanted to throw them around her. "To think, we were looking for you, and all this time you were right in front of us. I'm sorry you missed your sisters, though I'm glad you're here."

"I don't even really know what it means to be a Norn," she said. "I wanted to come as myself. Marlis. To fight for what I believe in, what I used to think my father believed in. I don't want my country to be ruled with *lies*, and I don't even know who to trust anymore. I just know it isn't my father or anyone who was in on his plans."

"I am sorry about your father," Sebastian said. "I know how that feels." Whatever might be said about this prince, he could certainly sound earnest. She felt dangerously disarmed by his words, because she so wanted to be understood.

But he also wanted to rule *her* country. Where would she fit in here?

"I believe some of my father's men would fight under my banner," Marlis said, trying to hint that she would bring plenty to the table and intended to work with him, not merely for him. "I'd be willing to lend you what help I can if we can agree on a plan."

She had expected him to push back—instead he just clapped his hands around the arms of the chair and said, "I'd like you to attend a meeting with my advisers and first in command."

"I wish I'd gotten to you before you decided to destroy the arsenal," she said, a little flustered at his sheer agreeability. "I still think that was stupid."

"I'm sure you do," he said. "At least you don't have to worry about getting hold of those weapons."

While she could tell he thought she was going to be a handful, he didn't say so, and that was enough, she supposed, to work with.

THIRTY-SEVEN

Thea listened to Sebastian's speech. However shaken he seemed in his office, he summoned an authoritative calm when he spoke of Ingrid's betrayal. Soon eyes turned her way with expressions of sympathy and horror.

I can't face this.

Nan's clothes were gone. There was none of her here now, except her rumpled covers. Thea sat on Nan's bed, wishing she could soak up some of her friend's strength. She stretched her left arm, then her right. Comparing. She spread her right hand, admiring her fingers. She remembered occasionally a customer would tell her she had nice hands, even though they were always a little rough from washing dishes at home. Her right hand was like a widow now, lost without its mate.

She briefly shut her eyes, thinking of her parents.

Her heart thumped hard as she pulled the bandage away from her left arm. Blood spotted the bandage when she got to the layer beneath, but the little wounds where Yggdrasil's roots had dug into her were already beginning to close. The arm looked clean, like she'd simply been born without a hand. She felt like she was breaking some rule, just looking at herself. She could hear her mother, tugging her away from armless and legless men who begged on the street, saying, *Don't stare.*

Sebastian's men could have been those men on the street, once. The thoughts of beggars were too close. Sebastian wouldn't turn her out, supposing he retained power. What would he have her do, though? It had been hard enough just finding a place in the world when she was whole.

She started crying ugly tears. A hand pounded on the door. "Thea?"

Freddy. *No. I don't want to see him. I don't want to see anyone ever again.*

"I heard what happened," he said gently, through the door. "I've been worried sick about you." She shut her eyes. Tears burned behind her eyelids.

Finally, she threw a blanket around her arms, covering the injury, and let him in. She couldn't meet his eyes. "I'm sorry, Freddy," she said. "I know I've been acting strange and . . ."

He put a hand on her shoulder. "It wasn't the real you. I knew that."

She glanced up at him, her head clear now, remembering all they had shared, from the first glimpse of his strange silver hair all the way to the kiss. She was also still thinking of Sebastian: the ink stains on his strong hands, his arms wrapped around her, his easy confidence. It was different from the way she felt around Freddy, and she didn't think she would forget it anytime soon.

"How did it go?" she asked. "With the Chancellor?"

"Well, they tied my hands to his corpse and told me I wasn't going anywhere until I brought him back to life. So, just another day I suppose."

"Bad day for hands all around." Her voice came out too small and scared for a joke, but it brought a little light to his tired eyes.

When he tried to touch her cheek, she stiffened.

His hand fell to his side again. "Are you in any pain?" he asked.

She shook her head, biting her lip. "It's clean." She pulled the blanket away. "See, it's—like it was never even there."

"Thea . . ." He wrapped his hand around the end of her arm and drew it to his heart, drew her closer. Her skin still shivered at his touch, and at the idea that he wasn't afraid, that he looked at her as if she was as beautiful as before.

She didn't know what to do. Was this feeling enough? Something had changed between them. Or maybe something had always been missing.

"You want to meet us downstairs?" he asked. "Sebastian is holding a meeting in the basement."

She nodded, relieved that he wasn't addressing their relationship just now. As he left the room, she dug up her favorite dress. Her reflection in the little mirror above the bureau in the room, cut off at the shoulders, was the same as it had ever been, with the same things she had always liked about her appearance: skin other girls in school had envied, cupid's bow lips, a nose that was cute but not *too* cute. She put on some fresh lipstick and tried to look confident.

Downstairs, the men were all buzzing about the appearance of the Chancellor's daughter. Aleksy was standing guard at the basement door. He nodded her through. She didn't try to call attention to herself, but Freddy and Sebastian both looked at her. The single lamp in the middle of the table cast a sallow glow on their faces. Marlis had been speaking, then she trailed off when she saw their attention slip. Sebastian pointed Thea to the empty chair next to Freddy and motioned for Marlis to go on.

"Before I came here," Marlis said, "I'd been speaking with Wilhelmina Wachter, the wife of General Wachter, about allowing magic to be used within the military."

So strange to see Marlis here. She looked exactly like her pictures and exactly as Thea would have imagined—an inch on the tall side, wearing the same drab gray dress the newspapers had described. "He's always seemed to be a very reasonable man, and I think he might be convinced."

"Wachter is an experienced commander, and certainly an asset in that regard," Sebastian said. "The trouble is that he is strongly associated with the old regime."

"Mightn't that be spun as an asset, as well?" asked the thin suit-clad man sitting beside Thea. He must have come with Marlis. "If someone like General Wachter publicly declared that he supports the revolution, many people who thought they liked things just fine as they were would be more likely to reconsider."

"It's true, bringing a few of the old leaders into the fold has its advantages," Sebastian said. "And we do aim to distinguish ourselves from the radical UWP. Wachter might be too close, however."

Marlis's foot was fidgeting under the table—Thea could hear it knocking into the legs of her chair in the silence. "How are you going to distinguish yourself from the UWP if you won't work with my allies and you won't make it known that you are the prince of Irminau? You must do something *bold*."

"Bold, yes, but not foolishly hasty. I could ruin myself if I reveal my identity now. If there is one person people hate more than . . ." He faltered, obviously on the brink of saying *the Chancellor*. "We need to get everything settled down, to shift the balance of power. Freddy must let go of the Chancellor."

"You mean, my father needs to die."

"Brunner is itching to make a move already," Sebastian said. "There seems to be no reason to put it off." He looked at her—asking permission, it seemed. Thea thought it odd that he was so quick to trust the Chancellor's daughter.

Marlis stood up, waving one hand at the table. "Let him go, Freddy. Now, before I can think."

She climbed the stairs without saying anything else while Sebastian sighed heavily, massaging his temples.

"We can trust her?" Thea whispered to Freddy.

"She's a Norn," he said.

"A *Norn*? Are you sure?"

He nodded grimly. "Yes."

"Well, that doesn't mean we can trust her. Look at Ingrid."

"Marlis has a tough outer shell, but I know this betrayal by her father has rattled her through and through. She would have to be serious about joining us to take Volland with her." He motioned to the thin, scholarly man who was now going up the stairs after her. "He was one of her father's top advisers, and it's a huge risk for him to sneak out of the Chancellery."

Sebastian's adviser stood up, and Sebastian nodded to him,

then glanced at Thea. He half-smiled. She dropped her eyes, nervous now, and stood up. "I should go," she told Freddy. "I need to—to write Mother. I'll visit her soon, of course—I just don't want to break the news in person."

"Yeah," Freddy said. "Of course."

He knows something's wrong. I'm not acting right. I can't remember how to act.

She hesitated, but didn't know what to say. To either of them.

THIRTY-EIGHT

Stupid, stupid. Freddy punched the stone wall of the basement stairwell so hard that his entire hand throbbed.

Who cares? You've known this girl for—what—two weeks?

But what the hell else is there?

As far as he was concerned, the entire world might have been two weeks old. The men who had raised him, the people he had known, and the life he had lived—all gone. His bed—gone. Familiar maids? Gone. Books? The clock he'd been repairing? Clothes that weren't borrowed? Letters from his parents? All gone.

He had seen the way she looked at Sebastian. Whatever had compelled her to dance with him before, it wasn't only enchantment.

Not that he could blame her. Sebastian was undeniably handsome, and much stronger than Freddy. Of course, right now he could barely walk, but he'd still gotten the benefit of a first impression. *What was wrong with your first impression? Let me count the ways. You had to act fake because Gerik was*

*there, your touch gave her a terrifying vision of her dead father,
you had never been out of the house before . . . and basically you
still haven't.*

Why wouldn't she want someone worldly? Someone who led
arsenal raids? Someone with the respect of hundreds of men?
All Freddy had was creepy magic, no friends, no experience
outside of books. He couldn't help that—and she probably
couldn't help wanting something else.

He punched the wall again, in the hallway now. He remembered he had an immediate duty as well, to let the Chancellor
go, and the less time he spent with his magic tied to that man,
the better. It sounded like it should be a momentous event,
not something done in a manner of seconds in a quiet hallway. However, he didn't want to honor the Chancellor with
any ceremony.

Just a snip of the thread, and that was the end.

He did feel obligated to tell Marlis, though. Some sympathy
was in order, and this was certainly not a situation addressed
in etiquette books. He stepped out into the garden behind the
house. He hadn't been out here yet, but he knew the gardener
was a witch who was still harvesting baskets of vegetables
despite the freezing temperatures. Sure enough, a man was put-
tering around with a wheelbarrow full of compost.

"Hello," Freddy said. "You're the gardener?"

"Yessir."

"Do you have any flowers?"

"A few."

Freddy already saw them—a patch of little sunflower-looking

blooms. He didn't know the names of many flowers. They didn't seem appropriate for mourning—maybe it was better that way. "Can I cut a small bouquet?"

"Of course." The gardener was barely paying him any attention. He was wearing a dirt-streaked cotton shirt with the sleeves rolled up, despite the frigid temperatures. Freddy lingered a moment, watching him work fresh dirt into the soil. The cold wind stirred the leaves of lush heads of greens and carrot tops. It was like peeking into another world, where everything worked differently—where magic brought only beauty.

He found Marlis sitting on the floor of Ingrid's room with an open trunk full of books. Handwritten, by the looks of it. She was reading one, her shoes kicked off, her elbow resting on Ingrid's bed.

"What are those?" he asked.

She looked up from the book, finally. For a second, her expression was far away and she didn't look like Marlis at all. Her face had a curious radiance, like her blood was made of the same silver as his hair. Then she blinked out of it. "These are my journals, from all my years. I remembered them last night. They're the reason I knew I had to leave, how I knew it was real. I needed to see if they were here."

"Anything useful?"

"Oh *yes*." She noticed the flowers, and the light in her eyes faded. She held out her hand. "I know what those mean."

"I'm sorry."

"I doubt it. I wouldn't be, in your shoes." She grabbed the flowers out of his hand and frowned at them. "I don't even want to believe any of it. My father, I can almost accept that he would lie to me, but *Mother* . . ." She shut her eyes briefly. "I—I pitied you. I looked down on you. At least you know who your real parents are."

"What you are really goes beyond parents, doesn't it?"

"I don't know if that's any better." She smoothed the brittle pages of the book in her hand. "I've just been reading and reading. These books go back to King Albert the Fifth. Almost four hundred years ago! I *wrote* all these. It doesn't seem possible."

"Are they triggering any memories?"

"Just bits and pieces. No better than dreams." She huffed.

He sat down on the bed. "Be patient. Maybe you're not ready to remember it all immediately."

"I don't have time to be unready." Now she flipped through the pages, too fast to be reading them, like she wanted him to go away.

He leaned back on one elbow. "I know it's a lot to take in. You said you knew the name Urd, but . . . you didn't know what it meant, did you?"

She paused. "I knew the sound . . . the wyrdsong. I hear it all the time. I used to ask Papa about it when I was little, and he would give me medicine so I didn't hear it for a time, and I stopped telling him or even talking about it."

"How come you never talked about any of this?" Freddy asked. "It amazes me that even as a kid, you were so reserved."

"You were, too, don't you think? You were just nicer about it. You never talked about the magic you had to do, or how it made you feel. How *did* it feel when they started putting you in front of dead people every day when you were, what, seven or eight years old? You didn't want to talk about it, did you?"

"I don't even remember what I felt."

"Well, you said nothing at the time."

"You would've written about it in your diary if I had, wouldn't you?"

She was plucking petals off the flowers, biting her lip hard. "You're right," she said. "I don't know anything."

"I never said you didn't know *anything*."

"How could I not know I was a Norn? I've been reading these books for hours. In the past, it seems like I always *knew*. These books say the wyrdsong has the power to influence men's thoughts. A lot of good that does me—it doesn't say how to use the power, or what direction I'm supposed to influence them in. Seems like I'm just supposed to know. And I don't. If I had known, I'm sure I would never have let my father do what he did to you and all those people underground."

He grabbed the flowers from her. "Look at these poor things. They aren't going to have a petal left."

She wrapped her arms around her knees, looking into space with red-rimmed eyes.

"It's not your fault," he said.

"According to these books it is," she said. "I should be protecting magic."

"According to these books, you were supposed to know who you were. Something must have gone wrong. Nan and I already suspected that might be the case. I don't suppose the books offered any clues?"

"Maybe." Marlis put the old book aside and opened a different one, with a relatively clean cover and modern binding. "Read the last entry." She opened to a page and handed it to him.

June 8th, 3rd Year of King Otto I

The blight on Yggdrasil seems to be spreading. Men from Urobrun have been poking around, getting closer to the tree than any time I can remember. We have handled these scouts so far. They are hired men, easily persuaded. But . . .

We might have to enlist King Otto's help to protect Yggdrasil from Urobrun. I hope he proves reasonable, though I have doubts. He strikes me as arrogant, and some of his policies make me suspicious. They seem intended to track magic users.

It is getting more difficult for us to protect the tree and its children in the face of today's weaponry and communications.

Sometimes I am not sure how all of this could have a good end. All things must die in time . . . even Yggdrasil . . . even us.

When he looked up again, Marlis was staring into the dark corners of the room with hollow eyes.

"This is the last entry?" he asked.

"As far as I can tell."

"Yggdrasil had a blight? Does that happen often?"

"The books imply that was the first time. Apparently there is a barrier of magic around Yggdrasil and normally no one can get near it, but the barrier grew weaker and black blotches appeared on the trunk."

"If Yggdrasil was already dying when Urobrun destroyed the tree . . . but Ingrid brought it back to life—" He halted. "What if Ingrid didn't just plant a new tree? What if the tree was revived? And just as people become different when they are brought back to life without serum, the tree's magic has become twisted? The limbs are its own way of feeding itself?"

Marlis caught her breath. "If that's the case, is Ingrid in control or not?"

"I don't know. And if Yggdrasil dies, will you and Nan die, too?"

"I think the part of me that is human would still live. And that would be that. If my writings are true, magic would be gone."

"I suppose I could have a normal life," he said.

But the way she looked at him, he knew she understood. It was one thing to wish for a normal life when you thought you could never have one—it was another thing entirely to lose your power.

THIRTY-NINE

The next morning, Thea had barely woken up when Sebastian wanted to see her in his office.

"I have an opportunity for you, if you want it," he said as soon as she walked in the door.

"Good morning to you, too," she said, still rubbing sand out of her eyes.

"Sorry. Good morning. I'm bad at preamble. Too much to do."

"I'm not a morning person."

"I'm getting that impression. Anyway—I know you want to do more than waitress, but I found you a waitressing job."

This was not something she expected—or welcomed. "Are you kidding?"

"The reason is, the proprietress herself is a rustic, and she gets a lot of Irminauers in. Some of them might be sympathetic to my father. It's easy for me to know what the factions within Urobrun are doing, but the news from Irminau is slower and less complete. I want to know what my father's up to, as much as possible. If you could play the part of a rustic girl, chat it up with those customers . . ."

"I can't do it like this! Sometimes I wished for a *third* hand at work."

"They do make very functional prosthetics. Some of the men who lost arms in the war made do very well with hooks."

She felt the color drain out of her face. "Hooks? How am I supposed to play the part of a flirtatious waitress with a hook?"

"The same way you did before."

"It's awkward and ugly!" Sebastian could really be dim about some things. "Besides, when does this job start? I'm certainly not ready now."

"Well, you're really working as a scout for my intelligence. They aren't in desperate need of a waitress, so you have some time. Say, a month?"

She started to cross her arms, but even that felt awkward without her hand. "Where is this job, anyway?"

"Café Scorpio. I know the proprietress. I've only been in there once. It's a small place. Quirky. I'm sure people, being people, will stare sometimes—but eccentricity is welcomed."

"I've heard of it." Thea was at least passingly familiar with every nightspot in Lampenlight, but Café Scorpio was on the fringe of the district, with a night act consisting of belly-dancers and the vamp Ina Brand, nicknamed "The Sultry Serpent" for the snakes she wore like accessories. "Is it a nice place?"

"Would I send you into a bad place? Of course not. It seemed nice enough to me."

Thea wondered if Sebastian was the sort of person who would really notice whether it was nice or not. She could imagine him having nonstop conversations about politics and barely noticing the decor, the performers, or the staff.

Someone rapped on the door. "Sebastian, sir, Mr. Huber is downstairs."

"Ah, that's the prosthetist," Sebastian said. "Send him up."

"Already?" Thea was certainly having no trouble shoving aside her romantic feelings for Sebastian on this particular morning. She usually liked that he got right to the point, but not when it came to something so personal.

Sebastian's secretary Kircheis rushed in and thrust papers into Sebastian's hand. "Still no announcement of the Chancellor's death," he said, "though Brunner was asked to meet with some of the ministers."

"So they want to negotiate a compromise before they make the announcement. Brunner isn't taking them up on it, is he?"

"No, he's holding firm. That paper is the latest pamphlet the UWP is circulating, and it doesn't pull any punches."

Sebastian skimmed the pamphlet.

"You should have warned me," Thea hissed at Sebastian. "I'm not ready for—" She cut herself off as soon as his eyes rose to hers. *He's been through all this,* she thought. She didn't want to demand anyone's sympathy, but she wouldn't mind if he offered her a little. Some space, at least, to mourn.

"It's just a fitting," he said. "It won't hurt."

Thea composed herself as best she could. Maybe at least they could give her a false hand that would look normal if she covered it with a glove, then she could go out without the dreaded stares. She wondered how bulky it would be.

"Good morning, Mr. Huber." Sebastian lifted his hand as

the man walked in, a balding fellow with reddish hair and bright blue eyes.

"Good morning, Mr. Hirsch. I could hardly make sense of your message. What on earth happened here?"

"I had a magical leg and Miss Holder here had a magical hand, and, to make a long story short, the magic went awry."

"I'm afraid I can't compete with a magical limb, though I'll see what I can do for you."

"That's fine," Sebastian said, waving the UWP pamphlet impatiently before putting it down. "I have an ordinary artificial leg now, I've just outgrown it. I don't have time for my body to get in my way—I just need something that fits, and as quickly as possible."

Mr. Huber *tsk*ed at him. "You need to take care of that body of yours, young man, or it'll get in your way whether you like it or not. You look like you haven't slept in days." He opened a bag and rummaged in it, bringing out a few measuring implements. "When you get to be my age . . ." He glanced at Thea.

"What about you, my dear? Are we making an artificial hand or a hook? Or both?"

"Both," Sebastian said. "She should have options."

Thea was starting to tremble. This just sounded so real, and of course, what happened was real. She thought she already knew that, but each new aspect felt like a boot stomping on her chest, leaving her short of breath and wondering what had happened.

She expected Mr. Huber to measure her arm, and was surprised when he also measured her shoulders. "To operate the hook," he explained, "you'll use your opposite shoulder with a slight motion that will come very naturally with practice. It's two hooks, really, that can open and close to grip things through the use of bands."

"That sounds bulky." *And hideous.*

"Not as much as you might fear. It will fit under most clothes without much notice, and you'll soon find you can do almost everything you used to do. I've helped men who lost both hands and are able to live quite normal lives. Thanks to all these conflicts, people have come up with very functional solutions."

There was that word again, "functional." No one described hands as functional, because they were so much more than that. Slender. Beautiful. Expressive. Deft. Soft. She forced herself to display good spirits as he took a plaster cast of her arm, but storm clouds gathered inside her. Mr. Huber had said she might have "quite" a normal life—she didn't need him to tell her that normal life was over.

FORTY

"My name is Marlis Horn. Most of you will know me as the Chancellor's daughter." Her voice echoed through the theater, hundreds of faces staring back at her in the darkness. She kept returning to Wilhelmina and General Wachter. *They actually came.*

She'd had no idea if they would even respond to her invitation. Wilhelmina looked confused, while Wachter kept surveying the surroundings—a drab but spacious venue in the bohemian district of Langstrasse—like he expected an ambush. Wachter had brought enough of his own men to fill three rows of threadbare chairs. They looked out of place in their sharp uniforms. She expected more were watching the place outside, but in here they were outnumbered by over a hundred revolutionaries and several hundred more common people.

"At least," she said, "that's who I *thought* my father was. Three days ago, he gave me this letter." She held the letter up as evidence. The audience wouldn't recognize his handwriting from their seats, but the very suggestion of its existence made

Wachter sit up a little straighter. Wilhelmina looked at him. Marlis couldn't make out their expressions in the dim light.

She read the first part of the letter aloud. "'And then we tried to capture the Norns. You were the only one we could find.' This, you see, was my father's dying confession to me."

The audience rumbled. The capitol had not announced her father's death yet.

Her heart was beating so fast, she had to pause for breath. She couldn't even look at the Wachters, only Volland standing on the sidelines. He gently nodded that she was doing fine. She'd been worried she might speak too fast.

"He adopted me to test whether or not magic was real, if legends were true, while never mentioning these legends to me. I grew up loving my father and this modern nation with all my heart—but I have always been different. At night, I heard strange music. Just dreams, he told me. My eyes are not always able to see colors. He told me it was a 'condition.'

"Whatever spark of strange power lived inside of me, my father smothered, just as he smothered my own voice when he asked me to give a speech on the radio to reinforce his lies."

Her voice shook. She paused to steady herself. She had lost herself so many times in the power of the opera house, she couldn't falter now that she finally had the stage. "I have learned the truth," she said, sweeping her eyes across them all. "I speak, for the first time, as myself. I am a guardian of magic and of the people. Some of you will have heard the legends of the three fates who protect the tree Yggdrasil, deep in the northern forest."

She sensed skepticism, but continued. "The Norns are reborn again and again. I am Urd. I have lived countless lives. I am also still Marlis, who loves Urobrun with all her heart."

When she paused again, an agitated murmuring of voices filled the room all the way up to the balcony. The sound was harsh, as this theater was only carpeted down the aisles. It was cold, too. Her hands were growing numb. She heard a few questions called from different directions and shook her head.

"Urobrun broke away from Irminau," she said. "And then it shook off the ancient tradition of emperors and kings. With each incarnation, we become better and bolder and freer. All I want from you is to fight with me for a world in which no one needs to live in suffering. Though I know most of you will not believe me, you deserve the truth after all these years of my father's lies. And his final lie? It was his own death. When my father was shot three days ago, I was there as it happened. I watched him die."

The rumbling rose. Wachter started to stand up. Wilhelmina clutched his arm, but she met Marlis's eyes, the question in them plain.

"Down with the Chancellor!" someone shouted. "Down with the Republic!"

Now Wachter did stand, and all his men stood with him. They sat near the front, so they all turned back to the revolutionaries in the audience.

What am I doing? Marlis thought. She had thought if the Wachters heard the truth straight from her, they might see the right path before them. But if they didn't . . . *This could turn into a bloodbath. The Wachters came at my invitation. If they open fire on the revolutionaries—*

Even though Sebastian had arranged for heavy security, she was no longer sure who had control.

"Listen!" She lifted her arms, trying to draw the room's attention back. The wyrdsong was a pulsing rhythm in her mind. Her diaries said the wyrdsong would show people the path of fate. This was the moment to share the song that her father had asked her to keep locked away.

But as Wachter looked back at her again, she struggled to believe she had ever been anyone but Marlis. Her arms lowered and her mouth was dry.

How do I share it with them, exactly? It doesn't have words.

Wachter motioned for her to step down from the stage. *Just come quietly, I don't want an incident,* his expression said.

Marlis faltered, unwilling to concede but just as unable to find her voice. The wyrdsong had always been with her. Papa wanted to have her as his daughter, he claimed to be proud of her, but he didn't want to face what she truly was. He wanted her to be just like her mother, brushing off her differences with lies. And as much as she had loved her mother . . .

I am different. I am more than you allowed me to be.

He had made her believe she had no power, except that which he was willing to give.

The wyrdsong burst into Marlis's mind. Her body became a willing vessel for that strange sound. Her mouth opened as visions of Yggdrasil crossed her mind. When she shut her eyes, the outlines of branches, bright as lightning, spread around her.

But the magic went beyond her voice. The planks of the stage beneath her feet vibrated like a small earthquake had rocked the stage.

Marlis tried to pull back, and at first the wyrdsong didn't want to let her go. It had a terrible beauty that left her torn between surrender and struggle. She wasn't sure how much time passed, with the entire theater caught in her thrall. It might have been one minute, it might have been ten. Time was meaningless in that stream of sound.

And then it suddenly passed like a thunderstorm moving on, leaving a silent theater.

Marlis hardly understood what had moved through her. She touched her lips, her face, as if she expected to have changed into some new form. She smoothed her expression, knowing everyone had seen her alarm.

Wachter stepped into the aisle. He staggered, like he was dizzy, and clutched his stomach. "Marlis." His voice shook.

"What do you think, General?" Marlis rattled the letter. "Did Papa do right by your men when he brought them back from the dead?"

He looked to Wilhelmina. She reached for him. He didn't return the gesture.

Marlis was braced for Wachter to launch an attack.

"No," Wachter said gently. "I don't believe he did. Nor did I."

Marlis watched in horror as General Wachter got down on his knees. "I knew who you were. I just didn't know the power you had. I didn't know." He lowered his head like he was waiting for execution. "I'm guilty. I'm guilty."

She had taken his shaking voice and his terrible expressions for anger, and now she realized that he was breaking down before her eyes. Marlis stepped down from the stage.

"Sir!" Wachter's second in command had rushed to his side. "What are you doing?"

"She's right. I have been an evil man."

Marlis could feel hundreds of eyes upon her as she walked down the aisle to Wachter's side. They were hungry to see someone pay for the city's sins. Their whispers combined into something like a low growl.

"General Wachter, I asked you to come tonight in the hopes that you would work with me." She spoke carefully. "You have valuable information and skills."

"Your magic brings up every sin, and I have too many." He suddenly coughed up a mouthful of blood. He reached out a hand, and she took it without thinking.

Visions cut through her mind. Wachter, in her forest. Wachter, giving the order to shoot the Norns on sight. Wachter's men, dragging the corpse of a woman to him, to show that it was done. Wachter commanding the body to be destroyed.

It was me.

Wachter, approaching Yggdrasil. She was inside his head, the moment he saw Yggdrasil's beauty, the heavy branches lush with leaves that seemed a brighter green than any tree in the forest. She felt his awe—his sorrow that he had been ordered to destroy it. She saw him standing rapt, thinking of comforting memories of picking berries with his grandmother. But those days were long gone. The men were somber, but they did what they had come to do. Yggdrasil was felled.

He killed me.

She saw herself again, now an infant in his arms, being presented to her parents.

My father made the decisions, but Wachter carried them out.

"I—want—this—" he choked. "It's too late for anything else—" He reached for Wilhelmina's hand. She looked sober, as though she expected this moment. "I'm sorry, Willa. I'm sorry . . . Marlis."

He slumped forward, Wilhelmina still holding his hand. She lowered his body to the ground gently. Marlis had her hands mussed into her hair; she looked at Wilhelmina. "I didn't know the wyrdsong would—"

All those hungry eyes were still upon Marlis.

Wilhelmina was a regal statue in a black dress. "He never forgave himself," she said, so quietly that Marlis could barely hear her over the shouting in the room. Then she abruptly turned away and left, as the chorus of revolutionaries cried, "He deserved it!" "Guilty!" "Bastard!"

Shots fired. Marlis didn't know which side had taken the initiative.

"Come on! Come on!" One of Sebastian's guards pulled a gun out of his coat and muscled Marlis toward the exit.

Doors swung open in the back of the theater. The army rushed around the aisles as the crowd flooded toward the exit. Marlis kept her head down and her grip tight around the arm of Sebastian's guard. An elbow jabbed her ribs, a man stepped on her foot, as some people struggled to reach the doors and others rushed to fight.

One of Wachter's soldiers fired at Marlis—or close to her, at least. It was difficult to tell in the chaos. A woman screamed nearby. Marlis covered her head with her hands.

Sebastian's guards fired back, catching one soldier in the leg. Some of the UWP rushed in to provide Marlis further cover. Marlis sucked in the night air as they fled out of the theater toward their car. At last, she flung herself through the door, unsure whether she had been a hero or a villain.

FORTY-ONE

When she safely reached home, Marlis locked herself in her room to be alone with her diaries and her rattled nerves. Freddy knocked on the door, but she turned him away.

"I feel sick," she said.

"Do you need anything?"

"Only to be left alone."

She didn't sleep, but stayed up reading the diaries, searching for solace that she never found. The person she had been in the past never seemed conflicted, even when she had to dole out punishment.

In the morning, Volland came to see her, and although she had been so glad when he agreed to follow her here, now it was almost painful to see a familiar face. She wanted to cry to him, and she didn't have that kind of relationship with Volland. She didn't have that relationship with anyone.

"Marlis," he said gently. "It would not have gone well for General Wachter anyway. You know the revolutionaries are going to dredge up every detail of who did what and who knew what, and then hold trials. Every person who had a family member laboring underground will demand that. He wouldn't want to be executed or imprisoned or exiled. It's just as well."

"I knew him all my life . . ." She didn't even know what to say anymore.

Volland gave her an awkward shoulder pat. He hesitated, searching for words, before saying, "It was a brave thing to do." Then he left. She did feel better from this, but it wasn't enough.

When she emerged from her room, Sebastian approached her in the hall. He was only limping a little now, so he must have gotten a properly fitted leg. And he looked excited. "Well, well. The city is all abuzz about you this morning," he said. "A copy of your speech is already circulating. I'm not sure everyone knows what to make of the Norn story, but we can put out our own literature and get it sorted out. Are you all right?"

"You must have heard about General Wachter."

"Yes, I talked to Volland. He said you were fairly close to Mrs. Wachter."

She nodded, but no explanation quite captured her feelings. She tried to shake it off. Nothing to be done now. "Is there really a copy of my speech out there? I'd like to see it."

"I'll obtain one for you."

⊙-⊙-⊙-⊙

In a manner of days, Marlis had the political attention she had always wished for. Her words circulated throughout the city. First, the copy of her speech—full of inaccuracies that made the revolutionaries sound better. Then she released an official transcript, adding additional material on the history of the Norns, drawing quotes from her diaries.

One afternoon Freddy approached her with a poster rolled up in his hand. "Looks like someone has become the poster girl for the revolution."

"Oh no."

"Lucas just brought it in." He unfolded the paper to reveal a stylized modern girl with severe black bob and round glasses, lifting her hand in the revolutionary salute, with bold lettering that said THE FACE OF MODERN MAGIC.

"I would never do the revolutionary salute!" She tried to grab the poster, but he lifted it out of reach.

"No use ripping it up," he said. "They said it's plastered everywhere. Shouldn't you be proud? What did you want that speech to accomplish, if not something close to this?"

"Hmm," she said, not wanting to admit he was right.

"I know. Sometimes getting what you want isn't quite as good as it sounds," he said.

She wanted even less to admit he was right about that as well.

⊙–⊙–⊙–⊙

The last pieces of her world crumbled in the few weeks following her speech, now that so many pillars of the old guard had fallen—Roderick Valkenrath, Vice Chancellor Walther, her father, General Wachter. Gerik was taken to trial. Others resigned. Brunner was appointed chancellor in a hastily arranged election, and UWP members took all the minister positions.

Sebastian insisted on patience as this unfolded. "We have to let the dust settle," he said. "Your strategy has been perfect. You're above all this ugly negotiation. If Brunner goes down, he won't drag you with him."

"But we must design some better posters," she said, "where I am not giving the UWP salute!"

She didn't listen to a word of Brunner's inauguration. Deep down, the UWP would always feel like her enemies, and she hated being lauded for killing Wachter. The new poster-girl Marlis felt as fake as the one who had given a speech for her father.

Her father's words had never felt more true. *All politics is a game.* Even when you told the truth, it seemed that truth had a life of its own.

FORTY-TWO

"Do you recognize this place?" Ingrid asked, as the spires of a town came into view in the valley ahead. She did not usually walk beside Nan on their travels, but stayed with her men, leaving Nan and Sigi guarded but set apart.

The entire landscape was deeply familiar to Nan. They had walked through thick forests that smelled of evergreens and clean snow and memories. They crossed rolling pastures and passed farmhouses with cheerful lines of wood smoke reaching straight for the cloudy winter skies. But the town that lay before them did stir something even deeper with its particular makeup of church spires and the crumbling stone walls wrapped around it.

For a moment, as she looked at the town, the soft colors of winter bloomed in her vision. The sky was not pure gray, as she thought, nor the snow only white. Both held layers of blue: gray-blue clouds across the sky, purple-blue shadows beneath the trees. The snowcapped roofs of the town reflected the setting sun, turning golden.

The vision was there only for an instant.

We were happy here, Nan thought. The sight of this town seemed to promise a warm fire and good food.

"Did we live here once?" Nan asked.

"Close," Ingrid said. "This is Rauthenburg. The Mariendorfs lived here. They were friends of ours across several lifetimes, who gave us a place to stay when we traveled between the north and south—or Irminau and Urobrun, as we know the regions now. Urd always thought them a little too loud, but then, she thought that of most people."

"Will we stay with them now?" Nan asked.

"I lost touch with the current generation, and I wouldn't impose when we have such a large group. We'll stay at a hotel."

As they walked into town, the memories grew thicker. Small shops and vendor stalls crowded the main street. Witches once sold charms and potions here, but she didn't see any of them now. She remembered a cloth vendor that she had particularly liked, although she couldn't recall what kinds of cloth she used to buy.

"I'm feeling so oddly homesick," she whispered to Sigi.

"For the past?" Sigi asked.

"I don't know. For this town. I don't know if you can be homesick for a place when you're in it, but I am. I'm a stranger now."

Nan had barely been outside of the neighborhood where she'd grown up, much less the city of Urobrun itself. Just as a part of her was homesick, another part of her felt it was all new. She was delighted at the sight of old frame cottages and the narrow, curving streets that followed the natural slopes of the hilly landscape. It grew dark so early now that it was near the shortest day of the year, and streetlamps turned the snow bright. Doors and balconies were decked with evergreens. It was all like a scene from a storybook. Thea would have been peering at all the pastries and dolls in shop windows.

The charm was finally broken when six men in uniforms, with epaulets and tall boots, approached Ingrid as if they had been expecting her.

"Lady Skuld," the one in front said, bowing. "Baron Best." His clothes were finer than the rest, with an array of medals pinned to his chest, a cape, and a peaked hat edged in fur, but he was a ferocious-looking man. His dark beard fell across the collar of his uniform, and his eyes were pale. "King Otto told me you were coming. Some of my men shall escort you to the capital. For tonight, I have the pleasure of entertaining you."

"Thank you." Ingrid didn't bow or curtsy in return.

"You all must be tired. We have reserved space at Traveler's Hotel for tonight."

Ingrid nodded. "Lead the way, Baron."

Nan felt pinched inside at every mention of his status. They had really arrived, to this land of royalty. Baron Best didn't look or sound like the Irminauers Nan was familiar with. He must come out of the far north, where snowcapped mountains cut a rugged border between Irminau and the small countries beyond, which were even more wild and strange. When he walked down the street, people scurried out of the way. He was almost seven feet tall with his hat. He and all his men were armed with pistols and sabers.

"Whoa, it's the Six Swordsmen of Salandra," Sigi said, referencing a swashbuckler movie from last year.

Nan grinned. "But Remy Paul is only a hair over five feet in real life," she said.

"Did you ever serve him, then? At the Telephone Club?" Sigi asked.

Nan nodded. "Once. He was very nice. And he tips well, too. But his favorite waitress was Pauline."

"Really? I thought you'd tell me he was a cad. Nearly all the famous actors I've ever met were. I used to pretend to be Remy Paul when I was a kid, back when he was in *Master of the Seas*. My mother was very chagrined that I used her makeup to paint a mustache on my face."

"That explains your adventurous streak." Nan tried to relax into the chatter and not think of the fact that the Irminau army had joined them.

The sun was setting as they followed Baron Best to the hotel. Royal flags fluttered from the roof of the white-and-gold building, and electric lights shone on the snow heaped around the sidewalks. The hotel had probably been built twenty or thirty years before, but compared to all the older houses and shops in the rest of town, it seemed almost offensively new, and the lobby smelled of fresh paint and furniture polish. A portrait of King Otto hung over the desk, a sharp-eyed, dark-haired man wearing an ermine robe, who bore a faint resemblance to Sebastian.

Bellhops took their bags, and the baron showed them into a dining room that had been reserved entirely for their party.

Nan was not invited to Ingrid's table—or was it really Baron Best's table? She could see them from afar, the baron leaning toward Ingrid, while she seemed even smaller than usual, listening to him speak with a steady, unreadable gaze. Her body language did not suggest trust.

Waitresses brought around plates heaped with food and glasses of wine. The room was already noisy with the men talking, and the arrival of food did nothing to slow the conversation. This was good, because she could barely hear the man beside her, and had to lean in to speak to Sigi. It was the most privacy she and Sigi had had since they'd left.

"So," Sigi said. "Here we are. Irminau. Should we have another toast? To our own insanity?"

"Why not." They clinked wineglasses.

"I didn't expect to be met by the military," Sigi said. "This is already unnerving, and we just got here. He seemed to expect Ingrid."

"I'm sure she's been sending messages as we travel," Nan said. "She seems well connected."

"I don't know how that happened," Sigi said. "She rarely even talks!"

A curtain had risen on a stage with a prop cow. Now a girl in a very short milkmaid costume swished out and began to sing a flirtatious song about being lonely on the farm, fluttering her eyelashes at various men in the audience. Sigi snickered and then turned back to Nan.

"This reminds me so much of Mitterburg," Sigi said. "We used to go up every single year in the winter to the lodges for skiing and the hot springs. In fact, my father got me my first camera so I could take pictures on vacation. I always liked being there, the way the air smelled."

"Are you saying you're a country girl at heart?"

"Quite possibly. I'd miss my friends if I left the city, but it was strange being around them, anyway."

"You seemed in your element."

"I guess I'm good at pretending. And I love my friends. I just felt odd the whole time. And Urobrun has such bad memories now. I'll always think of what happened underneath the sidewalks." Sigi picked the large forest mushrooms out of her meat, apparently disliking them. "I try not to let on how much all that haunts me. We have enough to worry about."

"If Irminau and Urobrun did reunite, do you think you'd want to move out of the city?"

"Maybe. I could get a little apartment over a shop, like the ones here. Work in a café or someplace nice, and take pictures."

"I used to say I'd be a dressmaker," Nan said, "and Thea would be my assistant. I wanted to rescue her. She worked so hard, and she was so worried all the time. But it would never happen. I knew that."

"It could happen, when this is all over."

"When this is all over . . ." Nan tilted her wineglass, watching the dark liquid glow in the candlelight. "I find that hard to imagine."

Sigi and Nan had barely touched each other since they met up with Ingrid again. She was trying to pretend to agree to Ingrid's wishes, and Irminau was a more conservative country besides. But Sigi's hand suddenly clasped Nan's under the table. "It'll work out."

As they crossed through the lobby after dinner, a man jostled past her with his suitcase. Nan thought nothing of it until she felt a mysterious paper in her pocket. One of Sebastian's messengers?

She says it lives, but it must feed.

Nan instantly suspected the meaning of the note. The "she" must be Ingrid. The "it" must be Yggdrasil, which she claimed she had saved from death by planting a new tree.

It must feed. The way the revived workers needed serum, or they would crave human blood. Was this note from Freddy?

The Norns could return from the dead, but perhaps that was because of Yggdrasil's magic. If Yggdrasil was the source of magic, then where did the magic to revive the tree come from?

FORTY-THREE

The apartment door swung open, and Mother's eyes welled on the spot. "Thea. I got your letter, I—"

"I'm okay. Please don't cry." But Thea had to wipe away tears herself. "I—I would've come sooner, and I know I should have, but I've been trying so hard just to be strong, and I worried it would all collapse if I saw you." Thea walked in, going slightly limp at the sight of home. She felt like she hadn't seen this place in years.

"Have they been taking care of you, the revolutionaries?"

Thea nodded. "Like I told you in the letters." She noticed one letter, sitting on the table, looking crumpled, as if Mother had balled it up in her hand. Maybe more than once. Thea had been writing since the day after she broke free, but now weeks had passed. "Sebastian's making sure I'm all right. We're in the same position."

But Mother could spot a lie. "Are you?"

"Well, he understands, anyway, on account of his leg."

"He got you a job."

Thea shrugged one shoulder. "I'm not working yet, but I will be, soon."

"It seems much too soon for you to go to work."

"Everyone is working so hard. I can't just sit around feeling sorry for myself."

Mother nodded. "I suppose so. I just don't want you to suffer any more than you already have." She suddenly put her arms around Thea. "Oh dear. I have to hug you. You should've come sooner."

"I couldn't. I didn't want to cry." She was crying now. "I missed you so much, but it's easier to be tough with strangers."

"You don't have to be tough all the time. Not with me, not anymore." Her mother pulled back to look at her and smooth her hair, but Thea looked down. It was so painful here. She didn't know how to explain that it was too late. She'd been tough for so long, sadness didn't feel allowed.

"Sit down," Mother said. "I don't suppose you want anything to eat?"

"No."

Mother had put her winter arrangement of pinecones on the table. Thea smiled that Mother still bothered to make the house festive, even when she was living alone and the city was on the brink of war. That was how she used to be, before the bound-sickness. "I wouldn't mind some tea, if you still have that."

"I do." Mother put the kettle on, then stepped back toward the dining table. She glanced at Thea's hands, which were still in her pockets. She'd had them in her pockets the whole time.

Thea frowned slightly. She didn't know how to show her mother what had happened. She didn't want to make a big deal of it. She certainly didn't want to make her cry, but she feared that was impossible.

"Do you feel you'll manage the job all right?" Mother asked.

"I've been practicing. I can fit a tray between my elbow and the prosthetic and serve from there." She had trouble saying the word "hook," much like the word "stump," although she was blunt with herself within her mind. She added, trying to be reassuring, "It isn't quite as hard to use as I thought it might be."

"The hook, you mean?"

Thea nodded, trying not to cringe. "Or maybe I'm just determined. That's what Sebastian says."

"Sebastian is rather young, isn't he?" Mother asked, and now Thea could tell she must have given something away by the way she said his name.

"I guess," she said, noncommittally. Mother obviously wasn't fooled, but the teakettle was whistling, and she took it off the gas and poured out a cup.

"Just be careful," she said. She set down the teacup. "You're allowed to take your hands out of your pockets. I promise I won't cry."

Thea, feeling hot with discomfort, pulled out her hands. In plural, they were still hands to her. She had been trying to wear the hook most of the time, since Mr. Huber had brought it, even though it had felt frustrating and cumbersome, especially at first. The hooks opened when she extended her arm or moved her right shoulder, and it wasn't intuitive to move her right shoulder to use her left arm.

"Your father would be proud of you." Mother took the chair

next to her. "We had to face all this when he was called up to fight—the prospect that he could be injured. When you say good-bye to a soldier, you don't know how they'll come back. And they try to be brave, but . . . they're just young men. It's not an easy thing, but it will get better with time."

"I know," Thea said gently. Mother was obviously not speaking just to Thea, but to her own struggles as well.

Mother smiled a little. "I suppose you're tired of comforting speeches by now. It sounds like Sebastian may have given you a few."

"Well, it's not the same," Thea said. "I'm glad you're getting better, too." She squeezed Mother's hand, and they drank their tea.

⊙–⊙–⊙–⊙

Thea could manage the days. It was the nights when the weight of her losses and the uncertain future crushed her. She woke from nightmares into a dark room.

She took to stepping outside the room and walking up and down the hall. At least a few men were always up downstairs, listening to the radio, waiting for messengers who might come at any hour. She didn't join them, but she listened to the sound of their voices, just to know she wasn't alone, and after a while she would calm down enough to sleep.

One night Sebastian found her pacing. "Thea? What's wrong?"

"Nightmares." She drew her robe closer around her pajamas. "I'll be glad to work at night again. The sun would rise just a few hours after I came home. It was easier to sleep when it wasn't so dark and quiet. I felt safe hearing kids going to school and birds chirping."

"I understand." He looked hesitant.

"Why are you up?" Thea asked. "Do you ever sleep?" He was even still wearing daytime clothes, albeit wrinkled ones.

"I nap."

"That can't be good for you."

"'You need to take care of that body of yours, young man.'" He mimicked Mr. Huber's aged voice and shook his finger.

Thea smiled. "Well, he was a little bit right."

The hesitancy was back as he scratched his head. "The— um. I mean, do you want to . . . if you can't sleep anyway . . . have a cup of coffee with me?"

She hadn't seen him much in the month since Ingrid left. Once the Chancellor's death was known, everything had happened very quickly, and he needed to keep up. Many of the existing officials surrendered, a few fled, several more were killed or captured. There was a constant round of messengers and meetings, and he had spent much of his time at UWP headquarters, keeping abreast of the latest developments.

"You drink too much coffee," she said.

"I know I do. We might run out. How about cocoa, then?"

He cut a strong figure in the dim hallway, with broad shoulders and a slim waist. His hair grew more unkempt as the revolution turned toward the serious business of governing the country, and his stubble was now halfway toward a beard. It seemed unfair that he was still wearing regular clothes while she had on faded pink pajamas with a scraggly bow tie in front and thick gray wool socks. She covered the end of her left arm reflexively.

"Come on, no sense in lying awake thinking dark thoughts." He held out his hand. She took it, her face growing hot even as her feet froze against the wooden floors.

Due to electricity restrictions, just a few lamps lit the downstairs. Sebastian picked up the one by the entrance hall. She heard a card game going on around the radio.

"If you want to wait in the parlor, I'll get the cocoa," he said.

She felt along the walls and stumbled around the furniture until she reached the curtains and opened them to let in the moonlight. She sat on the sofa, bound up with curious anticipation. Her mouth was dry. She tried to straighten out the bow on her pajamas.

"Here we are." He walked in with two mugs. She didn't care about drinking the cocoa so much as simply holding something warm. She missed the feeling of wrapping both hands around a warm mug on a cold night. He sat on the other end of the sofa, but he didn't seem to know what to say.

It wasn't easy to talk about nightmares and insomnia and political coups.

"Thea, I—"

She looked at him expectantly.

"I feel like I haven't seen you much lately," he said.

"I've been around. You've been busy, if you haven't noticed."

"I've been too busy to notice. But . . . I wondered if maybe you feel differently about me since you found out who I am."

She tugged nervously at the bow, ruining her earlier attempt to fix it. "It *was* a surprise."

"I'm still the same person," he said, the slightest undercurrent of desperation running beneath his casual tone.

"Of course. It just—it does change some things."

"Does it? It doesn't have to."

"I guess it depends on how we felt about each other. To begin with."

He coughed like he'd swallowed his cocoa wrong. "I . . . I want to say that when we danced, that one night, I know we were both enchanted. I was trying to figure out what Ingrid had done to you—that is, I had a sense of dread even though I couldn't think straight to place it."

"I remembered you mentioned feeling haunted."

"Yes. Well—I just want to say, I liked dancing with you. And I'm always happy to see you."

She looked at him shyly, pleased that he was flustered.

He continued, "I know I threw a lot at you as soon as you lost your hand, suggesting you go back to work in public. I thought about when I lost my leg and I hid in my room and moped for some months. I didn't feel better until I started doing things again. Maybe it was presumptuous of me—"

"No, you were right," she said. "It helps to have a goal."

"Good." He gazed at her a moment, and shifted his hand a little closer, like he was thinking of touching her face. "Thea, I—"

She smiled a little. "Sebastian . . ."

"I think Freddy is a good sort. We have a lot in common. And I certainly wouldn't want to get on his bad side, with powers like his. I don't want to say anything to you when I'm not sure where you stand with him."

She looked down. "I did have feelings for him. I mean, I still do. But it's different with you." She had never liked Freddy so much that she felt sick to her stomach like she did now.

Sebastian put down his mug, and then he took hers and put it down, too. Thea's skin tingled as he leaned in closer and kissed her. He slid his fingers into her hair and around her back, and his warm mouth met hers. Her body seemed to know just what to do even though she'd never kissed anyone like this before. Her leg draped over his knee, and he leaned into her, his weight comforting as she fell back against the arm of the couch. She ran her palm across his rough cheek and then she clutched the dark hair that fell, a little too long for fashion, to his collar. This felt so wonderful it frightened her.

She had already lost so much.

When he pulled back, her mouth felt bruised. He looked at her, a wicked spark in his eyes. "You . . ."

"Me? You started it."

"Yeah, I did."

"You've probably kissed a lot of girls like that before, when you were Mr. Ski Daredevil."

"Nah. I'm actually shy with girls."

"I can't tell."

"Well, Mr. Ski Daredevil was only sixteen. I didn't know how to make a move. And when you're heir to the throne, girls—and their mothers—are often scheming to get close to you. . . ."

"I see," she said, sobered by the reminder of his position.

"I don't want that anymore," he said softly. "I'm not sure

I even want to unite the countries and lead them. That was Ingrid. She whispered those things in my ear."

"Really? But you seem to genuinely like being a leader."

"I do. I like the *work*. That's why I work too much. I am genuinely interested in how the UWP is currently handling the rebuilding of government, and thinking about what I want to do differently, and strategizing the impending war. But the position? That I hate." He rubbed his face like he was trying to snap out of a bad dream. "I didn't think I'd admit that to anyone. Don't talk about this."

"Never."

"If so many people weren't counting on me . . ." He leaned back, but slung his arm around her. "Well, I can't back out now."

"You *could*," Thea said. "You're not at the forefront right now. Why not just support the UWP? Stick with political writing?"

"I'm fickle, Thea. I want to call the shots, I just don't want the attention. Sometimes I feel like Prince Rupert is another person who has been hunting me down for years, and I never know when he might find me."

"Sometimes anticipation is the worst part, though. It's like going to work after losing a hand. At least, I hope the anticipation is worse."

"It is, I promise. You're right. We build up these things in our minds." He took her left arm and held it to his chest, much the same way Freddy had. This brought back a new surge of guilt and worry. She didn't want Freddy to be hurt. She knew that day when he came back and found out what had happened, he had reached for her arm because he wanted her to know he still found her beautiful. Freddy was kind and brave and empathetic and strong, and she didn't know why he paled next to Sebastian. She felt like a terrible person, especially for having kissed him. It would be a little easier had she not made that bold move.

"Sebastian . . ." She drew back. "I am worried about Freddy. He lost everything. I'm afraid if he loses me, too—"

"You won't do him any favors by stringing him along."

"I know. But I've led him to believe that I just can't think about relationships now. I feel like . . . if we could find his parents, at least. I don't want to be so cruel as to carry on with you right in front of him when he has no one else."

Sebastian made a noise of frustration. "You're right. I can make inquiries about his parents. I don't think they'll be a substitute for you, though."

FORTY-FOUR

Standing in front of the mirror, Thea tucked her left arm behind her.

Now you look the part. For her first night at work, Thea wore a dark crimson dress with black buttons, paired with a plain black hat with an asymmetrical brim in the new style that fitted close to the head and curved around the forehead, both darker than her usual clothes. She had done her makeup a little darker, too, to match the image of Café Scorpio.

But when she brought her left arm forward again, the hook was all she could see. She couldn't imagine her customers' eyes would be any more forgiving.

Remember your first day at the Telephone Club? She had never had a beau, just that one school dance with a boy named Peter—she'd liked him but had not talked much because she didn't want him to know about her home life. And suddenly, there she was, talking to dozens of strange men. Some of them leered or said scandalous things. Her fellow waitresses seemed so worldly wise.

This still isn't the same, she thought, a lump rising in her throat. She had learned to act worldly wise. But she could never get her hand back. She rubbed her left arm, regarding the prosthetic. Before Mr. Huber brought the hook, she had imagined some monster's claw, but the reality was practical, almost dainty in comparison to her imagination.

Of all the things I've faced, why does having people stare at me seem the hardest? It certainly wasn't the worst. She would give up her other hand to have her father back. *And you wouldn't want to hide away forever.*

She faced the mirror again, keeping both arms in view. This job was far different than the Telephone Club, anyway. She wasn't there to be pretty, but to wheedle out as much information from patrons as she could. Perhaps if people asked about her injury, she could use her story to get them to confide in her. A real spy would use every angle at her disposal. This was her first step toward a life that mattered, a life that went far beyond serving drinks in a cute dress.

She grabbed her purse and hurried to the door before she lost her resolve.

Freddy and Sebastian were hanging around downstairs. She smiled nervously. Sebastian winked at her.

"Thea," Freddy said, catching up with her as she was leaving. "I just have to say . . . you look amazing."

"Thanks. Really." She hesitated, trying to think what to say. "Too bad I'm going to ruin it when I put my coat on." The only coats she'd been able to find at the stores were hideous, so she was now the proud owner of a green-and-gold plaid coat that didn't match anything.

"Be careful out there," he said.

"Sebastian's sending a guard to escort me there and back."

He nodded. "Good luck."

Sebastian's right. I can't string him along. But I can't tell him I like him less. What possible way could I say that? He already has to deal with his awful magic; he can't even leave the house.

She had to stop thinking about it.

A light snowfall had just ended, and the dirty piles from prior days surrounded the sidewalks. Thea drew fresh air into her lungs, savoring the sharp cold. A few young people were milling about on the street, looking at the house. They were probably hoping to see Marlis. Every day people came around wanting to see her with their own eyes, after all the posters and pamphlets and rumors.

But it was a little eerie how empty the city still was only days before the winter holidays. Normally people would fill the sidewalks to shop the markets and ice-skate on the river, and windows would glow with light from evening parties. A lot of the wealthier people, the ones with second homes in the country, had moved out of the city until the situation was more secure.

Nor was Lampenlight the place it had been. The street-lamps shone, but all the bright, dancing neon signs that had once defined this strip of the city were out, thanks to the harsh new decrees on electricity usage. The dancing legs over the Demimonde Club were now just severed limbs looming dark over the building. The moon, for once, was bright in Lampenlight, no longer drowned by human invention.

Café Scorpio was closer to the north end of the district than the Telephone Club, occupying the basement of a narrow brick building. Incense burners hung from brass poles on either side of the entrance, sending wisps of smoke up into the bluish light of dusk.

Thea walked into a small foyer with an empty hostess desk. A beaded curtain suggested exotic wonders beyond. Lamps with frosted globe shades set in intricate iron mounts ran along the wall, and the walls themselves were made of wooden panels with equally ornate edgework. Thea pulled the bell marked "For Service." The proprietress, Miss Helm, had asked her to come early for orientation, so the building was quiet.

The beads clinked softly as Miss Helm stepped through them, her hair a cloud of black frizz streaked with white. Heavy black kohl ringed her eyes, and pale makeup didn't quite hide the wrinkles around her mouth. Her dress was plain black but cut unusually, with a capelet and a sharp ruffle over each shoulder.

"Hello," Thea said a little warily. "I'm Thea Holder, here about the job."

"Yes, yes. I know all about you from Mr. Hirsch." Miss Helm motioned her into the back.

"Good things, I hope," Thea said, trying to sound light-hearted.

"You might be his agent, but I'm still going to treat you like any of my girls."

"I mean to take the job seriously," Thea said. "Did he tell you I worked at the Telephone Club for a year?"

"Oh I wouldn't have obliged him if you didn't have any experience. And we're never as busy as *that* place." Miss Helm plainly didn't think much of the Telephone Club. "How about your hand? Mr. Hirsch also warned me you might be self-conscious."

"He certainly had a lot to say about me."

"He did." Miss Helm smiled, making Thea wish she knew precisely what he had said. "But I want to assure you that I treat my girls like family. If anyone is cruel to you, I'll show them the door."

"I hope it isn't necessary," Thea said, feeling jittery again.

"Well, just know that I delight in yelling at people, when warranted. Now, I need to run the rules by you, and then I'll show you around the dining room."

The rules were nothing unexpected—codes of dress and conduct. Café Scorpio was much smaller than the Telephone Club: Not even fifty tables filled the floor, and three private rooms stood to the side. There was no dance floor or band pit. The room was so poorly lit, Thea worried she might stumble into things.

"With the power rations we can only light the stage and the exits," Miss Helm said. "But before we open, the waitresses light the candles on every table. And through these doors are the kitchens—I'll give you a menu. A lot of things simply aren't available anymore, I'm afraid. Lately our most popular item is a potato soup. Can you manage the plates and such?" Miss Helm asked, gesturing to Thea's hook. "I know you've had a few weeks by now, but I'm not sure how difficult—"

"I'll manage."

Miss Helm walked her through a food and drink order, and just as she had practiced at home, she held the tray between her left elbow and the edge of the hook, but she wondered how it would all go when she had hungry people staring at her, jostling, some of them tipsy.

FORTY-FIVE

Freddy watched Thea walk away to her new job, wishing he could walk away, too. He couldn't leave the house without risking being captured by Otto's spies, and while he should have been used to it, he had tasted freedom.

"Freddy?" Volland approached as Freddy backed away from the window, embarrassed at being caught staring out like a restless house cat. "We've received a message." His tone implied it was something serious, and Freddy tensed as he took the paper from Volland's shivering hand, worried something might have happened to his parents.

The message was brief, beneath the new Chancellery seal:

Have captured an Irminauer spy. She took poison before questioning. Mr. Linden's presence requested.

"Brunner wants me to revive?" A lump settled into Freddy's stomach.

"Clearly. I think this is worthy of discussion. I'm not sure we should just cave in to this demand."

⊙–⊙–⊙–⊙

Marlis was furious when she saw the note. "He can't just ask for Freddy any time because a spy poisoned herself!"

"It does say 'requested,'" Sebastian said. "It's not a threat."

"But it is very firm," she said.

"Besides, what would he think if I said no?" Freddy asked. "He's known I've existed this whole time, and this is the first time he's requested my magic, so I'm sure he's trying to be reasonable."

"So you want to do it?" Marlis said.

"No," Freddy said. "Not at all. They're trying to question a spy who was prepared to die rather than give answers—what does that mean? Torture? And she won't have an out the second time. It seems such a violation."

"You are right, though. Refusing has its own ramifications." Sebastian had walked in carrying a deck of cards for some reason, and he shuffled them absently as he spoke. "Besides preserving our relationship with Brunner, who *has* been very reasonable, I do wonder what information this spy has? For all we know, it's the one pivotal piece of information we need to win this war."

"I am well aware," Freddy said. But that didn't change the deep resistance that churned inside him. "I don't see how I can refuse. Brunner knows I'm here; I don't want him to get ideas about kidnapping me."

"I'm going with you," Marlis said. "I want to make sure they understand that they can't use you any way they want to."

Considering the tense nature of the mission, Freddy

welcomed backup. "So only you're allowed to use me any way you want to?" he said, unable to resist a jibe as they climbed into the car.

She cut him a sideways look. "I owe you," she said.

At the prison, they were met by several agents, headed by a Mr. Tiersen. All the men had several inches over Freddy, and their muscular shoulders strained their suits. Freddy supposed this group had been hired to intimidate captured prisoners, but it was working just as well on him.

"Thank you for coming, Mr. Linden. This woman was apprehended this morning by our forces in one of the border villages after she was caught searching the base and tried to flee."

"We have no guesses as to her identity?" Marlis asked.

"Possibly Rosa Watts Lang, a known spy, but she doesn't quite fit the descriptions we have. Of course, spies can be tricky that way. She has already proved herself willing to die rather than talk, so I assume it will take time to break her. We'll send a message when she can be released."

Marlis glanced at Freddy.

Freddy already regretted agreeing. He would always regret agreeing, he suddenly realized. He would feel as if he had tortured Rosa Watts Lang with his own hands.

"Sometimes I can feel what they feel," Freddy said. Tiersen was looking at him sharply.

"Define 'sometimes,'" he said. "Do you feel their pain unwillingly, or when you concentrate on them?"

"When I concentrate, but—"

"Then I'd suggest you don't concentrate."

"But when I bring her back . . . things that will kill a living person won't kill her anymore." Freddy faltered as Tiersen's eyes stayed focused on him like the barrel of a gun. "This is wrong beyond what you need her for."

"What did you think would happen when you came here?" Tiersen asked. "She isn't going to talk unless we torture her. We obviously wouldn't do it just for *fun*." Tiersen's shoulders relaxed, so he looked less a brute. "Maybe we should have a drink or two first, relax a little, and we'll talk about what we know now and what we need to know, so you can feel better about the purpose of this interrogation."

But the lump remained in Freddy's stomach. "I know the purpose. Let me just see her." He didn't want to spend any more time with Tiersen than he must. It was useless to fight anymore. They had a corpse full of secrets on their hands, and they would wear him down. He had always known it was useless. He shut the door on his emotions as he followed Tiersen into the room.

The woman's corpse was slumped in a chair, her hands tied behind her, her feet bound as well, the pose already suggesting that she would live again, and she would *talk*. She was small and athletically built, with dark, messy hair and a strong brow. Since her hands were bound, he touched her chin to bring her back.

Her eyes opened and rolled up to look at him groggily, and then struggled against her bonds with sudden panic. Freddy stepped back, turning his gaze to the wall.

"No!" she screamed, as she came further out of the fog. "You *bastards!*"

"You will talk this time," Tiersen said calmly. "You are no longer able to commit suicide."

She shut her eyes, and when she spoke again, her voice was choked with hatred. "The reviver. So it's true."

Freddy moved to the door. Only the insatiable hunger that always followed using his magic kept his dinner in his stomach.

One of the guards quietly opened the door and let him out into the hall. If he concentrated, he could still hear Tiersen's voice in the woman's ears. *If you tell me what your king has planned, this can go easily. If you do not . . . you may want to consider just how much your body can endure.*

Freddy closed himself against her thoughts.

"You don't have to do this," Marlis said in a low voice.

"But I do. If they're willing to torture a woman for information, they aren't going to go easy on me either. It's just that I never used to feel my magic the way I do now. I don't feel her pain physically, but . . ." Freddy lifted a hand to the door. "We could go home now, and I'd still be in that room."

A scream ripped through him—he heard it on the other side of the door, and he felt it deep inside him. He turned his mind to steel. *She works for Otto, and Otto kills magic users. She doesn't deserve my mercy.* But when it came to the moment of touching her skin, giving her life, feeling the invisible bonds between himself and her . . .

A second scream tore out of her mouth, more pained than the last, and—

He cut it off, breaking the spell so violently that it twisted him inside, and he vomited on the cold stone floor.

The door burst open, Tiersen emerging with a brisk step and a face of stone. "We weren't ready to let the prisoner go."

Marlis straightened, tilting her head slightly in a way that very much made her seem like a displeased queen regarding her subject, despite Tiersen's height. "Mr. Tiersen, this will not work," she said. "We can't torture the dead. As Mr. Linden's magic grows more powerful, he is also developing too strong of a connection with the subjects of his spells. We'll hurt him along with them."

"Well—can you bring her back again and we'll try being more . . . patient?"

"No," Marlis said. "He cannot. His magic doesn't work that way."

"We need that information!" Tiersen said. "You should have told me up front not to hurt her."

"I did!" Freddy cried.

"No, not explicitly. You told me not to abuse her revived state."

"There will be other spies," Marlis said, "and we're lucky to have a reviver at all. We have to be careful: If we abuse him, then what did we overthrow my father for?"

Tiersen relented with a minuscule relaxing of his eyebrows. "Well, I hope next time will prove more successful, seeing what's at stake. You know what's at stake, Miss Horn," he said, and Freddy wondered if he meant King Otto or the alliance with the UWP itself.

"I know."

FORTY-SIX

I can't believe I'm about to walk into *Neue Adlerwald.* The motorcars of King Otto's guard had only a short distance to go, down a wide boulevard flanked by white statues, before passing through the royal gates. The palace reached out with two wings that curved around, embracing a formal garden. `Although covered in snow, the shapes of fountains and hedges were apparent.

Nan was piled in with Sigi and four men. She had no idea where they were headed exactly, but the line of cars pulled around to a side entrance and a few men dressed in long coats, tight white pants, and tall boots directed them inside with white-gloved hands.

"Madam, this way, please." Just inside the doors, someone pointed Nan, Sigi, and Ingrid one way while all the men were herded down the opposite corridor. The corridors were long, with high ceilings, so they seemed empty even with sixty people in them.

"Where are we going?" Sigi asked.

"The king wishes to outfit you for court before you enter the palace proper," their attendant said. He was dressed very nicely, and every look he gave them showed his awareness that they were not dressed nicely at all.

"What does *that* mean?" Sigi asked.

"We are rather dirty, I suppose," Ingrid said. "But we would like to keep it as simple as possible."

The attendant said nothing, merely opened a door. At first, Nan was startled to see so many people in the room, but then she realized a row of mannequins was lined up in front of the window clad in jewel-and-brocade costumes inspired by a prior age. If Nan ever had dressmaking nightmares, they might take place in a room like this—even the furniture and curtains had frills and smelled like perfume. Two old ladies with makeup caked on their faces awaited them with placid smiles.

The sight actually stopped Ingrid in her tracks, even as one of the old ladies approached her, bowing slightly. "Welcome, Skuld. I am Margit. You and your ladies must be weary from your travels. Perhaps you would like to bathe before we begin?"

Nan had never seen Ingrid look so out of her element. Then she said, with a threatening note in her voice, "Please tell the king I would prefer to present a humble appearance."

The woman ignored her. "His Majesty is throwing a ball in your honor tonight. He has already selected your gowns. We have been asked to attend to your toilet. Please—Anna will show you to the baths."

"I had a bath last night in the hotel," Sigi said, like she thought the water might poison her.

Nan played along. She didn't want to draw attention. In the bathroom, they each had their own claw-foot tub, separated by privacy curtains. Anna and Margit offered to wash their hair for them, in a tone that suggested they might not know how, but they all refused.

From the baths, they were shown back to the dressing room. Nan was relieved as the two old women brought out modern beaded gowns that fell to the knee; she had feared she might be expected to wear the heavy, antiquated gowns on display with a corset, maybe a powdered wig.

Ingrid stared at the dresses as they came near, her eyes cold as if she'd been betrayed. She backed away when Margit came too close. "I don't wear things like that. I want to see Otto now. I didn't come here for a ball."

"But kings always have balls," Sigi said. "All rich people do, whenever anything good happens."

Ingrid looked at Nan, and Nan suddenly understood her anger. *I know this man, Nan. He is toying with me. He wants me to feel uncomfortable before I even see him.*

Until this moment, Nan had suspected Ingrid might have made some deal with Otto in the past, but it was clear now that whatever their past, she didn't trust the man at all.

Nan nodded at her, very faintly, the same way she nodded to Thea—knowing she would be understood. "I don't mind dressing up tonight," she told Margit. "But Ingrid—or Skuld—is truly a creature of the forest. She wouldn't be comfortable. You have to let her stay in the clothes she has."

"His Majesty does not like anything around him to look shabby and unpleasant," Margit said, but she was twisting her hands, as if trying to decide how much this battle meant to the king.

"She isn't human," Nan said. "Would you tell the trees of the forest they look shabby and unpleasant?"

"No . . ."

"Anyway, the king will have plenty of beautiful gowns to admire," Nan said.

Ingrid sat on the sidelines without further harassment, while Nan and Sigi were dressed. Sigi endured it all with the expression of a wet cat, but Nan couldn't help admiring the gown. She couldn't afford to make beaded gowns like this one. The beads formed a faux belt that crisscrossed her waist, and panels of black tulle gave the skirt a little volume.

"What color is it?" she asked Sigi, when Ingrid wasn't paying attention.

"Mostly black, but the lighter beads are blue and gold," Sigi said. "And mine's *peach*."

"Peach sounds pretty."

"It's a wishy-washy color, if you ask me. I hate pastels."

Anna hustled up behind her and jammed a fan into her hand. "You had better not talk like that around the king."

Once dressed, the palace attendants directed them back to the private cars just so they could drive back to the entrance of Neue Adlerwald. The men were all cleaned up and dressed in nice suits.

Guards stood at attention at the front. The attendants opened the doors—all their movements formal, without words of welcome. The hall beyond the doors was almost completely dark. Nan was a few heads back from Ingrid, who entered first, holding her fair head high and moving with slow formality, even though she was still wearing a homespun dress. Passing under the doors felt like a point of no return, and they were such tall, thick, heavy doors, intricately carved.

Stepping inside, Nan realized why the hall was dark—to showcase a series of large paintings running down both sides of the walls. Each painting occupied its own recessed niche, with lights placed to illuminate the scene, but not to bring it into the stark everyday world, where paintings were merely pigment on canvas. In the darkness of the long passage, the paintings glowed with a life of their own. Each depicted some romantic scene of dragon-slaying or long-haired maidens on a craggy mountaintop or a woman weeping over a slain man in a funeral procession.

At the end of the hall, another set of doors opened to a great entrance room. The ceiling was painted with angels and clouds, and a huge chandelier with thousands of crystals caught the light of tall windows around a balcony above.

At the top of the stairs stood the king with one hand on the stair rail. "Skuld the Norn," he said, his voice similar to Sebastian's, but deeper and more debonair. Maybe Sebastian's accent had grown rougher in his years away. "What happened? You didn't like the clothes I provided? I apologize if I offended in some way."

She remembered that voice, when it had belonged to a younger man—when it had been softer, for her ears alone.

It was definitely the man she had seen in all those paintings, and no disappointment for anyone expecting a regal king. He was perhaps six feet tall, with thick dark hair, sharp eyebrows, and pronounced temples. But she also saw the much younger man in her memories, who had threatened her and locked her away.

"Maybe this plain dress does suit you." King Otto took Ingrid's hand and kissed it. "But I'm told you can't dance?" His fingers still grasped her small wrist.

"If you know anything about the Nornir, sir, you know human music is of no interest to us."

"What a waste. You look like a ballerina. Human food, I hope, is a universal delight. I have planned quite an evening." He snapped his fingers at one of the few servants visible on the sidelines. The castle felt very empty overall, like a museum with Otto as the curator more than a home.

"An evening of productive discussion, I hope," Ingrid said. "I didn't come here to be diverted by pretty clothes and light entertainment—not when Urobrun and Irminau are at war and the fate of magic is at stake."

"One night! One night won't hurt anyone. Your men could use the rest, I'm sure." He narrowed his eyes as he took them all in over his shoulder. "What a ragtag band you have here, but at least it's interesting." He finally noticed Nan. "What are these girls? They aren't—"

"This is my sister Verthandi," Ingrid said, "and her friend."

"You didn't tell me you were bringing your sister." The king reached for her hand and kissed it, too. She was rigid, wondering if he knew she was the same Norn he had killed in the past. Maybe she should have forced a smile, but she considered it an accomplishment to get through the moment without yanking back her hand.

The king led them through a series of fancifully decorated rooms—the first few were painted in light, delicate shades, with artwork depicting young heroes bearing swords, riding horses, and courting ladies with heavy braids. "The rooms of my palace tell a story," he explained. "The salon and the music room represent the innocence of childhood and the idealism of youth."

The next room had walls that were a deep red—Nan saw flashes out of the corner of her eyes like warnings—with swords and armor decorating the walls.

"This room, of course, is innocence lost, man's realization of his power," Otto said.

As they moved through the palace, a few ladies of the court appeared briefly down halls or from balconies. They never joined the party, but watched from afar with shy smiles and whispers. Their modern clothes didn't seem to fit their behavior.

The dining room was nautical in theme, with carved fish on the chairs and a centerpiece of a long wooden boat sailing through a sea of fruit and candy, and here they were asked to sit, with Otto, Ingrid, and Nan at one end, with a few of Otto's men separating them from the rest. Sigi gave her an apologetic wave as she was shunted off to sit next to Andre and Marco, familiar faces among Sebastian's men. She would probably have a much better time than Nan.

"You have traveled so far through this ghastly cold," the king said. "Please, make yourselves at home. Hopefully we'll have the beginning of a fruitful partnership for Irminau and Yggdrasil." He raised his glass.

Ingrid raised hers as well, and then everyone at the table followed.

The mood was nervous. These men were unaccustomed to royal dinners, and Nan wondered if some of them had unpleasant memories of Otto stirring in their enchanted brains. Someone knocked over a wineglass. Everyone looked at the mortified fellow, who started mumbling apologies and trying to mop it with his napkin.

"Oh, don't worry about that," King Otto said. "I welcome the chance for my sorcerers to display one of their talents." A number of servants stood around the wall like statues. Nan had assumed they were maids and footmen, but now one of them moved forward and picked up the empty glass. She waved her hand over the spill and the wine was back in the vessel again.

"Very impressive," Ingrid asked. "A water witch?"

"Of course."

"What sort of witches do you have here?" Ingrid asked. "Lots of healers, I expected. Garden witches."

"Yes. Common types, mostly. A few who can boost strength, a fire witch . . . You know we just don't have as many as we once did. Sad days for the magic collector."

Nan looked more closely at the water witch and the other people standing so silently along the wall. She wondered how they felt being spoken of as a collection.

"Lady Verthandi," Otto said. She snapped her attention back to the food. "I am surprised to see you. I wondered if the Norns would still be reborn after Yggdrasil's destruction, but it appears Skuld's efforts to preserve the tree have saved your life."

Nan smiled uncomfortably. She was reluctant to drink or eat anything here.

Ingrid sipped her wine slowly, and Nan wondered if she was suspicious, too. "I would do anything to save my sisters," she said. "I was lost without them. Your Majesty, all I want is to have a frank conversation with you about our mutual goals. I know that many years ago, when you were newly crowned, Verthandi came to you and tried to tell you not to keep magic users in your palace."

Nan raised her eyebrows.

"Mm," Otto said, cutting up his—no doubt magically grown—white asparagus.

"But we have since realized that we were wrong to ask this of you," Ingrid said, looking at Nan sharply. "If we are to protect Yggdrasil properly and regain control of Urobrun, you must have all the power in the land at your disposal. If you are to be our king and protector, we were wrong to try to take away one of your greatest assets."

"Sensible," he said.

"All I want is your protection," Ingrid continued, "and my men and I will help you win this war."

"Do you agree, Verthandi?" he asked. "Because the last time I saw you, you seemed more willing to let Yggdrasil die than to allow this."

"I—I do agree," Nan said. She wasn't sure what else to say, on the spot. "Protecting Yggdrasil is the only thing that matters."

"I think we've had enough of this talk for one night," the king said, waving a hand to signal someone. "We'll have days upon days to discuss politics. Let's have a show."

The lights dimmed until the room was black, and then thousands of tiny lights came on above their heads in the shape of constellations and a full moon that illuminated the ship centerpiece. The oars began to move, and little sails rose up the masts. Nan had no idea if it was magic or clockwork. The room filled with the sound of the ocean—that must be magic for sure. At the top of the wall above King Otto's head, little doors opened like a cuckoo clock, revealing a woman sitting inside clad in a costume of fish scales and coral. She began to comb her loose hair and sing as if she were luring the sailors on the boat to their doom.

Under the dim light, the footmen gathered the soup bowls so quietly that not a single spoon clinked, then brought the fish course.

Nan struggled to eat a single bite under the pain of the woman's singing. She suspected it was already an eerie song by the way the men had gone so quiet, but to her it was a tuneless wailing that echoed all around. As the song went on, one of the sorcerers took a step forward and sent lightning crackling along the ceiling.

What a waste of magic, Nan thought with disgust.

As the song ended, the table itself opened up and the ship began to sink through it, the lightning still flashing. The cuckoo clock doors shut, as the siren was apparently satisfied by the sinking ship.

"Bravo, my dear," Otto said, applauding. Everyone else began to clap when he did, though many of Ingrid's men looked bewildered. Andre whispered in Sigi's ear, and she replied with a smile. Nan hoped Sigi didn't anger the king, but he didn't even seem to notice.

Near the end, as the coffee and dessert were served, King Otto barked, "This is *much* too hot!"

One sorcerer hurried forward and quickly touched his fingers to Otto's mouth while another took the coffee and waved a hand over it.

After the meal, King Otto led the party to a ballroom, where they joined the rest of the men and dozens of other members of the court under another chandelier formed of faces holding electric candles in their open mouths like they were being force-fed. An entourage of ladies joined them so the men had dance partners. A large band was already playing light airs in the corner, while waiters circulated with drinks.

Nan was caught in a round of introductions for a while. She even met the queen, which was quite a surprise to her, because Sebastian had never spoken of his mother. Even the Irminau papers almost never mentioned the queen. She was tall and shy, retreating to the sidelines with her ladies after the introductions.

"What an awkward court," Sigi said, once they were finally free. Sigi had gotten a martini somewhere. "It would make for a very interesting book. I've been gossiping."

"You'd better not be getting yourself in trouble."

"No, no. Mostly just listening to them go on about who's having an affair with who." She gestured to a group of women in a cluster near the bar. "I was asking about the queen. Apparently Otto never talks to her. Bad marriage? Homosexual? Or maybe he's just too caught up in ruling, but you'd think he'd want more heirs in that case."

"I don't think it matters," Nan said.

"I don't mean to stereotype, but I'm thinking he's really into decorating the place. I almost feel bad for him. Wouldn't it be awful to be royalty, with all that pressure to marry for alliances and produce heirs?"

"We need to stay focused."

Sigi tapped her chin. "Or do we? We'll seem suspicious if we stay focused. The best thing we can do to blend in is to take an interest in anything *but* magic and war so we can quietly gather information. That is the plan, isn't it?"

"If I can't think of a better plan to rescue Ingrid . . ."

"Let's get a drink in your hand so at least you look relaxed and not so scheming."

"I don't want any more drinks," Nan said. "I want to keep my head."

"One drink won't even make a dent in your head, darling."

Nan's cheeks warmed. Thea had called her darling before, but Sigi never had. Sigi had grown up as Arabella von Kaspar's daughter; she knew how to navigate a society party. It was not easy for Nan to let go of her focus, but she tried to follow Sigi's lead. She held her drink, and Sigi introduced her to the other ladies. Nan stayed mostly quiet, laughing when appropriate at stories about this baron sleeping with someone else's servant girl or whatever else, but keeping an eye on Ingrid all the while.

She noticed Ingrid suddenly leave the room alone. Nan followed her down the hall. One of Otto's guards who was posted by the doors trailed behind her, while another walked a distance ahead, following Ingrid, but they didn't interfere. She turned when she heard Nan's heels behind her.

"Nan?"

"Is everything all right?" Nan asked, trying to be gentle. An evening of court gossip reminded her that Ingrid was indeed her sister, with no patience for this either.

"Urd was always the one who could stand this sort of thing," Ingrid said, as they climbed the steps. The upstairs seemed colder than downstairs, as if the radiators had been shut off, and only an occasional light was kept on. The palace was relatively new, but it smelled of antiques, of objects very slowly rotting away. "I don't like these games, these rules, all this *talk*."

"Here is your room, Lady Skuld," the guard said, opening a door. A fire already crackled gently in the hearth. "Shall I show you to yours, Lady Verthandi?"

Nan would never get used to this "Lady Verthandi" business. "Not yet. Let me talk to my sister a moment."

When the door was shut, she spoke softly. "Do you plan to control him? Is that it?"

Ingrid sat down on the floor by the fire and pulled off her shoes, then stared into the flames.

"Ingrid?" Nan crouched beside her. Her stocking feet and her pose, like a girl settling in to pick daisies, suggested the old Skuld as much as anything she might have said. "Please. If you do care about me at all, reconsider this plan. Otto might shake off the enchantment, or he might do something awful to you before you even get that far. When I came to see him, he imprisoned me all alone and kept me in a stupor so I couldn't use the wyrdsong. You said yourself, he's not a good man. There must be another way."

"You and Urd wanted the tree to die." Ingrid's voice sounded small. "I was so scared that if it did, you wouldn't be reincarnated. We would lose our magic. I would be alone."

Nan took her hand. "But I'm here now."

Ingrid wouldn't meet her eyes.

"Is the tree dead?" Nan asked. "Are you keeping it alive with this dark magic?"

Ingrid remained unresponsive. Her eyes were wet.

"Ingrid, what did you do?"

Ingrid finally looked at Nan. "The greatest magic always comes from sacrifice." She took off her stockings. "I want you to see me as I really am."

Her skin seemed to shimmer. A layer of illusion dropped away. Her legs were made of the same carved wood as Thea's hand and Sebastian's leg. Her arms were made of wood. And when Nan turned to look at her sister's face, blank wooden eyes looked back at her.

Nan thought she might be sick. "What happened?"

"Yggdrasil's life and mine have become one now. If I die, it dies. If it dies . . . there isn't much left of me. It was the only way." Her face was eerie with tears falling out of her dead eyes. "I asked for Otto's help to save the tree."

"Did you know he had killed me? Please—tell me what happened."

"The tree was sick. And Urd said maybe it was dying. We thought maybe it was because King Otto and the Chancellor were searching for magic users and making use of them. So you went to King Otto to ask him to change his ways and help us. I guess he didn't like that. But you and Urd felt that it might be a futile quest anyway. That maybe the world was—" She sniffed. "Growing out of magic, or something."

"Why?"

"Urd said, with all the new inventions—like the motorcar, and the telegraph—the world was changing. Magic could no longer remain a gift that belongs only to those who need it, and our powers weren't enough to protect magic anymore. Technology was becoming more powerful than us. You agreed with her. But I was so scared. I wouldn't give up, no matter what. So when you and Urd were killed, and the Urobrunians destroyed the tree—"

"You went to Otto," Nan said, heart sinking.

"I borrowed a horse from the nearest village and I rode all night, because if I wasn't quick, magic would have died, and—" She wiped her nose. "I wouldn't be able to find you and Urd again. Otto had a reviver at the time, so he sent him with me, and the man revived Yggdrasil, but he said it was sick, so it was just going to die again. I didn't know what to do."

"So you fed the tree with your own body . . ."

"Yes. I read of a dark healing spell in the books Urd had left behind, and made myself limbs from the wood of the old Yggdrasil, so its roots could feed off my life. But I wasn't enough; Yggdrasil was still weakening. When I heard about Prince Rupert's accident, I thought maybe I could help him and he would have to help me. And then it worked so well. The tree grew stronger. I just kept going."

She shivered and the illusion returned. Her blue eyes blinked the last of her tears, and she started to laugh in a low, pained way. "See? There is nothing you can do. I can't be saved, not the way you want to save me. And I won't be stopped. I've already given up everything I have."

Nan nodded, feeling numb, of both mind and body, as if her toes and fingers were turning to wood as well. She shifted, as if to stand, and then she thought, *I might never talk to Ingrid again. Not as my little sister.*

"Ingrid," she said, swallowing back tears. "You should have just let us be reborn as humans. You did this so you wouldn't lose us, and now you're losing us anyway. And we're losing *you*."

"It was a mistake," Ingrid said hoarsely. "I know it was now. But I have to keep going. I don't want to die."

"I do remember you," Nan said. "The girl you were, across all your old lives. I love that girl. And as long as I live, I will never forget you, and us, and our happy days in the forest."

"Wait—Verthandi, don't say good-bye!" Ingrid cried, grabbing her arms, digging her fingernails into Nan's skin, like she had suddenly realized that Nan really was going to let go. "No—no, don't. There must be some way you can help me. Please, help me!"

"But I can't. The tree was dying. This magic you've done— it's dark. I don't even know how much power I have now to stop you. All I can do is beg you to end this."

"You *always* knew how to fix things." Ingrid drew her legs in and dropped her head on her knees, sobbing in a choked way. "I can't end this. I need you."

Nan looked at the ceiling, colors flashing as she blinked away her own tears. Part of this journey was saying good-bye to all of it. Not just Skuld, not just Yggdrasil, but Verthandi, too, and all her memories.

She pulled back from Ingrid, leaving her there on the rug, sobbing and broken. There was nothing more to say. It tore at every fragile, human part of Nan's heart, but she knew . . . Ingrid should have listened to fate.

She should have let Yggdrasil die.

FORTY-SEVEN

Guards hovered outside Ingrid's room, ready to usher Nan to her own room or back to the dance floor. "Whatever you wish," they said, but obviously they were also watching her closely. She wouldn't be able to leave Neue Adlerwald without a fight.

She returned to the dance to grab Sigi and explain it to her under all the noise provided by the band.

"That's the saddest story I've ever heard," Sigi said.

"But she won't give up on keeping the men enchanted and the tree alive, unless she has a change of heart after she sleeps on it, but I'm not hopeful."

"Do you know how to stop her? Or should we just go home?"

"If she has Otto on her side, and she has all the men she brought with her—and none of them can be injured—well, that might give Irminau the edge when they invade Urobrun. But I don't want to kill her. Why did she have to put me in this position?"

Otto glanced over at them and smiled, showing his teeth. Nan forced herself to smile back.

"Well, while you were gone I asked about the Mausoleum."

Nan frowned. "You don't think that's a suspicious question?"

"The girl I was talking to asked if I was with you—well, 'Verthandi.' Apparently you're a bit of an underground hero. A lot of people remember the last time you were here, and they feel that you came to save the magic users and Otto killed you for it."

Nan hadn't even considered that angle. "So she's on our side?"

"Seems so. She said the Mausoleum is where magic users go when they're too spent and sick to work anymore. It's in the east wing. We have to try and find it."

"I wonder what Jenny could do to help us, if she's that weak."

"Regardless of Jenny, I thought I should try to get photographs of the Mausoleum. Sebastian could use them for articles to show Otto's cruelty."

"Good plan. But I imagine it's guarded."

"Yes, and I need daylight to be sure of good pictures, so it can't be during the night."

"I think daytime is best anyway. Easier to give an excuse if we're caught." Nan swept her eyes around the ballroom. Like the rest of the castle, it seemed too vast for comfort. The dancing couples had too much space to move. Had this room ever been filled? Nan just wanted to get out of this place, but she couldn't balk after coming this far.

"Sigi, the girl who told you about the Mausoleum . . . maybe she could tell us how to get in. I don't want to trust anyone here; I'm not sure what else to do. We need an ally."

The girl was the Lady Marie, a young woman with a serious

face that didn't match her cheerful blond curls. "I've never seen the Mausoleum myself," she said. "Prince Rupert told me about it."

"Did you know the prince?" Nan asked.

Lady Marie nodded. "Of course. I saw him every summer and winter holiday. What a shock when he died. I know he would have abolished these practices the moment he became king." She was speaking in the barest whisper now. "It will be guarded, but I'll see what I can do. I'll try and find you tomorrow."

"All right," Nan said, hoping the timing would work out and this girl was trustworthy.

⊙–⊙–⊙–⊙

True to her word, Lady Marie approached them while King Otto was showing Ingrid the gardens, even in the brutal winter wind. Nan and Sigi were along for the tour, at the back of the group, while Otto talked about winter berries and showed off his pen of reindeer.

"Why don't you come with me and warm up?" Lady Marie offered. Looking over her shoulder, she hurried them into one of the palace's back doors, bringing them into a servants' entrance.

A stout maid with her gray hair in a bun was waiting for them inside, holding a plate of food. "Hurry," she whispered, starting to lead them down the corridor.

"Good luck," Lady Marie said, before going back out the door. Apparently she was willing to show them this far, but not willing to get caught. Not very reassuring, but at least it was one less person to worry about if something did go wrong.

"The guards are sympathizers with the resistance movement here," the maid said. "But we'll have no excuse for you to be in the Mausoleum if you're caught."

"Thank you for trusting us," Nan said.

"But you are Verthandi! We haven't forgotten you."

"Are many of you in the household against Otto?"

"Oh yes," the maid said. "But we stay quiet. He's very popular outside the household."

"I'll never understand how tyrants can be popular," Nan said.

"I do," Sigi said. "Everyone seemed to love my mother, and I could easily see her turning into a tyrant if she'd been given the chance."

"Hush now," the housemaid said, adjusting her tray of food into one hand as she opened the door into the hall and peered out, then motioned them forward.

They approached a room in the far corner of one of the palace wings. They passed through warm squares of sunlight that fell upon the marble floors, formed by huge windows at the end of the wing. Another maid was just coming out of the door carrying a stack of empty trays and dishes. The guards at the door ignored them.

Behind the door, a record played classical music that Nan expected was soothing to most ears—even to her, it came close to sounding pleasant. The beds had grand, tall headboards, and carved wooden partitions blocked the room into private spaces for the beds' occupants, while still allowing a sense of open space with the soaring ceiling above, which had been painted with scenes of clouds and rosy-cheeked people dancing along the border.

The people in the beds, however, looked deathly ill. Fragile skin stretched over their bones. Every thread of hair on their heads was silver, and a few had no hair at all. One of them slept with a rattle in his chest with every breath, another slowly lifted a spoonful of soup to her mouth.

The maid was still edging around the room nervously, and Sigi got out her camera, wasting no time. Luckily she had already been carrying it for the garden expedition.

"Jenny is here," the maid said, motioning Nan forward while Sigi snapped pictures. Nan was struck by the contrast of Sigi, her eyes alight with the prospect of capturing a powerful moment, and the witches who laid here near death. She was almost shy to approach Jenny—as if, deep down, a part of her was responsible for her suffering. The Norns were supposed to protect magic users. Her powers should have left her when the tree died. None of these people should be here.

Jenny's brittle silver hair was in a braid that fell across her shoulder. She was sitting propped up on numerous pillows, with a book on her lap. Seeing Nan approach, she shut it and set it aside, lifting it with effort although it was of ordinary size. Nan shuddered to think that Freddy had been headed to this state.

"Are you here to help me?" she asked, but she sounded doubtful.

"Maybe. Rupert sent me and told me to check on you." But Nan could see Jenny was beyond help.

"Is Rupert well?"

"Yes, he is."

"You're the Norn, aren't you? I was a young woman the last time you were here. People still talk about it." Jenny coughed. She seemed worn out even by this short conversation.

"Do you know anything about Yggdrasil? I was told that a reviver helped bring it back to life."

"Yes, he did. But that man died, years ago."

"So the tree doesn't need the reviver." Disappointing, but not surprising. "I came back here because I was trying to stop King Otto from abusing magic users anymore, but I'm not sure I can do anything now. I need to return to Rupert. If you have any information that could help him . . ."

"Hurry," the maid said, constantly looking over her shoulder.

"If I was younger and stronger, I could have helped you fight," Jenny said. "I could have killed him. I should have killed him . . . tell Rupert . . . not to hesitate to kill him. He should not feel guilty because it's his father. He's an evil man, and we all know it is so."

Nan felt a chill, wondering if this advice should apply to her as well. *Should I have killed Ingrid already?*

The maid tensed at the sound of voices in the hall beyond.

One of the door guards stepped in and said, "The king is coming."

"The king never comes to the Mausoleum!" the maid said. "You need to hide!"

FORTY-EIGHT

Sigi and Nan climbed under Jenny's bed. Luckily, the expensive beds were quite spacious. The maid nudged Nan's arm with her toe, pushing her farther out of sight.

"Here," Jenny whispered, and then a blanket dropped over the side of the bed.

Sigi was breathing hard. Nan laced their fingers together. They couldn't move without potentially shifting a limb into view.

The voices outside the room came closer until they were through the doorway. Judging by the footsteps, Nan guessed at least twenty people were in the party. The maids greeted Otto with, "Your Majesty, to what do we owe this honor?"

"This is Lady Skuld," Otto said. "She says she can help these poor souls."

"Yes," Ingrid said. "I can restore their strength."

Nan's eyes widened. Was Ingrid going to—?

She heard—and felt, through the floorboards—heavy objects set down. Lids creaked open. These must be the several trunks

Ingrid's men had carried all the way from Urobrun. Ingrid said gently, "I will help you" to one of the witches near the front of the room, and then she spoke to the rest. "There will be no pain, but you may want to turn away if you're squeamish."

Nan saw the plan clearly now. She had assumed Ingrid would target Otto first. But this approach made more sense. These magic users were useless, weak as they were. She must have promised him that she could restore them. All they had to do was make one small sacrifice of their broken bodies. The trunks must hold the wooden limbs.

A woman groaned weakly as a saw ground through bone. Ingrid hummed a low note. Nan gripped Sigi's hand tighter as Sigi looked queasy. This couldn't have taken long, but the grinding seemed to go on forever.

"Ohhh," the woman said, her voice dry and fragile. "I see the sacred tree."

"Yggdrasil," Ingrid said gently. "My Yggdrasil. Look upon its beauty and take it into your heart, and your strength will return to you." Something fell with a small, solid weight onto the floor.

"Get that cleaned up," Otto directed someone in a low tone of restrained irritation. "Let's not have blood staining the floors, shall we?" There was a brief scuffle of footsteps.

"My king, just a little blood is a small price to pay to have your witches regain their strength," Ingrid said, and she sounded a little irritated at him as well, for caring about his floors in the midst of her spell. "Come, madam, see if you can get out of that bed now."

The bedsprings creaked. Stocking feet moved softly on the floors. "I can walk," the woman said. "Will my hair grow back, too?"

"In time, if you are careful," Ingrid said. "You can only use your magic sparingly. But you won't die here."

"Oh my lady."

Nan was tensed, ready to move. She couldn't let Ingrid exploit these witches on their deathbed and gain all their power. But if she made a move, it was just her against Ingrid and Otto both. If she could just take what she had learned, along with Sigi's photographs, back to Sebastian, that might be the best she could do.

Or am I just being cowardly?

Her bones ached from resting against the hard floor, staying so still. Ingrid's feet came into view as she approached Jenny.

"Don't touch me," Jenny said.

"You don't want to be strong again?"

"Not for this price," Jenny snapped.

"Stubborn," the king said. "No use talking to her, Lady Skuld. Just do what needs to be done."

Jenny groaned with effort. Her feet hit the floor and the blanket that had helped conceal Nan and Sigi tumbled to the ground. Nan pressed closer to Sigi to stay out of view.

"Jenny," the king said warningly. Nan heard a few guns pulled from holsters.

"Just shoot me, why don't you? I don't care anymore."

"Shh." Ingrid's slippers shifted, inches from Nan's face, and springs creaked as Jenny sat down hard on the bed. "Is that any way to talk? I understand your anger at the king, but I'm here to help you begin your life anew, without any pain. Only beauty." Her voice had slipped into its most bewitching cadence.

Ingrid took a step toward the end of the bed.

Jenny's body shifted slightly on the mattress. Ingrid was singing the wyrdsong, but it didn't sound as Nan knew it. It was the siren song that drove men mad and the low growl of a beast in the shadows. As soon as she thought she knew what she heard, it changed into something else, as if she never quite heard it at all. It ground into her mind, deeper by the moment.

Damn it.

Nan scrambled out from under the bed. "Ingrid! You must stop!"

Ingrid stepped back in surprise, the wyrdsong dying, her bloody bone saw in hand, about to touch Jenny's wrist. Jenny's eyes had gone blank. "Verthandi? You—you can't stop me. I'll hurt you."

Nan's only chance was to reach for her own power, the power she barely understood and would soon lose. But what was her power, now? Her Yggdrasil had already died. She could only pray that the brighter forces in the world would still work through her.

There is only one Yggdrasil, Verthandi. The words stepped into her mind, an answer to her prayer. *And it wants you to set it free. The time of magic has ended.*

The walls rumbled with Nan's wyrdsong. Was she singing? Was she speaking? Her consciousness stretched out beyond her body. She was one with the air, one with the floor and the walls. Ingrid clenched her fists, her mouth open like she was screaming. Her wyrdsong responded, a roar of fury and pain.

Lightbulbs shattered in the wall sconces from the force of their power. King Otto and his entourage stepped back, drawing closer to the wall. The floor was covered in bloody footprints.

What power we would have had, when we fought together, Nan thought.

Please. Don't make me kill my sister.

Ingrid's song began to wither, as if she had heard Nan's words. Some of her men and the sorcerers she had just bound to her were gathered close around her.

"Go," she said.

"She can't go," Otto said.

"Go!" Ingrid repeated. "She will go, and it won't matter. We will conquer Urobrun. My powers are greater than hers. But I want a fair fight."

Nan looked at Jenny. She was too weak to travel with them. She shook her head and waved Nan away like she had become a nuisance. "Just go, go with my blessing. Do what you can, don't waste yourself on what is impossible."

Sigi had climbed out from under the bed, hesitantly. Nan grabbed her hand, nodded at her sister, and then she flew out the door.

FORTY-NINE

Thea still couldn't help a brief flash of resentment that she was now relegated to a tiny, odd club at the end of the district, but the girls were all friendly, and the welcoming atmosphere made the Telephone Club seem in contrast like a factory where her personality was a product pumped out by the hour. The waitresses there moved in cliques and competed for the best tables. Occasionally they stooped to catty rumors and shoved shoulders in the hallway.

The first day, when Thea's nightmare came true and she dropped a glass onto the floor, Hedda immediately appeared at her side. "What was it? I'll get another one." She came back in moments with a new glass of wine and a dustpan and broom to sweep up the glass.

There were only three full-time waitresses besides Thea. They had all worked there at least six months. Her old boss wouldn't have considered any of them perfect enough to hire. Lori was a very freckled redhead—even her lips had freckles—with an alien quality to her ice-blue eyes. Ruthie was too tall; she could imagine her old boss saying, "A man doesn't like a woman who can look down at him." Hedda had a faint scar carved down her cheek and a severe beauty. Thea imagined most people would've thought Hedda was the spy if anyone was.

Hedda could be very sharp with customers, but she was sweet to Thea, like a big sister. She seemed to sense Thea needed reassurance. On her first day, she said, "We'll start you with a table of university professors. They're so nice, and they just talk about dinosaurs." If it was slow, she doubled up with Thea and helped her serve. Lori and Ruthie were just as nice, even though Thea got huge tips from the very first day.

Pity tips.

Thea tried so hard not to do anything pitiable, but apparently just existing was enough. A lot of people did ask her about her hand and if she'd been injured in the riots. She said she was. It was the easiest explanation. So they often saw her as a hero, who'd been brave enough to go out and stand for the revolution.

But she didn't feel like a hero either. "I expect most heroes just stumble into it," Hedda said.

Half an hour into the evening, the curtain would rise and the café's star, Ina Brand, stepped onto the stage, wearing a short dress made of silvery fringe. Her arms were bare and sleeved with tattoos. Thea had never seen a woman with tattoos. Her black-rimmed eyes bugged with dramatic effect when she performed, and her hair was a short, wild mop. Sometimes she wore a peacock feather headdress. And she started the show with a serpent draped around her arms. It was quite a presentation even before she opened her mouth, but she also had a sultry voice, and all the men seemed riveted by her. Thea kept watching her, too—she wouldn't want to have tattoos and a serpent, but she had always been drawn to performers and their utter composure, the way they could take the stage night after night and create a mood and a character and have hundreds of people watch them.

All in all, she enjoyed the job, but night after night she came home with nothing to report to Sebastian.

"I didn't see anyone who looked like they worked for the king," she told him, sitting on the edge of his desk. "Again. Are you sure they go there?"

"It's only been a week. But you know I like to hear everything."

"Well, two of the men were talking about Marlis's New Year's party," she told him. "They were Brunner's men. They seemed excited about it."

"Really?" He groaned.

"You don't think it's nice for us to host a party? It'll build goodwill."

"I just don't enjoy the attention. Isn't anyone talking about my last pamphlet? I thought I had some amazing points about labor laws. Did you read it?" He opened a drawer. "Maybe you could ask people if they've read it."

"Sebastian, parties are so much more exciting than pamphlets. Pamphlets aren't illegal anymore, so no one cares. And Marlis herself is exciting. The Chancellor's daughter has declared herself a mythological being. How can you top that?"

"I *could*." He sighed.

"Well, I understand that you don't want to be Prince Rupert, and you don't want anyone to notice you're Prince Rupert, but that does limit your ability to be exciting. Maybe you should wear a serpent around your arms. It seems to work out pretty well at the café."

⊙–⊙–⊙–⊙

"That sure is a shame, pretty girl like you saddled with a thing like that." Café Scorpio was packed on her second Saturday night there, and Thea was already feeling harried. She'd heard similar comments already, but not with a leer—like this guy was thinking he'd go home and tell his friends, "Guess what girl I hooked last night? Ha-ha."

"How'd you lose it?" he continued.

"Gunfight," Thea said, which was not untrue.

"That sounds like an exciting story. I like my women a little dangerous. I don't mind this." He reached for her left wrist, and she yanked her arm back.

"No need to be shy," he said.

"Oh, I'm not shy." She pressed her hook to his cheek. "I don't mind putting your eyes out."

"Whoa." He sounded rattled. "I was trying to give you a compliment."

She had probably overreacted, but she didn't feel bad. She had never liked men like him, but now she had no tolerance for them. She'd probably lived through more harrowing experiences than he ever would. Anyway, the hooks weren't sharp, or she would have put her own eye out by now.

He leaned closer. "Hey, I'm sorry, sweetheart. Can I buy you a drink and make it up to you?"

326

Beneath the edge of his shirt, she saw a silver necklace—with Otto's crest. He was a tall, strong fellow, with rustic features and clothes that looked travel-worn and a little unpolished, like they were sewn by a woman at home. Irminauer clothes.

Curses. Part of the problem with trying to gather crucial information was that no one was going to walk around announcing themselves as Otto's spies, blabbing crucial information right at their table. She had to coerce it out, but she couldn't do that without some clue they might work for Otto to begin with.

"Maybe," she said.

He relaxed a little. "You work for the resistance around here?"

She shrugged.

"Seems like everyone does," he said.

"Not everyone. I flirted with it."

"How did that go?"

He was trying to get information out of her, she thought, while she was hoping for the same. "I was intrigued with Arabella von Kaspar. Do you know of her? She died the night the workers escaped. I'd gone to some meetings of her group."

"I've heard of her."

"Of course, when she died, that's when this Brunner fellow came into power. I'm just not sure about him. He made a lot of concessions to the old regime."

He was starting to look a little bored, his eyes grazing her curves. Maybe he didn't want information after all. "Beautiful rustic girl like you shouldn't be caught up in all this," he said. "Why aren't you married?"

"I'm not interested in being a housewife," she said, a little disturbed that he thought she was old enough to ask that question—but girls did marry at seventeen in Irminau. "I'd rather work. Speaking of which, let me get you a drink."

He'd probably be worse with liquor in him, but she wanted a minute away. She didn't want to get information out of him anymore—not when he kept looking at her hook and then her body, like he was weighing them against each other and had decided she was worthy of his attention, and maybe ought to be grateful, to boot.

She took a deep breath. If he did work for Otto, if he knew something, she could use his attention to her advantage. He had no idea how much she had faced, how involved she had been, who she worked for. She wouldn't let him scare her from her duties just because he had poked at her insecurities. And Sebastian's guard would be waiting for her when she left, so she didn't even have to fear him pursuing her.

She brought him the drink and lingered a moment at the table while he took a sip.

"Good?"

"Perfect. You don't skimp on the alcohol around here."

"I made it myself." She leaned against the table. "This is your first time here, isn't it? You aren't from the city?"

"No."

"Irminau?"

He nodded.

"My parents were from Irminau. I've always wished to see it. I'm so tired of the big city."

"You might not like Irminau. Women don't work there. They get married and have babies."

She doubted this was entirely true. "There are no waitresses in Irminau?"

"None like you."

She turned her head, as if shy, although really she didn't want to have to force some smile. She left him for a little bit, so he wouldn't take her presence for granted, although it was hard when she was impatient to be done with him.

When she noticed his drink was empty, she returned. "So tell me more about Irminau. My mother always says the pastries here never compare."

"Your mother is right. Have y'ever had gooseberry gateau? With vanilla cream . . ." He was getting tipsy, and she was feeling more anxious that she might be wrong and maybe he was an ordinary rustic with nothing to do but ogle girls and tell her things she already knew.

She asked if he would be in the city next week.

"No." He sounded apologetic. "I'm headed north day after tomorrow."

"Back to Irminau? Why?"

"I've got something to do."

"I wish I could see Irminau."

"It'll be dangerous."

"Oh no, why?" She tried not to sound too eager. "Anyway, I don't care, I've been in a gunfight, remember?"

"Well, I don't think you want to go into battle."

"I heard the armies aren't going to move through this snow."

He shrugged.

"You're not really going into battle, are you?"

"Nah, I hope not."

"Well, could I write you a letter? To boost your spirits?"

He brightened. "Would you really?"

"I'd love to. For the glory of my mother's homeland."

⊙–⊙–⊙–⊙

"Hustenburg." Sebastian smiled.

"Is it helpful at all? I tried to get him to tell me more about why he was going there, but—"

Sebastian held up his hand. "Oh no. This is very helpful indeed. Do you know where Hustenburg is?"

"No."

"It's tiny, right on the border of Irminau, just a few miles north of Lingfeldt. And Lingfeldt is a supply base that has been traded back and forth more than once between Irminau and Urobrun, right where the Urobrun River splits into a tributary. It's actually on the Irminauer side of the river, but Urobrun has control of it." He was sounding excited. "Lingfeldt's supply base holds a large stockpile of weapons—ammunition and heavy guns. They're meant to defend the border. The problem is, manpower at the base is too short for defense now. The Urobrunians could over-whelm them, take the weapons, come over the bridge, and get a foothold in our lands there. I know it's been on Brunner's mind, but we assumed—no, let's say we *hoped*—they wouldn't pursue it during the snows. But I'm sure that's their target."

"So this is bad news, isn't it?" It was hard to tell when he was talking so much, grabbing papers and looking eager. "They're planning an attack?"

"And soon, if your man's time frame is to be believed."

"*Don't* call him 'my man.'"

"How about 'your target'?"

"Better."

"I should talk to Marlis and gather up a unit quickly. It seems I'm going to miss her New Year's party."

"You might want to try not sounding so delighted about it when you tell her."

"Oh, she'll probably be glad to handle all the diplomacy herself."

"Are you going to meet the Irminau army? Personally?"

He crossed around to the front of the desk. "It should be a fairly simple operation if we can get there in time. I'd just be supervising the defense. Don't worry."

"I'm not," she lied, but she reached for his jacket and pulled him closer. "But I think I'm tired of pretending I don't have any feelings for you for Freddy's sake. If you did die, I would think about all the moments I'd missed."

"Not many, with how busy we've all been." He cupped his hand around her hair. "But I know."

She stood on her tiptoes to kiss him, throwing her arms around him. She wasn't sure if she would have a chance to say good-bye later, if he intended to move so quickly.

"I can't bear losing one more thing, Sebastian. I really can't."

"I'll be back before you know it. I promise."

"In one piece," she added, feeling suspicious about promises.

"As much as that is possible. And promise me you'll enjoy yourself at the party and keep Marlis from doing anything too insane."

"As much as *that* is possible."

FIFTY

I hear you're headed for the border," Freddy said, in a considerable understatement, what with the sudden hubbub of preparations throughout the house. "Will it be dangerous?"

"If we make it in time, we won't even have to engage. But if we don't, it could be." Sebastian had his hands spread over the map thoughtfully.

"I'd like to go with you," Freddy said.

"You would?"

"I've been trapped in this house for weeks. If we do go into battle and I could help turn the tide, that's a better use of my power than bringing back spies for the UWP to torture."

Sebastian's eyes brightened, but he put his hands on his hips. "I worry about your capture."

"Will the enemy even know I'm there? If I revive men behind the walls of a base? They can fight out the duration if I revive them."

"I won't turn it down, of course. I just wanted to make sure you mean it. You've never been in a battle before." Sebastian wiped his glasses on the edge of his shirt. "There is the potential for us to be vastly outnumbered."

"I was out the night the workers died," Freddy said. "Not only was that ugly, but it was very personal. I don't want to sit around uselessly waiting for the next time Brunner demands to see me, when I could offer you real help. And I have magical protection on me, so that does lessen the risk."

Sebastian nodded. "Brunner doesn't even know I'm doing this, you know. I want those weapons for our use."

"He isn't going to like that."

"To say the least. But this is my chance to grab some glory without having to use my family name." Sebastian started looking at the map again, so Freddy moved to the stairs.

Sebastian waved his hand. "But, Freddy? I'm sending someone to get hair dye. Make that your evening project. No need to make yourself too obvious."

⊙–⊙–⊙–⊙

In the morning, forty-five men piled into the trucks they'd captured from the arsenal. Freddy tried not to lose his nerve as he climbed into the truck. Most of the men who weren't going, plus Thea and Marlis, stood out front to wave good-bye. He watched them grow smaller and smaller until they turned the corner.

Aleksy was driving; he had a picture of his girl stuck in a crack in the dashboard. Freddy had heard him talk about her before, and the snapshot of Ilse and her sunshine smile, messy hair, and homespun sweater matched the stories. She was an

Irminauer girl that Aleksy hoped to return to when the war was over.

It set Freddy to brooding. It would be easier to go to war if he had a girl to return to. He kept wondering if Thea and Sebastian had a relationship. If he had kissed her. *I just want to know.*

Sebastian rode with them; he kept taking out his map and putting it away just to take it out again, musing endlessly on possibilities. "Depending on how many men they have . . . we might not even have enough drivers to transport all the weapons out. It's probably better to have the sheer volume of ammunition than to save *all* the heavy guns . . . but then, how many heavy guns does Otto have? He'll want those especially—he does enjoy big things."

Once they were out of the city, the landscape opened into barren fields sparkling with snow, broken by occasional stands of trees and farmhouses. Freddy had never seen the landscape outside the city before without Gerik next to him, when they went on rare visits to his parents that brought more sadness than joy. They could never speak honestly, with Gerik there for every word, and each year they interacted more as strangers. The prospect of a battle ahead wasn't as bad as that.

I certainly hope they found safety in Irminau. He had almost given up on finding them, and was ashamed at how little it seemed to matter. He had never had a relationship with them, thanks to Gerik. He hoped to build one, but it was hard to miss something that was already absent.

Snow-covered roads slowed their progress. Two of the trucks had been outfitted with plows to lead the way. The weather was largely kind, the skies clear, but when they set up camp in the shelter of an abandoned barn, Freddy shivered through the night in his sleeping bag, and the ground was so hard he seemed to have grown extra bones, just for the sake of them jabbing into the old planks.

Sebastian must have had some sympathy for leaving behind a pampered existence, because he woke Freddy with a cup of hot coffee and a bowl of porridge. "Sleep all right?"

"No." He laughed, and then coughed. The dry air made his throat sore. He could see his breath in the barn. The sun wasn't even up yet.

Sebastian was sitting behind him, already bundled up to go. "My first night on the road was not a good one either. I was used to a feather mattress and a warm fire and my dog, Falk. When I left with Ingrid, all I had was a scratchy wool blanket, and she didn't make coffee for breakfast, I can tell you. She brewed leaves into some horrible tea."

"You didn't bring your dog?" Freddy was still missing his cat. Amsel used to keep him warm, too.

"I couldn't bring a handsome purebred dog along while I was trying to hide my identity. But leaving behind a faithful dog is the worst: You can't explain it to them. Also, you're going to make me cry, so let's not speak of it anymore. Now, get out of your sleeping bag so we can pack it up."

Supplies were quickly packed back into the trucks, and they set off just after sunrise—which came late, this time of year. Ice on the roads hampered progress, and one of the trucks slid off into a ditch and had to be pushed out. Sebastian had hoped to reach Lingfeldt in two days, but by nightfall they were still two hours away, and with the poor roads, Sebastian reluctantly gave in to another night of making camp. Usually Sebastian was the first one to put up his feet and enjoy a meal when the occasion called for it, but even while everyone else was eating, he was still looking over the map, and while they ate, he reviewed everyone on the lay of the land at Lingfeldt and where they would each go if a battle was already in progress when they arrived.

Freddy slept better that night. The still air smelled of fir and pine and buried memories. It was a homesick feeling, but in a good way. In the morning, excitement pervaded the camp. Freddy had never understood why anyone would choose to be a soldier, but as he rolled up his sleeping bag and wolfed down his breakfast with the other men, he felt a part of something important and invigorating. The prospect of impending death brought everything to life.

As they drove, the foothills of Irminau rose in the distance out of low, soft clouds, dark with evergreens, while the Urobrun River ran along the road to their right, with the train tracks between. Before long, they reached the bridge that crossed a tributary of the Urobrun River and led right into Lingfeldt. This little wedge of land, bordered by rivers on two sides, rested in former Irminauer territory, and it looked Irminauer right down to the little thatched-roof houses among the modern military buildings.

As they pulled in, the base guard was already approaching the trucks. Just as Sebastian had warned, the complex of large buildings, surrounded by walls and guard towers, looked nearly empty, though it stirred to life as Sebastian's men climbed out of their trucks. The base commander shook Sebastian's hand. He looked like a man who wasn't easily impressed—but his mouth was hanging open now.

"Are you the reinforcements I requested?"

Sebastian saluted. "Sebastian Hirsch."

"Thank god. Commander Opitz. We don't have much time."

"How much?"

"Two hours at best. I sent a message to Urobrun, but I figured you wouldn't be able to get here in time with the roads as they are. Were you stationed nearby? I've heard of you, Mr. Hirsch—you're the young one. Wasn't your father a baron in Irminau?"

Freddy had almost forgotten Sebastian's false origin story. "Yes," Sebastian said.

"Your enemy is a baron as well," Opitz said. "My intelligence reports that the enemy commander is Baron Best, from the north."

"I know Baron Best—he's formidable. One of the king's closest comrades. They call him the Wolf of the Woods."

"Chancellor Brunner . . . he didn't send you, did he?" Commander Opitz had a careful tone now. Freddy couldn't tell if he liked Brunner or not, the way he said his name.

"No, I have my own contacts. I left as soon as I suspected. Brunner is stretched too thin to assist."

Commander Opitz was quiet, regarding Sebastian with a weathered face, clearly twice the age of the young man who had come to offer help outside of the Chancellor's command.

"My men are veterans," Sebastian said. "At Brunner's order, I led the command to take the arsenal in Urobrun. We'll help you hold the base long enough to get the weapons to safety and destroy the bridge. Otherwise, as I'm sure you're aware, Best can take them and use them against us."

Opitz's face was somber, unmoving as a statue. Freddy could imagine what he must be thinking. Even if he knew Sebastian's name, Freddy understood how hard it was to trust anyone with the government so fragmented. But after a pause, he nodded. "I'd already started loading the weapons onto the trucks as soon as we knew they were coming, but our numbers are a problem."

"How many here?"

"A hundred. They must have at least two thousand, probably closer to three thousand."

Sebastian didn't react, although Freddy knew this was the upper end of his expectations. "Well, we don't have to defeat them, we just have to hold them off—and we have, by far, the better position and superior weaponry. Besides that, I have a reviver—and all my men are prepared to die twice. I will leave it to your men to decide if they are also prepared to do so."

The commander stiffened, and his expression was hard to read. Opitz's men were looking over Sebastian's crew with renewed suspicion, and Freddy forced a stoic expression on his face. Sebastian hadn't introduced him yet, but the moment would come soon. When he was kept secret, he never had to endure such scrutiny.

Freddy wondered if he'd be willing to die twice for his country. He never thought what it would be like to be on the receiving end of his magic, but the people he revived were often disoriented. *I have to stay calm. Maybe it will help them, too.*

"If one man can live another day because of another man's sacrifice—I'd say that's the code we live by, and that includes magic," Opitz said, glancing around with his ragged gray eyebrows furrowed, but if anyone was afraid to be brought back from the dead, they didn't admit it.

Sebastian nodded. "Let's move quickly, then."

On the supply base's north side, a high wall faced Irminau, with guard towers at the corners. Freddy was stationed here with the front line. He knew much of what to expect from Sebastian's maps and meetings. A low hill blocked them from viewing the horizon, so they couldn't yet see the advancing forces. Fir trees and snow made for a restful scene on these gentle slopes, and yet it was so much larger in scope than it seemed on the map. He had read of battles, but he'd always imagined "the battlefield" as some designated place, as if every town had one parked outside waiting for the next war. Now he realized men would spill blood on the peaceful path ahead.

Within the base, most of the men were working quickly to load crates of guns and ammunition into trucks, while others pulled out with heavy guns on the back of trailers. Although the men worked at a frenzied pace, driving out the trucks drained their numbers. He felt as if he'd only been watching the operations within the base for a few minutes when the rumble of enemy movement drove a low note of danger into the still white forests.

Freddy was nearest to two men he knew; Samuel and Adalbert. Everyone was exchanging blank faces of acknowledgment, shifting the position of weapons, taking one last look at photographs of loved ones, leading Freddy to wonder again, *Just who am I fighting for? My own freedom . . .*

It sounded all right, but you couldn't take a picture of it.

He put his hand on the wall of the rampart, grounding himself in the feel of cold, hard stone penetrating his glove. His heart hammered in his chest as the sound grew more defined, taking the shape of slow-moving artillery coming around the distant bend. Sebastian had been overseeing operations on the ground, but now he was up on the wall next to Freddy.

The artillery opened fire.

"Duck!" Sebastian shouted, and all the men dropped beneath the wall. Aleksy was on the other side of Sebastian, lending him an arm to help him get up and down quickly without drawing attention.

"They're just trying to rattle us!" Sebastian told Freddy over the sound of shells hitting the ground outside. The echoes bounced off the hills, making everything seem as if it was happening many times over. The wall absorbed some of the vibration of impact, but he still felt each hit under his feet. A low cloud of smoke drifted over their heads.

Freddy's magical protection didn't feel very comforting just now—he felt small next to all the noise. He covered his ears and tried to breathe.

When the artillery ceased, Sebastian's men slowly raised back up. During the barrage, the enemy had gotten closer. Now the men in front took a few probing shots at the top of the wall.

"Fire back sporadically!" Sebastian ordered. "Hide our numbers! We don't want them to know any reinforcements arrived."

Sebastian's side was cautious as they opened fire, the enemy less so—of course, their numbers now filled the road ahead as far as the eye could see, hundreds of them marching, with more heavy guns at the back. On either side of Freddy, two men went down almost at once. The first one got up and clutched his shoulder, but the other one stayed on the ground. Freddy rushed to his side and took his hand.

His magic flowed; he shut his eyes and tried to block out the noise and the unfamiliar chemical-sweet smell of burnt gunpowder, reaching for the calmest place inside him, trying to help this stranger get back on his feet.

Emotions flashed across the revived man's face as he realized what Freddy had done—confusion, panic, understanding, determination—all in seconds. He went back to his post, firing again.

Freddy's hands were shaking.

The man was the first of several to go down from the first wave of direct attack, including two men Freddy knew.

"Thank you, son, I won't waste it," one of them said before he got back to work. Freddy squinted, shoving aside tears. They weren't all so prepared for a heroic last stand. The fifth man he revived got a little hysterical at first, crying and sputtering, "No, no—"

Freddy had let go of his hand when he came back, but now he took it again, trying to force calm. He couldn't let anyone panic. His presence on the battlefield wouldn't be much of an advantage then. "Listen," he said gently. "You're a brave man, to be here today fighting. I can't truly save you, I wish I could, all I can grant is the chance for you to save others. The men fighting beside you, and everyone in Urobrun who will be safe from Irminau."

"My family—"

"Your family is going to be taken care of." Freddy met his eyes, trying desperately to impart some great courage.

The man turned back to the battle, and Freddy unclenched muscles he barely knew he had.

He glanced behind him during a lull in the fatalities. The trucks were still moving out of the base, one by one—so slowly, it seemed, that this day would never end.

As a few light flakes of snow fell from the gray-white sky on what was otherwise a fairly warm day for the season, Baron Best's second wave was getting closer to their walls—now with the heavier guns. Some men were running up between them.

Sebastian lowered his binoculars. "They've got explosives," he said, thrusting his arm forward. "Now, open full fire! Don't let them breach the walls!"

The men followed orders, raining shots on the ground. Due to the hills, most of Best's men had been funneled into a fairly tight space and were an easy target, although some of them were clambering up the rocks and trees to get height. As their men fell, the bodies were roadblocks to be tripped on and hamper the movement of the guns.

But casualties mounted on Sebastian's side as well. Freddy was running back and forth now, hardly able to keep up with the fallen men. He counted in his mind as he touched each hand—five, ten, fifteen men down today. Had he ever revived fifteen people in one day? Maybe once or twice. His strength was holding up much better than it ever had with the Valkenraths. It must be because he wasn't holding on to thousands of people, and because he was fully willing to use this magic.

His stomach still grumbled fiercely, but in the rush of adrenaline, he didn't care about hunger.

"Guhh!" Aleksy staggered back from the wall, dropped to his knees and then the ground.

"Aleksy!" Sebastian had been looking through the binoculars again, but now he dropped—almost fell—to the ground. He pulled back Aleksy's shirt, finding the spreading red stain. "Damn it."

"I'm going," Aleksy said, closing his eyes.

Sebastian's mouth twisted. Freddy already had Aleksy's hand. His eyes fluttered open again and looked at Sebastian.

"Don't lose morale," Aleksy said. He clapped his hand over his jacket where Freddy knew he kept the picture of Ilse. "Please. You need to live through this."

"I know," Sebastian said.

Aleksy helped Sebastian to his feet again, but Sebastian kept a hand to the wall, looking like he was in pain. Freddy knew, whatever Aleksy might say, Sebastian was shaken by so many losses.

"Sebastian," Freddy said.

"I don't know why," Sebastian spoke so softly Freddy read the words from his lips, "but it's worse when they come back."

"It is. But you'd lose more if they didn't."

Sebastian clapped his shoulder and looked grim, as if to comfort himself by comforting Freddy, then turned his attention back to the fighting.

But the battle was slowing down. The defenders had been successful in holding against the first wave. The few Irminauer soldiers remaining were trying to clear the bodies of their dead out of the way while just a few men defended them. Freddy had a chance to devour the rations he carried in his pocket to fortify himself for more magic, though at this point twenty of the men on the ramparts and in the guard towers were dead, and a few more had retreated from injuries.

"They made a determined effort to keep the road fairly clear," Sebastian said, "as if they have something on wheels. But as far as I know, Otto's behind on technology."

One of the guards in the towers interrupted him. "Commander Hirsch, sir, there's something approaching the bend. It looks like crude self-propelled guns."

"Hmm. Armored?"

"Yes, sir. Iron boxes on wheels, from the looks of it. Steam-powered."

"I'll be damned." Sebastian almost looked intrigued. "But if they work, we might be in trouble."

FIFTY-ONE

"Boy, they must have cobbled those together recently," Sebastian said, as the guns finally rolled into view on rows of what looked like carriage wheels, dark-gray smoke puffing out the stacks on the back of their iron-riveted bodies. They looked as if they might have been outfitted from old steam-driven tractors.

Their crude bodies didn't detract from the tension of watching their slow approach as they rolled forward. The steady clack of their engines seemed to build the closer they came. Another wave of soldiers walked with them.

"We need a report," Sebastian said, looking back toward the base. "How many more loads until we have to move out of here?"

One of the men ran to check and returned quickly. "Sir, there are nine trucks left, but four are the ones we came in, so they'll only take a small load of ammunition. We can't take the remaining guns."

Sebastian rubbed his palms together rapidly. "We'll try and hold, but tell Opitz we don't have much longer if we can't take out those tanks. He should start making preparations to blow up what's left and move out."

"Yes, sir."

No sooner had the messenger departed than one of the armored vehicles stalled out. This was obviously not intentional; immediately a few of the men on the ground stopped to poke at it while the other two vehicles kept moving.

"Ha!" Adalbert jeered. "What do Irminauers know about tanks, anyway?"

The men cheered from the wall as the crew of the vehicle climbed out. "What a piece of junk!"

"If they all broke down it would be our lucky day, but I wouldn't bet on it," Sebastian said. The other two tanks were almost within range, while a striking figure appeared at the bend, his plumed hat and shaggy black horse visible from a distance.

"Let me guess—Baron Best?" Freddy asked.

"What? Oh—" Sebastian shifted his view. "Yes. That's him, all right, and his horse, Brigand." He turned his back to the army briefly. "I was hoping he'd stay in the back."

"Do you think he'll recognize you after all this time?"

"If he thinks I'm dead, I don't think he'll recognize me— not from a distance like this. But if any rumors have leaked out, well, that's another matter if he's actively looking for me." Sebastian tugged his scarf away from his neck, like he felt choked at the thought of encountering anyone from home. "Could they load those trucks any slower?"

"Well, every time one drives out, that's one less man," Aleksy said.

"I know." Sebastian checked on the guns. "They're almost in range. Men, ready your weapons! Try to hit those guns in a weak spot—we can't let them reach the walls!" He tapped his hand against his thigh restlessly, as if he now wanted the vehicles to move faster. *"Fire!"*

Freddy realized his heart was pounding along with the guns, but his emotions felt like they had ceased functioning in the heat of battle. There was no room for fear or sorrow—that could come later, when he was no longer needed. The infantry on the ground fired back, trying to protect their heavy equipment, and Freddy's internal count resumed. *Twenty-two down, twenty-three down . . .*

A bullet smacked him in the head. His hat offered slight protection, besides the spell, but it still knocked him sideways, leaving him dizzy. Stars danced in his eyes.

"Freddy?" Samuel saw him struggling to pull himself up on his hands and knees as the world whirled. "What happened?"

"A bullet got me in the head . . . I'm protected, but . . . it grazed my temple."

"Just sit a moment and recover. I'll bring them to you."

Freddy sat back, watching the dancing lights in his eyes recede as he heard another man grunting slightly, carrying a body toward him. Freddy always feared the next man down might be Sebastian, even though he was keeping back, and that fear was heightened by his disorientation, but it was one of Opitz's. He touched his face.

Around him, men were screaming, "Commander, their armor is resisting our bullets!"

"Try to get the wheels, shoot between cracks—anything you

can—just keep at it!" Sebastian's voice moved closer to Freddy. "You all right?"

"I'm getting there. Just give me another minute."

They kept bringing him fresh deaths.

Twenty-six down . . .

Twenty-seven . . .

Almost half their initial number were now dead or injured. His vision had cleared, and although he still felt a little dizzy, he staggered to his feet, waiting a moment for the swirling to end. The chugging engines were growing alarmingly close now, and when he glanced out he could see them rolling over fallen bodies, and how large their guns were.

"Best's hanging back, but he keeps pointing up here," Sebastian said. He frowned. "I think we need to evacuate."

"Sir, they're loading the last truck! Commander Opitz wants to know if you can hold them off for fifteen more minutes."

"We can try. Give them everything you've got! We can't let those guns breach the gates!" Sebastian looked uncertainly at Freddy. "Freddy, maybe you should retreat now."

"Not if you aren't." A man was down on the other end of the wall, and Freddy was already making his way. In this moment, the whole world existed inside of this battle and the men he had revived to fight. He might walk out of this, but they fought knowing they would never see their loved ones again. He wouldn't leave them. He owed them this much.

His ears were beyond ringing now, the guns deafening as everyone poured their ammo into the guns that were now almost close enough to knock on their doors, but even as bullets shot off the iron bodies, the first gun fired point-blank, rocking the wall. Sebastian was shouting, waving his arm to keep up the attack. *Twenty-nine down . . . thirty . . .*

Freddy couldn't hear, but he saw Aleksy grab Sebastian's arm and speak to him frantically. The gist was plain: *You need to take the survivors and go.*

Sebastian grimaced, grief barely restrained in his eyes, as he quickly embraced Aleksy and thumped his back. He approached Freddy, his expression resolved. *They know you're here,* he mouthed.

"They do?" Freddy supposed he shouldn't be surprised; everyone in Urobrun seemed to know.

"All right, men, if you can fight another day, retreat!" Sebastian motioned for the stairs, even as another assault from the guns knocked him off balance. Aleksy, still keeping an eye on him, caught his arm and steadied him. "Move!" Sebastian shouted, as Freddy took one long look at the men he had revived. He would never have a chance to thank them.

He took Sebastian's arm to help him hurry down the stairs as one of the guns breached the gate. Now all the men, living or dead, were rushing to the ground, some of them to escape and others to hold off the army. Sebastian stumbled, jerking Freddy's shoulder.

"Damn my stupid leg!" Sebastian snapped. "You go ahead of me."

Freddy glanced around, but no one else was near to help Sebastian. In the chaos, some of them had run ahead; a few others had joined the defenders at the gate.

"Don't worry about it, just keep moving," Freddy said.

"You're steady. Just don't outrun yourself. We both need to come back."

Something fell from the sky, ripping through the roof of one of the smaller buildings at the base, blowing out the windows in shattering glass.

"Artillery?" Sebastian cursed vehemently. "Move, move!"

Another explosion threw up dirt. A man's body flew sideways. Freddy forced his eyes ahead to the bridge, breathing heavily with exertion, but he barely felt his own feet. He kept his arm around Sebastian, trying to shield him—if anyone shot at them, the bullets wouldn't hurt Freddy like they would Sebastian.

The last truck drove across the bridge. Freddy fixed his eyes on the bank ahead—true home soil, not this little stolen piece of Irminau. Across the way, men were setting up explosives, waving the escaping men forward with wild gestures. Freddy could taste safety as they set foot on the bridge—the sounds of shooting and screaming were behind him.

Not halfway across the bridge, another explosion dropped from the sky, the force knocking Freddy sideways—Sebastian grabbing him, stumbling over the guardrail—both of them losing their anchor to the world as death rang in Freddy's ears. He threw his arms tightly around Sebastian and looked at the sky, trying to be the one to hit the cold rock-studded waters below, in that longest second of his life as they both blew off the bridge together.

FIFTY-TWO

Freddy's body plunged into rushing, cold water, scraping rocks. He lost hold of Sebastian, or maybe Sebastian tore away from him. He couldn't tell. *I can't swim.*

"I've got you," Sebastian panted, and Freddy realized that although the water was rushing around his head, his face was above the surface. Sebastian had a hold of him as the current pushed them forward, but Freddy had never felt so helpless. His body was breathing fast in uncontrollable panic, while his mind was still trying to grasp what had happened.

"Play dead!" Sebastian's shouts seemed thin against the rushing river. "Just do it, quickly! I've got you."

Freddy forced his body to go as limp as he could, but his teeth wouldn't stop chattering, his body shivering. Sebastian had an arm around him and raked his other hand through the water quickly to steer them away from other rocks.

"Now, let the dead go! Make them think *you're* dead."

Freddy wanted to question this decision—the dead men were still defending—but Sebastian knew more about the Irminauers than he did. The frigid dark water surrounding him made him feel so close to death himself that severing ties to his magic came easily. As he let them all go, it felt as if their spirits were floating away with the current.

"We have to get out of this cold river!" Freddy said.

"Yeah, I'm aware!" Sebastian glanced back, just as the river began a gentle curve ahead, the water glinting in the moonlight below the tall, shadowed banks.

"Your men are going to think we're dead!"

"I'm aware of that also!" Sebastian loosened his hold on Freddy. "Can you swim?"

"No."

"Just paddle and don't let go of my hand. Follow my lead."

Freddy wasn't so sure there was a leader here, except the river itself. As they fought their way to the bank, his toes briefly touched the bottom but were swept away again. The cold was quickly sinking deeper toward his heart, and he wondered how long before hypothermia set in, but he shoved that thought aside and kept kicking and paddling until he found the river's bottom for good and they managed to clamber out onto a wide, flat rock large enough to set up camp on.

If only they had a camp. A warm fire and dry clothes—he fixed on that thought, drawing some suggestion of warmth from his imagination. Now the open air was a fresh assault on his soaked and heavy garments, every little breeze like a thousand knives. He offered Sebastian a hand. "How's your leg?"

"Still here. My glasses, too. Now I know we're going to live because clearly I have a guardian angel." They spoke through violently chattering teeth. "Move."

Freddy wasn't sure of their prospects of climbing the six-foot slopes that led up from the river, but a quick glance at their surroundings revealed a path carved up the riverbank. A railing made it visible even though it was covered with snow.

"Maybe someone lives up here," Sebastian said.

"But we need to get back—"

"We're not going anywhere until we warm up. That river must have swept us a mile already."

The path led to a cottage; perhaps a little vacation getaway or fishing shack. The door was locked, but they were able to push up a window and climb in. The cottage held little of value to protect, but there was a bed with blankets, and a fur rug on the ground. They immediately peeled off their wet clothes, and Sebastian spread the fur rug over the bed. Once in bed, Sebastian unfastened his leg and put it on the ground.

"Well, we're not going anywhere for a while," he said.

"What happened?" Freddy asked, once his teeth stopped chattering enough to talk. "Why were you so adamant I let the dead go?"

"You didn't see because you were busy working magic, but Baron Best had his binoculars, and he was pointing excitedly at the men you revived. Aleksy and I were both sure he'd figured out what it meant: He knew you were there. If he thought he could get a hold of you, he'd do anything to bring you back to my father. But if you let them go abruptly, he'd probably assume you were dead. Unfortunately, as you pointed out, our people might also assume we're dead."

"You aren't worried how people will react if they think you're dead?"

"I am worried," he said softly.

They stared at the ceiling for a moment.

"Thea—" Sebastian began.

"No," Freddy said. "You don't have to explain." He wasn't sure he wanted to hear it anyway.

Sebastian took a deep breath. "We would have been in huge trouble without you today. We all owe you our lives."

"Yeah, well . . ." He kept thinking of Thea's name on Sebastian's lips. She was waiting for Sebastian to return. Not Freddy. But his pain felt stupid at this point, his feelings illogical and out of control. He should have been able to just shove Thea's face out of his mind. What did she really mean to him? A shared experience, a new world, but it was sheer coincidence that they had gone through all that together.

But whenever he thought of Sebastian with his arms around her, he felt possessed by demons of jealousy that just wanted to punch things.

"Freddy, I feel very uncomfortable making use of you in my army, and . . . you saving my life, when—"

"You saved my life as much as I saved yours," Freddy interjected.

"Maybe. I just need to tell you. Thea doesn't want to hurt you, but I don't think—"

"I know what you're going to say, for god's sake. We don't need to have an official conversation. It isn't as if I didn't suspect she had feelings for you from the moment we arrived. I thought at first it was the enchantment, but I know better now."

"I try not to pay attention to girls," Sebastian said. "Everything gets more complicated when romantic feelings are involved. But they have a way of sneaking up on you. And I couldn't ignore Thea. I feel responsible for her losing her hand, for unleashing Ingrid on the world in general."

Freddy understood this. He felt responsible for the workers who labored underground, including Thea's father. He could try and reason these feelings away, and he could tell Sebastian that Ingrid wasn't his fault either, but feelings often defied reason.

He had a lot in common with Sebastian. They could be good friends. Only he didn't know if he could stand to watch Sebastian's relationship with Thea develop.

"Look, I'm glad Thea's happy. That's really all I can say," Freddy said, his tone sharp.

"I know how it feels to be lonely," Sebastian said, in almost a whisper.

In the following silence, Freddy crashed into sleep, the after effect of so much magic. He woke in a room that had the gentle brightness of white snow falling in the night. He could just make out the silhouette of Sebastian sitting on the floor, pulling on his undershirt.

"Sebastian?"

"Our clothes are drying out. We should spread out the coats."

Freddy, holding the blankets to his neck, propped himself up on one elbow to look around the cottage. It was not an inviting place, between bare wooden floors and drafty windows. Even if there had been firewood ready, they couldn't dare start a fire just in case Baron Best hadn't given up that easily.

Freddy pulled on the legs of his long underwear, feeling like some unkempt mountain man—who broke into cabins and slept in strangers' beds, at that. Although the dry air and howling winds that leaked into the cracks of the cabin had sped up the drying, they still felt damp and almost crackly, as if turning into ice. He yanked a blanket off the bed and wrapped it around himself like a cape.

While Sebastian spread out their clothes, he searched every drawer, shelf, basket, and crock in the cabin, finding matches and candles, and a bit of usable food. A mood of grim determination pervaded the cabin.

"Peas and crackers for dinner, pumpkin and crackers for breakfast?" Freddy said, regarding the selections.

"Sounds . . . sensible."

Freddy frowned at the kitchen tools. "You know how to use a can opener, right?"

"Hand it over."

Freddy stepped out to fill cups with snow, and they used the candle to melt them into water as they sat around the table wrapped in blankets. Sebastian regarded his bowl of cold peas and handful of stale crackers, the flickering candlelight adding to his skeptical expression. Freddy was hungry enough to find them almost delicious. The wind gusted and howled around the cracks in the windows, snow sometimes hitting the windowpanes.

"What did you say was for breakfast? *Pumpkin?*"

"Yes. A can of pumpkin."

"I really hope they sent a search party."

FIFTY-THREE

An urgent message for Freddy arrived shortly after the men left for Lingfeldt.

"Do you suppose we should open it?" Marlis asked Thea.

"Open his mail?" Thea frowned. She already felt she was keeping secrets from him; she didn't want to invade his privacy on top of it.

"But it's marked 'Urgent.'" Marlis decisively pulled up the edge of the envelope and slashed it open with her thumb.

The letter was from Freddy's parents, letting him know they had heard he was with the revolutionaries, that they were safe with friends, and they would let Freddy know where as soon as they could.

I hope we will finally get to know you as we should have known you all along, the letter said near the end, and tears came to Thea's eyes. The tragedy of her own father being alive without her knowing seemed parallel to Freddy being torn from his parents.

"Isn't it good news?" Marlis asked.

Thea pulled herself together quickly, ashamed at having had

such an emotional reaction in front of Marlis. "I just feel so bad for him that they are such strangers."

"He'll be all right. I don't think he needs you feeling sorry for him." Marlis sounded a tad defensive. "You don't even know him that well."

"I know him."

"I know you went on a date or two."

"And we went underground and found the workers together. That wasn't a *date*."

"No, I imagine not." Marlis let the matter drop, but Thea felt oddly provoked by this conversation. She hadn't realized Marlis knew she had a romantic history with Freddy, and now she thought, *Marlis probably also knows I dropped him without explanation.*

Thea had thought herself a direct person. She didn't know why this was the one thing she couldn't seem to face.

That night at work, when Ruthie said she had found kittens in her neighborhood and needed to find homes for them, Thea impulsively agreed to take one home. Freddy had seemed very fond of his cat that had died; maybe it would be a nice surprise when he returned. That night she carried home a tiny white creature with black markings that reminded Thea of a tiara and necklace.

She brought it into Freddy's room, since she wanted it to get used to him. The kitten crawled under the bed and wouldn't come out for an entire day, and when Thea pushed food under the bed, the kitten let out a tiny hiss, but the plate was empty later. All the men who were familiar with cats assured her this was normal. It was nice to have something to fret over, rather than the empty feeling inside the house with Sebastian and so many others away.

She had more to fret over than she could have imagined the morning of the party, when the Lingfeldt unit returned with the horrifying news that they had lost twenty men during the battle, and Sebastian and Freddy had gone missing.

"It was getting dark by that time, and they were escaping the base. We think they fell off the bridge when the opposition destroyed it."

"Did no one search?" Marlis demanded.

"We left behind four men, but we couldn't spare more with so many losses. We had to get the weapons back. Those were Sebastian's orders. If they've been found, we wouldn't know right away, of course, but all the men Freddy had revived went silent right after the attack. And the water's frigid . . . their chances would have been slim, Miss Horn. I'm so sorry."

Thea felt like she had been dropped into an icy river herself. Everyone began to speak of canceling the party, to mourn the men who had died, and murmur of what would be done with Sebastian lost, as if the matter was certain. They kept saying, *No one could survive on a cold winter night like that.*

"Sebastian isn't the type to just give up," Thea said. "And Freddy, he—he's protected by magic, and he would have let the dead go anyway if the battle was over!"

A number of skeptical, battle-hardened faces turned to her. They all seemed to say, *Poor girl, she doesn't get it. War doesn't care who it claims.*

"Listen!" Marlis said. "The party should go on. It will be more of a somber gathering now, but if Sebastian is dead, we mustn't let his work be in vain. Sebastian's vision for this land went beyond what our current leadership can offer; if we retreat into mourning, we might give up our chance to join the fight."

Marlis had a gifted tongue; listening to her, Thea was almost swept into this impromptu obituary.

Whether or not Sebastian had actually died, Thea realized he had given Marlis an excellent chance to take the leadership role. Her calm, firm speech seemed to promise that the mission would go on uninterrupted, that she had control of the situation.

"Please, tonight we need to hold ourselves together and carry on as before," Marlis said. "The guests will be arriving in mere hours—we have to show them that we remain as strong as we ever were."

FIFTY-FOUR

Marlis ran the scenario over and over in her mind.

The river would have been freezing cold. Can they even swim? I can't think when Freddy would have learned. How fast is that current? They'd have to get out quickly and find shelter. Would Sebastian's leg have come off in the fall? Maybe he couldn't even walk. It would have been dark, they'd have no place to go.

She saw them thrashing and drowning in the cold, their bodies carried up the river, battered by rocks, and ultimately frozen under the ice, to be found in the spring thaw.

Her gut still rebelled against the news. Sebastian and Freddy wouldn't have died in such a way. Of course, it had given her the perfect opportunity to have what she'd always wanted: to step into Sebastian's shoes and use her newly built reputation to lead.

She retreated into Sebastian's office, ostensibly to plan her speech for the gathering, but the room seemed so alive with his presence. She looked over his papers, his slanted and nearly indecipherable handwriting, his empty coffee cups. These signs of recent life mocked the terrible news and sent her running over the possibilities once more.

And I'll have to write Freddy's parents and tell them.

That thought almost broke her. She did know how much Freddy missed them, and she used to think so poorly of his parents. Papa always said such things about rustics, so she imagined them as simple and backward. She had made comments that hurt Freddy's feelings. She had snapped at Thea earlier when she really wanted to snap at herself. *How could I have been so cruel? I should have been above all that. Why didn't I know?*

Her human side had been stronger, all along. Her attempts to grasp at her power now had left her feeling so hollow.

Because I'm still acting like a human. Like Papa. Selfish. Power-hungry. Freddy is the one person who has been constant, and now he's gone.

Tonight, she vowed to change. She would not use the wyrd-song to gain power. She would not begrudge Sebastian the trust he had earned among his men. But she did have to do something to keep the ground they had gained, and unfortunately she could only think of one thing.

Someone pounded on the door. "It's Thea."

Marlis shoved the chair back, dabbed any trace of tears from her eyes, and opened the door.

"Can we talk? I mean—do you have a plan?" Thea asked. "You really want to let this party go on? Brunner will be here, and the men just came back with the weapons from Lingfeldt. He's going to want them to go into the government arsenals."

"I know. But consider if we don't have the party: Morale will be low, and word will get out that we've lost our leader. Clearly, I would need to do something. To gather everyone together and, well . . . I think I have to tell everyone he is the prince," Marlis said.

"But what if he isn't dead?"

"Then we will give him a hero's welcome."

"He dreads nothing more than being the prince."

"This moment is too pivotal," Marlis said. "We need an immediate surge in Sebastian's popularity to have any hope of keeping Brunner from seizing the weapons. He'll say they belong to the government by rights, but Sebastian is the one who risked his life to get them. If we don't keep support on our side, then even if Sebastian comes back, the thing he fought for will be gone."

"I know."

"It's our secret for now," Marlis added. "I don't want the gossip to spread beforehand. I know this is an unfortunate situation, but this will define our group and us, and keep us in the running for taking control of Irminau."

Thea nodded, standing straight. "I'll get dressed."

Marlis twisted her hands. "Thea? I've never dressed for a party without the help of a maid."

"Do you want me to help you?"

"If you could. I really don't know the first thing about all that stuff."

"Of course."

Thea despaired a bit at Marlis's party dress, which she had purchased with the intent of looking both intimidating and financially conservative in these lean times. It was black and unadorned.

"But the skirt rustles," Marlis pointed out. The skirt was cut at the sides, with poufs of net. "That's fancy, for me. Although it was the only one they had. The new style, I suppose."

"You should enjoy it," Thea said. "The next new style won't waste fabric like this."

Thea lamented that Marlis hadn't given her enough time to curl her hair, but as she did her makeup, she didn't nag her about her skin like Marlis's maid, who felt women should never go outside, and that Marlis had committed a grave sin by acquiring a few freckles and sometimes even a full-blown tan in the summer.

"You have lovely collarbones. I wish we had some diamonds you could wear. What is this?" Thea asked, pointing to the gold chain around Marlis's neck.

Marlis pulled out the gold heart. "My mother gave it to me, before she died."

"What is it?"

"A human heart."

"Oh! Of course it is." Thea looked sheepish. "I guess I didn't pay enough attention when we studied anatomy. You should wear it on the outside."

"It's a strange thing to have."

"But it's from your mother. She died a while ago, didn't she?"

"Yes, half my life ago. We were very much alike." Marlis suddenly yanked at the chain. "But she wasn't really my mother. Everything was a lie."

Thea lowered her hand. "I'm sure not everything." Her

brows furrowed with concern. "I don't know you well enough to say much, but you must have loved your mother if you've worn it all this time. That's worth holding on to. Life is so short. . . ."

Marlis dropped her hand, letting the heart hang free. Nothing felt concrete enough to hold on to at this moment. "I wonder if I'm doing the right thing today. I always wanted to go into politics, but not by taking advantage of Sebastian."

"If he is dead, what are we fighting for?" Thea asked. "I suppose that's the question. He wanted to bring Irminau and Urobrun together as a unified republic. But besides that, are our goals much different from those of the rest of the UWP?"

"The UWP was still quite willing to use Freddy's abilities," Marlis said. "If magic is lost, the point is moot, but there are other things to consider. If Chancellor Brunner and King Otto go to war and one nation conquers the other, I think the winners will abuse the losers, who will be bitter for generations. Sebastian was right: We need to try to unify our countries as peacefully as possible, and whoever rules the new nation has to value what each side has to offer."

"Then that's what tonight is all about. And every night after that," Thea said. "That goal. I'm not sure Sebastian was that good with goals."

"No?" Marlis said, although she knew just what Thea meant.

"He was so afraid of being the prince. But you're not afraid, are you?"

"Only a little." Marlis half-smiled.

⊙–⊙–⊙–⊙

She had invited an eclectic group, from soldiers of the old republic who had been low enough on the rung to escape scrutiny, to people she had met through her recent public appearances, and, of course, revolutionary leaders, both within the radical UWP and from other fringe groups like Sebastian's. Some of them were Sebastian's friends, not hers, and she had to struggle through awkward greetings without his introduction. They had no idea of the news when they arrived, and so they came in their best winter finery, shedding fur coats to show off beads and sequins, glittery jewelry, and feather headdresses.

Brunner came alone, no lady on his arm, and gave Marlis's hand such a vigorous shake that she almost winced. "I finally meet the famous Norn. Who would've guessed you had such a secret?" With his small but merry eyes and a bushy beard, he looked uncomfortable in a suit, like he'd rather have boots and rolled-up sleeves. He certainly looked the part of the working man's hero even more than Sebastian did, and he had a broad Urobrunian accent.

Volland stayed beside her in lieu of Sebastian, but he kept looking at her suspiciously. He knew her well enough, unfortunately, to sense the anticipation mixed with the sadness.

"Are you up to something?" he whispered in a quiet moment.

"I'm always up to *something*."

He let her leave it at that, but didn't seem convinced.

Thea seemed to be working the room well. She was wearing a dark blue dress with a black beaded headband over her auburn waves, and shoes with silver accents. Whatever grief she felt over Sebastian and Freddy didn't show. Marlis thought she must be holding out hope they would return.

The band played music that was not quite funereal, but gentle to frayed emotions. Wine flowed freely; Marlis had instructed the servers to open ten more bottles than originally planned, but she didn't touch a drop of the stuff herself.

Brunner, she noticed, was talking to Lucas, Sebastian's head adviser. Now Brunner looked to be asking the tough questions; she sidled over when she saw him frowning.

"I'm not in a position to discuss that," Lucas was saying.

"What is this, now?" Marlis asked.

"I'd like to talk to Mr. Hirsch's second in command, if I may."

"That would be me," Marlis said. Some of the men might argue, but she could handle that later.

"But, ah, who did he leave in charge of military operations?"

"Me," she insisted. "What is the problem?"

"I hear you've recovered a number of weapons from Lingfeldt, and I wondered when you planned to tell me about it."

"Chancellor Brunner, of course we planned to tell you, only we thought the chances of success were so slim. When Sebastian found out he had to rush out the door that very moment to have any chance of reaching the base in time, and as you've heard, the losses were heavy. We've had no time to see what we've recovered or sort it out."

Brunner's friendliness slipped away now. "The weaponry is the property of the government. It should be delivered directly to our base without you needing to 'sort it out' first."

"I'll see what I can do."

"I appreciate that," Brunner said, but his eyes followed her even as she moved away. She wondered if he would send someone to confiscate the weapons. Her plan felt thin, without Sebastian here. *His memory won't be enough. They won't follow me. They won't follow anyone but him.*

She forced her fears back. Thea had asked what she was fighting for. She had to focus on that. A unified nation, with a vote and a voice for every citizen—like the nation she had imagined her father governed, when she was younger and naive.

"Everyone!" She lifted a hand, stilling conversation, and stepped up onto the dais. "I'd like to thank you all for coming, despite these sad circumstances. I know I take comfort, on this sad day, in your support."

The room collectively murmured condolence. A few ladies dabbed their eyes with handkerchiefs, while Sebastian's men lowered their heads.

"Sebastian had originally planned to tell you all something tonight, until he was called away for this swift and brutal attack from Irminau. You will understand how personal this was to him. Sebastian, you see, has been living under a painful secret. He wants nothing more than to be one of the people, and he considered Urobrun his adopted home."

Now, her audience was almost dead silent. A few glasses or plates clinked as people set their refreshments aside.

"Sebastian's real name is Rupert, and our enemy, the king of Irminau, is his father. Or, must I say . . . was." She wasn't sure many people even heard that over the sudden gasping and exclamations spread among her audience, but she felt suddenly adrift, remembering that this wasn't some event she had staged, but that Sebastian really was most likely gone.

"That's impossible!" some of Sebastian's own men were shouting. "His father was only a baron!"

"That was only a story," Marlis said, "to explain his well-bred accent. He gave himself the most humble origins he could."

"A story? I'll say," said Yann, Brunner's adviser. "Lost princes and magical trees. Stories would seem to be your forte, Miss Horn."

"She's telling the truth," Lucas said. "He didn't tell many people, even among his own men. If we figured it out, we kept the secret, because he really didn't act like a prince. He was one of us. We respected that."

"His death was always suspicious," one of the women said. Heads nodded.

"Now that I think about it . . ."

"He does look . . ."

"Older, of course . . ."

"Sebastian's heart was here in Urobrun. I tell you his secret now," Marlis said, "because I intend to do everything in my power to keep his dreams from dying with him. He devoted his life to this revolution."

She let the crowd's chatter take over. In many ways, Sebastian's stubborn insistence on not revealing his identity was now an advantage. If he had told them himself, Yann might not have been the only one questioning the story. They might have wondered, Why now? But tonight, it was a heroic tale people wanted to believe.

Brunner was glancing around with a furrowed brow. He hadn't guessed either. As she moved back into the crowd, fielding questions, she saw him arguing with one of her men.

"What's wrong, Chancellor?" she asked, trying to sound pleasant—but with an edge.

"Marlis Horn, those weapons are still property of the Urobrun Army."

"And I have always had an excellent relationship with the Urobrun Army. Besides, if not for Sebastian's sacrifice, Irminau would hold those weapons."

He tugged his beard. She could see he was trying to think of a good response, but craftiness wasn't Brunner's forte. In some ways, she felt sorry for him, because he was just the tip of the UWP at large, elected for being a hardworking fellow that everyone could agree on. "I see what you're trying to do here," he said.

"I suppose you do."

"It will buy you a few more weeks of attention."

As if he thought she was just a spoiled rich girl who wanted attention. "Not much, is it? So, I suppose you don't mind, then." She smiled, and let out her breath.

FIFTY-FIVE

Thea thought, at first, that the wailing and chanting voices were in her dreams. But she woke to see Freddy's kitten—*my kitten, now, I suppose*—with her tail puffed with alarm at something before she ran under the bed again.

She parted the curtains. Outside, a crowd had gathered—girls with their hats bent together in mutual support, rustic men with tear-streaked faces. The front of the house was piled with flowers.

Her stomach twisted oddly. Were they crying for *Sebastian*?

An old Irminauer woman with a shawl over her head was clutching a photograph of young Prince Rupert to her chest, a burning candle in her other hand. Yes, they were holding vigil for Prince Rupert. *But haven't they already thought he was dead for three years?*

Thea dressed quickly and ran downstairs.

"You underestimate the power of royalty," Marlis said. "I suppose when the same family rules the country for centuries and centuries, people get funny about it."

Thea could hardly eat breakfast. It still didn't feel like

Sebastian was really dead, and now all these strangers had appeared to cry over this person he used to be years ago. Marlis went out to shake their hands and try to comfort them. Thea couldn't handle the thought that they were crying for her Sebastian. All those people. *All those people.*

How did I ever get swept up in such a thing?

But she wasn't. He was gone. At least he and Freddy had died together.

She left early for work, battling her way past the crowd, so she could spend some time with her mother.

"Why don't you just come home?" her mother said.

"I can't. I need work, and Marlis will keep me employed," Thea said, but she realized the revolution had gotten under her bones. She hated the thought of not hearing the latest news as it reached headquarters. "Anyway, I can't just walk away from what all my friends fought for. And Nan will come back."

She didn't tell Mother she had cared for Sebastian—maybe later—but Mother was very sad to hear about Freddy. Thea felt better just having a shoulder to cry on.

At work, Sebastian's death was all anyone could talk about. Miss Helm tried to send her home early because she looked so pale.

"Please, I don't want to go home," Thea said. "There are all these people outside acting like Sebastian was a saint and it's—it's going to be like sleeping inside a funeral. They didn't even know him."

"Why don't you just work with Hedda, then? Keep busy, but you don't have to talk to anyone unless you want to."

When she returned in the wee hours, the crowd had thinned

but a few loyal people lingered, hands clasped in prayer in the bitter cold. Some Irminauers were very serious about their mourning vigils.

⊙–⊙–⊙–⊙

She woke to a pounding on her door. "Thea!" Sebastian shouted.

For a moment she thought, *This time, it really is a dream.* But the world felt much too real as she rubbed her eyes. She flung open the door. He grabbed her to him before she could even get a good look at him. His clothes were still cold from the outside.

"Oh god," she gasped. "It's really you."

"It's me."

He just looked at her for a long moment, and she looked at him. His face was pale and drawn. She touched his cold cheek, lightly. Her Sebastian.

But he wasn't just her Sebastian anymore.

"I can't stay," he said. "Everyone wants to talk to me." His eyes were frantic, a little angry, but mostly sad.

"Is Freddy alive, too?"

"He is, though he's caught a cold. He'll be fine. I just hope I will." He scowled at the window.

"Everyone said you couldn't possibly have lived."

"Well, they don't have very good imaginations! Or much patience. You didn't think to wait a day? A week, even? Give a man a chance to climb out of the damned frozen river and warm up? I told you not to let Marlis do anything crazy!"

The crowd outside was no longer crying, but shouting his name or "Your Majesty!"

"Truly, it didn't matter if you had lived or not," Thea said. "When the men came back with the weapons but you weren't with them, Marlis had to do something to keep Brunner from taking them. When she told everyone you were Prince Rupert, the mood shifted immediately and it would have made him look bad to demand them from her right then."

"Yes, well . . ." He looked over his shoulder, as if the past were a person hovering behind him. "I see her reasoning, but . . ." His hands had dropped to her arms, sitting heavily a moment before grasping. She had seen the way people had simply appeared at the first mention of his name, with pictures they must have kept all this years, and faces of sorrow for someone they had never known.

She had already understood why he didn't want to be Prince Rupert, but she hadn't grasped just how scary it could be to have people love you. Not when they wanted something. Not when they loved the idea of you, and not the reality.

FIFTY-SIX

A warm bed had never felt so good. Freddy was dull-headed with fever. His throat was scratchy, and piles of blankets couldn't stop him from shivering. Climbing the stairs to his room had been an effort, but now he was safe in familiar surroundings and someone had handed him a letter from his parents.

They were alive and so was he. He didn't want to think about where to go from there, how to close the immense gap of unfamiliarity between them, but it was enough for now to know he had a chance.

Still, the sickness only added to the feeling that he was weak. Of *course* he caught a fever while Sebastian came back unscathed.

When Thea walked in his room with a tray, he barely opened his burning-hot eyes to see her before closing them again.

"Freddy? I brought you something."

"I don't want anything now," he said, figuring it was tea or soup, but then he heard a tiny peep of protest and opened his eyes again. Thea put a kitten on the bed and took a step back, looking nervous.

"If you don't want her, I'll keep her. But I was thinking about how you had brought your old cat back from the dead—"

"Amsel," he said. The kitten was stumbling over the covers now, wiry tail in the air. He couldn't even remember when Amsel had been this little. The kitten let out another small cry, and he slid his finger under the covers. It immediately developed an interest in the mysterious motion, getting very still, eyes riveted.

"Does she have a name?" he asked.

"Of course not, I got her for you. Do you like her?"

The kitten certainly wasn't Amsel, who had been big, black, and lazy. "I like her," he said. "Thank you." He coughed, and the kitten dropped off the bed in blind terror at the sound.

Thea laughed and scooped her up. "She's shy, but she falls asleep on my lap now. She's already been in your room a lot because I wanted her to be comfortable here. I brought you some tea, too."

"Thanks." He sat up a little more. He wanted to say something to her, he just wasn't sure what. "Thea . . ."

She was lingering, too, her pose pensive, ankles and arms half-crossed. "Freddy, I'm so glad you're safe. I need to talk to you."

"Sebastian told me about you two."

She looked at the floor. Then at him again, with a slight frown. "I should have been honest with you. But I didn't know how. I still don't. Marlis said I don't even know you, but I don't think that's true. I think I've seen your essential character, and based on that, I'd trust you with my life. We shared things that no one else will know or could understand."

"Yes."

"But I shouldn't have kissed you. I feel like I misled you. I mean, I wanted to kiss you." She scratched her head. "Hell, I don't know how to say it. I kissed you because I wanted to feel like something good came out of all those terrible things."

"We're both new to this," he said. "Life's too short to feel bad about this. I almost died. And so did Sebastian. So, really. We're fine." Everything he said was true, but she was also so sweet to have brought him a kitten and so beautiful that he felt like he'd swallowed shards of glass.

She stepped closer and put a hand on his head. "I don't have a lot of people in my life either. I think that's why this is so hard. I'm really scared to lose you, Freddy."

"You won't." He gave her a slightly pained smile. "I mean, now you're the mother of my kitten."

She laughed. "I hope so. We've gotten close, kitty and I."

He dropped his head back onto the pillow, trying to cover his hurt with exhaustion, and she left quietly. He tried to sleep, as best he could with a kitten who decided it was now time to jump all over him, climb the curtains, and swat all the objects off the desk, just like Amsel used to do.

Marlis came to check on him some hours later. She didn't bring kittens and tea, but she did look worried. "How are you feeling, Freddy?"

"I'll live. You don't have to check on me."

"Well, someone should, in the absence of proper servants. Has anyone taken your temperature?"

"Right," he said. "I forgot you're Miss Hospital Volunteer."

"I thought you were dead," she said. "I thought—" She stopped.

He sat up again and tried to rake his hair into a semblance of respectability. Marlis was not someone he wanted to see when he was sick in bed.

"I never told you I was sorry," she said. "For forcing you to revive my father, and treating you the way I did."

He shook his head. "You were grieving—"

"No. I'm sorry for everything. I'm sorry that—when we were growing up together—I knew my father was killing you and I didn't tell you. You were one of the only kids who would play with me, and I didn't treat you like an equal—I treated you like a servant. I shouldn't have even treated the servants like servants, but especially not you. Please forgive me."

"It's fine." He felt uncomfortable at this declaration. "I appreciate the apology, but we were also kids, so don't beat yourself up."

"I'm not a kid, I was never a kid, I'm hundreds of years old!" she cried, and then her face crumpled slightly.

"You didn't remember being hundreds of years old. You had a tantrum when I grabbed your trains, you pretended the sofa was a horse, and you slid down banisters. You *were* a kid."

"I had a tantrum because you *broke* my train."

"I didn't break your train. That was Peter von Dorin. I just made it worse when I tried to fix it."

"You made it a lot worse. It came apart." She clasped her hands behind her back and tapped her foot restlessly. "We grew up together, you know."

"I noticed."

"I'm not sure I did. I was so caught up in wanting to be smart and successful and make my parents proud, and you didn't seem like you had anything to do with my ambitions. So I didn't think about you much."

He shrugged, and suppressed a cough. "I'm sure your father and the Valkenraths would have been alarmed if we'd gotten close, anyway."

"But it was nice, actually, when we did just have fun. I wish I'd enjoyed myself more often."

He was surprised at how long she was talking to him like this. Of course, he had seen a change in her since her father died, but for once she really looked like a young girl, awkward and shy.

"Thea gave you the letter from your parents, didn't she?" Marlis asked.

"Someone did, as soon as I walked in."

"Do you think you'll go back to them, once this is over?"

"I don't know."

"I thought you might finally get a chance to be a clockmaker."

"But my father stopped making clocks when the Valkenraths were giving my parents money. I guess he didn't really love clocks that much. Maybe he'll do it again, since they've probably lost everything, but I'm not sure I want to be his apprentice if he gave it up himself. I love clocks because they reminded me of him, and that might ruin it for me. I don't think I'm meant to make clocks."

"What, then, I wonder? If your magic is gone? It's hard to imagine you without it."

"It is, isn't it?" He didn't like to talk about that. "Well, you might laugh at this, but I was thinking I'd like to learn more about gardening."

"Why would I laugh?"

"Because it's rustic and peasantish, and it's not some grand ambition. If I'm lucky enough to grow old at all, I'm afraid I'll be referred to as 'the kindly old gardener.' "

She smiled wryly. "My mother was very interested in plants, learning about their medicinal purposes, or how to develop new species, or more efficient ways to grow food. All sorts of things. Plants are quite powerful."

"Urd would know, eh?"

"Urd would know. But I'm still figuring it all out."

FIFTY-SEVEN

As news spread of Prince Rupert's heroic life and dramatic near-death saving the Lingfeldt weaponry, so many people thronged the street around the Schiff house that the city police had to assist in managing the crowd. The newspapers and radio spoke of nothing else, and reporters swarmed the house trying to speak to him. No matter where Thea went inside, she heard people screaming and crying outside, and although she knew they were supporters and not enemies, after a while the sound made her feel so rattled that her hands were shaking.

Sebastian stepped onto the balcony of the house to address the throng. Thea stayed well behind him, out of sight of the crowd. He still wore his ordinary, rumpled revolutionary clothes. She heard the roar of excitement when he appeared. Women screamed both his names.

Sebastian held out his arms, trying to quiet them. "Good afternoon!" he projected over the din. But that wasn't enough. "Good afternoon!" Finally, "Listen! Listen, listen."

The roar of chanting and cheering cut in half. Several indecipherable questions were screamed at him.

Thea imagined that most people still wouldn't be able to hear the speech, but he just forged ahead, confirming the stories and rumors. He was Prince Rupert, he had faked his own death in Irminau, and he had come here as Sebastian Hirsch to aid in the revolutionary effort.

The speech was tentative at first, but his confidence seemed to build with the crowd's enthusiasm, and at the end, he was starting to sound like himself, but with an extra dose of swagger. "King Otto might have superior numbers now, but I know we can hold him off if we mobilize. How many of you were born in Irminau? Well, you probably left for some of the same reasons I did. Growing up, I always heard stories of Urobrun: It seemed like they had all the newest and shiniest stuff, and I wondered why we were so behind. I wanted to find out what made this place tick, and then when I did, it was terrifying. But we have a chance to make this place what we hoped it would be. We need willing people, hard work, efficient government."

His style of oration was more laid-back than Marlis's, with occasional jokes. He was the same person she had grown to know and love over these past months, but it was so strange to see him engage with people this way.

When he finished speaking, he walked back into the room from the balcony slowly and was greeted by a round of compliments from his advisers, who seemed relieved he wasn't trying to run away from his identity. He met Thea's eyes before slipping off to his office without talking to anyone.

The next few days were such chaos that she barely saw him. He accepted some of the requests for interviews and spoke on the radio and had meetings with more potential allies and government officials. The meetings had grown too serious for her to be sitting in like she once did. Thea continued going to work, and the mood had changed drastically. She couldn't believe how jubilant people seemed. The conversation was similar at so many tables:

"Brunner's a good chap, but he's soft. Rupert, on the other hand, he has a real backbone, going to Lingfeldt like that."

"He ought to know just how to deal with Otto, wouldn't you think?"

"I'd sure like to see Otto's face when he heard about this."

"God wouldn't have saved him from that river if he wasn't meant to save this country, I'm sure of that."

Thea felt a little like the ant beneath Sebastian's feet the way people spoke of him and barely paid attention to her. She didn't want attention, but he didn't either, and here it was, everywhere she turned.

But the excitement was also infectious. Sebastian could really do something wonderful if he harnessed the power of so many people's hopes and dreams. She would never rule the country or command an army, but she had a part to play. Even when she feared Sebastian was lost, she still felt an independent sense of belonging—that the revolution meant something to her, and she meant something to it.

Thea saw her reflection in the washroom, radiant and bright-eyed. She felt beautiful in a way that had nothing to do with a new dress or the way she fixed her hair. It burned inside her like a light switched on.

Returning home, she found Sebastian sleeping at his desk, head in his arms like he'd meant to just rest for a moment, but he was breathing so deeply she thought he might be dreaming. She ran her hand through his hair, which was shorter now; he'd finally gotten it cut to appear more professional for the public.

He suddenly flinched, jerking his head up.

"Didn't mean to scare you," she said, "but maybe you should actually sleep in a bed."

"I can't. I just lay there and panic. It's better here."

"You're doing a wonderful job," she said. "Everyone loves you. It's all anyone could talk about at work today."

He stretched and yawned. "They love this Prince Rupert persona."

"You've put in a lot of hard work. Give yourself some credit."

He took her hand, kissed it, held it to his lips. "If our relationship was public, you couldn't work anymore. You'd be scrutinized. People will say I need to make a strategic match. I don't want to lose you over this."

"You want to lose me over something else?" she teased.

He raised an eyebrow at her. "The potential of taking the throne, it's huge."

"But you're prepared for it, aren't you? I know this is scary to you, but you said yourself, you like the work. You *can* do this, and I think you should."

"It doesn't scare you because you don't know what it's like yet," he said. "You're still anonymous, but if that stopped, everyone would know your name, and no one would see you as a person anymore."

"I didn't say I wasn't scared." She straightened a mess of papers on his desk, thinking of the right words. "I thought my father died when I was eight years old, but he didn't. It was so much worse. My mother developed bound-sickness, and I had to care for her like she was the child. This country should be ruled by someone who is *good*, who wouldn't have done that to my family. And I will do anything to have a world where that doesn't happen, even if it means that I'm scrutinized. Even if it means I *lose* you. Who have you done all this work for?"

He was quiet for a long stretch.

"Not for Ingrid?" she said.

"No." He looked down, his glasses reflecting the lamplight and hiding his eyes. "My first nurse, Jenny, the woman I told Nan to look for in Irminau? She was like a mother to me. My own mother was distant, but Jenny was always there. She played with me, she taught me to read, sang me songs, held me when I cried. But she was also a skilled healer. She was the one who healed all my cuts and scrapes. The magic aged her, and finally, my father replaced her."

"And she went to this place—what did you call it?" Thea remembered the name had been ominous, but that night was a blur.

"The Mausoleum. In the north wing of the palace was a row of lovely, expensively furnished rooms. I had never seen them until I heard they had taken Jenny there. I snuck in to see her and found . . ." He faltered a little, the memory still painful. "Jenny was too sick to leave her bed. She comforted me as best she could, but she told me never to come back. She didn't want me to see her like that. And what must she have felt, an invalid at such a young age? Ingrid helped me to forget she ever existed."

Thea put her arms around him, but he had gone rigid. "You're right, Thea. This is bigger than us."

FIFTY-EIGHT

It took three harrowing weeks for Nan and Sigi to make it back to the threshold of the revolutionary headquarters. When Ingrid let them go, they had almost nothing of value. They found a place to exchange Sigi's Urobrunian money for Irminau coins, but it still wasn't much, and miles of rural country pelted by frequent snowstorms stood between them and the border. They walked down country roads, praying not to be caught in a blizzard. They washed dishes at an inn in exchange for a bed. They went out of their way to avoid Irminau guards, in case Ingrid had changed her mind.

News was often sparse in Irminau; they heard word of Prince Rupert, but in Irminau's papers he was described as "the treasonous prince." Nan didn't really know what had been happening at home, but as she and Sigi came into the city, she immediately noticed posters of Sebastian and newspaper headlines that stated 5,000 TROOPS TO JOIN PRINCE RUPERT, and they both picked up their pace.

"Nan! *Nan!*" Nan had just stepped in the door when Thea

came rushing down the stairs and threw her arms around her. "You're safe!"

"Yes!" Nan broke into a spontaneous smile, realizing Thea seemed happy. "And you—you all seem safe as well?"

"We are, but so much has happened since you left." Thea hugged Sigi now. "Did you go to King Otto's palace?"

"Believe it or not, as long as we've been gone, we were only there for one night," Sigi said. "But that was one night too many for my taste."

"It took you this long to get back?" Thea asked.

"Yeah, between weather—"

"Oh god, the *weather*," Sigi interjected.

"—and trying to keep a low profile. But we do have some information for Sebastian, and Sigi has photographs. Or do we call him Prince Rupert now?"

"He still likes Sebastian better," Thea said.

Another girl hurried down the stairs—a girl Nan had also heard rumors of as she traveled home. She had seen posters of her plastered on buildings on the city streets along with Sebastian. Marlis Horn, the Chancellor's daughter.

Urd.

"Verthandi," Marlis said.

Thea was still saying something, and Sigi was talking to Freddy, who had just walked in the entrance room from the side, but Nan didn't hear them. For a moment, she only saw Urd—the other girl in her memories, the other guardian of Yggdrasil. Urd, who made the best soups and wrote everything in her diary. Urd, serious and dependable.

"You remember me, too?" Nan asked. "And Skuld?"

"Yes," Marlis said. "I'm sorry I missed you before. I feel as if I know everything about you already. Skuld had all of my diaries, and I've learned so much from them to fill in the gaps of my memory. But what a curious feeling. I'm actually somewhat nervous."

"Do you know the tree was dying?" Nan asked.

"Yes. And we suspect—well, did you get the note that Freddy sent?"

"That it needed to feed?" Nan nodded. "The tree was revived. Ingrid's magic is keeping it alive."

"Skuld was supposed to—"

"To let it die. I know. I *know*." Nan took a deep breath. "And I should have killed her, in Irminau, before she spread her magic farther. But I couldn't kill her. It was—it was just too sad."

"We need to talk this out."

Nan and Marlis sat together with the diaries. The longer Nan looked at Marlis, the more details sprung to mind.

"Didn't you buy a horse once, named Ashes?"

"Do you remember the time we tried to sneak into Queen Lizbetta's summer house? I didn't write down what we were looking for."

"You were very bossy about bonfires, as I recall."

"According to this, we *both* masqueraded as boys at that point. For five whole years. I'm sure it made things easier, especially in those days."

Marlis was just as Nan remembered Urd. She was more talkative than Ingrid, but in a serious way. She was not quick to laugh, and when she did, it was low and restrained. Her slender hands reminded Nan of cursive letters, the way they gestured in small swoops when she spoke, as if she was always writing in her mind. She remembered butting heads with Urd while Skuld usually floated above the arguments. But they were always together in the end, all three of them.

Until now.

Marlis grew very quiet when Nan told her about Skuld. "I feel the bonds between the three of us breaking," Marlis said.

"I sensed the heart of Yggdrasil when I used the wyrdsong against her. It needs to be set free, and she's become a part of what's trapping it here. So that's all we can do. It's our job. Our final job. But it still feels wrong to abandon her, when she made such a sacrifice for us."

"She made a poor choice," Marlis said. "We honor her by setting her free from it."

"You're always so calm." Marlis's calm was familiar to Nan, like finding a once-beloved possession that had fallen behind a bookcase years ago.

"I am holding on to calm for dear life," Marlis said. "Do you feel as if you're changing? Thea told me you were more emotional than Ingrid, that you didn't want to be a Norn."

"I *have* changed. Did your books ever mention us having feelings for people? Falling in love?"

"We had feelings occasionally, but it seems we were always able to turn away from them."

"Did Thea tell you I have feelings for Sigi?" Nan laughed nervously. "I don't know what you'll say to that."

"I think I'm afraid of those kinds of feelings," Marlis said.

"Romance seems too far from my nature. I wouldn't know how to navigate it."

"That's how I feel, except I can't seem to help them creeping in."

"I loved my parents," Marlis said. "I think I always knew I was different, and that made me absolutely desperate for my father's approval, as if it would make me not different anymore."

"I understand. I tried to hide my strangeness, too, but it didn't matter. People could *see* I was different before I even said a word."

"But we're powerful, Nan. We've had an amazing life. If Urd and Verthandi are barely alive and soon we will only be Marlis and Nan . . . Well, we owe it to them to appreciate what they've given us."

Nan had never seen it quite that way before, but it made her feel better knowing that Marlis had struggled with the same feelings, that Nan was not alone. And Marlis was right—part of her was so heartbroken over the idea of killing Skuld and what was left of Yggdrasil that she wanted to hide from it, her final duty.

She also learned that, in her absence, not only had Sebastian's identity been revealed but he had received such a groundswell of support that Brunner and the UWP were now behind him. He had the whole Urobrun army at his disposal and the assistance of their leading commanders.

But everyone wondered if it would be enough to withstand Irminau. Although Urobrun was the more technologically advanced country, Irminau's army outnumbered them substantially. Urobrun's army had been so fragmented by the months of revolution, and their weapons were limited. Some spoke of negotiating a truce, but Sebastian felt that his father had been dreaming too long of getting Urobrun back under his rule. Otto would not give up this chance, especially with Ingrid's aid bolstering his confidence.

The rest of the winter was filled by attempts to organize and train as many soldiers as possible to lend support at the border as King Otto moved more of his men closer. Nan knew she would have to face Ingrid again. A few of Sebastian's men took her under their wing to improve her skill with weapons, but in the end, it would come down to the wyrdsong.

FIFTY-NINE

The river ran with melting snow on the final day of March. Otto's border army had spread into Urobrun land like a stranger quietly stealing the armrest at the theater. They had made camp at a large state-run farm right on the line, taking grain, milking cows, and clearing out the henhouse.

Sebastian's army was positioned close enough to see them in the distance, putting Freddy on constant edge, as he never forgot that Otto's army would surely love to seize him for their own. He was under guard at all times.

No one had made a move yet. Troops were still arriving by the day, on both sides. Sebastian had a handful of magic users by now, including a powerful wind magic user who had escaped from Irminau. He was just a few years older than Freddy, and his hair was silver, too.

"Otto made me control the weather over Neue Adlerwald," he explained. "Of course, sometimes there wasn't much I could do. I can shove aside a summer thunderstorm, but I can't control a blizzard. Otto hates not having control over anything."

"I hear you can't even spill a drink in his palace," Freddy

said, having heard the stories from Nan and Sigi. He tried to keep the conversation casual, because the stories of how Otto treated magic users were enough to keep him up at night.

No one knew how many magic users Otto had, but Sebastian said true offensive magic was rare, and technology might tip the balance. The Urobrunians had seven tanks, the artillery from Lingfeldt, and most glamorously, two airships: The *Falcon* had once served as a passenger ship, but it had been converted for military purposes; the *Invincible* was built specifically for war. Freddy was so fascinated by the airships that he made the crew give him a tour. Sigi took a slew of pictures of them.

"They look so forlorn," she said.

"Forlorn? They're exciting," Freddy said.

Sigi shrugged. "I guess they seem so lonely in the clouds."

Freddy still saw adventure when he looked at the airships, but he understood what Sigi meant. The prospect of death and war produced funny thoughts; one evening he lifted a chunk of potato from his tasteless stew and stared at it for a while, thinking, *What if this was my last meal, this potato?*

Sometimes he couldn't believe he was in this position again by choice, on the brink of battle, and yet there seemed no other path.

"Otto has more troops coming down from the north; if we don't get more storms, they could get here by week's end. While I had hoped to muster more troops ourselves, it seems we will have to make do with what we have now." Sebastian addressed the commanders that evening. Freddy was standing along the side of the room with Thea, Nan, and Sigi.

"They outnumber us, but don't be dismayed by the sheer numbers. Our equipment is better, our morale is higher, and fate is on our side." Although Sebastian spoke convincingly, everyone knew victory was by no means assured. Word was that Otto's men outnumbered them three to one.

Marlis stood beside Sebastian, sharp in a navy suit. "One of the most dangerous elements are Otto's magic users. We know he will have unexpected tricks up his sleeve. Be on the lookout for anything unusual." Their army had a healer for every unit, and a handful of offensive sorcerers, but Freddy himself would be among the most useful magic users in the army.

If all went as anticipated, Ingrid would die in this battle and take Yggdrasil with her. This might be Freddy's last chance to use his magic before he turned ordinary. For all his dreams of a quiet life, nothing compared to the thrill of his power.

⊙–⊙–⊙–⊙

Ten thousand men were in their places that morning, marching behind seven medium tanks. Freddy could hardly fathom the coordination of armies, but Sebastian seemed unusually calm. Freddy accompanied him in a small military vehicle so they could get around the battlefield quickly. The tires drove through a thin layer of snow, moving slowly with the front line of soldiers.

The open farmland rolled gently, and as they crested the next slope, Otto's army was visible in the distance. The sheer numbers were hard to comprehend—that this many people would gather in one place to kill one another. Reviving twenty men wouldn't even make a dent in armies of thousands. This was no Lingfeldt, but two oceans of men clashing tides.

Sebastian was taking it all in through his binoculars. "Yep, those are the same armored vehicles we faced at Lingfeldt. It doesn't look like they've made any improvements at a glance, though they've fancied them up a bit."

Otto's steam-powered tanks stood in an offensive line, holding their ground as Sebastian's forces approached. They had only faced two at Lingfeldt, but now Freddy counted fifteen. The seven Urobrunian tanks should be able to handle them; the infantry divisions were of more concern. Freddy looked up toward the hill where Marlis and Thea were stationed with the long-range artillery. Although the hill was an excellent vantage point for them, to Freddy it looked vulnerable rising above the soldiers on the ground.

The airships were at camp waiting for their orders; Freddy was excited to see them fly. The anticipation of first fire was almost unbearable as the tanks trundled slowly into position. It seemed to take hours for Sebastian's army to approach—long enough that Freddy had time to consider the clotted gray clouds that sailed across the sky and the patches of brown field appearing between the melted snow.

Eventually they drew close enough to Otto's army that the painted crests and adornments on the steam-powered Irminauer tanks were visible. While the Urobrun tanks were pure aggression, painted white to match the snow, the Irminauer tanks had embellishments, painted scrolls, and gold ornamentation like one would see on a passenger locomotive.

"Almost there . . ." Sebastian said.

No sooner had he said this than Otto's tanks took the first shots. The next few minutes were a blur of activity, the blasts of the powerful Urobrun guns' return fire pounding deep into Freddy's ears. Dirt sprayed from the ground, clouds of smoke rose. Several of the Irminauer tanks were destroyed quickly. The foot soldiers held back for the initial barrage; their guns were not yet in range.

Early that morning, Marlis had told Freddy, "Make sure Sebastian stays in the jeep for his own safety." But Sebastian was already leaning out the jeep window looking around, his hand clutching the door handle.

"You'd better not start roaming," Freddy said. "Marlis will kill you. And you don't want to tire out your legs like you did at Lingfeldt."

Sebastian waved a hand dismissively.

The radio operator sat behind them, relaying messages to the commanders of their units. "Sir, a report from the crew of tank six: They are withdrawing to make repairs." And then, "Tank One is down."

As the tanks continued to fire, it was clear the Irminauer vehicles were indeed outclassed. Several of them came apart in dramatic fashion, painted plates of metal flying sideways and wood underneath exploding into toothpicks. While their destruction drew some cheering from the Urobrun men, many more Irminau tanks remained. Otto's tanks managed a few strikes while the Urobrunians were reloading.

"Tell the airships to move in for bombardment," Sebastian told the radio operator.

"Is this going about as well as expected?" Freddy asked.

"Yes. But I was hoping for better than expected. We could really use it."

The *Falcon* and the *Invincible* rose over the horizon behind them, their engines small and softly whirring in comparison to the bulk of their silver skins. Eight hundred feet long, the crew had told Freddy during the tour. They looked gentle, like whales swimming through the ocean. They swept over Otto's army, flying low so their machine-gun crews could run swaths of bullets through the enemy. They dropped explosives that tore up the landscape, scattering chunks of dirt and rocks. From Freddy's vantage point, the bodies looked like tossed dolls. The sense of death was thick in the air.

On the ground, the Irminauer tanks were all destroyed or damaged, while Sebastian had two remaining. But Otto's army was swarming toward them, pitching grenades that ripped through turrets and tracks, until the tanks were nothing more than husks surrounded by the remains of their useful parts, like dismembered bodies.

The infantry divisions were beginning to engage, the loud and more infrequent firing of tanks exchanged for the constant noise of soldiers' weapons. Sebastian's vehicle moved forward to keep up with the front line, staying far enough back to avoid most of the danger but close enough that Sebastian could keep an eye on proceedings and Freddy could revive. Men started dragging bodies to him, and soon he had a line of them waiting. Magic burned hot down his arms. He grabbed their hands, two at a time, barely aware now of the chaos around him.

"What the hell is that?" Sebastian stopped panning his binoculars.

Freddy glanced in the same direction, seeing what appeared to be a person flying up to meet the *Falcon*.

"Send a message to the *Falcon*: Take out whatever it is flying toward them quickly!" Sebastian told the radio operator. He got out of the jeep for a better view.

"A flying magic user," Sebastian said.

He had only time to say this before the person reached the airship's hull, which was filled with bags of flammable hydrogen. For a moment, they lost sight of the distant form.

Then fire sparked in one of the gas bags, spreading in seconds through the entire hull, stripping the airship's skin away to the metal framework, but even that was crumpling as the burning ship sank. Some of the crew jumped from the ship's cabin to escape the explosions. Otto's men were running from the blaze; even from here Freddy could hear the shouting and panic.

"Get that magic user!" Sebastian screamed, as if anyone in earshot could help. "Tell the *Invincible* to shoot them down! Where did they go?" He tore his hat off and dashed it into the snow. "Damn it. No one warned us about this. Where the hell did he get a flying witch?"

"It might be an air witch, sir," their driver suggested. "A really talented one. Or even a dual elemental."

"Good god." Sebastian slapped his hand on the roof of the vehicle. They were all watching the sky, looking for the witch.

"That was quite a blaze when it went up," Freddy said. "Maybe they got caught in it. Wait—"

The witch was in the air again, shooting for the *Invincible*. Everyone around watched, completely still.

A fierce round of shots came from the *Invincible*. This magic user was on a doomed mission from the start, Freddy thought, wondering if the sacrifice had been willing. The witch hung in the air for a long second, as if held by the hand of the wind, then dropped like a stone, limp arms lifting above the head. Freddy instinctively shut his eyes when the body struck the ground.

Sebastian grabbed his hat and got back in the jeep, drawing a deep breath. "All right. Report from the *Invincible*?"

"They're fine, sir. They've taken out five divisions, but they've maneuvered out of position in order to strike Otto himself. Should they circle back around?"

"Yes. Hopefully he doesn't have two of those! Freddy, how are you holding up?"

"Fine," Freddy said, although stopping to watch the airship had broken his momentum, and he felt a little dizzy when he had a chance to think about it. He must have brought back a hundred men already.

"Good," Sebastian said. "We're going to need every last man. Get back in the jeep, we need to move up."

SIXTY

Marlis wondered if she'd ever be able to wipe the sight of that burning airship from her eyes. Such a beautiful thing, gone that quickly.

With the tanks all knocked out and one airship down, the battle had descended into man against man. Marlis stood on the hill behind hastily erected ramparts, watching the valley turn into a churning mess of shooting and shouting and bodies. She kept picking out Sebastian's jeep in the crowd, but was too far away to identify him or Freddy.

They shared the hill with the artillery from Lingfeldt, and Marlis kept moving back and forth, checking on the artillery commander and getting the latest reports, then joining Thea at the wall to keep her eyes on the fight.

Sigi snapped photographs of the battlefield, complaining that their vantage point was poor. They were removed from the fighting up on the hilltop, with a broad view of men spilling across the valley, churning up dirt with the snow. The rear of the army was closest to them, so the fighting was mostly distant and she didn't see many fallen men, but as time passed,

Otto's men mixed in more with Sebastian's, and blood stained the slush. Sebastian's men were being slowly pushed back, she noticed—not a good sign.

Nevertheless, the radio operator said, "Prince Rupert reports that we're holding our own." Sebastian's ranks had swelled so much since he had been revealed as the prince that hardly anyone called him Sebastian anymore, but Marlis still had a hard time getting used to it.

"Good," she said. But she felt a little useless. Nan had asked her to stay out of the fighting.

"I'll take care of Ingrid," Nan had said. "One of us should stay back in case the battle doesn't go well."

"But it seems cowardly," Marlis had protested. "We should do this together."

"You've been a symbol of hope for Urobrun so . . . you really need to take care of yourself. What if Sebastian died? They need you."

"If Sebastian dies with Otto at our doorstep, I'm not sure all the speeches in the world will save our morale," Marlis replied.

"You always were the pessimist, weren't you?" Nan gave her a knowing smile before leaving her behind.

Papa, for all his failings, had never showed pessimism. He kept his brash confidence until the end. If she couldn't believe in Nan and the soldiers of Urobrun, who would?

"Can you see Sebastian and Freddy?" she asked Thea, returning to the wall.

"It's just so hard to tell since Freddy dyed his hair. They all look the same from here."

"I suppose it doesn't matter when we're too far away to do anything," Marlis said.

"You wish you were down there, don't you?" Thea asked.

"I just pray it all goes well. I'm not sure what I could possibly do to save Urobrun if they all died, and I'm not sure I'd have the spirit for it, either."

"Any word from Nan?" Sigi asked.

"No. Sebastian said the *Invincible* is swinging back around and aiming for Otto's camp. Maybe one of the explosives will take out Ingrid." Marlis wrapped her gloved hands around the hastily erected defensive walls. "It would be easier that way. Nan shouldn't have to be the one to kill her."

The *Invincible* seemed to be moving into position again, but before the guns could fire, a bolt of lightning streaked across the sky.

No, not the sky exactly. Its violently bright light raced from Otto's camp to the *Invincible*'s engines.

"Oh no," Marlis breathed. "How many elementals do they *have*?" She was waiting to see the *Invincible* go up in flames the way the *Falcon* had, but it was a more advanced design, with better defenses—more guns, more responsive engines, and an armored hull.

"I told him to change the name of that airship," Thea said. "It's just asking for trouble."

The airship remained true to its reputation and stayed in the sky, only it was drifting off course. "It's lost power," Marlis said. "Maybe our air witch can steer it to safety."

"Can it still attack?" Sigi asked.

"I doubt they'll risk it. One air witch doesn't have that kind of control," said Marlis, recalling the scenarios they had gone over in numerous planning meetings. "They'll need to repair the engines."

This meant the *Invincible* would be unable to bomb Otto's main camp. Only a weapon of substantial magnitude could possibly penetrate Ingrid's magical barriers. Nan would have to face Ingrid and her men.

"I think I should go down there," Marlis said. "I should help Nan."

"No," Thea snapped. "She told you to stay here! If you walk down there, everyone will wonder what's going on, and they might do stupid things to protect you."

As Marlis glared past her, she noticed odd ripples in the snow in the distance. "Wait." She held up a hand. "Look, there."

They all turned. Thea had her binoculars at the ready.

"What is that?" Sigi asked.

"Something is moving through the snow," Thea said. "Almost like . . . footsteps?"

Marlis rushed straight for the radio operator. "Hurry and send a message to Sebastian. An enemy unit appears to be approaching fast at his right flank—and they're invisible."

"Yes, miss."

But this wasn't enough. Within minutes the invisible army would be within range of their men, and they would be caught off guard by shots they never saw coming. She turned to the artillery commander. "We need to take out that approaching army as fast as possible."

"As soon as Prince Rupert gives the—"

"He's going to say the same damn thing. We do *not* have time to wait for messages to come through." Marlis pointed toward the field. "Ready them *now*."

It would still take crucial moments for the artillery to change their target. Marlis watched the tamped-down snow move ever closer, the wyrdsong thrumming through her mind, but her power was useless from such a distance. The *Invincible* was drifting back toward the base, a crippled behemoth, and Sebastian's right flank started getting the first round of fire from their unseen ambush.

The battle seemed like a disaster played out in slow motion. A whole section of men went down without hardly knowing what hit them. As the front lines began to turn their attention to support the right flank, the entire Urobrun army was driven farther back. The fighting was getting close to their hill now.

"Thea, Sigi," Marlis said. "Maybe you should get away from the wall now, just in case. I can keep watch."

"No," Sigi said. "We aren't in half as much danger here as Nan is down there."

"Don't be stupid," Marlis said.

"We don't want to be shuffled off where we can't see what's going on," Thea said.

Marlis remembered her frustration at being shoved in the Chancellery basement. The girls she used to know would never have stood on the ramparts with her. Sigi and Thea might not be soldiers, but they were just as invested as anyone. She stopped arguing. The artillery was firing on the invisible army now, the men suddenly appearing as they died and the spell broke.

But it would still take a miracle for them to win, Marlis thought.

Nan is the only chance we have.

SIXTY-ONE

Nan was determined not to think, not to feel. She couldn't let herself remember Ingrid's innocent smile or her begging for Nan's help. With an army behind her, she felt the weight of the whole country's need for a new world. Yggdrasil was already dead and Ingrid had chosen her path.

You're thinking. Stop thinking. Just find her and take her out and think later.

She couldn't charge right past enemy lines; she had to wait out the battle stage by stage. Only after the armies were scattered and the main camp was exposed could she get close. Until then, she waited restlessly in one of the military jeeps. The wind sorcerer had been with her until he was called away to work his magic on the airship; now she was left with the driver and a radio operator.

By the time the sun was beginning to climb back down the sky and the battle had waged for hours, she could tell they were barely managing to hold their own. The field was littered with bodies, probably more than all the workers underground—so many that after a while she had stopped feeling anything when she saw them. They were just part of the landscape. But all the while her gut twisted tighter and tighter, and it all felt more senseless as the day went on. Why couldn't they just talk? Why did thousands of people have to die?

She had no idea how it could have been prevented, though, just like she couldn't help Ingrid.

Sebastian's jeep came driving across the field and pulled up beside her. "Nan," he said. "Otto's camped at that barn up ahead. We've cleared a path, but we can't hold that much longer. We won't have enough ammo to win this, and our numbers are down by half."

"That bad?"

"They've lost more than half, but they also have more reinforcements on the way who will be here in a few days."

The unspoken message was that they would soon have to retreat.

This was it, then. They didn't have much more ammo back in Urobrun or anywhere else, thanks to the destruction of the arsenal. If she couldn't take out Ingrid with the wyrdsong, Otto's advantage would be insurmountable. *It might still be.*

She couldn't think that way.

"You're going in with the revived soldiers," Sebastian said. "They're stronger."

The jeep crossed the battlefield, weaving around piles of the dead until it met with the assemblage of revived soldiers. Nan saw familiar faces among them—all of them now doomed. They hurried forward, approaching the camp. Military tents were clustered around an old barn with its thatched roof sagging. Several horses were tethered outside, and some of the chickens the Irminauers had appropriated from the Urobrun farm were running around. If Otto was in the main camp, he was hiding.

From behind farm equipment and hay, soldiers appeared, waiting for Nan's group to come within range. The revived men closed in ahead of her as they approached, shielding her from the attack.

Both sides opened fire almost at once. Nan recognized the Irminauers—Sebastian's men who had gone with Ingrid. She had traveled with them. She knew many of their names. When Ingrid didn't need them, they talked and laughed as normal, but their faces were blank with enchantment now.

The Urobrunians had no protection, except that they were already dead, but the bullets still hurt. Some of them went down, screaming and writhing. They were willing to suffer just to give her a chance. They had already *died* for her, for Sebastian, for Urobrun.

Nan stormed forward, the wyrdsong pouring from her, their cries giving her fuel. She chanted the sounds, but just as before, the song came from all around her. The ground was singing, the sky was singing, even the barn and the hay and the tents seemed to be singing. The whole world was made of her orchestra, and she lifted her hands to conduct.

"Skuld!" she cried. "Come forth! Show yourself to me!" Her voice barely seemed her own; it was Verthandi now, speaking in the cadence of an earlier age.

The flaps of one of the tents parted, and Ingrid stood before her. Her face had no expression, and she didn't move at first. Then, with the slightest narrowing of her eyes, she looked briefly alien and cruel, and her glamour fell away again, showing her wooden limbs and eyes. She let the gulf between them widen until Nan felt she would tumble in.

"I told you to go, Verthandi," Skuld said. "I gave you a chance to let me take care of Yggdrasil on my own. Now we'll have to battle to the death."

"I know."

Skuld spread her arms. She didn't open her mouth, yet her wyrdsong burst forth in dark glory, so strong that Nan tasted bitterness on her tongue. It screeched and growled in her ears.

"If Verthandi wins, all of you will lose what I have given you, everything that makes you strong," Skuld told the men surrounding her. Gun barrels that had been pointed at the revived soldiers now fixed on Nan.

"That isn't true," Nan said. "I've come to free you! Ingrid has given you nothing and taken your freedom and your memories. She's taken your pain, but she's also taken everything you love. She's forced you to protect something that is already dead."

"It isn't dead," Ingrid said. "It lives *because* of all of you."

"Ingrid is the true Norn." One of the men moved to Ingrid's side. "You've betrayed your sister and your destiny."

Memories spiraled out of Nan's mind and into the magic surrounding her, more than she could hold at once. She saw Yggdrasil dying and Yggdrasil in the height of its beauty. The wyrdsong pulsed like a beating heart around her, and dimly she heard the battle still raging on the fields behind her, but no bullet could touch her in this moment. *This is all I have. This is all we've shared. This is the end of what we've been.*

The colors brightened and sharpened. Nan was ready to let go.

But Skuld fought for her life. Her stance shifted like she was holding out against a harsh wind, but her wyrdsong raged on in response. The chickens had all run away, the cattle lowed in fear.

In the midst of it all, Max stepped forward, and as he did, the magic on his hands fell away and then the hands themselves began to detach from his arms, sliding slowly out of his sleeves until they dangled by the roots. They dropped to the ground.

"Max, you don't want to do this," Skuld said.

"I want to be *free*." His voice was ragged with anger. "She cut off my hands, and she made me shoot your friend so she could keep feeding her powers, feeding and feeding . . ." He clutched his arms around his chest, and one of the revived men reached for him, pulling him to their side.

Nan sensed a crack in Skuld's magic caused by this betrayal, and when she felt it, she reached with her magic to all the men under Skuld's thrall.

Jenny suddenly pushed out of one of the tents, missing a hand now. She stumbled through the muddy snow to Nan's side. Other men shook off wooden feet, leaving behind a shoe, or pulled off an arm. Despite their limping and the dropping of weapons as they shed the wooden limbs, relief showed on many faces, like they had been released from a long imprisonment.

But not all of them responded to Nan's song.

A woman with a withered face suddenly pushed her way

forward and flung lightning from her fingertips at Nan. Nan jumped out of the way, and one of her own men shoved her farther back just before the lightning struck him instead.

"Skuld set me free," the lightning witch said. "Otto stole everything I had, and Skuld has given me back my power. This is our second chance."

Skuld smiled.

The witch released another bolt of lightning, and this time Nan didn't escape. *Protect me, Yggdrasil, this is my chance to save you,* she thought, feeling her skin glow with power. The lightning jolted through her and raised every hair on her body, leaving her on the ground. Jenny grabbed her hand, pulled her up.

"You need to get out of here," Max said. "Ingrid is too strong."

"She isn't! I have to destroy her, I have no choice!"

Skuld dropped to the ground, raking her wooden fingers into the dirt, as if drawing power from the soil like a tree's roots took strength from the earth. She stared at Nan with her dead wooden eyes. "Your powers will never be strong enough. You wouldn't help me, so Yggdrasil belongs only to me."

SIXTY-TWO

The wyrdsong swelled in Marlis's head, but it was not the slow, soothing tone of her dreams anymore. It sounded like bow strings raked roughly across a large, deep instrument, and she clutched her head.

"Are you all right?" Thea asked, walking to Marlis's side.

Marlis's stomach convulsed. Usually her digestion was as disciplined as the rest of her. She shut her eyes against the pain, and when she opened them again, the world was more colorful, but stars danced at the edges. "Nan's fighting Ingrid. I think— it's happening. The end of magic. Or maybe the end of my magic. They're fighting with the wyrdsong."

She blinked back the colors and the stars. "I don't care what Nan said. I need to go down there."

The driver of the nearest jeep looked worried for her health—she must have turned a sickly color—but when she gave an order, he followed. Two gunners came with her, keeping enemy soldiers away from the car as the driver maneuvered around the mess of the battlefield.

When Marlis saw the crowd of men surrounding Nan, she lost all thoughts of her own safety and rushed out of the vehicle. Ingrid was sitting on the ground, but she didn't look injured. She seemed to be drawing power. Her face lifted to Marlis's approach, but even though Nan had warned her, she didn't expect the wooden eyes that made Ingrid's face seem blank and blind.

"Urd," Ingrid said. "I wondered if I'd ever see you. But I hoped I wouldn't."

Marlis stepped back. "Why?"

"The Chancellor's daughter." Ingrid's face was pointed at her, the carved pupils of her wooden eyes staring. "You never realized who you *really* were? You never heard the wyrdsong?"

"I did."

"Well, you must not have listened. It's supposed to guide you. It should have told you your father was your enemy."

"Skuld, the tree was already *dying*," Marlis said. "My father's men wouldn't have even been able to get close if it wasn't already a lost cause. The wyrdsong failed me because it's been corrupted. The books said—"

"I don't care about the *books*. You didn't even come to see me." Ingrid swallowed back tears. "You were going to let Nan kill me without saying good-bye."

"I had other duties, to my people."

"Your *people*. We are each other's people. We live together, fight together—*die* together."

Marlis and Nan glanced at each other.

She's willing to die . . . but she wants to drag us with her?

Maybe this was fitting. Maybe they were supposed to die together.

Ingrid shut her eyes, and rolling waves of dark music seemed to come from her body as a vision unfurled above her small crouched form—of Yggdrasil . . . or was it? The shimmering image had the rough shape of the familiar tree, but the bark was too smooth—almost like skin, covered in short dark hair like a man's arms, and then she realized that fingers and toes sprouted from its branches like growths. What she had first taken for knots were actually eyes and even an ear.

Every piece of a person Ingrid had ever stolen had become a part of their tree.

"What is this?" Nan asked, her voice barely above a whisper. "Is this what Yggdrasil looks like now?"

"Can you see it?" Ingrid asked. "I wanted to show you. I wanted to bring you back to our forest, but this vision will have to do."

"This is growing in our forest?" Nan switched to shouting.

"Yes. It will grow stronger and more beautiful—if you let it."

"Beautiful? It has *fingers*," Marlis said. "It's monstrous. How—how could you?"

Ingrid raised her arms like branches, shutting her eyes, the vision wavering and shifting until the fingers and toes disappeared, the bark turned dark and rough, and the leaves grew brighter. "Here it is," she said. "Yggdrasil's spirit is with us. We're all together. Let's go together, Urd, Verthandi. Let's go together." Tears streaked her face. Marlis edged closer to Nan, and they locked hands.

Marlis's wyrdsong had already killed one of the men she thought she admired; now it might kill her own sister. Was she acting with courage, or was she selfish to wish for a human life?

The wyrdsong poured through them, more than a song now, but the rawest, purest power Marlis was capable of, and she felt Nan must be giving the same, standing against Ingrid's darkness. They were going to take her life, and Yggdrasil's with her.

Am I selfish? Am I? Am I? She wanted to turn away, even now. Let someone else do the deed. Through her many lives, she had felt the hand of fate telling her what to do—to reward one man, to punish another. To take lives, to influence human events, to protect Yggdrasil.

This was different. This was a human choice. It felt right, but also wrong. It would haunt her. She could have pulled back.

But she didn't.

I will do my best to live a human life worthy of my Norn life. To do what is right. Please. Let me have that chance.

I'm sorry we couldn't save you, Skuld.

The vision of Yggdrasil shrunk away into Ingrid, and she collapsed forward, her wooden limbs detaching from her body. Her song died. The world seemed to break open in Marlis's eyes, becoming a blinding white and then clearing, colors turning two shades more vivid.

Nan dropped to Ingrid's side and turned her over so her wooden eyes faced the sky. Marlis thought she was already gone. But then Ingrid's lungs drew a ragged breath. "It's dark now and I'm so cold. Don't leave me, Verthandi."

"I'm here." Nan gathered her body onto her lap. There was

so little left of her. Marlis stroked her forehead, and her eyes closed. She let out a small sigh.

"I'm sorry, Urd. Verthandi, I'm sorry. I'm sorry."

"I love you," Nan said.

"We both love you," Marlis said, but she bit her lip. She loved Skuld, but not Ingrid.

"I love you, too," Skuld whispered.

And when she died, magic died with her.

SIXTY-THREE

In that moment, Freddy's magic felt like a ghost that had possessed him since birth and had become a friend—a friend that was gone in an instant. Every man he had revived fell where they stood. He had brought back over a hundred, and when they were gone, he felt—not weaker, not stronger. Just strange. Like a different person altogether.

It's gone. It's just gone. Like that.

"Tell the fifth division to cover Nan and Marlis as they get out of there," Sebastian told the radio operator. "Quickly, quickly, before Otto regroups."

Freddy climbed into the jeep and stared at his hands. All the tingling heat in his fingers and the prickling sense in his temples that always occurred when he was around the dead was gone like it had never existed.

"Freddy?" Sebastian clamped a hand on his shoulder, making him jump. "Are you all right?"

"Fine. I'm fine." He forced himself to think only of the

moment at hand. "Are we going to try and get Otto? If Ingrid's gone?"

"We're almost out of ammo," Sebastian said. "Nan and Marlis did what they needed to do, but . . ." He surveyed the scene. The center of the field was opening up as Otto and Sebastian's scattered men drew back toward their sides. "They do seem disoriented. They still outnumber us, though not as badly as before. Should we attempt one final push? Losing magic should have hit their morale more than ours."

Another jeep pulled up next to them with Marlis and Nan inside, but the first to climb out was a silver-haired witch with one hand. Her face was drawn and weak. *This must be one of the magic users from the Mausoleum.*

"Jenny!" Sebastian ran forward to embrace the woman. He looked close to tears when he pulled back. "I'm so sorry. Not your hand, too . . ."

"Rupert." She was firm. "Don't be sorry for any of this. You're still so young, to challenge your father's armies like this. You have done all you could and more. Support for you in Irminau grows by the day."

Sebastian looked grave. "Do you think his army would surrender to me?"

"I want to address them now." She coughed, her thin body rattling.

"We're low on ammo. I think I have enough for one last stand, but it's a gamble."

"I'm going back to face Otto, even if they are the last steps I take," Jenny said.

"For what it's worth, I think we should try," Freddy said.

"We've lost a lot of men, but they've lost more, and you are the prince." Seeing Jenny and the other magic users who had come back twisted him with guilt; he would survive this, but they wouldn't come back from the state they were in. Jenny was surely thinking she had nothing to lose.

Marlis had stepped out of the jeep while they were talking; she watched quietly.

"Marlis," Sebastian said. "Do you mind taking care of things here, making sure the injured make it back safely? And if the worst happens to me . . . you're in command."

She opened her mouth as if to protest, then looked at Nan sitting in the jeep with Ingrid's body. She nodded.

Then, quickly, she kissed Freddy on the cheek. "For luck. That's all," she said, and climbed back in the car.

The touch of her lips left a tingle of surprise; he rubbed his cheek.

"I don't get one?" Sebastian called, even as the vehicle was pulling away.

"You already got something similar back at the base, I'm sure," Marlis said.

Sebastian took one of the guns from the revived men who had fallen nearby and handed it to Jenny. "For protection," he said. "Don't do anything rash."

They climbed in the vehicle, and he addressed the men directly with the radio. "This is Prince Rupert speaking. You've all done a fine job; their numbers are substantially reduced. I'd like to avoid further bloodshed. I'm going to try and work out an agreement. Please provide cover but hold your fire unless necessary."

The Irminauer soldiers were closing in around the vehicle. Sebastian picked up his megaphone.

"Let me say something first," Jenny said. She grabbed the megaphone and stood up to address the soldiers across the field while Sebastian still looked unsure about this plan.

"Men of Irminau! I have been working for King Otto since I was fourteen years old—and not by choice. I was unlucky enough to be born with magic, and for that I was forced to spend my very short life under Your Majesty's nose. I'm still shy of my fortieth birthday, and I look seventy. He doesn't care about you. All he cares about is his own power and glory, and he'll stomp on you to get it. But here with me now is Crown Prince Rupert. He is here today fighting you, but what he is really doing, whether you know it or not, is fighting *for* you. This is the side you should be on."

Sebastian stood up and Jenny handed him the megaphone. "Irminau is my homeland. I'm here to fight my father, because he is, truly, the enemy of my country." He hesitated. "I am the leader of the Urobrun Army, and I'd also like to serve as your king. I want to see a strong, wealthy nation like we once were. King Otto can force Urobrun to fall in line, or I can bring about a peaceful union."

A very long moment occurred in which no one moved at all, and then an old woman—*no, not old,* Freddy thought, *just another poor magic user*—slowly hobbled out into the center of the field. Looking at Sebastian, she dropped with difficulty onto her knees, and then her arms. Finally, she dropped her forehead to the cold ground, prostrate to Sebastian as if he were the king.

Another pause, but shorter, before another man joined her, a young soldier this time.

And then it was like a spell had been cast—or broken. A few more came, and then more, and then the entire Irminauer army was on their knees.

Amidst this, in the distance, a figure emerged. Unlike Sebastian, Otto had not been at the front lines. Freddy picked up the binoculars and found him. He was wearing a fine uniform with gold braiding and medals. He was speaking to someone. Then he mounted a horse and rode forward.

"Move up. We'll meet him in the center," Sebastian told the driver.

"Rupert." King Otto looked imperious on his horse, but his hands twitched, and the horse stepped sideways and had to be reined back in.

Sebastian climbed out of the car. "Father, the era of magic has ended, and your men seem to agree it's time for a new regime."

King Otto's eyes were pure rage. But he lifted his hands.

Jenny started to move, and Sebastian clutched her good arm.

"He's a liar," Jenny hissed.

Sebastian looked at his father again, still holding Jenny's arm.

"He should die," another man called. "He killed my sister. Don't you dare spare him just because he's your father, Prince Rupert, I beg you. Get justice for everyone he sacrificed."

422

Freddy thought this an alarming statement, coming from someone who had been fighting for King Otto moments ago. He hadn't considered that people would fight for someone they hated if they were afraid to do otherwise.

A counter-rumble was beginning, some people defending Otto's actions. This could get ugly quickly, Freddy thought.

He lifted a hand. "I'm a magic user myself; I've dyed my hair, but it's pure silver. I was used by Chancellor Horn the same way Otto has used his sorcerers here. But we can't build a new country by executing someone without trial. That is the right of every citizen in a modern nation."

Otto had clasped his hands during this conversation as if in prayer. "My son, I am grateful for your mercy. Considering how long I have thought you to be dead." He had replaced the fury with almost tearful repentance.

"No. No trial." Jenny's voice was so low, it was like she muttered to herself. She pulled her arm away from Sebastian, who snatched his hand back as if she'd caused him pain. "No trial," she repeated, firing the gun. The recoil knocked her back into Sebastian's arms, and blood sprayed from Otto's chest. He stayed mounted, his eyes widening with surprise. One of his healers rushed toward him, but she must have forgotten that magic was gone. A few other men helped him down from the horse. He was looking at his own hand, his white glove now bright red, but then they couldn't see him anymore for the crowd surrounding him.

"He's dead," one of the men announced.

"Long live King Rupert!" someone cried, and then the whole crowd began to take up the chant until it was a roar.

Jenny looked at Sebastian. "I'm sorry," she said. "But you're too kind, my dear Rupert. You haven't spent ten years trapped in bed while your hatred poisons you. Now it's not on your hands. And I won't make you put me on trial either. My life is over. Yours must begin fresh."

She turned the gun on herself.

SIXTY-FOUR

Nan had wrapped her coat around Skuld's body, bringing her back to the camp. This didn't feel like a victory. Cries and groans of pain came from every direction as injured men were treated right on the ground, as soon as a doctor could get to them. The healers were useless now. Bright red blood was everywhere—spattering the snow, turning the slush pink, staining clothes, and matted in hair.

Nan stood still amidst the commotion, overwhelmed by the color and sound. Everything seemed so different.

"Nan." Marlis looked torn. Volland was already waving for her attention. "I need to make sure everyone's attended to. But—"

"I know you need to help here," Nan told Marlis. "I can bury her alone. If you don't mind."

"I've said my good-byes." Marlis hastily wiped tears.

Nan walked outside of the camp. A stand of evergreen trees rose up at the edge of the field, along with one deciduous tree with a thick trunk, reminiscent of Yggdrasil itself. She put Ingrid's body down among the roots and tried to sing the wyrdsong, but it was gone. She couldn't even quite remember how it sounded. After a faltering moment, something else came out instead—a note of human song. Just like the color green, she recognized the sound, as if it had been waiting for her to find it.

She heard footsteps squelching behind her. The field was getting muddy with the snowmelt. Sigi walked up to her with two shovels.

"Marlis said you might need these. I don't know if you want some help, too. I think digging a grave might be pretty hard work."

"I do."

"Were you singing?"

"Trying to. Maybe you could teach me a song."

"I can teach you a lot of songs." Sigi leaned the shovels against the tree. "How do you feel?"

"Strange. But I see all the colors, too." The sun was sinking low in the sky, and everything looked golden.

"This is the most beautiful time of day," Sigi said.

"It is beautiful, and I dreamed of this, but it's also . . ." There were no words for the feeling of losing that life.

Sigi held out her hands. Nan took them. They were ice cold. She realized Sigi was just wearing a wool dress with no coat.

"Aren't you cold, Sigi?"

"Watching that battle was so terrifying I warmed up. I am a little cold now, but shoveling will take care of that."

Nan leaned her head on Sigi's shoulder and cried. For once she didn't feel like the strong one, and it wasn't a bad way to feel.

SIXTY-FIVE

Thea watched the battlefield anxiously through her binoculars until she saw the Irminau army bow to Sebastian. She could finally breathe again.

By this time, the camp was full of the wounded. She picked up her medical bag to help. Familiar faces were starting to walk in—the men Ingrid had tied to her by enchantment. Men with missing hands were helping along men who had lost feet.

Marlis spotted her. "Thea, can you go to the infirmary and get all the crutches we have?"

"Of course."

"Thea . . ." A voice interrupted her. Max staggered out from the crowd, missing both his hands, looking so haunted she took a step back from him. "Thea. Please, I didn't mean to frighten you, but when Nan used the wyrdsong, the spell broke and I remembered everything. I hurt you."

"It wasn't your fault. It was Ingrid. I'm more worried about you."

"I used to remember, when I drank enough, but even when I became aware of the spell, I didn't break it."

"Here." She grabbed his arm. "Walk with me. I need to get those crutches."

He started to follow her, but he seemed distracted, almost slipping on the ice. "If there is anything I can do to make it up to you, ever, just say the word."

Thea stopped walking, took one of his arms, and rolled back his sleeve, revealing the stump of his arm and the small bleeding wounds left behind from the roots. She took out the bandages and wrapped him up, hook and hand working together. She was just as quick as she would have been with both hands by now.

"Max," she said, "it's okay."

She didn't try to reassure him about his own condition. Although she was in most ways grateful for Sebastian for trying to keep her moving instead of grieving, she remembered what a blur of devastation those first few days had been.

She got the crutches distributed among the men, and then stew, and Sebastian still had not returned. But she heard approaching commotion and cheering, and then it seemed to happen all at once that the camp was full of Urobun and Irminau soldiers in a celebratory mood, cheering for King Rupert. She couldn't get close to Sebastian, but the story spread around quickly that the commander of the Urobrun Army had appointed him king right there on the battlefield, to be followed by a proper coronation in Irminau.

She cheered with everyone else, joyous that her loved ones were safe and the country could rebuild in peace. But Sebastian was so swarmed with people every moment, that as the evening stretched on into feasting and music, she still had not seen him.

At one point, he caught her eye across the room, but kept talking to the Irminauer man beside him. It was not until very late, when she tried to slip away from the celebrations, that he caught up with her.

His footsteps crunched heavily through the snow. He didn't say a word, just put his arms around her.

"I thought you might have forgotten me," she said, trying not to sound as concerned as she felt. She noticed a few guards had followed him, even to this quiet part of the camp, and were pretending not to watch them embrace.

"Never. I need you." His back shuddered with a silent sob. "I need you more than I should."

"Sebastian . . ." She stroked his hair. "You're allowed to cry."

He drew back and shook his head violently. "Not yet. I don't want to risk anyone seeing weakness." He swallowed. "It's—it's really too much, even for me. But I just keep thinking of everyone I'll have a chance to help."

"I'm committed to this," she said. "I think it will be like everything else. We'll take it one day at a time, and it will get easier."

He pulled her close again and kissed her, suddenly and forcefully. His breathing was rapid. He smelled like gunpowder and sweat. She gripped him tight, trying to convey how she meant to stay by his side. "Sebastian . . . Sebastian . . ." He was shaking all over, and he stayed like that until her touch finally seemed to reach him.

"I suppose I really am Rupert now."

"Rupert," she whispered, testing it now, with a hint of laughter.

"I feel these are not the most romantic syllables," he said. "Roo-pert."

"Ruperrrrrt," she purred into his ear. "Maybe more like that."

"No."

They both laughed now.

"Too bad, I kind of like it," she said. "But Sebastian can still be your bedroom name."

"Ohh . . . something to look forward to."

"There will be a lot to look forward to. I'm not afraid."

"I don't quite believe you."

She tilted her head to the side so her hair fell into her right eye. "You think I'd lie to you?"

"I think you'd lie to yourself. I would if I could." He pushed her hair back again, his hand lingering to graze her cheek. "But I suppose if we can summon three-quarters of our confidence, we can work with that."

SIXTY-SIX

Marlis never imagined she would cross the threshold of this house again, but here she was, coming home to stay just a month after the battle. She wasn't sure she liked the feeling. And yet, when Brunner, who was now serving as the mayor, suggested she reclaim the home she had grown up in, she couldn't say no.

She walked upstairs and looked at her favorite painting, of the children playing in a square of sunshine on the floor while their mother tended the hearth. Their smiles were still real after three hundred years.

Three hundred years later, and we're both still here.

She put her things down in one of the guest bedrooms. Redecorating was certainly in order. She didn't want to spend time in her bedroom, or her father's, when they looked the same as they did when Father was alive.

The new furnishings would be modest, though. Times were lean. Marlis rather enjoyed lean times, as long as no one starved, and she would do her best to that end. The prospect of work was exciting. But this house . . .

Now that she was standing in it, it seemed so big just for her and the servants. She'd offered that Nan and Sigi could live with her, but they had decided to follow Thea and Sebastian to Irminau.

You won't even have time to be lonely, Governor Horn, she thought, giving her reflection a smile. It had a nice ring.

⊙–⊙–⊙–⊙

Marlis's inauguration was the next day, under a clear blue sky. She had seen many springs, but never a spring like this, where the flowers were so brilliant and the trees turning such a vivid green. Every color in the rainbow was two shades brighter now. As she gave her oaths and King Rupert made the official appointment, while the people cheered for her and waved the Urobrunian flag, she couldn't shake the feeling that she was an impostor, that this was all a mistake.

"I know exactly what you mean," Sebastian—he was still Sebastian in her head—told her later at the official ball, after they shared one of the first dances and picked up glasses of champagne. "I feel like that every day. And I still have so much to learn. For all I've done in my life, I'm certainly no elder statesman with years and years of experience."

"I feel as if I'm just a figurehead," Marlis said. "The people wouldn't accept a female governor, and certainly not my age, if I hadn't proven my power and age as Norn. I know they're going to expect Brunner is making all the actual decisions."

"I'm sure you'll prove them—"

One of the Urobrunian delegates interrupted excitedly. "Your

Majesty, I just wanted to thank you for everything you've done over these past weeks." He shook Sebastian's hand.

"Well, we'll see how that goes. Thank you."

"Thank *you*. Congratulations, Governor Horn."

"Thank you."

"I hope we get a chance to talk at some point about public health. In my district . . ."

Sebastian surreptitiously rubbed his hands once the man left. "I thought I had a strong handshake, but they're proving me wrong. Anyway, as I was saying. Yes, I was going to tell you that I think one of the hardest parts for me has been accepting how much I don't know. This might be hard for you, too. In some ways, right now you *are* a figurehead. I appointed you governor because I know Urobrun will also appreciate that comforting combination of familiarity and freshness. But, I also know you'll pour your soul into this country."

He somehow managed to get out that entire speech before two of their generals and their wives approached for more congratulations.

I certainly will pour out my soul, she thought, *but I wonder how much it will be appreciated.* With the wyrdsong, with the shield of her diminished emotions, she had possessed more confidence. Sometimes this felt hopeless. Urobrun didn't want to be led by a severe young woman, and they would forget this brief war and the Norns in no time at all. Anything she did accomplish would be credited to Brunner or Sebastian or whoever else happened to be at hand. She knew how these things worked.

Freddy caught her eye across the room. She had barely seen

him since the battle; he had gone to visit his parents as she was swept into the whirl of political negotiations over Urobrun's autonomy. He had sent a postcard while he was gone with a picture of her doing the revolutionary salute and the message: "Ha-ha, you're even famous (infamous?) out in the woods." The dye had washed out of his hair; it was silver again now.

"Governor Horn," Freddy said. "How does that feel?"

"Getting what you want might not be as good as it sounds, but people are aching for a change, so I think I will have less old-guard sentiment to battle with at least."

"The battles will come later, I'm sure."

"Such an optimist."

"You'll enjoy it, won't you? You can't tell me you hate conflict, quick as you are to pick a fight."

"I don't pick fights. You're picking a fight." But she could tell he was teasing. She didn't mind it as she once had.

She glanced at the couples moving around the dance floor in an energetic newer dance. The older officials were frowning on the sidelines. "Are you going to Irminau, then, with Thea and Nan?"

"I suppose it depends on who might offer me a job." He raised an eyebrow at her. "I'll give you first crack for old times' sake."

"Or is it just because Sebastian stole your girlfriend?"

"How kind of you to remind me."

"I am already thinking I need to conduct a survey of the government-subsidized farms surrounding the city. Hunger was a problem this winter; it will only get worse if we don't make sure we're maximizing our usage of those lands. I could have you go around and make a report on that."

"I see. I wanted to work with plants and so . . . farm inspector. That's very glamorous. I thought maybe you'd just hire me as your gardener."

"You really don't know *how* to be a gardener."

"How hard can it be?"

"There are century-old prize rosebushes in this yard, so I'd rather not find out."

"All right. If you want to send me on the road . . . I thought you might want some human company, but I guess you'll just have to look after my cat."

"Oh well. Maybe I can find you something here." Marlis looked at him sideways. "Still, you can't be my *gardener*. For heaven's sake."

SIXTY-SEVEN

While Thea was, theoretically, Sebastian's date, she still could hardly get near him. This was his first trip back to Urobrun since the coronation, and the officials were falling over themselves to speak to him. Of course, she was certainly having more fun, gossiping with Nan and Sigi and eating "Austerity Cake." Marlis had instructed the servers to be sure everyone knew she was not serving indulgent food at her inauguration while people were hungry.

"Why didn't your mother come?" Nan asked.

"She said it sounded like too much." Thea was disappointed when Mother refused the invitation, but she understood.

Right around midnight, Sebastian managed to break away and come over to them. "Let's get out of here."

"Can you do that?" Thea asked.

"I'm the king, I can do whatever I want."

"So far that has been the opposite of true."

"Ooh! I definitely vote for sneaking out," Sigi said. She'd been cross all night because her father had somehow gotten invited to the party, apparently by a few politicians who had commissioned paintings from him, and he was drinking a lot and being very loud. "Is there an after-party? With better music?"

"There sure is."

They grabbed Freddy and Marlis and piled into a car together for a short jaunt to Lampenlight. The lights were still dim thanks to the electricity restrictions, but the streets were absolutely packed with people celebrating. Thea laughed. "Don't tell me: You're putting us to work as waitresses again?"

"The guys rented out Café Scorpio tonight," Sebastian said. "That is, the ones who aren't fancy enough to go to the ball."

"Lucky them," Sigi said.

"The ball wasn't that bad," Nan said. "Marlis, was the Austerity Cake something you and I used to make? It tasted so familiar."

"I found the recipe in the books! We made it during some terrible wheat famine. It has potato in it."

Inside the dim, smoky club, the band was hopping and Ina Brand was dancing on one of the tables. One of the men was holding her snake. Bottles of wine and trays of food covered every table so the waitresses could dance with the men instead of serving. Thea saw her mother in the corner talking to Walter, the pianist. When she saw Thea, she raised a glass of champagne in greeting.

A deep pang shot through Thea at the thought of leaving this city, leaving Lampenlight. But she had seen Urobrun now, the mountains and forests that her ancestors had known.

Maybe she would see something like Lampenlight grow up in Irminau, and she would be one of those glamorous patrons she used to serve.

"Thea!" Hedda ran up and gave her a hug. "You lucky thing! I can't believe you never told us you were dating the *prince*. Are you going to be the queen? Do you need ladies-in-waiting?"

"Oh goodness. That's a horrifying thought. Do people still even have ladies-in-waiting?"

"Well, they must have a lady's maid."

Hedda's tone was joking, but Thea understood the real fears that came with working as a waitress. Thea glanced at Sebastian. He was still getting mobbed with congratulations, but at least he'd been able to sit down with a glass of wine. "It's definitely premature for me to hire a lady's maid, but I won't forget about you."

"Then again, there are about a hundred handsome men in here," Hedda said. "Maybe I'll beat you to it. Your success inspires me."

"Please do. I'd love it if you came to Irminau."

She slipped away from Hedda and joined her mother. "Mother! You said going out would be 'too much.'"

Mother smiled. "I wouldn't fit in with all those government luminaries, but this night is a nice way to remember the city before we go," she said.

Thea knew her Mother struggled with leaving the home she had shared with Thea's father, but at least they would stay together, and they still had family who had never left Irminau. Thea was eager to meet her cousins.

Thea danced with Freddy, who was a terrible dancer, and she was a very popular partner with all of Sebastian's men who had lost a hand or arm—or two in the case of Max and a few others—and were now adapting to new prosthetics themselves. They weren't so nervous with her. *Meanwhile, I had to face losing my hand without any company in my misery,* she thought a bit grumpily.

Except, of course, Sebastian. Not that he had ever shown much misery. But that was what she loved about him.

When she was tired and a bit tipsy, she dropped her head on Sebastian's shoulder and watched her friends. Hedda flirting shamelessly, Mother making new friends in the crowd, Freddy and Marlis stepping on each other's feet, Sigi and Nan kicking their heels. The future was, perhaps, no more certain than it had ever been, but in this moment, she was exactly where she wanted to be.

ACKNOWLEDGMENTS

First, to Su Mon Han, who should have been in the acknowledgments of *Dark Metropolis*. Never write your acknowledgments at the last minute! She gave me an amazing critique and some wonderful ideas for the first book between rounds of edits when I was feeling tired and burned out, and helped me feel energized and excited again. Some of these ideas have bled through into this book as well. *Arigatou, Su-chan*, I know how busy you are!

I always have to thank my partner, Dade Bell, but especially with this book. How do I write battle scenes? I go to Dade and say, "I need X and Y to happen, HELP," and he plans out the whole thing complete with diagrams and maps. He is amazing and I don't know how I could have done this book without him.

To my editor, Tracey Keevan, for editorial notes that are wonderfully detailed and smart, but not intimidating. It's been such a pleasure working with you. And to the whole team at Hyperion, for beautiful covers, marketing, copyedits, and everything else you do.

I did a lot of research for this book, much of it never used, some of it most definitely applied, and I appreciate everyone around the Internet and in real life who answered a question for me.

And as always, to readers and fans, from the kid who picks up my book at the library to the book bloggers who keep my chin up on a bad day. I can never thank all of you enough for choosing my stories out of all the books in the world.